GROUND RULES

Ground Rules

Richard Whittle

ISBN: 9798621318529

1

The car Curtis sent for me slithered to a stop on wet cobbles, its blue lights strobing the mews. That it arrived so soon after he phoned me caught me off guard. I wasn't ready. Almost everything I owned, including my forensic kit, was still packed in boxes.

I opened my front door to beating rain. A running man, one hand on his head as if holding his hair on, jogged from door to door checking the house numbers. Seeing me, he changed direction. He changed, also, from a stooping Dickensian beggar to an upright, uniformed man.

I opened the door wide and he dashed inside. I half expected him to shake water off his coat like a spaniel emerging from a pond but he just stood there in my hallway, panting and puffing, rain from his soaked hair trickling down his cheeks. Wiping his face with his hand he fixed me with a stare.

'Doctor Spargo? Doctor Jessica Spargo? I have a car for you.'

I was nervous. I'd been expecting the car but this was all new to me. I had never been to Curtis. Curtis always came to me.

Flustered, I ran to my kitchen, grabbed a waterproof jacket and returned to the man at a controlled, refined pace. Then, spoiling any impression I was trying to make, like a three-year-old child I put my arm down the wrong armhole. The policeman stood quietly, watching me. He even offered to help.

I was assisted into the back of the car by that ducking-down, head-shove thing they do with suspects and bad guys. Then we were away before I'd strapped myself in, slipping and sliding on what I'd called cobbles but which were actually stone setts – those polished stone blocks our forefathers used before that Scottish engineer, John MacAdam, invented tarmac.

We turned out of the mews and the car surged forwards, a floodlit fairground ride through the city with horns blaring and headlights pulsing. The few cars that remained on the streets at such a late hour swerved to one side or pulled over.

To me, pinned back in my seat, we travelled at the speed of sound. Before I knew it we were well west of Edinburgh, heading towards Glasgow on brightly lit motorway, changing lanes rapidly and cutting up cars. I sat upright and rigid, gripping the seat as if perched on a cliff edge. When blocked by cars, the driver overtook on the inside, scattering stones as he shrieked down the hard shoulder.

We swung onto a slip road. My view of the world changed from brightly lit motorway to dark country roads. The driver could see the road, he had a clean windscreen and bright headlights. I could not. I had a side window smeared with swept-back raindrops. All I saw of the countryside were trees, stone walls and hedges in ghoulish, pulsating blue. Childhood fears flooded back – fear of darkness, fear of the unknown.

A ghost-train ride without ghosts.

None yet, anyway.

Because I am a geologist I tend to know places better by what lies under the ground than by what sits above it. If my brain-based GPS was functioning correctly we were probably travelling above an exotic mix of volcanic rocks, shown in bright purple on geology maps but disappointingly brown in real life.

I had known Tom Curtis for years. I knew also that this time he didn't want me for my geological knowledge. Five minutes before the car arrived at my door he'd phoned me and asked me two questions: Did I know Charles deWit? And, if so, did he work with me?

On reflection, perhaps I should have said no to both.

The driver braked hard. Compared with the speed we'd been doing to get here, we now moved at the pace of a snail. The country roads became lanes, the lanes became tracks. Angling my head to peer between the car's front seats I saw lights in the distance, torches waving and hand lamps swinging. Headlights too, from vehicles perched at odd angles, some on the track and others in field gateways. Surely not a serious car smash, not in tight lanes like this?

Lit by our car's headlights I saw Curtis's car, the only vehicle parked neatly, the only one with its lights switched off. Thankfully he'd had the foresight to send a car for me. This was a wild place, real bandit country, a location I would never have found at night without divine intervention. Or perhaps a good satnav.

Lamps on the roof of an unmarked van threw their light sideways over a tall gappy hedge, illuminating the field beyond. Shadowy figures, some in uniform, glanced in my direction as I stepped from the car. A woman in white coveralls broke away from her colleagues and trotted towards me, beckoning impatiently with a wagging hand.

'Doctor Spargo? Detective Chief Inspector Curtis wants you right away.'

She beckoned again and I followed. Before long I was clad like her in white coveralls, matching white bootees and thin latex gloves – the kind of kit that, had this been a professional callout, I would have brought with me. Accepting directions from a uniformed constable I stepped into the lit field through a gap in the hedge. I was seriously ill equipped. The woman had given me coveralls, she hadn't given me wellies. Under the slip-on bootees I'd been given I was wearing my trainers, wholly unsuitable footwear for conditions like this. My walking boots were, like the rest of my kit, still in removal boxes.

A uniformed constable pointed. They had *established a corridor*, he told me – police-speak for *marked out a path*. He told me to follow the field boundary, to keep close to the trees. I hesitated for so long that he said he would come with me to show me the way. Out of sympathy, I suppose.

The lamps on the van cast long shadows that hindered rather than helped. Hindered, like the policeman, who walked well ahead of me, switching his torch on and off as if saving its batteries, lighting-up the grass and mud only when he thought necessary. Necessary for him, that is. I remained in the dark in every way. To me, it was like following a car with bad wiring.

The man didn't take me the whole way. Either he'd had enough or he decided I was a big girl and could find my own way. He said it would be easy, that the van's lights would help. It wasn't, and they didn't. I lost both overshoes in mud. Couldn't have found them if I'd wanted to.

Feeling useless and helpless I followed the flight-path of marker tape across muddy, ploughed ground. Had Curtis wanted me in my capacity as a forensic geologist this would have been a disaster. I would have had to take samples, make sketches and take photographs. I would have had to find, and assemble, my field kit before I left home. That, assuming I could even find it all, would have taken time. I resolved to get my act together for next time.

2

The further I walked the clearer things became. At the far end of the field wispy ghosts worked in hazy white light like moths around a candle. I made straight for them. My first impression was that they stood in the entrance to a small barn. This, I soon realised, was a trick of the light. There was no building, just tree branches overhanging tall floodlights.

The undergrowth was dense, there was no room for a tent. Instead, they had slung ropes and tarpaulins from trees, improvising an awning to keep off the rain. Rainwater, caught by the tarpaulins, ran off them in the manner of badly blocked gutters.

A large van had been driven across the field and was parked some way off. A generator close by hummed softly, powering the lamps that floodlit the scene. I plodded nervously towards them in my own little world. I still had some way to go when I heard my own name.

It was Curtis, ordering me to stop – the kind of command a hunter might give if I was about to come face to face with a bear. I froze. My feet, no longer moving, started to sink in soft mud. Ice-cold water crept slowly and deliberately through my trainers, soaking my socks in the way a particularly efficient irrigation scheme might water the roots of plants.

My weak attempts at humour weren't working. Since clambering from the car I'd had a childlike desire to be somewhere else; the adrenaline rush I'd felt when Curtis phoned me had given way to dark thoughts. The floodlights didn't help. Perched on tall tripods, they looked down from on high like alien ships and they fuelled my fantasies, making the scene more unreal.

Adjusting my eyes to the light, I saw Curtis. He is a tall man. His white disposable suit, made for people as tall as him but much wider, gave him the appearance of a worryingly thin polar bear in a hoodie. He faced me and watched me, his hands on his hips in that way of his. Behind him, deep in the trees, faint zigzags of light revealed other white clothed figures, searching the woodland with hand lamps and torches. I didn't envy them. I knew from experience that the undergrowth at the edge of woodland can be dense and impenetrable. My own searches in such places had been simple and innocent, searching in daytime for exposures of rock. God knows what those shadowy figures were searching for.

Curtis came towards me and I mumbled a greeting. It should have sounded confident but it came out cracked.

'Mister Curtis?'

'Charles deWit. How well do you know him?'

He reached me, stopped, turned and looked back towards the lights. I shook my head. He didn't notice. 'I don't know him, not particularly. He's a lecturer. He used to be one of my students.'

'Used to be?'

'Isn't now.'

'But he's university staff, like you? You would recognise him if you saw him again?'

'You don't mean that. You mean would I recognise him dead.'

It sounded crass and cocky and I don't know why I said it. I was feigning confidence. Without replying he walked back the way he had come. I followed him.

I already knew there was a body, I had seen its bulk, flat on the ground in trampled-down bushes. Two hooded, white-clad figures crouched over it. One of them moved away and I saw clothing, green and brown. Charles deWit was a big man, he didn't wear flimsy fleeces, he favoured heavy-weave jackets of dull plaid just like this one. The jacket I particularly remembered had leather elbow-patches, things I hadn't seen on jackets for years.

One of the hooded figures stood up. Tucking back strands of long hair that had escaped from her hood, she looked at Curtis and then at me, holding the gaze for several seconds, the way children do when outstaring each other.

I looked away, so she won. She gave Curtis a quick nod. 'I'm done here.'

'The rain doesn't help,' I murmured.

They ignored me. I asked how long the body had been there. Curtis shrugged. It was none of my business but he answered anyway.

'It's not recent.'

'Days? Weeks?'

The shrug again. 'Been here some time.'

I felt nauseous. And horribly cold.

Curtis stayed. The others moved away, became shadows. It was, apparently, my turn for the limelight and I had stage fright, I had to identify deWit and I didn't want to go closer. Whoever said *it is better to travel than to arrive*, got it right.

I had strange, mixed feelings. Just because I disliked deWit didn't mean I wanted him dead.

I assumed – hoped – that if I had been called to a real forensic job rather than to identify a corpse then things would have been different. Earlier in the year, in a rare relaxed moment, Curtis admitted to me that when things got really bad the job simply took over and he worked like an automaton, doing what he had to do. The personal feelings came later, he said, like grieving. At the time I'd wondered what he meant by *really bad*.

'Are you ready for this?' Words said quietly so the others wouldn't hear.

'No.'

'There's no need for you to go right up. Just get to where you can see him properly.'

I took a step forwards and then stopped. Then stepped forwards again. I had deliberately ignored the body by looking down at my feet, pretending to see where I was treading. Now, a glance at the victim told me he lay flat on his back, his head near the edge of the field and his feet beneath chopped-back undergrowth. The police had cut back branches to give themselves better access.

I did an out-of-focus appraisal of the body, first the boots and the legs and then the trunk. Had it been in the middle of a cornfield I might have mistaken it, even from so close a distance, for a fallen scarecrow. I could make out a hole in the chest where, had it been a scarecrow, the straw stuffing might have burst out. Finally I focussed. In this case it wasn't straw, it was the pale ends of smashed ribs. I swallowed, glad I'd spent the evening unpacking removal boxes and hadn't had time to eat.

There was no blood, not now. I guessed that with such a huge hole there had been a lot of it and the rain had washed it away. The body was so wet it might well have been dragged from a pond. What little bare flesh I saw was bloodless, the colour of a butchered carcass.

I gathered up courage and looked at the face. From my surreptitious glances I already knew that the head was turned sideways, as if looking away from me. Curtis's remark about not having to go right up was meaningless. Unless I did, I couldn't see who it was.

From somewhere in the shadows, Curtis was talking. I'd assumed he was speaking to the others but he was speaking to me. I caught the last bit.

'...as soon as you are sure, Doctor, just say. It's not a formal ID. I just want to know if it's deWit.'

Not taking my eyes off the body, I nodded. The arm nearest to me was twisted unnaturally, locked under the body. I stared at the plaid fabric and the worn leather-patches. It was definitely deWit's jacket. To see the face properly I bent over the body. I could see more bone than flesh. The soft tissue around the eyes, the nose and the mouth was gone, no doubt the work of birds and animals – rooks and crows, foxes and badgers. I let my eyes focus and then jumped back. Not because of what I'd seen but because Curtis spoke unexpectedly.

'You all right there?'

The breeze had carried much of the stench of decomposition away from me. I now caught it for the first time and my stomach heaved. Somehow I managed to control myself.

I nodded. 'I'm okay.' I was definitely not okay. I felt nauseous.

'Can you tell? Is it deWit? Are you absolutely sure?'

'No.'

'No you're not sure?'

'No it is not Charles deWit.'

Curtis swore softly. I guessed that for him it was back to square one. For me, called out in foul weather to identify the body of Charles deWit (who, however much I disliked him, I sincerely hoped was alive and well and a long way from here) it was over. Or so I thought.

As if the remains weren't illuminated well enough already, Curtis went for a hand lamp. When he returned he shone its beam at the remains of the face. He repeated his question.

'Are you absolutely sure?'

I tried to answer but my voice dried. I nodded, feigned a cough and tried again.

'Absolutely. Charlie doesn't wear a gold earring. Charlie doesn't have black hair. Charlie – '

Curtis interrupted me. Perhaps he was afraid I was about to list every difference I could think of. Perhaps I was.

'Right. Yes. Fine,' he said. 'But it looks something like him?'

I looked down again. It was not an easy question to answer.

'Same build. Same jacket.'

'Thank you for coming, Doctor Spargo. I am sorry if I spoiled your evening.'

I mumbled 'No problem.' In such situations, lying comes easily.

Neither of us moved. Curtis stayed quiet, staring down at the body, an uncomfortable silence that I wanted to break. There were things I wanted to know but wasn't sure I should ask. Wasn't sure I would be told anyway. Finally I spoke.

'What made you think it was Charlie?'

Curtis shrugged. 'I'm finished here. I'm returning to Edinburgh. Can I drive you home?'

He hadn't answered my question and I didn't answer his. Something had clicked in my brain, nodes linking together to make meaningful patterns or whatever it is that goes on in there. I took a cautious step towards the head and crouched down. Curtis made a move to stop me but changed his mind.

'What? What is it, Doctor?'

I was on the wrong side of the body. I couldn't see what I was trying to see. I moved unsteadily and went to step over it. Curtis shook his head, grabbed my arm, and guided me around the feet and legs. I stepped gingerly along the other side of the body and crouched by the head.

'What?' he asked again.

I needed a frontal view of the face but that wasn't possible. Also, the strongest set of floodlights was high up and behind me. What little remained of the face lay in my own shadow.

'I need a light. The hand lamp is too big. I need something smaller.'

He attempted to put his hand in his pocket but remembered he was wearing the coveralls. Unzipping them from the neck he reached inside, produced a small Maglite and switched it on.

His *What?* became a *What is it?* then, 'What are you looking for, Doctor?'

'I need to see his other cheek.'

'Why is that?'

If the other side of his face was as bad as this side then I was wasting my time. The smell had been bad enough before, but up close I was having trouble coping. In the hope I could filter it through my handkerchief I groped for a pocket and realised, like Curtis, that I wore coveralls and gloves. I probably didn't have a handkerchief anyway, it would be at home, like everything else I should have brought with me.

I took a deep breath. I wasn't low enough, I had to kneel. As I did so I felt the soft ground, flooded by water from the tarpaulin, ooze up around my knees. Hesitantly I shone the torch at the face and brought the features into focus. There wasn't much of it left and it was too much for me. I jumped to my feet and stared hard at Curtis. I was taking long deep breaths and shaking my head in frustration.

'I can't!'

'Can't what? Tell me what you are doing. What are you looking for?'

I pulled myself together, trying to convince myself that the victim was no longer a person but an empty shell. As a philosophical argument it was probably sound. As a confidence booster it did nothing at all.

'I can't see him properly,' I said. 'I need to see the other side of his face.'

Without hesitating Curtis did what he'd forbidden me to do, he stepped over the body. He bent over, put his hands around the head and lifted it an inch or so off the ground.

'That enough?'

The skin around the neck had been protected by the collar of the coat and I could see it properly now, grubby white and the texture of latex. The old two-inch scar on the neck that I was seeking stood out like a ridge. The romantic in me, now stifled, once supposed it was the result of defending himself, or someone else, in a fight. Far more likely it resulted from ham-fisted stitching after a childhood operation. I handed Curtis his torch. He was frowning.

'So?'

'You didn't tell me why you thought it was deWit.' Though the coat had made me think it was Charlie, that couldn't have been Curtis's reason.

He didn't answer. Beckoning me to follow, he walked towards the van. He climbed into the back and returned with a small clear bag that he held out to me. In it was what looked like a credit card. I took the bag from him and held it up so it was lit by the floodlights. The card had a photo in the bottom right corner that I couldn't see clearly. I could, however, see the name printed across the middle of the card.

'DeWit's university card,' Curtis said. 'It was in the jacket. It looks old, the photograph has faded, it's not much use.'

I nodded. The cards were university issue that gave access to libraries, departments and exams. Somehow Charlie had managed to hang on to his when he became a lecturer.

'So?' Curtis said. 'Changed your mind? Is it him? Is it deWit?'

I hadn't changed my mind. Though the earring and black hair rang bells with me, they could belong to any number of people I knew. It was the scar that clinched it for me.

'It is not Charles deWit.' I said. 'His name is Demitri Morini.'

3

I can't say I really knew Demitri Morini. What I did know was that he was a researcher or lecturer in another department, Chemistry, I think. As for deWit, I knew him well. He was a waste of space. I hadn't liked him when he was a student of mine. Since he became a lecturer I liked him even less.

DeWit shared my office for a while, though the story he put around was that I shared his. Not content with the shelf space I cleared for him, he gradually encroached on my own. Personal, geological maps went missing. Books I'd had for years transferred themselves mysteriously from my shelves to his. He claimed that one of them, a geological classic given to me by my father on the day I was awarded my doctorate, belonged to him. He had even written his name inside its hard-bound cover, something I would never have done to a one-hundred-year-old book. Especially one I didn't own.

Things came to a head after I returned from a week's conference in London and discovered that he had rearranged my office. My desk, previously facing the window and overlooking tall trees, now faced an internal wall, hemmed in by a barrier of bookshelves, filing cabinets and my multi-drawer map cabinet. I had opened the door of my room to find DeWit sitting at a larger desk than he'd had before – a desk that now faced the door, reminiscent of a miniature version the US President's Oval Office. Rather than engage in a petty squabble with the man I turned on my heel and returned to my room with the Head of Department. By mid-afternoon I was again the sole occupant. I am not without influence.

Though I can't say I knew Morini, I did know that he and deWit used to hang out together. Sometime in the past they shared a flat. Perhaps they still did. Both were in their mid-thirties. Both a lot younger than me.

I told Curtis these things while he drove me home. No marked car this time and no blue lights. I took the opportunity to ask him the one big question that puzzled me. Why, when he found deWit's student card, did he call me rather than call the university?

'Obvious, Doctor,' he said. 'I'm surprised you asked. It's pointless trying to contact them at night. Much easier to call someone who would know.'

Personally, I suspected he'd phoned me because for months I'd been pestering him to call me out to crime scenes rather than simply pass samples to me later. I had told him more than once that scenes of crime officers didn't have my experience and that whenever geology was involved, however obscurely, they didn't take samples in the way a geologist takes samples, they merely collected and bagged-up. I'd grumbled to him that they inadvertently destroyed evidence, and that to do geological material justice I needed to see it in context. In short, I had to take the samples myself. Being called to identify a rotting corpse wasn't quite what I'd had in mind.

At home I stripped off and packed my clothes into my washing machine. When I showered, all of the dirt and most – but not all – of the smell went down the plughole. The memories of what I'd seen did not. I suspected that, rather like a first date, the experience would stay with me forever.

Poor comparison, I know.

Sleeping was out of the question. Still wrapped in a bath towel I slumped in front of the television and watched a documentary about penguins, anything to get my mind off of Morini. I fell asleep and woke up a lot later, turned off the TV and dragged myself to bed.

Despite everything I slept well. I had no idea what I dreamt about but I woke with an image of Curtis lifting a severed head by the hair, the way a gladiator might lift a trophy. Thankfully it wasn't the head I had seen in the field. Nevertheless, it was a bad start to my day.

You have no doubt heard of those stress factors, things you should do one at a time or preferably not at all. Recently I messed up on that big time by managing to move house, change jobs and split up with my long-term partner all in the space of six weeks. I moved house, into the mews, and also took a long lease on a disused church hall that would eventually become my new office and laboratory. Probably too much, too soon.

Before moving house I lived in a bay-windowed apartment that had belonged to my parents. It overlooked Bruntsfield Links, an expanse of grassed parkland conveniently close to the university, theatres, museums, and Edinburgh's main shops. If you can't imagine the area, think Muriel Spark… *Morningside ladies… Miss Jean Brodie.*

My decision to move house triggered another decision, one I had avoided for years. I decided to go it alone, to set up as a consultant. All of these life-changing moves were driven by the fact that my Bruntsfield apartment sold for a small fortune, giving me cash in hand to spend on my dreams. With it I bought a neat, two-up and two-down mews cottage on the edge of Edinburgh's New Town, much less spacious than my former property but more than adequate for me. It even has a small garage.

The church hall – my new office and lab – felt comfortably small and needed little attention. It has thick stone walls, a heavy front door, and windows wire-meshed against vandals. All of which conspire to block calls to my mobile.

My clients approved of my changes. When I first started forensic work my laboratory was at the university's King's Buildings on the south side of the city, a portable building in the yard at the back of the old geology block. Curtis hadn't liked it. When he first came to see me there he'd inspected the door locks and window catches, expressing his concern that every Tom, Dick and Harriet seemed able to wander in wherever they liked. Also, if anyone wanted to break in, they could simply take a saw and cut through the walls. Not, he'd said, the kind of place to store forensic samples.

Security is no longer a problem. The church hall is practically bombproof. Its entrance must have been made by a maker of dungeon doors, it has lion-cage hinges and a treasure-chest lock. Apart from the front door, the hall has, or should I say had, one other access – a narrow door at the back of the building. I say *had*, because somebody, years ago, mindful of the possibility of a break-in or perhaps to prevent another one, nailed it shut with long iron pegs.

The morning after my callout by Curtis I spent the day in my new lab. I was there before nine, pacing around, working out where to place my mobile phone to get a hint of a signal. So far, the phone company had connected me at home but not at my office. Because the church hall never had a phone, somebody would have to string wires.

At exactly one thirty my mobile rang. I grabbed it and ran outside. It was Curtis.

'Where are you now?'

'My new office.'

'Where's that?'

'Up from Dean Village. The old church hall. I'm sure I told you.'

Silence from Curtis. Probably tactless of me to say that I'd told him.

'I need to see you. Where can we meet?'

Before I had chance to answer he suggested a coffee shop at Tollcross. It was a five-minute walk from where I used to live, but many more minutes than that now.

'What is it? Still about Morini?'

If it was, I didn't want to know. Giving free information doesn't pay bills. I could hardly charge Curtis for the time I spent identifying Morini's body.

'I can't say.'

'Not on the phone?'

'Definitely not on the phone.'

I didn't protest. Curtis was my lifeline. Since I set up my own business the bills had come in faster than the cash needed to pay them. The work done on the hall cost me more than expected and I needed a cash-rich white knight to ride in and rescue me. Tom Curtis was no white knight but he would do for now. If didn't keep on the right side of him my business would never take off. I hoped it wouldn't always be like this. Perhaps there just wasn't enough crime.

The coffee shop was neutral ground and that mattered to Curtis. As I already mentioned, he always came to me, I never went to him. The reason, he admitted to me once in a roundabout way, was that he didn't want anyone associated with students anywhere near his office.

You get no points for working out that Edinburgh's Tollcross is a junction where several roads meet, one or more of which must have been toll roads. Many of the buildings nearby are at least one hundred years old and have three or four storeys. At street level there are shops whose facades have undergone numerous conversions, though many of them retain that mock-Woolworth look. The shop has gone. The style lives on.

I had no time to walk to Tollcross or to wait for a bus. The taxi I took cost an arm and a leg, though it meant that I got there before Curtis. Costa, by the way, is on the corner of Earl Grey Street, an irony missed by Curtis but not by me. From what I knew of him he didn't do humour.

I carried my coffee to a table at the back of the room. To pass the time I took a sheaf of lecture notes from my bag and thumbed through them. Though I no longer worked full-time for the university, I continue to hold twice-weekly seminars with my post-grads. This year's batch weren't exactly supercharged. I needed all my skills just to keep them awake.

I didn't see Curtis arrive, I saw him in the queue at the counter. He glanced at me but didn't acknowledge me. He looked tired. Solemn too, but for him that was normal. Like me, he was well into his forties, but today he looked ancient. Too much work, too little sleep. Paper cup in one hand and briefcase in the other, he came over to me.

'They thought you wanted a take-out,' I said with a nod towards his paper cup. 'They should have given you a proper cup like mine.'

As an icebreaker it failed. As usual there was no handshake and no smile. He placed his briefcase on the floor, tucking it against the wall so it couldn't be seen. He sat down, glanced at me for less than a second and then stared at his coffee.

'You look tired,' he said.

'Thank you. I was thinking the same about you. Only I didn't say it.'

Touché, Tom Curtis. So much for niceties. Even white knights should have manners – especially white knights. He looked at me properly and gave an on-off smile.

'I didn't mean it like that.'

'What you meant was that you were concerned for my well-being.'

He looked away, embarrassed. It was not a good start. He levered the plastic top off his paper cup, placed it top-down on the table and sipped at the coffee, vacuuming foam. He leaned forwards, rested the paper cup on the table and clasped it with both hands as if he was cold.

'Did I ever tell you that I joined the force in my early twenties?' he said. 'I can retire after twenty-five years. Not long to go.'

I did a double-take. Never, in all the years I'd known Curtis, had he opened up like that. He was a private person, a bit of a loner. I had judged right when I said he looked tired. Perhaps, last night, something between us had changed. He had called me there and I'd gone, despite the hour, despite the weather. Despite it not being anything to do with me.

'But you won't retire.'

He shrugged. 'That depends on what comes along.'

'Things don't come along. If you wait for things to come along then your life ticks away. Then before you know it, you're old.'

He shrugged again. 'Sometimes I'd be happy to stay on. Other times I yearn for the chance to do something else.'

'It's called life. It's what happens. Man first crawled out of the pond because he wondered what lay beyond.'

Curtis looked at me long and hard.

'Are you sure that first creature was a man and not a woman?'

I smiled. He was compensating for his *you look tired* gaffe and I appreciated it.

'When we became Police Scotland they moved me to St. Leonards, did I tell you that? Now the decorators have moved in. For a bit of peace I've moved back to West End.'

I nodded. It explained today's venue, a ten-minute walk from West End police station in Torphichen Street. Torphichen, in Gaelic, means '*Hill of the Magpies*'. Probably not that many magpies in Edinburgh's West End these days.

He placed his cup back on the table, slid it to one side and reached for his briefcase. I had seen the briefcase many times, a worn but heavy piece of leather that might once have been black. I suspected it was older than he was and that it might well have belonged to his father. He pressed down on its heavy brass catch, flicked back the leather flap and took out a clear plastic bag like the one that had contained deWit's card. He held the bag out to me. I took it from him, holding it between finger and thumb. A clear glass vial the size of a small test tube lay on the bottom of the bag. It contained a brown, gluey gunge.

He watched me. Saw my look of distaste.

'What is it?'

'Mr Morini. It's scrapings.'

'Scrapings?'

'From Mr Morini.'

'Ugh! Shouldn't that be in a fridge?'

'I don't have one on me.'

Rare humour from Curtis. My face must have contorted even more because he took the bag back.

'The organic matter isn't important,' he continued. 'I'm interested in the heavy sediment. As you saw, Mr Morini was shot – '

'It's *Doctor* Morini.'

'As I was trying to say, from the size of the wound we think he was shot with a sawn-off. So far we're not even sure it was a conventional gun. There is no shot. No pellets.'

I frowned. No shotgun pellets. More than just odd. How can you kill someone with a cartridge with no pellets? What came to my mind was a variation on that 'stabbed with an icicle' story. Perhaps no shot had been found because the cartridge was loaded with ice. Thankfully logic kicked in before I suggested it. I could think of a dozen reasons why such an explanation was nonsense.

'Point-blank,' he said. 'Just about. The jacket was zipped up and shows powder burns. The pathologist says the wound is unlike any he's seen before. He says it's more like blast damage than a gunshot.'

'Was the cartridge simply empty? Could wadding do damage like that?'

Someone once told me that shotgun cartridges contain packing material to force out the shot and protect the shotgun barrel from wear. I wondered if the cartridge used to kill Morini had no shot, only the wadding.

'There were traces of wadding. There was also this.' Curtis waggled the bag in front of me as if trying to shake up the contents of the vial, but they didn't move. 'It looks like glitter,' he said. 'I want to know what it is. I don't need to tell you to take precautions. Treat it like a blood sample.'

I winced. My nose was turned up and I maintained the expression. What was left of my coffee suddenly became unappetising.

'I don't do bodies,' I said. 'I'm a geologist, I look at rocks. If I'd wanted to look at bits of body I would have become a surgeon or a pathologist. Can't your lab separate the solid stuff and send it to me?'

That wasn't what he wanted to hear. He had another go at his coffee but gave up, shoved it away again and returned the sample bag to his briefcase. I sensed from the way he was fumbling with the brass catch that he was preparing to leave. If that happened, I might never hear from him again.

I backtracked fast. 'What I'm saying is that I'd be happy to help you but I can't work on pathological material. It has to be handled by a licensed lab.'

'I am aware of that. It's a problem for you?'

It certainly was. Probably not an insurmountable one, but one I had not faced before. I might be able to find someone at Uni to help me. Experience told me that it could be weeks before they got around to doing anything.

'The problem is delays,' I said.

'I'm thinking of results in hours, not geological time scales.'

More of that rare humour. The last thing I wanted to admit was that any delays would probably be university-related. I suspected he had come to me because he knew I was now independent.

'I'm talking about delays connected with handling and disposal of that,' I said, wagging a finger towards the now vanished vial. 'I don't have those kinds of problems with rocks and soil.'

'I came to you because our labs are bogged down with work. Key staff at Howdenhall are off sick. That vial isn't the only sample, there are three like that. Howdenhall has one. Another has gone to Gartcosh.' He reached down again. I hoped he was going for the sample again, and if so then my train was back on the rails. 'I want you to come up with results before the others do,' he continued. 'And I do mean hours, not days.'

I didn't respond. I heard what he said but my mind wasn't with him. I was thinking Carrie. Carrie – Doctor Caroline Fitzpatrick – did things with body parts. Not human body parts, animal body parts. Half-standing, I took out my phone, held it up and waved it.

'Do you mind?'

'Go ahead, Doctor.'

I made two calls. The first gave me the number of the person I wanted to speak to and the second connected me to her. I walked to the window as I talked and looked out at the traffic. Tollcross, always busy.

'I can have a preliminary result for you before the end of the afternoon,' I told Curtis when I returned to him.

His face brightened. 'Really? Are you absolutely sure of that?'

'I am sure of that.'

I chalked an imaginary tick on my equally imaginary success board. All I had to do now was to deliver. Curtis held out the sample bag to me. Concealing my revulsion I took it from him, trying hard to think of its contents as something minced from the belly of a chicken or scraped from a butcher's slab. Or roadkill. Unsurprisingly, that didn't help. It was, my heart told me, a good time to embrace vegetarianism.

Curtis settled back in his chair and nodded, slowly. With satisfaction, I hoped. I held the plastic bag up near the window. The tube lay on its side and a thin strand of sediment had settled out from the goo. What Curtis had said seemed right, it did look like glitter. But wasn't glitter plastic? Wouldn't it float rather than sink? With my earlier revulsion now mastered I reached for my coffee, sample bag in one hand and cup in the other. I took a sip and nodded towards the sample.

'Could they have broken up? The shotgun pellets, I mean. Pellets used to be lead, didn't they? What do they use now?'

'Non-toxic shot. Nickel. Possibly steel or tungsten.'

'No way those metals would break up. You found none of that in Morini? No metal pellets?'

'No. I already said. It's why you've got that. I want to know what it is.'

'Is there another cartridge? An unused one we could look at?'

'It's a murder, Doctor Spargo. We don't have the gun. Whoever did this didn't think to send us spare cartridges.'

Okay. Not just rare humour. Dry humour.

'Do you want this back or can I destroy it?'

I got a blank stare. Then, realising that I probably meant I might have to use acids and solvents, he nodded.

'Do whatever you have to do.'

I walked from the coffee shop with pride. I had secured my first job since setting up on my own. It wasn't the most palatable job I could have hoped for, but it at least it was simple.

Or it should have been. Maybe I should have asked Curtis more questions.

4

The call I had made on my mobile was to Carrie, a friend from my schooldays, now an experienced veterinary pathologist. She is also a strict vegetarian and I suspect there is a connection between those two things.

In the hope that Carrie could offer a solution to my little problem, I had asked her for advice. She did better than that. She told me that if I could deliver the sample to her within the hour, she would give me results by the end of the day.

After leaving Curtis I boarded a bus to Easter Bush, a business and science park south of Edinburgh. The stop-start ride took me out of the city through Edinburgh's Morningside. As the bus passed over the city bypass I peered out through steamy windows, looking for skiers on the dry ski slope at Hillend, the northern end of the Pentland Hills. I saw none. Skiing through light drizzle and mist wouldn't be my idea of fun either.

The Dick Vet at Easter Bush is an institution, not an individual. Officially it is The Royal (Dick) School of Veterinary Studies, the original school having been established in Edinburgh many years ago — no prizes for guessing the founder's surname. The new school is an impressive building, part of Edinburgh University and surrounded by green fields. Carrie once told me that on the campus they have facilities for dealing with animals of all sizes. *All sizes*, she'd stressed, *including elephants* – probably not an animal they encountered that often. Compared with the size of problem they are able to deal with, my little phial of gunge seemed mere trivia.

I phoned Carrie from the bus as it passed the entrance to the dry ski slope. Shortly afterwards I called her again, this time from a bus shelter at Bush, checking I'd got off at the right stop. It wasn't that I was getting paranoid, it was just that I'd made promises to Curtis that I wanted to keep. Also, I wanted to be sure Carrie could still deliver, that I hadn't missed a slot or something.

Okay. So that's paranoid.

Carrie came out for me. She stood in the doorway, attracting my attention by waving both arms. After customary hugs she hauled me into the dry, telling me I was lucky I hadn't called her last week.

'Drove down to Yorkshire,' she said. 'Gaping Ghyll.'

'The cave.'

'The pothole.'

Of course. Caves tend to go in sideways, Carrie once told me, whereas potholes tend to go straight down. Years ago she introduced me to what she calls a sport, though thankfully not at Gaping Ghyll because I didn't fancy being winched down its one hundred metre deep shaft. It turned out that I didn't fancy caving very much. I had only attempted it because my father, a mining engineer, had spent much of his working life underground and I wanted a similar experience. After three or four trips into caves I'd chickened out. Seemingly bottomless holes in the ground scared me silly.

'That shaft, Carrie! Rather you than me.'

'The shaft isn't the only way in. Promise you'll join me sometime? Get out of the city for a change? So where is this sample?'

I handed over the vial and explained what I wanted. I then kitted up in disposable coveralls. In my lab I do it solely to avoid contaminating samples. Here I felt I was doing it more to prevent samples contaminating me.

Curtis's vial looked different under the laboratory's bright lights. My bus trip had buzzed it around and the sediment had gone into suspension and really did appear glittery. I asked Carrie if she had a magnet, and from a desk drawer she took a traditional, horseshoe shaped, red painted one. She handed it over and I touched it to the glass. The sediment stayed put. It was a simple test. But one that in these days of electronic analysis can be overlooked.

'So, not magnetic,' she said.

'You don't mean magnetic. If it was magnetic it would attract iron and steel things to it.'

'I'm a pathologist, not a physicist. As you said, whatever it is it must be heavy. Look at it. It's starting to settle.'

'Can we float off all the gunge so we are left with just the heavy stuff? I only want the sediment. The rest can go.'

'What is it, brain tissue?'

'Can't tell you. Police Scotland stuff.'

'They have their own labs.'

'Their own labs have been given similar samples.'

She found a kidney-shaped dish, shook up the gunge and tipped it out. After she'd added water I picked it up the dish and swirled it around over the sink. When I tilted the dish the floaters went over the edge and the heavy stuff stayed put.

'Simple gravity separation,' I said. 'Heavy stuff sinks. Light stuff floats away.' She gave me a look. 'Sorry,' I added. 'Teaching granny to suck eggs.'

'Not heard that expression for a while. And less of the granny, I'm the same age as you.'

It had taken me longer to kit-up in the suit than it took me to do the separation. The sediment, less than half a teaspoon-full, lay in one corner of the kidney dish as if cemented there. It had a shine, and a complete absence of tarnish. I knew what it was. As did Carrie.

The fragments were not much bigger than sand grains. Carrie sterilised them with something that killed all known germs and which smelt like lavatory cleaner. Then she dried the sample and corked it in a glass tube.

While waiting for the bus back into Edinburgh I phoned Curtis and told him I had found gold.

'There isn't much,' I said. 'There's so little of it that I was scared to sneeze in case it vanished.'

'You didn't sneeze, I hope?'

'I didn't.'

'Are you sure it's pure gold?'

'I didn't say pure, but it's definitely gold. Gold doesn't tarnish like most other metals.'

'So how did it get there?'

That wasn't part of my brief. That was his job, not mine. I had done my bit. I had identified the sediment. I waited, hoping he would say something else. He didn't.

'Could it have been in the cartridge?' I offered. I was answering a question with a question, a thing I often did with my students. 'Like a gold bullet?'

'I'm not with you.'

'Symbolism. They kill vampires with gold bullets.'

'Wrong precious metal. You're thinking of silver. And unless you know something I don't know, Dr Morini was not a vampire.'

'I've only done a visual inspection so can't guarantee it is one hundred per cent gold, there may well be other metals with it. I should really look at it again, in my lab.'

'Hold fire on that for now, Doctor.'

I hadn't analysed the stuff, hadn't subjected it to tests. If I did, it would mean more work for me and hopefully I might even get paid for it.

More silence from Curtis.

'You have given me your opinion as an expert. Do I need more than that?'

'It depends how far you want to go with this. I can inspect it for impurities. I can detect microscopic patterns to see if the gold is mixed with different metals. In some cases it is possible to say where the gold was mined. Or you may want – '

'Not yet. If I wanted this other stuff what would it cost me?'

'A few hundred.' And if I had to use university equipment then it would cost much more, with most of it going to them rather than to me. 'If I did more on the – '

'Leave it for now. I appreciate what you have done, dropping your other work to do this. I'm sure working for yourself isn't easy, juggling everything.'

'No problem. Can I keep the sample?'

'Why?'

'In case you want me to do more tests.'

Juggling everything was the last of my worries. My problem was not having anything to juggle with. I thought about that. Being called out by Curtis had caught me unprepared. If I was to make a success of my business, that must not happen again. I was not new to this stuff, I had years of experience, I'd been doing geological bits and bobs for the police for years. Until now I had been doing it under an academic umbrella. Now it was all up to me.

5

I spent that evening unpacking boxes and finding new homes for their contents. I was not finding it easy. The good thing was that for the first time in my life I had a garage for temporary storage. Not a car, just a garage filled with boxes. No room at all for a car.

Curtis phoned me next morning. I had continued to unpack poxes, this time in my lab. I had set up the few pieces of electronic analytical equipment that I possessed – most of them purchased at knock-down prices from various university departments. I grabbed my mobile from its home on the windowsill and took it outside.

As usual with Curtis there were no niceties. This time he didn't get straight to the point and I wondered what he wanted. Clearly, it wasn't anything to do with Morini. Nor Morini's gold.

'I read something a few years ago about a newspaper reporter who claimed he'd found human remains in ancient rocks.'

'Interesting it was a journalist,' I said, 'and not a professor of geology.'

'So it isn't possible?'

'How old were the rocks?'

'Two hundred and eighty million years. I just looked it up.'

'The first hominids – that's apelike creatures with human characteristics – appeared only twenty million years ago. So whoever said that was around two hundred and sixty million years out.'

'The report was from Pennsylvania.'

'It doesn't matter where it was from. It's nonsense. No doubt the newspaper sold a lot of copies that week. Do you mind me asking why you're telling me this?'

'I think I might have something similar.'

It was like extracting teeth.

'Similar?'

'I'm not saying that I believe it.'

'Believe what?'

'What do you know about drills?' he asked. 'The kind they use to check the ground under construction sites.'

'Try me.'

I knew a lot about site investigation drilling rigs. After getting my first degree I spent a year working for a ground investigation company. It was dirty, wet work.

'There's a construction firm drilling on a site east of Edinburgh. It seems they have found something odd.'

'Where is it?'

'The site? It's miles from anywhere. The nearest town is Haddington.'

'And?'

'And I'd like you to look at something there. Are you free?'

'What, right now?'

'Right now.'

He picked me up and drove me to site. To avoid road works we turned onto the Edinburgh bypass and headed east, keeping in the nearside lane and driving steadily and courteously. I have to admit that after my high-speed trip two nights earlier I'd hoped for more of the same, hoped Curtis's unmarked car would have blue lights hidden behind the front grill or one of those magnetic things with curly cables that they clamp to the car roof in old movies. If he had any of these things, he didn't use them.

Courtesy came to an end at the huge roundabout at Sherriffhall. To the accompaniment of car horns Curtis crossed all four lanes without warning, inside to outside. Blue lights would have helped. From what I was seeing of Curtis's driving, I was beginning to wonder if I should buy him some.

I had hoped the journey would give us time to talk, but Curtis's thoughts seemed miles away and I left them there, didn't want to interrupt what was going on in his mind. From the little I knew of detective work there wasn't much time to sit and think. I knew he would talk if he wanted to.

Despite having lived in Edinburgh for most of my life, the country east of Edinburgh was not well known to me. From Curtis's woolly description, the site might have been anywhere in the vast tract of countryside between the Firth of Forth to the north and the Lammermuir Hills to the south. Today, the thin eerie mist didn't help, nor did the tortuous route Curtis took once he left the dual carriageway.

The sign fixed to the site's high fence said Kevron Construction. The fence itself would not have looked out of place around a grizzly bear enclosure at a safari park. Like the site's wide double gate, it was topped by coiled razor wire. One of the gates stood open to allow a delivery lorry to drive in and Curtis, impatiently, drove in behind it.

Kevron occupied prefabricated site offices. Curtis, having been there before, drove straight to car spaces marked VISITORS. I stepped from his car and followed him, crunching my way across loose gravel, in through the office double doors and along a short corridor.

I wondered, not for the first time with Curtis, what I had let myself in for – and also, just as importantly, if I would get paid for my trouble. If he had already decided to pay me by the hour it might explain why he was walking so fast. He paused at a door.

'We are meeting the site manager, James Blackie.'

'Are you going to tell me what this is about?'

'Not yet. I'd rather you came into this fresh and made your own judgement.'

We paused in a doorway. Access to Blackie was controlled by a secretary, a late middle-aged lady in a knitted two-piece. Her office, a narrow anteroom with a desk, three chairs and two filing cabinets, was decorated with printouts and flowcharts. She looked up as we entered.

'Ah! An inspector calls…'

'Tom Curtis for Mr Blackie.'

'I know who you are, Chief Inspector.'

She pressed a button on a box and said, so loudly that she didn't need the intercom, that Mr Curtis was here, *'with a woman…'*

An inner door opened. Instead of us going in, James Blackie came out. What he lacked in height he made up for in width. His shoulders, encased in a yellow hi-viz jacket, seemed almost as wide as the doorway. Curtis held out a hand but Blackie ignored it. Stopping at the secretary's desk he picked up papers, glanced at them and dropped them back.

'I've got a meeting in ten minutes,' he said, doing the same with more papers. 'How long will this take?'

I had been standing behind Curtis, half-hidden by door jamb. Blackie noticed me for the first time.

'Who's she?'

'Dr Spargo. The geologist I told you about.'

'If it wasn't for bloody geologists we wouldn't be in this mess.'

I looked at Curtis and he looked away. Blackie barged past me and charged up the corridor. Pausing at the front door, he wagged a finger at coat hooks.

'Jackets. Hard hats. I want them back. Don't touch the boots, you should have brought your own.'

Appropriately clad – apart from proper footwear – we followed him out. Unhindered by a slight limp he walked fast, keeping well ahead of us on a hard-packed, gravel road.

'The man's a pig,' I said.

'He's an acquired taste.'

'Like eggshell in omelette.'

'Don't let him get to you.'

'Too late. What did he mean by that? The geologist thing?'

'You'll see.'

The secrecy annoyed me. I didn't like being put on the spot, but I'd learned long ago not to push Curtis too hard. I also knew that sometimes he told me more than he should. In the great scheme of things it balanced out.

The Kevron site was not a green-field site. Whatever was here before had been bulldozed, leaving only massive concrete slabs and a grid of dirt roads. A network of long trenches had been newly dug for drains, water and power.

It wasn't a public holiday and yet the place looked deserted. Two excavators stood idle. The only humans I had seen, on what seemed to me like an immense site, were the man on the gate, James Blackie, and his secretary – that's if Blackie was indeed human. Way across the site, not far from the boundary fence, stood a drilling rig mounted on the back of a lorry. It, too, wasn't working. The only sound I could hear was the thump-thump of a distant water pump.

We kept several paces behind Blackie. It wasn't deference. The man walked with a robotic swagger, his arms flailing the air as if clearing the way. We walked on a contractors' road, a temporary road that curved gently upwards towards a row of multi-coloured shipping containers. As the slope steepened, Blackie appeared to change gear, maintaining the same speed but with his trunk and head leaning back, as if his legs were ahead of him.

The road split into three, one to the left, one to the right, and another, the one we were on, led to the row of containers. These sat side by side on what once had been grass, all but one with their double doors closed and padlocked. Storage sheds, I guessed. Or perhaps site huts for workers.

'Marie Celeste,' I mumbled.

Curtis said, 'The whole site is on-stop. Yesterday they sent everyone home. They couldn't work, not with all the TV cameras.'

'What cameras?'

'They've gone now.'

'Why were they here?'

'You'll see.'

The last container, battleship grey and newly painted, sat well away from the others. Instead of steel double doors it had a single wooden door, its top half glazed with wired glass. It also had a long window in the side overlooking the site. Blackie produced a key, attached to a wooden tag by a length of twisted wire. Having opened the door, he stood aside to let us in, his only act of civility so far. He followed us in and pointedly inspected his wristwatch. Most of the ten minutes he'd allocated had gone already. If he genuinely had a meeting to go to, then there didn't seem to be anyone to have it with.

I had expected the container to be some sort of site office because it was, after all, the only container with a window. Also, after my recent experiences with Curtis, I half-expected to see another mutilated body. I was wrong on both counts.

Surprisingly I was in familiar surroundings. Heavy steel racks lined the back wall of the container. Along the opposite wall, under the window, stood a long metal table. The other furnishings, if that's what they could be called, included an old wooden desk and two tubular metal kitchen chairs.

We were in a core shed, a sample shed, a hut used by geologists to examine soil and rock samples brought in from site investigation drills. Blackie flicked a switch. Fluorescent tubes on the roof pinged and flickered, flooding the shed with white light.

The place was untidy. Removal men's boxes, flattened and caked with dried mud, lined the floor. Now, in better light, I saw another item of furniture, an armchair – that might well have once been fly-tipped – had been rammed back into a corner. Piled on it were several large, clear plastic sacks of clay.

'Core shed,' I said.

Curtis raised an eyebrow. I didn't know why, it wasn't as if he didn't know I what I did for a living. I stood there waiting, expecting explanations. None came.

The racks held long narrow boxes, some made of strong plastic and others of wood. I knew that inside them would be columns of rock – rock core – removed from the ground by site investigation drills. It might be a mysterious world to Curtis but it wasn't mysterious to me. I had spent many hours describing core in huts like this.

A similar box lay on the long metal table. It was closed and padlocked. I frowned. Who on earth bothered to padlock core boxes? Blackie reached up, ran his hand along the top of the window frame and took down a small key. He removed the padlock and opened the long, hinged lid.

No surprises so far. A wooden core box full of core – two long cylinders of arm-thick, solid brown rock, side by side in trays, recovered from somewhere beneath the site by the drill I'd seen. To protect the rock and hold it together if broken, the drilling process had encased it in a strong tube of clear plastic. Someone, no doubt the site geologist, had slit the plastic to expose the rock.

I glanced at the core. There was nothing nasty, no bits of body. This was rock. I knew all about rock.

'How do they get it like that?'

It was Curtis. Both men looked at me. If all they wanted from me today was an explanation of how rock core was drilled from the ground then I was onto a winner. Though I suspected they wanted more than that.

'If you are asking me how they recover the core, they use a hollow drill bit on the end of a steel tube. The tube is called a core barrel.' I spread my arms wide. 'Most are about this long. The drill bit is impregnated with diamond dust or diamond chips and is screwed onto the end of the core barrel. When the drill bit is rotated by the drill it cuts into the rock and a core of rock goes up inside the barrel. The core barrel itself is on the end of drill rods or drill pipe. To go deeper the drillers add more pipe.'

That was just about as simple an explanation as it was possible to make. Even Curtis, frowning hard, had followed it.

'Like forcing an apple corer into an apple,' he said.

'Right. Except that the corer rotates as it cores. Inside the barrel, behind the hollow drill bit, is a plastic sleeve.' For emphasis I tapped the clear plastic.

Curtis again: 'So the string of drill rods, with the core barrel on the end, goes down into the ground. What stops the core sliding back out when they pull it all back out?'

'It passes through a one-way steel sleeve.'

Blackie muttered something about teaching grandmas. 'It's called a core lifter.'

I had forgotten about that. I did my best to ignore him.

'Yes Mr Blackie. The drillers pull the rods from the hole, unscrew the barrel from the end of the rods, slide the core from it and put it in a box like this.' I pointed to numbers, written in black marker on the plastic. 'They mark the depths on the box.'

'To show the depth.'

It was Blackie again. I stared at him. 'For the Chief Inspector's benefit, Mr Blackie. I'm sure you already know it all.' I faced Curtis. 'Then they repeat all that. Core barrel down the hole again, on the end of longer rods. They drill deeper and recover another core. They continue doing it, down to the depth they have been told to go.'

'That must take time,' Curtis asked. 'Why? Why do they do it?'

'That's what I asked head office,' Blackie said. 'Why bother? We've dug trenches. We know there is three metres of clay above bedrock. Our foundations won't be that deep. We're building two storey offices, not skyscrapers.'

'What are they looking for,' Curtis asked. 'Old mine workings?'

'There were no mines near here. Bloody waste of time!'

Both men went quiet. Curtis looked at me. 'Why is so much of the rock broken into discs?'

'The beds of rock lie flat here. It's mainly sandstone with some finer layers. Imagine a circular pastry cutter going down through layers of pastry. Most stays unbroken. Some finer, weaker layers do not. Hence the discs.'

I could have gone into more detail but there was no point. Blackie was picking his nose and Curtis was now photographing the core with his phone. Children have such short attention spans.

'So why am here?' I asked. 'You didn't bring me here to explain site investigation techniques. Are either of you going to let me into your secret?'

Blackie looked at Curtis and Curtis looked at me. Blackie pointed to the middle of the box, to a short length of brown clay sandwiched between lengths of rock core.

'What do you make of that?'

'It's sandstone gravel. It's the same rock, broken up small. Mixed with some brown clay.'

'And this?'

He shoved his fingers into the mix and retrieved what looked like a thin disc of rock. He held it between finger and thumb and I took it from him. It was rust-brown and felt light, rather like plastic. It was also slightly curved, as if cut from a large ball. It had been scraped clean of clay and replaced in the box, presumably for my benefit. Earlier, I'd noticed a bucket of water under the bench. I reached down to it and rinsed the disc.

'It's bone,' I said, holding it up to the light. 'Definitely bone.'

Curtis was nodding. 'So you agree with their geologist. He said fossil bone.'

'No, I said bone. Definitely not fossil bone, not from rocks as old as these.'

Blackie stayed quiet. Curtis said the inevitable.

'Are you sure of that?'

'I am sure of that. When this rock was laid down as sediment, no creatures existed with body parts this size. This cannot be a fossil. It has to be real bone.'

Curtis was nodding, slowly. Blackie had folded his arms.

'So you agree with the driller,' Blackie said. 'It's a slice of dead dog the drill passed through. It was in the clay and got dragged down the hole. That's all I need to know. You happy with that, Curtis? Now I can get the press off our backs. Thanks to that bloody geologist they think we've uncovered Neanderthal Man.'

Curtis gave just a hint of a smile. 'Haddington Man…'

'Haddington Bear,' I mumbled. But I wasn't smiling. What Blackie was suggesting made no sense. He believed that someone, long ago, dug a shallow hole in the clay and buried a dead dog. By chance the drill had been set up over that same spot, drilled through its skeleton, and part of that skeleton had fallen down the hole. That, to me, was impossible.

I turned to Blackie. 'You said they drilled through three metres of clay and then into rock?'

He looked at me as if I'd asked a trick question. 'That's what I said. Three metres of clay. Samples are over here.' He stepped across the cabin to the clear plastic bags on the armchair. He lifted one onto the floor and then kicked it. 'Clay, see it? Clay from the same hole.'

'Have the bags been checked for more bones? If they were in the clay, then surely that is where you would expect to find them. Not in solid bedrock beneath the clay.'

Blackie shrugged. 'I've no idea. If they found anything in those bags I'd have been told. Anyway, it was a dog. The bone fell down the hole, that's how it got in the core barrel. That's the driller's explanation. I've known this firm for twenty years. They are the experts.'

I didn't bite. The length of time Blackie had used the drilling company had no bearing whatever on how good they were. I was about to argue my point. A glance from Curtis warned me off.

'I understand what you are saying, Doctor,' he said. 'What is your alternative explanation? How can bone from a dog, or possibly some other animal, be in rock a million or so years old?'

'Rather longer than that,' I said. 'This rock was deposited as a sediment at least three hundred million years ago. And we haven't established that it is a bit of dog. It looks human to me. It looks like a piece of skull.'

Curtis jerked. It couldn't have been more than a few millimetres but it was definitely a jerk.

'Are you sure it's not a fossil?'

'Absolutely. It's bone, look at its edge, you can see the structure.' He kept nodding, so I continued. 'What's more, if a piece of bone somehow fell down the hole, it could only have done so when the rods and barrel were out of the hole. It would fall to the bottom of the hole, which means it would be picked up when the barrel went back down. That means it would be at the top of this run of core, not right in the middle, inside the rock.'

Think about it, I said under my breath. Work it out. The bone hasn't fallen from anywhere. It had to be in the rock. But their eyes had glazed over. I had lost them.

Blackie said 'Doesn't have to be a dog, does it? Could be a cow or a horse. It was buried there and the driller drilled through it. Then the piece fell down the hole.'

Someone once told me that if you say something stupid for long enough you eventually believe it. Blackie had reached that point.

'How is it you people never agree?' he asked. 'You geologists? 'One says it's fossil bone and another – you – says it's not. I'm with the driller, he's the man with the experience, he says it's a dog then that's fine by me and I'm not stopping the site because of a slice of dead dog. You have no idea how much this delay is costing Kevron.'

I'd had enough. 'Is anyone going to tell me what this is all about?' I asked, 'Or am I going to stand here guessing?'

Curtis started to speak. 'Their geologist said he'd found –'

Blackie interrupted. 'He's not our geologist. He's on contract, like the drillers.'

'Whatever,' Curtis said, taking the bone from me. 'Doctor, the geologist found this. He called the local radio station and said he'd found fossilised human remains in rocks millions of years old. That was early yesterday. By midday the road outside was blocked by the media.'

'It must have been a slow news day. Where is the geologist, can I speak to him?'

'I stopped the drilling,' Blackie said. 'Sent him off site, told him not to come back. He had no right to do what he did. His name's Smith. Do you know him?'

I shrugged. 'Smith. Okay. Do you happen to know his first name?'

'No idea. Media blocked the roads. Concrete trucks couldn't get in. You know how much it's costing us? The concrete's useless. They go back and dump it before it sets in the truck. And we had a crane due, who the hell knows where that's gone now? Head office went ape.'

I was having second thoughts. Perhaps I was wrong. What looked like bone might actually be a concretion of some kind, a build-up of mineral – think stalactites and stalagmites – or a slice from a vein of a white coloured mineral. I always carry a small hand lens and I took it out of my pocket, held the disc up to the light and inspected it. It was bone. I could see the trace of a suture where two halves had knitted together.

Blackie mumbled 'Sherlock bloody Holmes' and then laughed at his words.

I glared at him. I'd had enough. I made a curt comment and we started to argue. Curtis defused it by asking me what more I could do. Instead of answering, I returned to the core box and poked around in the gravel patch using my fingers. If the geologist was sloppy enough to have called this fossilised bone, he may be sloppy enough not to have checked for more fragments.

I found a few small bits that I rinsed in the bucket. All of them turned out to be rock. I was about to give up when I felt something vaguely familiar. I picked it out, rinsed it in the bucket, and held it up.

It was a tooth.

I won't repeat what Blackie said. I wasn't sure if it was directed at me or the tooth.

'You saw where it came from,' I said, more defensively than I meant to. 'It's definitely canine.'

Blackie's face changed from angry-dour to I-told-you-so arrogant. 'Canine! A bloody dog! I knew it!' He was pointing, first at the tooth and then at my nose. The tip of his finger came so close I felt about six years old. 'Now, Doctor...' he said the word scathingly. '...don't you try to tell me that something this small couldn't have fallen down the drill hole.'

'Canine,' I repeated, opening my mouth and pointing to my front teeth. 'Canine, the dog tooth. The eye tooth. This pointy one at the side.'

My words were ill-formed, the way they sound when the dentist asks me a question and I attempt to answer with all that dentist-stuff in my mouth. I was beginning to enjoy myself.

'I'm a geologist,' I said. 'Not a dentist. But I think you'll find this is human. Are you going to suggest it was left there for the tooth fairy?'

My attempt at humour fell flat. Blackie was tight-lipped and Curtis had things on his mind. Miles away, he was stroking his chin. Finally he spoke.

'Are you absolutely sure these bits are human? There is no possibility that you are wrong?'

'No possibility at all.'

'Are you certain it is real bone? I have to say, it looked like fossil bone to me.'

'How many fossils have you seen? And don't forget the tooth. That is no fossil.'

'Point made, Doctor.'

Then I went a step further than I should have done, saying that the fragment of skull and the tooth belonged to someone small, not an infant but someone in their teens. Blackie went ape. I didn't know how old the bone fragment and the tooth were but what I did know for sure was that Blackie himself was a Neanderthal.

He didn't bid us goodbye. He stormed off in a huff, leaving us in the shed.

Curtis seemed perplexed, saying that if the samples turned out to be human, he wouldn't just have the press on his back, he'd have the Procurator Fiscal's office to deal with as well. I said nothing more until we were in his car heading for home. Though he hadn't asked Blackie if he could take them, Curtis had the bone and the tooth in a sample bag in his briefcase.

'You could have warned me,' I said as he swung onto the bypass.

'About what?'

'Blackie, for a start. And some history would have helped.'

'I'm sorry.'

'There's no need to be sorry. It's just that I don't understand how you got involved with this. If everyone thought it was a fossil, how did the police get involved? Why didn't somebody call the Geological Survey? They have an office in Edinburgh. They would have come.'

'Blackie called us because he was besieged. He wanted the press moved away.'

'Surely that's a job for uniform, not a DCI?'

'It was. Uniform dealt with it. I got involved later.'

'Your superintendent plays golf with Blackie?'

'Doctor, you don't know how close you are. No, not Blackie, with Kevron's big boss down south. He knows my Super. Twice a year they play golf together at St. Andrews.'

I thought it best not to comment. Curtis was in the outside lane, driving fast. Unexpectedly he signalled, pulled into the nearside lane and slowed down. Trying to relax, he breathed out noisily.

'What you said just now… somebody did call the Survey. They drove into the site without asking and Blackie threw them off, said he didn't want more bloody geologists sniffing around. By late yesterday it was all over, the site was shut down, the site geologist wasn't to be found and everyone had been moved on. Blackie put it around that it was a hoax, that they had been about to dismiss the geologist and this was his revenge. Everyone lost interest.'

'Except you.'

'Not me, Kevron's boss and then my Superintendent. Do you know what the geologist said? He told the press that this was bigger than Darwin, that it overturned geological thinking and the whole of evolution.'

'Then he's a numpty.'

'Maybe. But he's a numpty that has stopped a huge development project in its tracks. Blackie says it's deliberate. Could it be?'

I hadn't thought about that. 'I don't see that. Not unless someone placed the fragments in that patch of gravel after the plastic sleeve was slit. That could only have been done by the geologist.'

'Is there any way the geologist, or anyone else, could have placed a piece of bone on the ground and got the drillers to cut through it? Then put it in the box later?'

'No. Anyway, that's stupidity, not conspiracy. If he was deliberately trying to fool people it wouldn't have been long before someone called his bluff.'

'Like you.'

'No, I don't think he was bluffing. He's a fool who's risked his career.'

'What if he was paid so much that his career no longer mattered to him?'

'To pay that kind of money to shut down a site for a day or so? That makes no sense.'

'Kevron's boss says the same. Nobody could possibly benefit from closing the site, not for a few days only.'

'So, as I said, stupidity rather than conspiracy. He really believed he had found fossil human bone. What he got wrong was to say it's fossil.'

'But you said it can't possibly be human, not in rock that old.'

'It's not in rock that old. It's sandwiched between rocks that old.'

Traffic was heavy. We ended up driving through Morningside behind a snaking queue of buses. He didn't say anything for over five minutes. I broke the silence.

'What are you going to do with the samples.'

'They'll go to one of our labs.'

I nodded. I wondered about Carrie, but she was busy enough already. And anyway, she did animals, not people.

Curtis really did need blue lights and horns. He finally overtook six buses in a row, forcing a courier's van into the kerb. He went quiet again. Didn't speak until he pulled up outside my lab.

'So how did the tooth and bone get there?' he asked. 'Surely you have some idea?'

6

I bumped into deWit next day. I had just given a forensic geology seminar, standing in for one of my former colleagues who called in sick. In it, I emphasised to my students that just because things you discover might not be good enough to be used as evidence in court, doesn't mean they can't be used to point an investigation in the right direction. *Pointers* and *Provers*, I call them.

DeWit stood in the corridor, taking up space, leaning one shoulder against the wall. I hadn't realised until then how closely his body shape resembled Morini's. Our eyes met. It wasn't a romantic thing. I was picturing Morini as I had seen him on Saturday night. DeWit could have no idea of the visions that swam in my head.

'Charlie…' I said, hesitating, unsure what to say. 'You have heard, haven't you?'

'Of course I have heard!'

DeWit is South African. He pronounces his words with precision, as if snapping off the end of each one. In retrospect my question was stupid, because news of Morini's death had spread like a bush fire. By then I had heard at least six different versions of events, none of which matched the facts even closely. However, I hadn't seen deWit since I was called out. There was always the possibility he hadn't been told.

'I'm sorry,' I said.

'Sorry? Why are you sorry, Jessica? I have had a visit from the police, they have been quizzing me. What have you been telling your policeman?'

I noted the *Jessica*. It seemed appropriate. Only my close friends call me Jez.

Charlie had been the kind of student destined to crash and burn. He was built like a heavy horse and was trouble from day one, attending as few lectures and seminars as possible and sometimes disappearing for days. Not only had he managed to hang on at university to work on his doctorate, he had managed to convince someone in authority to take him on full-time. I'd heard rumours of some kind of deal – a trust fund set up by his father's firm for a deWit prize in mineralogy. If that was true, then thankfully nothing had materialised. If the father wanted his son to be recognised, a deWit prize for Sulky Arrogance might have been more appropriate.

'DCI Curtis asked about you,' I said. I told him you were South African and that your father is a mining engineer working out of Johannesburg. And Curtis is not my policeman. He's a client.'

'My father? What the hell does my father have to do with you?'

His words were expressionless and knife-sharp. Curtis had asked questions about deWit and I'd answered them as truthfully as I could, including the information that deWit senior was a partner in a gold mining firm. Somehow it seemed relevant. Gold in the cartridge, etcetera.

'At the time Curtis asked me the questions he was investigating Morini's murder.'

'Then get your facts right. My father died last year and he never worked out of Jo'burg. I suppose it was you who told them I am often seen around with Demitri? That is something else you got wrong. Have you talked to the press? How much did the parasitic bastards pay you?'

I wanted to walk away but pride wouldn't let me. His dislike for me showed in his face, a look best described as a sneer.

'I'm sorry about your father,' I said. 'And I've not spoken to anyone else about this. I did not tell the police I had seen you with Demitri. Anyone could have told them that. It's hardly a secret that you share an apartment.'

'What the devil is that supposed to mean? Get your facts right, woman! We do not. We shared when I was a student.'

Hair had fallen over his face and he tossed his head back. He had rage in his eyes and it scared me. I knew he had a short temper and that his bulk was all rugby-prop muscle, not fat. He started ranting again but ran out of steam. When he calmed down I explained my involvement.

'The police called me out to identify a body. They thought it was you.' Rather than tell him about the jacket and university card, I added *for some reason*. I splayed out the fingers of my right hand. 'There was a hole in your chest this big.'

His face didn't change. He was one of those people who, when they look at you, might be wondering how best to kill you or what to buy you for your birthday. Right now it had to was closer to the former than the latter.

'I did not know that.'

Clipped, staccato words. For a second or two I thought I sensed contrition but I was wrong. I got the sneer again.

'Back off, Jessica. Keep your big nose out of matters that don't concern you.' He turned, slammed both palms against the wall and blew a long sigh. 'Jesus Christ!' he said. 'This country!'

After my encounter with deWit I disliked him even more than I did before – if indeed that was possible. The confrontation was no real surprise. What I hadn't expected was the insult. I do not have a big nose.

I needed to speak to Curtis, not to tell him about deWit, but to ask if there was anything more I could do for him. I was running short of work. Many of the jobs I had done for the police in the past had been fairly mundane. The first involved stolen sand – lorry-loads rather than buckets-full – stolen from a beach on the Firth of Forth. The sandman told the police it came from a sand pit. The police went to the pit and took samples.

I had explained to Curtis that, when seen through a microscope, grains of beach sand are rounded, they have been battered by waves. Sand grains from pits are more angular because they were ground down by glaciers before being deposited in convenient, ready-to-dig piles. These piles, I told him, are called drumlins, also terminal and lateral moraines. Curtis had shaken his head. He wasn't one for such detail. There were other differences in the two lots of sand that I won't bore you with, elementary stuff for me but not for him. I'd sat him at a microscope so he could see the differences himself.

All that happened years ago and Curtis hadn't forgotten it. Showing him, rather than simply telling him, had been the right thing to do. He admitted to me at the time that he'd had his fill of experts who came to conclusions and then wouldn't – or couldn't – explain how they reached them. For a while I was deluged with work. I guessed he had recommended me to his colleagues.

Now, just as I was setting out on my own, that work had dried up. I had spent less than two days on the gold gunge and I knew there was more I could do on it. Somehow I needed to convince Curtis of that.

I spent time unpacking boxes. In the lab I set up my computer, my microscopes and my dated, but far from obsolete, analytical equipment. My electronic *black boxes* are nowhere near as fast as their modern counterparts but they are just as accurate. Speed, for me, is not a problem. I don't need kit that can analyse ten samples a second. One every half-hour is good for me.

The tooth and bone, Curtis said when I called him, were now at the lab. I suggested that if they were confirmed as human then he should have them dated, preferably in Glasgow by my archaeologist friend Rory Negus.

Curtis was in no mood to talk. The Kevron bone story had hit the local papers and TV news. All but one said the police – rather than the media, Curtis emphasised – were the victim of a hoax.

'I won't keep you,' I said. 'Just wondering what's happening about the gold fragments. Any more on that?'

'Nothing yet from our labs. I am sure they will confirm your findings.'

He hung up before I could respond. That was not unusual.

Confirmation of my findings was the last of my worries. I knew the sample was gold. Because gold does not tarnish, gold coins and jewellery from Saxon or Roman times are as shiny and attractive when dug out from muddy fields as they were on the day they were buried there. After being wiped clean, of course.

I considered following up my call to Curtis with an email list of things I could do to the sample. This would allow him to pick and choose. I decided against it. So-called *distance selling* of expertise like mine didn't work. My selling was done face to face.

7

With the exception of several small cans of beans and a bottle of brown sauce, I had run out food. My kitchen is small. When I moved in, I was unsure where to put my fridge-freezer. The removal men inadvertently but conveniently solved the problem by leaving it in the garage, next to a power socket and my internal, connecting door. The day after I moved in I had packed the freezer with microwavable meals. Now it was empty.

It takes me five minutes to walk to my local supermarket and fifteen minutes to walk back. The walk back is a slow uphill drag, made even slower when carrying food. Sod's Law says that when you are labouring uphill with heavily laden, orang-utan arms, your mobile will ring. Just as I was walking past a low wall, mine did. I settled all four bags on it and fumbled for my phone.

'Spargo…'

'Is that Doctor Jessica Spargo?'

A man's voice, well-spoken and with a west-country tang. Not West of Scotland, West of England. Somerset, perhaps. Maybe Devon or Cornwall.

'Speaking…'

A refuse lorry labouring up the hill made so much noise that I missed some of the caller's words.

'…the site,' I heard him say. 'The bones. I haven't been able to contact the officer who is dealing with it.'

Bloody journalists! Bloody media! I should have guessed. I sighed loudly and deliberately into the phone, wondering how they knew about me and how they got my number. Curtis knew it, Carrie knew it. Site manager Blackie knew it. I couldn't imagine any of them leaking it to the press.

'I'm sorry, I have nothing to say. You must use the proper channels.'

It's what Curtis told me to say. Though I'm not sure the popular press recognises the existence of proper channels.

'I'm sure Detective Chief Inspector Curtis won't mind us talking, Doctor. I understand that you visited the Kevron site and spoke to my site manager, Jimmy Blackie. He tells me you took away pieces of rock core.'

'That isn't correct. And you said Jimmy?'

'James. James Blackie.'

Whoever this was had got things wrong. I hadn't taken anything, Curtis had. And it wasn't a piece of core, it was a piece of bone and a tooth.

I had been steadying one of the carrier bags by holding its handle. So I could put a hand to my ear to block the noise of the lorry, I let go of the bag. It sagged, slowly. A plastic bottle of milk toppled, slipped out, fell off the wall and burst on the pavement in an impressive, semi-skimmed display.

I tried to ignore it. In all the chaos I finally realised I was talking to someone from Kevron, someone senior to Blackie. For me, that didn't change things. From what I'd heard of some journalists, they'd pretend to be your dead granny to get information from you.

'Tell me who you are.'

'Kevin Marshall, chairman of Kevron Construction. We are the design and build contractor on the site you visited with Detective Chief Inspector Curtis.'

'I'm sorry,' I said, still unsure. 'I thought you were the press.'

'That's understandable and I appreciate your caution. We have had similar problems.' He spoke slowly and clearly, as if my main language was Swahili or Serbo Croat. I hoped he wasn't doing that because I was Scottish. I let him continue.

'Are you willing to discuss this matter with me?'

The milk was now flowing down the hill in a dead-straight stream. It hit the edge of a raised paving slab, cut off sideways, trickled down a kerbstone and ran into the road. A woman pushing a buggy steered around it and gave me a look.

'That depends,' I said, slowly. I needed time to think. I didn't know how much he knew.

'I'm told you found a tooth. Also, that you don't think either item is a fossil.'

'I'm sorry. I really cannot discuss this matter further. I'm not sure I should be discussing it at all.'

'I didn't realise you *were* discussing them, Doctor Spargo. But as I said, I do understand. I would be obliged if you could contact Mr Curtis and tell him we have spoken. When you have done that please call me. I will give you my personal number, it will get straight through to me.'

Somewhere I had a pen and a pad. I did an unsuccessful one-handed search for it.

'I don't seem to have a pen.' It was an admission I shouldn't have made. A geologist without a notebook is like a dog without a bone – perhaps an inappropriate analogy in this instance. 'I'll get your number from my phone.'

'You won't. Not this number. Can you get on the Internet?'

'In about ten minutes.'

'Look up Kevron. Go to *Contacts* and call the Head Office number. Give your name to our switchboard operator and ask for me personally. I shall be here for the next hour.'

He went on talking but I didn't catch what he said. Gravity was now working on the rest of my groceries. The bags had no strength, all four were slumping. With sleight of hand a conjurer might envy, I caught a bottle of lemon juice as it rolled off the wall.

'I'll do that,' I said. 'Must go, sorry. I have a situation here…'

I did my best to clean up the mess and resumed my uphill trek. At home I sorted everything I'd bought, except the milk of course, into the fridge or freezer. Then I attempted to phone Curtis. I tried all three numbers I had for him, but had no more success than Marshall. I searched the Internet for Kevron and tapped a number into my phone.

To me, Kevron sounded like the name of a miracle fabric that was breathable, washable, crease resistant and could stop bullets. More realistically it was probably a partnership between Kevin Marshall and someone called Ronald.

'Dr Spargo...' Marshall said when his switchboard put me through to him. 'Thank you for calling me. Have you clarified matters with Mr Curtis?'

'I've been unable to contact him.'

'I'm sure he is busy man. Am I right in assuming you are now happy to talk?'

It wasn't a case of being happy. It was more a case of finding out what he wanted. 'I am still not sure how much more I can tell you.'

'I'm not aware that you have told me anything. Believe me, nobody understands the need for confidentiality more than I do. I have a construction site at a standstill because a sub-contractor's employee spoke to the press. We have suppliers breathing down our necks wanting to get on site.'

'I'm not sure what I can do. I don't know why the site had to stop work. Can't you just restart?'

'You didn't see what it was like. My site manager sent me a video. The place was a madhouse. First the press turned up, then the television news and then you lot. The police, I mean. I won't tolerate cameras filming everything we do, I am not willing to have my employees working under such conditions. The site stays closed until this matter is resolved.'

'The media has lost interest. I find it hard to believe they even bothered to turn up.'

'You underestimate the public's desire for sensational news, however ridiculous it might be. What I find disturbing is that a qualified geologist made such an unscientific pronouncement.'

'I understand he's straight out of university. You'd be surprised what some – '

'I'm not worried about that. I'm more worried about you saying that the remains are human. I accept your judgement. Are they old? Are they recent?'

'In geological terms they are definitely recent.'

Marshall went quiet. I waited. I didn't fall into the trap of asking if he was still there.

'So,' he said. 'We have found human remains under our site in rocks they cannot possibly be in. Isn't that the situation?'

I responded with a nod. Then mumbled a yes. Then, more clearly, 'In a patch of clay, between solid rock.'

'I'm told that the first three metres they drilled through is clay. They hit rock and continued another three metres. That's where the bone and tooth were discovered. Jimmy says a piece of old bone – and the tooth, I guess – fell down the hole.'

'I believe that is not possible.'

More silence. Then, 'You must be giving this a great deal of thought. Surely you have some ideas?'

He was right about both of these things. My brain had been working overtime, what with Morini, the gold, and now this impossible tooth and bone thing. Yes, I had ideas. But I had no intention of telling anyone what they were until I was sure. If you shoot from the hip you usually miss the target, despite what cowboys do. Hollywood has a lot to answer for.

Marshall spoke: 'I get the impression from Ken Ripon that the police have gone cold on this, is that your opinion?'

'Ken Ripon?'

'Detective Superintendent Ripon.'

Golf, I thought. St Andrews.

'I'm sorry, I don't know him, I only deal with DCI Curtis. He's told me that the bone fragment and the tooth are being examined and dated.'

'Are you not doing that for them?'

'It's more archaeology than geology. Pathology, if they're recent.'

'Of course. So, will you?'

'Sorry? Will I what?'

'Will you sort this out for me? What's the position with you and the police, are you under contract? If you are, there is no point in us discussing this further.'

'I'm a free agent.'

He went quiet. Again I resisted the temptation to fill the void.

'I need someone independent to investigate this properly,' he said. 'I want an inspired and well researched statement that stops this once and for all. I am talking days rather than weeks. I am anticipating additional problems when word gets out that these are human remains and I want to be ready with answers. Jimmy wants the site up and running again tomorrow, or at the very latest by this coming weekend.'

'There's nothing I can do by then.'

'I'm aware of that. I want to know if you are on-side.'

My instincts told me to say no. Reality, and my depleted bank balance, urged me to be more positive. However, if he wanted a replacement for his site geologist, then the answer was a definite no. Also a definite no if I was to be answerable to Blackie.

'I'm not sure I can help you.'

'If you can't help me, Doctor Spargo, then I don't know who can. I know about you. You have an enviable reputation.'

That was news to me. Though I felt flattered, it didn't change things. 'I'll have to consider it.'

'Then please consider it now. What more information do you need?'

'I'll not work for Mr Blackie.'

Silence, this time for much longer. I was sure I had just shot myself in the foot but I didn't care. I could not work for that man.

'You will work directly for me. Naturally I will have to inform Jimmy, he is responsible for the day to day running of the site. I shall instruct him to give you everything you need, including site access. You will submit all your expenses to me, also the hours you work. Is there anything else?'

My brain was in overdrive. What else was there?

'Yes,' I said. 'We need to discuss money. I don't come cheap.'

'I am sure you do not, Doctor Spargo.'

8

I suppose I should have been excited by Marshall's offer, but sometimes these things come with strings. If the core shed at the site was to become my responsibility, including supervising the driller and describing the core, then I didn't want to know. I have done that job. I have taught graduates how to do it. I did not intend to do it ever again.

After more failed attempts to call Curtis I set off for my lab, I wanted to finish my unpacking. The church hall, with its tall churchlike windows and tent-shaped, high timbered roof, still looked more like a church hall than a laboratory. That had to change. At great expense I had previously bought, and assembled along one wall, several flat-pack kitchen units. These gave me an impressive, continuous white worktop.

Lunchtime came and went. I needed a break. I filled my kettle, rinsed out a mug and made coffee. What I really wanted here was a proper coffee maker like at home. Or perhaps that was not a good idea. Today I'd had four cups already. If I went on like this would soon have to change to decaf. Or die.

When building the units I'd had the foresight to leave space for my knees under a short length of work surface. Though it reduced my cupboard space it meant that I no longer had to sit sideways, like in my old lab at King's. I placed my coffee mug on the pristine white surface, pulled my ex-charity shop lab stool out from its alcove, sat down on it and looked around me.

My day's efforts pleased me. Along from my coffee mug sat three microscopes, a computer and monitor and my various electronic instruments. Taken together, they all helped morph the old church hall into my new lab.

In all, a positive day. The big negative that remained was that the place had no central heating and I dreaded the coming winter. The windows were not double-glazed and there was no loft to lag. Also, but hopefully soon remedied, were the problems with phones.

My mind turned from coffee to Carrie. Curtis had needed results quickly. The tests we had done were basic and easy – I had picked one of the largest gold fragments out of the kidney dish with tweezers, inverted one of Carrie's tea cups and scraped the fragment along its unglazed bottom. The *streak* – the colour left when a mineral is used like a crayon – was gold. Had it been iron pyrite (Fool's Gold), or bronze or brass fragments, the streak would have been closer to black. As I said, basic and easy, the kind of test prospectors do when they believe they've discovered gold.

My jacket pocket still held the vial. My lectures to postgrads emphasise the importance of chain of custody and it was time to practise what I preached. I needed to book-in the sample and lock it away. Before doing that, I wanted to look at the gold more closely.

I took out the vial and weighed its contents. After transferring them to a small glass plate I slid them under my binocular microscope and adjusted my lights. Shifting my position on the stool, I made myself comfortable. Microscopes, like computers, are addictive, there is no such thing as a quick look. If you don't get comfortable at the start, half an hour later you will still be perched on the edge of the stool, your legs and back aching like hell.

The fragments looked stunning in 3-D. Through the twin eyepieces of the microscope I looked down at cubes, cylinders and pyramids whose surfaces reflected bright light like gold mirrors. I poked the particles with the point of a glass rod as I rotated the specimen. I re-focussed. Flew down Grand Canyons of gold.

The shapes of the fragments puzzled me. It was as if a microscopic celebrity chef had demonstrated his chopping technique on somebody's gold ring. Or on many gold rings, because not only were the fragments chopped up, they differed in colour. Some were brassy and others a copper-like red. Some were closer to silver. So, not all gold? Possibly some platinum too?

When I said that some of my equipment is old, I didn't mean Victorian. All my microscopes have built-in digital cameras connected to my computer and it wasn't long before I had saved several very impressive, high definition images of the magnified fragments to my laptop.

I got serious. I had been playing, finding my way. Now I measured and recorded the sizes of the fragments, their shapes and their colours. Some of the larger bits had grooves and ridges where something had sheared through them, so perhaps Curtis was right when he said they'd been cut from jewellery. Some fragments were tarnished, which meant they were not gold. I tried to scrape them clean with the tip of my tweezers but I failed. It was like trying to use a lamp post to scrape dirt off a plate.

Outside in the rain I called Curtis again, this time saying I'd spoken to Kevin Marshall. Also, that I had been looking at the gold.

'I know about Mr Marshall,' he said. 'I hear you are working for him now.'

I hadn't expected that. I took a few seconds to gather my thoughts.

'No, not exactly. I've been trying to call you. He phoned me, he wants me to work for him. He said you wouldn't object because there is no conflict of interest. I wanted to check with you first.'

He went quiet and so did I. I suspected I'd just contradicted myself and that if said more I'd be digging a hole. Mercifully he changed the subject.

'You said you had been looking at the gold.'

'Looking at it under a binocular microscope. It lets me see things in three dimensions.'

'I do know what a binocular microscope is.'

'Of course. Most of the fragments are around the size of pinheads. They look as if they have been cut. Have you ever tried cutting frozen butter?'

'I can't recall having had that pleasure.'

'It cracks and breaks in angular chunks. It leaves shiny faces. The gold looks like that.'

'Possibly cut from jewellery, yes. That's what forensics said.'

'Oh? You've had results?'

'Preliminary only.'

'What tests are they doing? The particle size distribution is peculiar, isn't it? What did they make of that?'

I was being mischievous. The reason I had looked at the sample more thoroughly was partly out of personal interest and partly in the hope that I would spot something odd that I could use to get Curtis's attention. And more work, of course.

'The what?'

'The particle size distribution.'

'In English, please.'

'There are pinhead size fragments and dust-size fragments, but no middle-sized ones. I could do a statistical analysis that would – '

I had hoped to give him a list of things I could do but he interrupted me. 'I don't want more work done.'

'There's something else. The smallest grains don't have the crop marks.'

'Crop marks?'

It was like talking to a parrot. 'Cut marks. They have been cropped from something larger, using metal snips.'

Curtis has that irritating habit of changing the subject, usually when he doesn't want to answer a question or make a decision. He did that now.

'What's the story with Mr Marshall?'

'It's a short-term thing. He wants me to sort things out.'

'If the remains prove to be human then it's not your job to sort anything out. It is a police matter. Tell me what do you intend to do for him.'

'He wants the press off his back. He knows they'll return when the specimens are shown to be human. He wants an independent statement ready for them. He wants to know how they got there.'

'Don't we all. I had hoped to have some input from you about that.'

'You were the one who involved me in this. You took me to site because you wanted a second opinion. You know I'll work for you. All you have to do is ask.' This time his long silence got to me. I really did think he'd hung up on me. 'Are you still there?'

'I'm still here.'

'There is no reason why I can't keep you informed. Whatever I tell Mr Marshall I can also tell you.'

I was giving him the option of hearing things from me rather than the roundabout route of me to Marshall, Marshall to Superintendent Ripon and Ripon to Curtis. He mumbled something I didn't catch and I made him repeat it.

He grunted. 'I'm happy with that.'

I punched the air. With Curtis, *I'm happy with that* was as positive as I could hope for.

'About the gold,' I said before we hung up. 'I've got some ideas. There are a few things I'd like to do…'

My secure place for samples is a large lockable cabinet, once used by a lawyer to store wills and deeds. I had intended to bolt it to the floor, but as it had taken me and three of my post-grads to drag it from the van I'd hired, I decided that bolting it down was pointless. While it wasn't quite the vaults of the Bank of Scotland, it would do the job. An ancient label said it was fireproof. From the look of the thing I'd say it was also burglar proof and bombproof.

The cabinet stood in the corner of an anteroom at the back of the lab. Unlike the lab itself, which was passably tidy, the anteroom resembled the inside of a small, tightly packed removal van. I had been using it as a store. The cabinet is in there because I had intended to use the room as my office.

I cleared boxes from around the cabinet, reached in for my sample book and entered details of the gold. Soon the vial and its contents would be locked away next to my copy of Curtis's chain of custody sheet. As the only two items in the cabinet, they looked lonely. I considered how less lonely they would look if they were sitting next to a disc of bone and a tooth. With luck, by now these might well be on their way to Rory Negus for dating.

Seeing the near-empty cabinet reminded me of how little work I had. I couldn't even call the vial paying work. Not unless Curtis gave me something in writing.

Checking my emails, I found a message from Kevron. I was pleased to see that Kevin Marshall was as efficient as he had sounded on the phone. His secretary had attached a letter that confirmed everything we had agreed, including expenses and a generous hourly rate up to a maximum that I was unlikely ever to reach. I was relieved that the letter said nothing about describing core samples for Kevron. Kevin Marshall would not be expecting me to do that, not at the high rates he was paying me.

There was also the all-important clause I had asked for – the one confirming that I report directly to him and not to Blackie. I noted the quaint English, telling me the site staff *would afford me every possible facility to aid me in the execution of my work*. Kevin, I decided, was not a young man.

Years ago, as a student, I worked on a site three or four times larger than the Kevron site. It was a summer vacation job. It was also an education. The site geologist was a real professional, explaining everything he did and the reasons he did it.

I learned so much in the time I was there, how to describe rock core, draw up core logs and construct geological sections through the underground strata. Then, watching while the ground was excavated, I could check if my predictions were right or wrong. After graduation I worked for a site investigation contractor, describing hundreds of metres of rock core of all kinds. There is no substitute for experience.

For Kevron, the clock was ticking. However much I wanted to work on the gold it had to take second place. I had paid work to do. I had to get my head around so-called Haddington man.

9

For most of my life I have lived within thirty miles of what was now the Kevron site, yet I hadn't paid much attention to that region's geology. I knew the basics. Around Edinburgh, some of the rock strata – the beds of rock – contain coal. They also contain oil shale, the beds that have been said by some geologists to contain gas reserves. The strata further east, around the Kevron site, are barren and have never been mined. Instead, the region is known for its fertile soils. Past generations laboured above ground rather than beneath it.

Several years ago I bought a collection of several hundred maps, journals and books from a post-grad. He decided, quite rightly, that his personal library of Scottish geology wouldn't be much use to him in his new lecturing post at Stanford University in California. He sold the lot to me for a song on condition that I took them all and didn't cherry-pick. So anxious was he to clear them out of his apartment that he even packed them into boxes for me and arranged for them to be delivered to my Bruntsfield flat. Before my recent move I had repacked them into boxes that I could actually lift.

The collection, still in boxes, now sat in my store. A few of the books were valuable geological classics, the kind usually seen locked in glass-fronted bookcases in antiquarian bookshops. What I needed right now was the booklet – the *geological memoir* – that dealt with the geology around Kevron's site. Thanks to nifty labelling on my boxes I soon found it. The booklet was over thirty years old but that hardly mattered. Geology tends to change rather slowly.

It was time to go. I tucked the booklet into my pocket, flicked up the row of brass switches near the front door and retrieved my mobile from the windowsill. Swinging open the dungeon door I stepped out into darkness and rain, slammed the door shut behind me and turned its great key in the lock. Whenever I put the key in my bag or my pocket I was reminded of those hotel keys with heavy tags, so cumbersome that you are forced to leave them at reception. My lab key is so big it doesn't need a tag like that. Also, it is quite ornamental. I had even considered wearing it on a leather thong around my neck.

Travelling in Edinburgh by bus is no problem. To travel east to the Kevron site I would need a car. Car hire is something I don't like doing. Firstly, I can't afford it. Secondly, parking in Edinburgh, like in any big city, can be challenging and costly.

Thanks to Kevin Marshall the first problem was solved. The second problem was not. When I returned home from the car hire firm I drove around for twenty minutes before I found a place to park.

Home again, I went to my garage, opened the freezer and selected a meal. Don't get me wrong. When I say *garage,* I don't mean a cavern-size space with up-and-over doors. Mine was built into the front of my small mews house well over one hundred years ago. It might well have housed a dog cart, or an artisan's motorbike and sidecar. If it ever housed a car, it would have been the size of a Mini.

Back in my kitchen I heated the meal in the microwave, grabbed a fork, tore the remaining plastic off the pack and ate while I emptied removal boxes. It was my new rule. Thirty minutes a day, unpacking and sorting, the only way I would clear them. Two hours later, curled in a chair, I picked up the geological memoir.

That the specimens found in the core were *fossilised* human remains simply beggared belief. It was an idea so unrealistic that the site geologist might just as well have suggested that the remains had been placed there by aliens. As far as I was concerned, such magical, irrational and convoluted explanations were out.

The driller's explanation – that the bone was part of an animal that had fallen down the hole after being drilled through – was one I had to consider seriously. However much I tried, I could see no way that remains from higher up the hole could end up sandwiched in the middle of rock core.

Then there was the possibility the tooth and bone were added by the geologist after he slit open the protective plastic sleeve. I knew he hadn't done that because he'd left the tooth behind, something he would not have done if he had put it there. To me, he was so startled by finding the bone, his so-called fossil, that he didn't bother to search further.

My own explanation, however unlikely, was that the remains were those of a dead miner, trapped underground and abandoned. Until now I had put this explanation on the back burner because I was sure there was no coal or anything else mineable under the site or anywhere near it. It was simply the wrong kind of rock.

The geological memoir confirmed my suspicions. The district had no known mineral resources that required underground workings. Like in other regions, it had surface quarries and sand and gravel pits, but nothing underground. This did not mean such minerals were not searched for. Before geology was properly understood it was common for landowners to explore beneath their land in the hope of discovering riches – especially if distant neighbours owned successful mines. Could this be the answer? Had a previous landowner employed some poor wretch to search under his land?

The memoir convinced me that if answers were to be found then they would be found on site, not sitting at home in an armchair. I had to go back there, I had to examine the core in the box, perhaps go through the samples of clay in the bags. I wanted to go there alone, unhindered by Curtis and Blackie.

I left home so early on Sunday morning that the roads were pleasantly clear. I was stopped at the Kevron gates by a young man with a fledgling moustache, who wore a peaked cap at least one size too big. He demanded my pass.

'Pass? I don't have a pass. I don't need a pass. Call Mr Blackie.'

Blackie, he said, was somewhere down south. In the United States this means Mississippi, maybe Florida. In Scotland it generally means anywhere between Gretna and Land's End.

'Then call Blackie's secretary.'

'It's Sunday. She's not in. I don't have your car number on my list.'

'That doesn't surprise me. I only just hired it.'

I ended up reading him my letter from Marshall. Reading it to him, because when I handed it to him he stared at it uncomprehendingly for a good ten seconds. He said he would let me in this time but it must not happen again. I had to get myself a pass or tell the office I was coming.

I nodded and grunted. Couldn't be bothered to argue.

I left my car in one of several visitors' spaces outside the office. I hoped that by parking where the security man could see it, rather than driving right up to the core shed, the car wouldn't be taken apart by him when I attempted to leave.

The site was noticeably quiet, with none of the bustle and noise that accompanies construction work. As I walked to the core shed I passed a truck discharged its rotating drum of concrete into a long, narrow trench. Nearby, a lorry with one of those built-in cranes unloaded sheets of steel mesh. The lack of activity suited me. I needed to concentrate.

Thirty minutes later I was back at the core shed, this time with the key. Stupidly, it hadn't crossed my mind that the core shed door would be locked. To get the key I'd had to produce Kevin Marshall's letter again, this time to Hamish Anderton, a stocky young engineer who had just arrived at the site office. Dutifully he asked me what I was doing there, why I was doing it, and did Mr Blackie know I was there? He insisted I sign the visitors' book, adding that I must not touch anything I shouldn't touch, or remove anything from site that I shouldn't remove.

I nodded. Nodded again. Nodded a third time. As with the security man, arguing wasn't worth the effort.

Rather than follow the site road back to the core shed I took a shortcut. Until then I hadn't realised how vast the site was. Most of it I hadn't seen before, including a part where they had been demolishing buildings. These had been huge, like hangars, constructed on the flat slabs I saw when I came with Curtis.

Way beyond the old buildings stood another drilling rig, different from the yellow one I'd seen mounted on the back of that truck. This one was a tripod rig, a three-legged thing, the kind of drill that can sometimes be seen working near road-widening schemes. I stopped and stared. I had made a mistake. A very stupid mistake.

I hurried to the core shed, unlocked the door and went in. Nothing had been disturbed and nobody had turned off the electricity. I had heat and light.

Geologists, when describing rock core, record their findings on core logs, either direct to laptop or on paper pads. The drillers also make progress notes and keep records of incidents, like when they pull out the core barrel, change drill bits, or add more drill rods. I sat at the desk and went through its drawers. In one I found clip boards, still with the drillers' rough notes. A quick check of them revealed that I had screwed-up, big time.

Driven by a need to confess I tried phoning Curtis. My phone had no signal. I was inside a steel container, so no surprise there. Outside again, I retried. Then a miracle happened. I got straight through to him. And on a Sunday.

'Sorry to phone you on a Sunday.'

'I work Sundays. It's the only time I get any peace.'

'Sorry.' Apologising sounded so unprofessional. I had to stop doing it.

'Why are you calling me, Doctor?'

'I messed up. Sorry.'

'What are you saying, exactly?'

'I'm on site. There are two drilling rigs. The one we saw, the yellow one, is not the one that drilled down through the clay.'

'And that is a problem?'

'Most definitely.'

'Perhaps you should start at the beginning?'

'The drill they used to drill down through the clay is a called a tripod rig. It's a cable-tool drill. It's simple. A winch lifts a heavy steel tube called a bailer and then drops it. It's like a massive version of one of those things used for planting daffodil bulbs.'

'That means nothing to me. I don't have a garden.'

'You must have seen tripod rigs. They used them to test the ground before they built the Queensferry Bridge.'

'Ah! Three steel legs?'

'You got it. They take the brake off the winch and the tube falls, cutting into the ground.'

'Do I need to know all this?'

'You do. It's important. The bailer has a flap on the bottom that traps the clay. They winch it back up and dump the clay. They bag some up as samples for the geologist to check. Those are the plastic bags in the core shed, the ones on that old armchair.'

'I remember. Go on…'

'Every so often they stop drilling so they can hammer steel tubing into the ground. It's called casing, it's done to stop the sides of the hole falling in.

Then they continue to drill down through the clay, except that this time they are doing it inside the casing. Every so often they stop, screw more casing onto the top and hammer it down a bit further.'

'Doctor Spargo – '

'Listen please. When they finally reach rock they leave the casing in place and then change to a coring rig. On the Kevron site that is the yellow one on the back of the lorry.'

'Ah, I see what you're getting at. By the time the rock core drilling rig is in place, the hole through clay is already lined with a steel pipe? Then all further drilling – the core drilling through rock – is carried out down through this pipe, this casing?'

'Correct.'

'So how can a tooth and bone drop down from the clay beds?'

I sighed. He'd worked it out for himself. 'You've got it. The bone and tooth can't have fallen from higher up. The driller lied.'

'Either that, or Mr Blackie got it wrong.'

'Blackie has been in the business too long to make mistakes like that. He wants the site reopened. If he can convince everyone that the remains are from a buried dog all the fuss will be over.'

'So why did you say you messed up? You started this by apologising.'

'I should have realised they would probably use a tripod rig to go through the clay. I should have known they cased the hole. I admit I was flustered by Blackie.'

'I see. Is everything solved?'

'All I've done is disprove the driller's story. The tooth and bone could not have been in the clay, they could not have fallen down the hole, they were definitely in the rock when it was drilled through. I still have no idea how they got there.'

'Have you told Kevron? Your friend?'

'If you mean Blackie, he's not here. If you mean Kevin Marshall then no, I thought I'd tell you first. And he's my employer. He's hardly my friend.'

Curtis stayed quiet. I was used to it. Then: 'Are you sure about this, Doctor? Have you been to the borehole? Have you seen this pipe, this casing?'

'The yellow drill truck is still there, it hasn't been moved. I'm walking to it now. I'll call you again when I'm sure of things.'

'No, stay with me. I need to know now.'

I was approaching the yellow truck rig. Compared with oil rigs this thing was a toy, a yellow painted lattice mast around five times my height, mounted on the back end of the truck.

'Just got to it,' I said. 'Hang on… yes, the mast is still in place, it's right over the hole. Before the drillers went off site they pulled out the drill rods and covered the hole with planks. Hang on a sec…' I shoved a plank aside with my boot. 'Moving them now,' I said, keeping him sweet. 'I'm looking at the top of a vertical steel pipe, about eight inches across. That's two hundred millimetres.'

'Yes, yes. Go on…'

'That's it. The casing is there, the hole is lined with steel. I know from the driller's records that the casing goes right down to bedrock. There is no way the remains could have dropped from the clay.'

'Yes, you said that. Perhaps you should now inform Mr Marshall.'

We ended the call. I didn't agree with him about calling Marshall. To say the driller was wrong, and maybe his site manager was complicit or incompetent, was not something he would want to hear. He wanted results, not grumbles from me.

Instead of calling him I used my phone to take photos of the rig and the casing. I wanted proof. I stood right above it, and used the flash on my phone to take pictures. Then I checked the photos. They showed the steel casing, of course. They also showed something else. Something I hadn't expected.

10

What I had expected to see in the photo was a bright reflection from water at the bottom of the borehole, perhaps a reflection so bright it would dazzle the camera. At a location like this the water table – the natural level of water in the ground beneath our feet – should be a couple of metres down at the most. But in this hole there was no reflection. The hole was dry.

To be absolutely sure I knelt down and used the torch on my phone to peer down the casing. I could see right to the bottom of the rust-coloured steel pipe, down to where the hole changed from a borehole through clay to a narrower one through brownish-red rock. I wobbled the phone light around, trying to get a reflection from any water in the rock hole. There was none.

Back in the core shed I again checked the driller's records, this time looking for a note about water. Drill rods are hollow. Water is pumped down them, through the rods and the core barrel, cooling the diamond drill bit and flushing the rock cuttings back to the surface.

By reading the driller's records properly for the first time I realised that not only had they not encountered water in the borehole, they had lost all their flushing water down the hole, perhaps thousands of gallons. Repeated through the driller's records were the words *lost flushing water*. Water went down. It didn't come back.

Back in the core shed I took down the key to the core box, wondering as I did so if it was Blackie or the geologist who decided to hide it over the window. Granted, it was out of the reach of short people. But it was about as secure as choosing *password* as a password.

I opened the box. If I were the geologist describing the rock core I would call it red-brown, perhaps dark red-brown. An interior decorator might think differently. *Burnt Earth*, perhaps? *Midnight Rust*?

Some rock core contains fossils or interesting minerals. This stuff looked boring, the same colour throughout and the same sandy texture. Above the gravel patch that had contained the bone and tooth the rock was broken into discs. Below it, the rock was an unbroken, continuous stick.

I took more photographs. Then, taking care not to disturb the core too much, I removed some of the discs of bedrock. Most of their surfaces had a thin coating of clay, which to me meant they had been broken many years ago rather than by the action of the drill. Some surfaces had been washed clean by the drill's flushing water – water that continued downwards, rather than back to the surface.

I replaced the discs of rock. To check there was nothing else in the gravel patch I poked around in it with a pencil. I found no more bone. No more teeth.

For me, geology has always been detective work, observing and sampling, piecing together evidence. In forensic work I have to answer the questions what and where, who and how, why and when. So far I could answer only one of these. We all knew *where*.

I was fairly sure that I also knew *what*. The piece of bone had to be from a crushed body. But what was the body of a young man – if it was a man – doing in rock, six metres underground?

I'd had a good day, I had proved to myself that the remains could not have fallen down the hole. To prove it to Curtis and Kevin Marshall – and in court if that ever became necessary – I would have to draw diagrams to show the different stages of drilling. That would not be a problem for me.

Knowing that the drillers lost flushing water meant that I also knew, though I did not have proof, that there was still an opening below ground, one large enough to hold a huge amount of water. Either that, or the water flowed away. If that were true, where had it gone?

That underground opening, whatever it was, had collapsed on the victim. The clues were all there. The drill had passed down through broken rock – broken because it had collapsed into the opening. It had then passed through a gravelly patch that contained the remains of the victim. Finally the core barrel cut into solid rock for the first time. Solid, because it was the floor of whatever that opening had been.

I wondered again if the remains were those of a miner. If so, then surely he would have known he was in the wrong kind of rock. These people might not have understood geology but that did not mean they were stupid. So, perhaps not a miner. But if not a miner, who else could it be?

I had just poured milk on my bowl of cereal when my mobile rang. It was Hamish Anderton, the site engineer, phoning on behalf of Mr Blackie.

'We're going to excavate. Mr Blackie says you need telling.'

I frowned into my phone. 'Excavate what?'

'The borehole site. We will pull the drill rig off and dig out the buried dog. Mr Blackie says that once we find it we can get on with our work.'

'You shouldn't do that.'

'I'm telling you what I've been told.'

When the call ended I called Curtis, repeating to him what I'd learned.

'They can't do that. I've got the lab results. I don't yet know about the bone but the tooth you found is human. Hang on, I've got another call. Doctor, I have to go.'

He hung up on me. I tapped in Kevron's head office number but got no reply. I knew Kevin Marshall started work early, but it wasn't yet eight. I tried again at five-minute intervals and when I eventually got through I repeated to him what Hamish Anderton had told me. Also, what Curtis had said about the tooth. He ended the call.

A few minutes later he called me back, thanking me for the prompt warning and saying the police had already called site to forbid any excavation work. He sounded stressed.

'The only excavation work to be done on site will be arranged by the police, not by Kevron. The Lord Advocate's office is demanding that the remains be exhumed. Why the Lord Advocate? Don't you have coroners up there?'

'We don't. The Lord Advocate has that responsibility. His Procurator Fiscal does the job of coroner. What do you mean, exhumation?'

'That isn't what I meant. I meant they want them recovered.'

'Are they aware that the remains are not in the clay? That they are six metres down in solid rock?'

'I'm not sure they understand that. I have spoken to DCI Curtis. He is arranging for a forensic team to work on site. Is it possible the remains are Ice Age, or something? I don't pretend to understand these things. The country was glaciated, wasn't it? Could there be a body that old? I'm thinking about that Ice Man they found in the Alps. Wasn't he four thousand years old?'

'If the remains were in the clay then I suppose there would be a remote chance of that. But they are in rock, well below any glacial effects. I have told Mr Curtis that I can now prove that nothing can have fallen down the hole during drilling. I won't bore you with the details. Please trust me.'

'If I didn't trust you I wouldn't have appointed you to do this for me. My contact up there tells me that DCI Curtis is inclined to believe what you are saying. How long will the excavation take, do you think?'

'To find a body in the clay? A body that isn't there? Who knows?'

'Dr Spargo, that is not helpful. Regardless of what you do or do not believe, I would like you on site while this is done. Will you do that for me?'

11

I had time on my hands. The team coming to site would need a day or so to prepare. Until I heard more from Curtis there was nothing I could to do. What I really wanted was to work on the gold, there were things I could do to it. Trouble is, for the first time in my life I was running a business. I needed to be paid for my time.

Though I had discussed the results of my microscopic inspection of the gold fragments with Curtis, I hadn't sent him the photos. Hoping that sending some to him might trigger a positive response, before leaving home for my lab I'd emailed photos to him. I added a one-liner that said *digital photomicrographs of the gold*.

My microscope had shown me the outsides of the fragments. What I now wanted to do was to see their insides. Slicing through grains the size of pinheads might sound difficult. I knew how to do it but I didn't have the equipment. Well, not all of it.

By midday I had encapsulated Curtis's gold in a disc of clear, quick setting resin. That bit was easy. I'd sprinkled the grains into a small flat-bottomed mould, mixed up resin and poured it in slowly. Once it had set, I eased the disc of resin from the mould. As I'd hoped, the grains had stayed on the bottom of the disc.

My mind wandered, concentrating not on what I was doing but on where the gold had been. Someone, a pathologist or an assistant, had searched Morini's chest for shotgun pellets and found this stuff instead. I shuddered. Invisible fingers stroked the back of my neck. Whoever shot Morini had opened a shotgun cartridge, tipped out the shot, replaced it with the fragments of gold and then sealed it again. My guess is that you don't use a bird gun to murder someone, you use a 12-gauge with twin barrels. That is one hell of a lot of gold.

I needed coffee. I found a passably clean mug and dropped in a teaspoon of instant. My mind wandered further. Curtis had said point-blank range. How far away is point-blank, I wondered, arm's length? Less than that? And where was Morini killed, at the edge of that field or elsewhere? If he wasn't killed at the field, why take the body there and dump it in undergrowth, perhaps leaving tyre tracks or footprints? It wasn't even hidden. Why not just dump it in the lane?

I didn't envy Curtis. I wouldn't know where to start. Thankfully it wasn't my problem. For all I knew, he had all the evidence he needed by now and had already arrested the killer. What I did know for sure about the killer is that he had blasted Morini with enough gold to have paid all my outstanding bills.

I had mentioned gold bullets to Curtis. It had been a tongue-in-cheek comment, but the more I thought about it, the more I was convinced that the murder had been a vendetta. Using gold had meant something to the killer. Curtis would be seeking answers to such questions. If, or when, he found those answers, he would not be sharing them with me.

I now had a resin disc. My next step was to grind down the end with the gold, not enough to grind it away, but enough to cut into the fragments. That sort of grinding is not a sandpaper job; at King's I'd had access to a lapping machine – a polisher that runs slowly and accurately. My budget didn't run to one of those and the best I could do was to grind it down on a sheet of plate glass. I had the plate glass. What I did not have was fine grinding paste and jeweller's rouge. This was, to me, too much like something my father used to say, *if we had some chips we could have fish and chips, if we had some fish…*

Edinburgh's Cockburn Street rises in a steep curve from Waverley Station to that part of the Royal Mile known as High Street. It is home to some fairly odd shops and Andy Kuzuk's is no exception. I remember the place years ago before Andy moved in, it was an occult shop of sorts, run by a heavily tattooed biker.

Andy's shop is so narrow that I swear it was built in what was once an alley between two buildings, one now a cafe and the other selling fancy dress, *'be a werewolf or vampire for the evening'*. Or maybe longer.

His shop door, set back one pace from the street, was normal size. The shop was not, it was unusually narrow. If I stuck my arms out either side of me I could almost touch each wall.

Ten years ago, in his third undergraduate year, Andy dropped out of geology. What the geological world lost was the art world's gain. The jewellery Andy designs is original, and painstakingly made. The last time I saw him he was supplying two London stores and negotiating with others in New York.

My presence was announced by the jangle of an ancient bell on a spiral spring above the door – a pointless jangle, because Andy wasn't there. A bead curtain at the far end of the shop divided the retail space from Andy's small workspace. This space, like the shop, was in darkness. From where I stood I could just make out the tall wooden stool beyond the bead curtain, on which Andy sat on while he worked. Just in case he was crouched down somewhere, I called out.

'Andy? You there?'

He wasn't. I walked down the shop. When I reached the curtain the doorbell jangled and Andy's lanky silhouette appeared in the doorway.

'Andy?'

He didn't know I was there. He jumped so much he dropped the paper bag he was carrying.

'Jez? Really?'

He retrieved the bag and walked to me. We stood face to face, simply staring. The last time I saw him here his head was shaved. The hairstyle I remember from his university days was now back again, sleek and dark and down to his shoulders. A Scots-Polish Richard III.

He squeezed past me, through the bead curtain and into his workspace. Switches clicked. Rays of light from spotlights above his workbench stabbed through the curtain like sun through a bare hedge. Beads clattered as I pushed through to him.

Andy works in silver, mounting semi-precious stones and attractive minerals in silver settings. His workplace resembles a blacksmith's shop in miniature, though without any horses or horseshoes. During my previous visit he explained to me that he fixes the bottom corners of his apron to the underside of the bench to catch filings and clippings from the precious metals he works with. All clever stuff.

'I thought you had closed the shop and forgotten to lock up,' I said.

'The door sign says closed.'

'Didn't see it.'

'I went next door for snacks.'

I nodded towards his displays. 'You left everything unlocked? All this jewellery?'

'My camera watches you. I was away a couple of minutes only. So what do I owe this… why are you here? I bet you are not just passing. Do you want to sit down, Jez?'

I shook my head. His stool was too high for me anyway. He reached for a folding chair propped against the wall and flipped down the seat for me. We sat there, him on his high stool and me on the low chair, staring at each other again. I felt uneasy. I guess he did too because he laughed.

'How long has it been, Jez? Five years?'

I had walked past the shop several times over the years. Either it was closed or I didn't have time to call in.

'Five or six. That's since I last saw you.'

'So why…?'

'I need your advice.'

'Wee birdies told me that you flew the nest.'

I wondered which wee birdies those were. Perhaps Andy kept in touch with his ex-colleagues.

'The birdies are right. I'm no longer with the department, though I still lecture there part time. I still have my postgrads.'

'That's Uni's loss. I didn't think you would do it, Jez. I thought you there for life.'

I didn't know how to take that. Andy was a plain speaker, he always had been. He once had a stand-up row in public with a senior lecturer, resulting in the head of department ordering him to apologise. He did not. It was, I'm sure, the reason Andy finally left the department. Whether it was his decision or theirs I never knew, but if the grapevine was right, he'd called the lecturer a *big fat bumptious bastard.* I'd admired the alliteration. And the truth of his words.

Andy was right about me. I was born in Zambia, schooled in Edinburgh, studied for my first degree at Edinburgh University, stayed on for my doctorate and then lectured. It took guts to leave, but I wanted to change my life. I had certainly done that.

'Were you around when I started the forensic stuff?'

He shook his head so I gave him the background and told him my news. I hoped it would give me a lead into why I was there.

'How about you?' I asked. 'How's business? Last time I saw you, you were about to supply two stores in the 'States.'

'Ah… it did not go well, Jez. I was sick for many weeks. I could not supply.'

'I'm sorry.'

'It turned out good. There was too much pressure. I am not short of customers here, Jez. I sell everything I make.'

'You should hire some elves.'

'No room for them here, you see? And I'd have elf and safety problem. Sorry. Old joke.'

'Fifty years ago that might have been funny.'

'What can I do for you, Jez? Something on your mind?'

He was right about that. I had too much on my mind.

'I need some grinding paste.'

'If it's for grinding-in the valves in your car engine you have come to wrong place. Try Halfords.'

'I haven't got a car. It's this…'

I took an envelope from my pocket and tipped the resin disc into my hand.

'What is it?'

'You tell me, Andy. You did geology.'

'Clear resin. Not sure what type. Polyester?'

'I'm not interested in the resin, I'm interested in this.' I turned the disc over and ran a finger over the surface. 'I want to polish it. I haven't got anything to polish it with.'

'It's gold, yes? Take it to Turtle. He'll put it in with others he makes.'

'He retired.'

Turtle – real name MacTurl – was a technician at King's. I'd considered asking one of the other labtecs to polish the disc for me, but I wanted independence from Uni. Also, sneaking stuff in to be polished is a good way to fall out with the head of department, I relied on her for income from my lectures and seminars. I could pay to have it done, of course, but that could take weeks. And there was another reason.

'I don't want to let it out of my sight.'

Andy nodded. 'Chain of custody.'

'You know about that?'

'Sometimes I watch TV.'

Knowing where a specimen had been and who has handled it matters only if used in a law court. Trouble is, when you take a sample you don't know if that will happen or not. With this sample I wasn't that worried. Curtis had more of it and he didn't want mine back. No doubt the disc would eventually end up in the demonstration collection I use for my seminars.

Andy was inspecting it, stroking his finger over the embedded gold.

'Looks like it's made in a kitchen. It's amateur.'

'I know that. I just need the paste.'

'Then you will do reflective microscopy to see what is there. Gold and perhaps other metals?'

'I don't remember you doing reflective microscopy.'

He shook his head. 'Couldn't.' He pointed to his eyes. 'I'm colour blind.'

I didn't know that. No reason why I should. Even the slightest hint of colour blindness would rule out identifying minerals the way I was going to do it. Polished minerals and metals, when seen through a reflecting microscope, have characteristic but very subtle colours. For the most part they are the kind of pastel shades you would get if you stirred a small spot of colour into a large can of white paint. Andy took the sample from me.

'Can I touch it? Is it a forensic sample?'

'Touching's no problem. The sample's what I call a pointer. There are pointers and provers. Pointers are bits of evidence that point an investigation in a certain direction but are too inconclusive to be used as evidence. Provers –'

'Help prove,' he said, holding up the disc, 'and possible to use in court as evidence. So what are you going to do with this?'

'I will borrow some grinding paste from you, spread it on a glass plate and polish the gold on it.'

'Borrow?'

'Semantics. Ask you for some. Not give it back.'

'Careful you don't grind the gold away, Jez. There is not much here.'

'I was thinking of using jeweller's rouge. That's if you've got any.'

'I have a better idea. Shall I do it for you?'

'Now, you mean?'

'While you wait.' He swivelled on his stool and nodded to what looked like a modelmakers lathe. 'I made this to polish flat faces on stones. I clamp the specimen this end.' He twiddled levers. 'Then I bring this rotating plate up to it.'

'Clever stuff.'

It took Andy ten minutes to polish the disc. He checked it often to be sure he wasn't polishing away too much gold. He cleaned it, passed it to me and I nodded approval. The surface was perfect. I tilted it so I could see the gold and it reflected Andy's spotlights as if it were a mirror. Though some of the smallest fragments had been ground away, sand-sized grains remained. The polishing process had cut into them and they shone like stars. He took it from me.

'I like it, Jez! It gives me ideas. I could do a lot of things with bits in resin, like this. Where did you get it?'

'Sorry. Can't tell you.'

'I don't suppose you can get more? No?'

I had a fleeting image of several Morinis in a row and a man with a pump-action shotgun.

'I sincerely hope not, Andy.'

12

While walking home from Cockburn Street I again thought about motive. Why would a murderer load fragments of gold into a shotgun cartridge? I thought again about gold bullets and silver bullets. If he was bumping off members of some dodgy devil-worshipping sect he would be well out of pocket by the time he'd finished.

I smiled as I crossed Princes Street. In my work I occasionally deal with dead things. The big difference between Curtis and me is that mine have usually been dead for hundreds of millions of years. What I'd told Curtis about bodies was true. If I'd wanted this kind of work I wouldn't have chosen geology.

'Those photos you sent. Is that right, the colours? It's not some lighting thing, making them so different?'

Talk of the devil. It was Curtis. I had taken shelter from a sudden heavy shower when he called my mobile. I had chosen the doorway of a hostel, not the most sensible place to stand. A constant stream of backpackers shoved past me, in and out of the doors.

'It's what the fragments look like under a binocular microscope,' I said. 'Except that I saw them in 3-D. The photos don't show that of course. Would you like to – '

He interrupted me. 'Did you get any indication of where they might be from?'

I was tempted to say Morini. 'Several sources,' I said. 'Probably.'

'There seem to be many different shapes. What does that tell you? Could being shot from a gun have caused that?'

'No. They were like that when they were loaded into the shotgun cartridge.'

'We haven't yet established that they were in a shotgun cartridge.'

I didn't argue. He was right not to assume such things. But as far as I could see, the only alternative was that they had been inserted into Morini one by one and that hadn't happened.

He stayed quiet. Then, 'I didn't know you were still working on this.'

'I'm not. I unpacked my microscopes and thought it worth a look. I wasn't thinking of billing you for my time.'

'That's not the point. The last thing I need is two labs coming up with different conclusions.'

I wasn't expecting that, not from him. It was the kind of thing Blackie said about geologists.

'I thought you would be grateful for any information that might help you solve your case. I'm not competing with other labs. I thought the photographs may help.'

'It didn't work on the Kevron site. Two geologists, two opinions.'

Okay. I found that offensive. Comparing me with that dimwit geologist was like comparing Curtis's detective skills and experience with those of a cop straight from college. And a dozy one at that. I held my tongue. If I won this argument I would lose much more.

'I was trying to help.'

'Perhaps it would be best if you returned the sample to me.'

I swallowed. Some of the sample was encapsulated in a resin disc and the rest was a grey slurry in a jar near Andy's lathe. The devil in me felt like popping the disc into an envelope and posting it to Curtis with my compliments. but to do such a thing might end my career. Before Scotland's police forces combined into one force, several of them had given me work. Now, if I fell out with Curtis, I fell out with them all.

When I didn't respond to his suggestion he changed the subject. Talked, instead, about my visit to site.

'Have you come to any conclusions about the Kevron business?'

'Only what I told you. About the different site investigation rigs.'

'Have you communicated your findings to Kevron yet?'

'About the casing? No, I haven't told Mr Marshall yet. Do you have any DNA information about the bone and tooth?'

'Nothing yet.'

We left it at that. He was having a bad day.

Kevin Marshall phoned me that evening. I was having time off, attempting to relax in front of the television with yet another ready-cook meal. That he called me so late in the day surprised me. Telling me that he wanted me in his office next morning surprised me even more. He had already booked me on the on the first flight of the day to Bristol.

I woke at an ungodly hour, drove to Edinburgh airport and left the hire car in the long-stay. Around three hours later, at Bristol Airport, a smart grey-haired man, somewhat older than me, held up a card that said KEVRON. We walked together through acres of car park and stopped at a large 4x4. He opened the front passenger door for me. I had expected to sit in the back seat, not in the front. Once we were strapped in, he turned face me. Held out his hand.

'Kevin Marshall,' he said, smiling. 'Sorry, Doctor Spargo. That was mischievous of me.'

I shook my head. I was not amused. Had I been overtired or just plain stupid I might have spent the last five minutes quizzing him about Kevron and asking him what he thought of his boss. I wondered if he played that trick on everyone he picked up.

'I thought you were your driver.' I said. A pointless remark. I had nothing else to say.

On the road all traces of flippancy vanished. There was no small talk, no asking about my flight. Marshall was down to business.

'DCI Curtis says they are going ahead with the recovery excavation. I want you on site the whole time they are doing it. Do you have a problem with that?'

'No, I don't. Except it's a waste of time. They won't find anything.'

'I respect your judgement, but that is not the point. I need to know what's going on, day to day. I'm told that they want to stop the whole site for the duration of the work. Is that necessary?'

'Who, the police?'

'DCI Curtis. Or the Procurator. I'm not sure.'

'DCI Curtis hasn't been very communicative since you appointed me. I can't see why they would want to stop the site. That borehole is well away from the main site work.'

I wondered what he wanted from me. If it was simply to see if I had any influence over Curtis, he could have done that by phone.

'I'm not sure how I can help you with that,' I said. 'Not if closing the site is the Procurator Fiscal's decision. Have you spoken to your friend, Curtis's superintendent? Can he do anything?'

He went quiet. Turning his head he regarded me inquisitively. My careless, unguarded remark had revealed to him that not only did Curtis know of the relationship, he had been indiscrete to mention it to me.

I detected a smirk. 'We still play golf, if that's what you are alluding to.' My little indiscretion had been forgiven – this time. 'Closing the site is not the reason I asked you here,' he continued. 'I wanted to meet you. Some things are best done face to face. Also, I have maps and plans that they do not have on site. I want you to look through them.'

I sat there, nodding. To my left, in the distance, was Brunel's suspension bridge, spanning Bristol's Avon Gorge. Such an impressive structure. Shame Brunel didn't live to see it built. That would have gutted me, designing something like that and not seeing it finished. If I remember correctly, he died before construction even started.

'Well? Can you do that?' Marshall asked.

Distracted by Brunel's creation I had missed a question.

'Sorry, I was miles away. Must be jet lag. I've never seen the Clifton Bridge before.'

'Jet lag? You were in the air for less than two hours. Well? Will you do it?'

So, not jet lag then. Just tiredness. I tried to unravel his questions.

'You want me there the whole time. On your site. At the excavation. Yes, I can be there. But I'm not part of the team. Have you considered the possibility that they might not want me there?'

He kept his eyes on the road, negotiating tight bends.

'The responsibility of everything that happens on site is mine. I shall ensure that DCI Curtis knows that I want you there, observing. Now, take me through it. How will they start?'

'I've been wondering about that. They will need somebody who can understand the ground in three dimensions.'

'Well, there you go. Is that you?'

'It won't be me. It's likely to be a team from Glasgow University. If it's headed up by who I think will head it up, he is more than capable.'

'How will they start?'

'That depends on what they are trying to do. If they really believe the remains are in the clay, then they will prob – '

'Forget about remains in the clay. If this team is as good as you say it is, they will soon be agreeing with you that there is no dead dog.'

'The borehole is cased. As soon as they see that, they will realise that nothing from the clay could have fallen down the borehole.'

'Oh?'

'The borehole was cased from collar to bedrock. There is a steel pipe – '

'I do know what borehole casing is.'

'The excavation team will soon realise that the remains are sandwiched in a collapsed underground opening.'

He was nodding again. 'Collapsed mineworkings, you mean? I know there were mines in that part of Scotland.'

'That's just it, there weren't, not that far east of Edinburgh. Had it been a mining district, and had the bone been in the right kind of rock, then yes, that would have been my suggestion.'

'Go on. What next?'

'Not easy. There are conflicts of opinion. We have two factions, one believing there is a shallow burial and another, perhaps just me, saying that the remains are deep within the rock.'

'And a third group, those with no expert knowledge of such things: DCI Curtis, the Procurator etcetera. Also myself, to some extent.'

'The casing proves that the remains did not fall from the clay.'

'You know that. I know that. Does DCI Curtis know that?'

'He does now.'

'But they have to hedge their bets. They have to consider the possibility that you are wrong. It would be remiss of them not to excavate the clay, would it not?'

I shrugged. 'It will mean stripping off layers of ground by hand, bit by bit and then sieving it. You must have seen those TV series.'

'I can't say I have. I don't have time for television. Tell me?'

'As they excavate they will look for signs of disturbance, discolouration of the ground and the edges of a grave or a backfilled pit.'

'And if you are right, there will be none of these things. What happens then?'

'That will be up to the Procurator. Presumably he will be advised by the police. After a while everyone will have to accept that the remains lie much deeper, in the underlying rock.'

'And then what?'

'Someone will have to decide whether or not to keep excavating. But into three metres of hard rock, not soft clay.'

He was nodding. 'I'm hoping that when the time comes you will help with that decision.'

I didn't like the sound of that. Such a decision shouldn't be mine to make.

'So,' he added. 'How long will all this take?'

I shrugged and gave a palms-up, *I have no idea* gesture. He was still peering ahead but for a second he flicked his head around and caught my eye. I was being paid for information. Shrugs were not acceptable.

I backtracked. 'That is difficult to estimate. It depends on what they decide to do. If the Procurator wants the whole skeleton recovered, which I'm sure will be his wish, that will need a shaft about four metres across.'

'That is assuming there is a whole skeleton. Why that wide? Why four metres?'

'The drill went through the skull. They will have to assume that the remains are lying flat, but they don't know in which direction. They won't want to sink a pit two metres across and then find that the main skeleton is lying in the other direction.'

I stayed quiet. He could work that one out himself.

'Because it could be lying in any direction, and is unlikely to be more than six feet tall?'

'You've got it.'

'Depth isn't a problem for us. We can excavate that clay in a couple of hours. Then we can attempt to rip out the rock.'

'They won't let an excavator anywhere near their dig.'

'Even when they realise the remains aren't in the clay?'

For the last mile or so of the journey nothing more was said. Finally we turned onto roads that skirted the city's redeveloped docklands and pulled up outside a glass-fronted, two storey building. A shiny, stainless steel sign said KEVRON in heavy black letters – an impressive sign for an impressive building. Kevron's offices occupied a recently modernised nineteen-fifties or 'sixties building, its original frontage replaced by dark tinted glass that overlooked a waterfront, once part of the busy harbour, now rebuilt and revitalised for tourists.

'Kevron,' I said. 'Kevin? Ronald?'

'Ron – Ronald – was my father. He set up the company in the nineteen-fifties. He died several years ago.'

'I'm sorry.'

'Don't be. He had a good life. About your visit, Doctor. Our site is design and build. We hire the architects, do the site investigation and the up-front research as well as the construction work. The former landowner passed documentation to us, some of it relevant to our work and some of it not. One of my engineers looked through it all some time ago and I want you to do the same. What was not relevant back then might be relevant now. We have a different situation.'

I had hoped to be shown around the offices but that didn't happen. At reception he introduced me to a young engineer who doubled as office librarian. She led me to a room on the first floor furnished with an impressively polished table and matching, upholstered chairs. Glass fronted bookcases lined the walls, some shelves dedicated to books and others to box files. A wide, tinted-glass window gave a panoramic view over the marina-like harbour.

I hadn't expected such furnishings. The engineer, sensing my surprise, explained that the library doubled as the boardroom. I should have guessed. In a wide space between bookcases hung a life-size photographic portrait of an elderly, grey haired man. The *Ron* in Kevron, perhaps? Kevin Marshall's late father?

One end of the table had been loaded with books, leaflets and maps. I hoped I managed to hide my dismay at the size of the pile. I had been booked on a flight home the same evening. To go through these documents thoroughly would take more than one day.

'A lot of stuff,' I said.

She nodded. 'Yes, there is. Feel free to call me if there is anything you need. I'm two doors down.' She pointed. 'That way.'

I soon realised that not all of the documents related to the site. Kevron had worked elsewhere in Scotland and some documents related to those sites. It seemed to me that at the start of the project everything possible had been collected together in case it was relevant.

I guessed that whenever the room was used for board meetings or discussions with clients, coffee was brought in to them. I had no such luck. During the day, periodically – and frequently – I made use of the automatic machine in the corridor. I had better luck at midday. For lunch I was offered a choice of sandwiches, brought to me by Kevin Marshall's secretary. Marshall, it transpired, had other things to do and that suited me perfectly. He dropped in to see me every hour, as regularly as if he had set a timer. Perhaps he had.

By the time the taxi came to take me to the airport I had winnowed the assemblage of documents down to one large pile of books, maps, and site plans.

Much to the consternation of the librarian, I had been given permission to borrow them and they arrived at my home next day, transported by overnight courier. I had offered to take some of them with me on my flight home, but Marshall wouldn't hear of it. After unpacking them I dutifully phoned Curtis and told him about my trip. I also told him that I had an assortment of documents from Kevron.

'It will take me some time to go through them all,' I said. 'I'm not optimistic. I haven't yet found anything in them that might help us.'

I used the word *us* deliberately. Him and me, working together.

'Have you had any more thoughts about the remains?'

'Only that Mr Marshall and I both believe that there must have been an underground opening of some kind. A shaft or a well. Perhaps an adit.'

'An adit is a mine into the side of a hill?'

'It is.'

'There aren't any hills. And I thought you said there weren't any mines.'

He was right. Apart from the gentle slope up to the core shed and steel containers, the ground was flat.

'Sometimes, rather than sink a shaft, miners drove an adit at an angle, down into flat ground. I know I said there weren't any mines, but that doesn't mean men didn't go exploring. Landowners couldn't believe their neighbours had been blessed with valuable resources and they hadn't. The other thing it could be is a well. Though as there is no water in that borehole, that's unlikely.'

Whoever Haddington Man was – I assumed it was a man – he must have dug through solid rock. The rock I'd seen in the core samples wasn't the hardest stuff around but I wouldn't have liked to have cut through it myself, even with modern hand tools. Was it something primitive man could have done? Probably only if he had tools of bronze or iron.

Curtis said nothing for a while. I could hear voices in the background. Then, 'Would they have made records of their excavations?'

'Mine plans weren't compulsory until the mid-1800s. Even then, just because the law said they had to be made doesn't mean they were made.'

'And if the remains are earlier than that, there won't be any plans?'

'If the remains are earlier than that, it's really academic who the victim is.'

Curtis grunted. 'You said *victim*.'

'Victim of an underground mishap. I'm not suggesting it's the victim of a crime.'

'Hopefully we'll know more about that soon. The Glasgow team will be on site on Thursday.'

'I didn't know that. Nobody told me that.'

'I'm telling you now. Will you be on site?'

'I have to be. Mr Marshall insisted.'

'Then I'll see you there, first thing.'

I spent time on the documents. Later that day I visited my lab, adjusting and then using my reflecting microscope. I had been itching to look at the resin block ever since Andy polished it for me. By late evening I had fifty or so images of the polished grains stored on my laptop. Also, I had many more unanswered questions buzzing around in my brain.

My mobile rang as I was getting ready for bed. It was Kevin Marshall, apparently unaware of the late hour. He apologised. Not for the late hour, but for abandoning me yesterday.

'Something came up that needed my time. Did you receive the documents?'

'They arrived this morning. Thank you.'

'Have you learned anything from them? Do they help?'

I made a few positive, noncommittal comments. I didn't want to admit that I'd opened the package but not spent any time on them. I'd had my fill of paperwork.

'Are you saying you haven't been on site today?'

'I haven't. The dig team won't be there until Thursday.'

'Ah! So you have heard. That's what I'm calling you about.'

'DCI Curtis told me.'

'I apologise. I asked Jimmy to tell you. He should have phoned you.'

Of course he should.

13

I arrived at the Kevron site at lunchtime next day. Hamish Anderton, the young site engineer, came out to meet me.

'The team is here, Doctor Spargo, I'll take you to them. Do you have boots? A hard hat? High visibility jacket?'

I pressed the car's remote. The car boot clicked itself open and answered his question. All I needed was there.

'And disposable coveralls,' I said. 'But I won't be needing those.'

'Not until they get down to the remains.'

Probably not at all, I thought. He walked with me across site. The yellow drill and its truck had gone. Someone, a skilled digger driver who was no longer there, had used the bucket of his digger to scrape the ground where the drill had been, skimming off stones, weeds, and surface mud so that the whole area now resembled a square, flat-bottomed, shallow dry pond. A short stub of rusty pipe – the borehole casing – stood exposed at its centre.

Two of Blackie's men had unloaded sections of large mesh fence panels from a dump truck and were busy erecting them around the scraped-off area. During our approach the fence grew in length with remarkable speed. Panels taller than me, locked into place one by one.

I saw Blackie, pacing and pointing, stamping his heavy boots to mark where the fence panels should go. He hadn't seen me. He walked backwards towards me, guiding panels into place, indicating where the entrance to the compound should be by swinging his arm sideways, like a gate. I had to step aside to avoid him walking back into me and he turned, surprised. Fixed me with a glare and said 'You!'

Another group, two men and two women, stood well clear of the action. I thought I recognised the tallest member as Cameron Thomson, a Glasgow-based forensic anthropologist – except that Cameron didn't have a beard... or didn't have one the last time I saw him. He called out to me.

'Jessica!'

'Cameron?'

Judging by their inappropriate clothing, two of the group were students, probably first-years. The fourth member, a woman, looked more like a postgrad or junior lecturer. I walked over to the now-bearded Cameron.

'Didn't recognise you,' I said. 'Sorry.'

'The beard you mean? You don't like it?'

'It's *your* beard, Cam. Doesn't matter if I like it or not.'

'I finally made Prof,' he said, stroking it. 'Thought it was time for big changes.'

It was a Drake-like beard. Without a moustache it didn't look right. A big Scotsman, with a name like Cameron, should have a big bushy one.

'*Professor* Thomson,' I murmured. 'Congratulations! Well deserved! I'm surprised I hadn't heard.'

I wasn't surprised at all. It must have happened recently. I was beginning to realise how out of touch I was with the academic grapevine.

He turned to watch the final mesh panel being lifted into place. Blackie's men walked back along the fence, straightening the panels. Cameron turned back to me.

'I understand from Mr Blackie that there has been some friction.'

'You could say that. We don't quite see eye to eye if that's what you mean. He has geolophobia.'

Cameron frowned. 'What's that?'

'Just made it up. He dislikes geologists. Though after the experiences he's had recently I can't say I blame him.'

'The core logger.'

I nodded. I had said enough. I didn't want to influence Cameron in any way, it was right that he should develop his own opinions. And anyway, it was time to stop talking. Blackie had finished and was walking towards us.

'I hope you are satisfied with that,' he said, addressing Cameron and avoiding my eyes. 'That's all the panels I have so it will have to do. I've been told to ask you if there is anything more that you want.'

Cameron looked over the man's shoulder at the fence and shook his head. 'Thank you, but no. For now we have all the equipment we need.'

'*Told to ask*?' Cameron said, when Blackie was out of hearing.

'His not too subtle way of telling you he isn't doing any of this willingly.'

Curtis called me to say he wasn't coming, but didn't say why. That suited me. I decided to spend time with Cameron rather than watching him from afar. I crossed the scraped-off surface and entered his team's newly-erected gazebo.

Watching Cameron and his team at work was like watching paint dry. I knew their procedures, knew how they worked. They were looking for evidence of boundaries, the edges of a shallow grave or pit. I knew they wouldn't be successful. However thoroughly you search, you cannot find what is not there.

After what seemed to me like half a day but was only two hours, they had scraped away the top few centimetres of clay to make two narrow trenches that crossed in the centre. The borehole's steel casing stood at the intersection of the trenches, standing proud of the ground.

Cameron came to me. Like the other members of his team he resembled a swamp creature. Dutifully I had been standing some way off, having declined his offer of disposable coveralls and inappropriate overshoes. Inappropriate, that is, for so much mud.

'Nothing?' I asked.

'Nothing yet.

'The remains came from within bedrock, six metres down,' I said. 'I'm sure you've heard that by now. No way could they have fallen down the hole.'

He frowned. 'Really? Our brief was that human remains in the clay had been drilled through and had fallen down the borehole. I have seen the tooth and skull fragment. They are definitely human.'

I stood open-mouthed, more for effect than surprise. Whoever called in Cameron and his team hadn't bothered to mention my theories. He stood stroking his beard while I explained what I knew. I asked him what he would do when he realised there was no shallow grave. The nodding head became a shaking one.

'That is not something I have even considered, Jessica.'

I had forgotten what a good listener he was. He listened to me without comment, his frown deepening as I told him about the casing. I took him and a member of his team to the core shed to show him the core and the gravel patch.

By the time we left site that day it was clear to all that there was no dead dog, dead human, nor a dead anything else in the clay. The team had excavated to a depth of around half a metre, enough to have detected a shallow grave. Had there been one to detect.

Although no bones were found, the day was not without incident. Shortly after a cloudburst swamped the dig, Blackie appeared. For a while he stood quietly, smoking a cigarette, watching the team but saying nothing. Once he had ground the cigarette stub into the clay with a wellington boot he called out to Cameron. I had already moved away and didn't catch what he said. Whatever it was, it provoked a prolonged, heated exchange of views. I stayed well away.

Before driving home I called Kevin Marshall and updated him, tactfully, on the absence of anything interesting in the dig. I said the same to Curtis, plus a curtly delivered expression of disbelief from me that Cameron Thomson hadn't been told of my theories.

'Cameron Thomson?'

'Professor Thomson. Forensic anthropologist from Glasgow. He's leading the dig.'

'Do you know him? Is he reliable?'

'Very.'

He hung up on me.

Though I was reluctant to admit it, I missed many of my university colleagues. I had thought that after working in my lab in the yard at King's for so many years I would be used to being on my own. The last assistant I had was poor company, a budding introvert who worked through the day wearing earbuds, blocking out the world with tinny music.

To be truthful I wasn't much better myself. I didn't need people around me while I worked. At King's, when I needed a break, I would leave my lab and walk through corridors with papers in my hand as if going somewhere important. Chance meets with staff or students were inevitable and they broke up my day. Now, in my new lab, that wasn't an option.

More than once over the last few days I'd admitted to myself that even a corridor encounter with deWit – *Mister Nasty* – might be better than nothing. Or perhaps a chat with a senior lecturer, who no doubt would, as always, and depending on the time of year, fill me in on a field trip recently undertaken. Once, these trips were nearly all in Scotland. In recent years they involved warmer climes such as the Seychelles and the smaller Greek islands. I used to feign interest. Now I missed even that.

My break with academia was deliberate. Academics tend to socialise with academics. For years I believed I was different, a belief that my association with DCI Curtis strengthened considerably – a belief crushed the day I overheard one of his colleagues refer to me as 'one of that academic horde'. I'd hoped Curtis would contradict him. He hadn't.

Sometimes, as a substitute for a break from work, I would grab what I was working on, walk home from King's and do it there. The thirty-minute brisk walk home served as a break of sorts, but more often than not my work would continue all evening. It still does. When you work for yourself it's difficult to know when to stop.

14

I had other things to do. Back in the centre of Edinburgh I parked the hire car at Waverley Station and walked to the station concourse, intent on buying wine. I was on my way to see Andy again and wondered if he still drank red, the heavy Cabernet stuff that strips paint. Me, I prefer whites these days but I don't buy them that often, I won't drink on my own because the cork – or screw cap, these days – doesn't seem to want to go back on the bottle.

The CLOSED sign on Andy's shop disappointed me. It was one of those ancient, white card things that hang on a loop of string that can be turned to say OPEN. Except it wasn't. I swore softly, checked the time and then swore again. It was later than I thought. I pressed my nose to the glass door and noticed a dim light behind the bead curtain at the far end of the shop. In case he was still there I tapped on the door. Then I tapped again, this time on the glass, with a coin. Just as I was wondering if he left a light on at night deliberately, the beads moved, the shop lights came on, and Andy appeared. Taking long strides towards me he unlocked the shop door, opening it just wide enough to let me in.

'Jez! Problems?'

'No problems. Everything is fine. I got you this.' I held out one of those colourful, slim bottle bags, this one printed with red sparkle. 'For the polishing job.'

'That's kind. There is no need.'

'I know that. I hope you still drink reds.'

We had stopped just inside the shop. He was peering into the bag.

'Open it now?'

I shook my head. 'No, it's for you.'

'You are not drinking?'

'I'm driving. My car's at Waverley.'

'Tea?'

'I'd prefer coffee.

'Sorry, Jez, I have only tea.'

'Tea's okay if it's weak.'

'You sure you are all right? You seem down. Work no good? Do you miss the department?'

He asked the last question tongue in cheek. I think.

'I miss the distractions. Can't say I miss the department.'

He was as perceptive as ever. Annoyingly so. How I felt or did not feel at the moment was not a topic I wished to pursue.

'The polished block was good? Did you use it?'

'I had a quick look at it yesterday evening. It's almost as good as those made by Terrance.'

'Turtle McTurl. Is he still there?'

'He retired last month.'

'Ah, you told me this, I remember. I think everyone is leaving the department. What will Turtle do when he retires? The department is his life.'

'He has already done it. He sold his house and moved to Ullapool.'

'Ullapool? That is as far as you go from Edinburgh before you fall off the edge of Scotland. Why did he go there?'

'His daughter and grandchildren live there. It's a puzzle, Andy.'

He had filled his kettle and was plugging it in. 'Turtle is a puzzle?'

'Sorry, no. I mean the polished section you made puzzles me. I examined it under reflected light.'

'No use you asking me. I told you, I can't do that thing.'

'It was once the best way to distinguish between different minerals. Some still think it is.'

'So, what's the puzzle?'

'What do you know about it? Do you know how reflective microscopy works?'

'I remember. You polish the surface of rock. You look at it through a microscope, a special one that is fitted with a light that shines on its polished surface. Different minerals show as different colours. I tried it once. To me the colours all looked the same.'

I nodded. He'd got it right. 'Most of the grains are gold, 'I said. 'But there are at least two fragments of platinum. I couldn't find much silver, which is strange if it comes from jewellery. There is lead, I think. And copper. Would you expect copper?'

'In jewellery? Perhaps in modern stuff. I don't use copper, it tarnishes, it turns green. You think there is lead?'

'Lead is usually easy to identify. Not sure about this stuff though. It's in thin layers between copper and silver.'

The kettle was blowing steam. Andy took a white pottery teapot from a cupboard, took off the lid, popped in two teabags and added water.

'Not too strong for me. One tea bag is good.'

'The lead is thin?'

'Very thin.'

'Is it solder, perhaps? A mix of lead and tin? Lead solder isn't used much these days. What you have was never jewellery, Jez. You have metals cut from electric switches and relays. Gold and platinum make best electrical contacts. Silver is used also, but it is not as good.'

While he poured tea I considered what he'd said. 'Are you thinking computers?'

'Old ones, not new ones, not modern ones. What is all this about?'

'You know I can't tell you.' I perched myself on a low cabinet and sipped my tea, wondering how much I could tell him without breaching confidences. 'Why would anyone load a shotgun cartridge with fragments of gold?'

'For real? Is that what this is about? The shooting?'

'You've heard about it?'

'Where have you been, Jez? Don't you watch TV news?'

'Not lately. I've been preoccupied. What was said?'

'They gave no name or place. They didn't say shotgun. Didn't say gold.'

'Nor will you or I'll be in trouble. Promise?'

He nodded. 'It has to be a vendetta. Has to be revenge.'

'I thought that.'

'Interesting, though. The killer knows he used gold but the victim does not. It's a big cost, too. Was it a 12-bore?'

'12 gauge, I think. Is that the same as 12-bore?'

He nodded again. 'If it was a 12-bore, the cartridge would need an ounce of gold at least. Perhaps two? That is one thousand pounds worth of gold.'

'That much?'

'A lot of trouble to make. Takes time to cut that amount from electrical parts.'

'Where would they get them from, a recycling centre? Those places always seem to be loaded up with old computers and televisions.'

He shrugged. 'Modern computers have small electrical contacts, microscopic, just a thin layer of gold. They are not big contacts like those you have. You want me to ask around?'

'I'd rather you didn't. I've told you more than I should.'

'You haven't told me anything. You asked why someone would fill a shotgun cartridge with gold. I said I didn't know.'

It didn't take me long to realise that babysitting the site team was a waste of my time. Cameron was a professional, he didn't need me looking over his shoulder. My time would be better spent revamping my Uni forensics course. When the Kevron job was over it would be my only paid work.

The solution came to me in the night – I would take my Uni work to site and do it there. I didn't particularly want to do it in the core shed because it would mean moving the core box off the bench to make space. I didn't want to do anything Blackie might bitch about.

Cameron had told me that Blackie had reluctantly agreed to provide him with a shipping container in which to store equipment. It hadn't yet materialised. Until it arrived he was keeping his kit in his small white van. I wondered if the container, if and when it came, would be a suitable workplace for me.

My hired car had become a hindrance. Parking it in my garage wasn't an option and I suspected that even if I cleared away all my packing cases, which

I couldn't yet do, the car wouldn't fit into it anyway. My house lay inside the city's meter zone so this morning, like every other morning when I don't want to leave for work early, I moved the car from a single yellow line to a hard-to-find meter space. Eventually I found one and eased the car into it, only to realise that I had no coins for the ticket machine. Edinburgh's meters also have card payment systems. I didn't want to use that, not for a hired car.

Furious with myself, with the car and the city, I drove to the hire firm's office, returned the car and took a taxi to site. It cost an arm and a leg but it was worth it. And, I hoped, rechargeable to Kevron.

A stiff breeze blew away overnight rain. Because of my car problems Cameron and his team were on site well before me. Rain from higher parts of the site, unable to soak into the clay, had channelled its way downslope to the dig and half-filled it with water. Cameron and his team stood bare-footed under their gazebo with their trouser legs rolled up high. They had tied up the gazebo's sides and were standing almost knee deep in water, scooping it up with buckets and hurling it away. That they were doing it surprised me. The last thing Cameron said to me as we left site yesterday was that I was right – the dig was a waste of time.

I called out as I approached them. 'They invented pumps to do things like that!'

He swung his bucket. A curving column of grey water arced towards me. Knowing it would fall well short I didn't bother to move. It was good to see a flash of the old Cameron. Back in the day he'd been a bit of a lad. Added responsibility had brought added seriousness.

He waded towards me, breathing heavily, wiping his beard with the back of his hand. Unfit, I thought. Too much time behind a desk.

'A pump, yes. Kevron's bringing one.'

'No frogs in there?'

'Wrong time of year. Wait until Spring.'

'What's your next move?'

He shrugged. 'Drive home? If it was up to me that's what I'd do.'

'But?'

'But it's not. The dating results are in. They did carbon fourteen on the tooth. It gave an age of nineteen-sixty. Plus or minus a couple of years.'

'Oh my god, Cameron! Surely that's impossible? You saw the tooth, it looked ancient.'

'Iron staining, Jessica. Just to be sure, they re-ran the test with a second sample, also the bone from the skull. It gave the same result. We have a recent death.'

I was shaking my head. It made no sense. 'Why did they go for carbon fourteen? Surely radiocarbon dating is for prehistoric stuff?'

'I suggested it. Belt and braces. I wasn't expecting anything useful from it.'

I walked away from him and called Curtis. He was, he said, about to call me. He'd just been handed the dating results.

'It says the victim was born in the early nineteen-sixties,' he said. 'Can that be right? That tooth looked to me like an adult tooth. We are born with baby teeth. We lose them and then we get adult teeth.'

'Not so. Our adult teeth are there at birth, they grow behind our baby teeth, eventually pushing them out.'

'Point taken, Doctor. Though when you first saw the remains you did say they were ancient.'

'I was mistaken. They were brown, they simply looked ancient. Iron minerals in the rock had stained them.'

'Tell me about this carbon dating. Can they really date that accurately?'

'Only if the subject was born between the mid-nineteen fifties and nineteen seventy. It's bomb carbon.'

'Go on.'

'Best if I send you a paper explaining it.'

'No it's not. Tell me now.'

15

I tried to keep it simple, explaining on the phone to Curtis that radiocarbon dating measures the amount of a particular kind of carbon in a sample – a naturally occurring, radioactive kind known as carbon fourteen. In archaeology, it is used to date archaeological finds between five hundred and fifty thousand years old.

'The post-war atomic bomb tests each released large amounts of carbon fourteen into the atmosphere,' I said. 'This extra radioactive carbon added to the amount of natural carbon fourteen in living things.'

'Are you saying it upsets the results?'

'Ironically, it does not. For biological things that were formed at that time it makes dating more accurate. The amount of this carbon can be linked to the date of each bomb test. It's very accurate for remains from those born between the mid-fifties to around nineteen-seventy.'

'So we have remains from an individual born around nineteen-sixty. That tooth looked fully developed to me. Does that mean we are looking at a teenage victim?'

'I'm not the person you should be asking. But judging by the curvature of the skull and the fact that the natural bone sutures were still visible, I'd say around fifteen or sixteen.'

There were no more questions. Not about radiocarbon dating, anyway.

'How are things on site? Are they excavating yet?'

'They started yesterday. They are taking things slowly. It's clear to everyone that there is nothing in the clay. As I've said, the remains are sandwiched in gravel, with rock below and above them.'

'Yes, yes. What's the next move?'

'Cameron has spoken to the Procurator's office. He's been told that the remains must be recovered.'

'I know that, I've been told that. How is he going to do it?'

'He's going to need a shaft.'

'Who pays for that?'

I had no idea. I was about to answer him when I heard a phone ringing in the background.

'I have to go,' he said. 'Procurator's office on my landline. If you haven't already informed Mr Marshall about the victim's age then I suggest you do it now.'

I didn't need him to tell me that. It was not something Kevin Marshall should hear from anyone else.

From the hollow sound of Kevin's mobile I guessed he was in his car. He listened while I gave him the same information I gave Curtis.

'It's a game-changer,' I said. 'The police will take over everything. It's no longer a matter of me providing you with words to say to the media.'

'I realise that. What is it you are telling me, exactly?'

'I suppose I'm asking you if you still want me involved.'

I waited for an answer. I could hear him talking, not to me but to someone in his car. I tried in vain to hear what they were saying.

'Dr Spargo, the police are happy that you stay involved. That's if you are still willing to do it.'

'I am very willing.'

'Fine. What happens now?'

'We need a shaft.'

'We?'

'Me and Professor Thomson.'

'We don't do shafts. We are builders, we don't pretend to be civil engineers. Until last year I had a mining engineer on my staff who could have done it. Leave it with me, I'll deal with it. When you see Professor Thomson tell him I will arrange everything.'

'He's on site with me now.'

'Have you spoken with DCI Curtis?'

'He seems concerned about who is paying for all this.'

'That is not your problem.'

We ended the call. That he was able to say the police were happy for me to continue made me think Curtis's boss must have been in the car with him. I returned to Cameron. He seemed anxious to talk.

'It changes everything, Jessica. If the victim had lived then he – or she – would now be around sixty years old. There are likely to be relatives still living. We must take them into account. We must find out who they are.'

I nodded. I knew that, I'd been subtracting dates too. 'That is not our problem, the police will do that. I've been talking with Mr Curtis. Is there any way we can tell how old the victim was when he died?'

'You are assuming it's a *he*. That has not been established.'

I had assumed the remains were of a male because I'd been thinking about miners and diggers of wells.

'To determine age we need a tissue sample,' he said. 'We are unlikely to get one. The tooth is fully developed, so it's not from a young child. We also get some idea of age from the curvature of the skull and suturing. Assuming normal growth, it puts the age at mid-teens.'

'That's what I told Mr Curtis. What about DNA?'

'If that's possible then the police will see to it.'

I stood quietly, thinking things through. Cameron was watching me, waiting for words.

'Penny for them?'

'Keep your penny. I'll give them freely. I had come to the conclusion that the victim was a young miner. That's miner with an 'e', not an 'o'. But youngsters worked in mines in previous centuries, not in the nineteen-sixties.'

'Nineteen seventies, Jessica. He was born in the nineteen sixties. If we are right about him being in his teens then we are talking mid-seventies.'

'Right. I get that.'

'This couldn't be a mine though, could it? It's too shallow. Also, you told me there were no mines this far to the east.'

'None that I know of.' I repeated to him what I had said to others, that just because there were no minerals around here didn't stop landowners exploring for them.

'Old exploratory workings, then? Workings the victim somehow got into and then became trapped?'

'I was wondering if it could be a well.'

'There's no sign of one, Jessica. The clay we are going through was undisturbed, there are no signs of any old excavation. Definitely no backfilled pits or shafts.'

'Some wells have side tunnels to collect more groundwater. What if there is a well somewhere nearby and the victim went down it and then along a tunnel?'

Cameron shrugged. Stroked his beard. I tried to remember what he did with his hands before he grew it.

'Either that or an old mineshaft. We simply do not know, Jessica.'

'But we do know that there is an underground opening of some sort. Or there was. You saw the rock in the core box. Above the patch of clay and gravel the rock was broken. Below it the rock was solid. To me that implies a collapse of the roof of an underground opening.'

'A cave, perhaps? Do you get caves in this kind of rock?'

'Not natural ones, not inland. This is all sandstone and you need limestone for caves. So what's your plan? You can't go much deeper in that clay without supporting the sides. What happens when you get down to rock? How are you going to excavate that?'

'We came here to excavate a metre of clay at the most. Now we're talking about sinking a shaft through rock. I can't do that, Kevron will have to do it. I haven't yet mentioned it to Mr Blackie, I go out of my way not to speak to him. He's a piece of work and no mistake.'

'I heard you both yesterday. What was all that about?'

'Childish. He made comments about us going slow deliberately. I'm not happy about going to him and asking for help. You know me, Jessica, I'm not much of a one for confrontation.'

'You won't have to ask him. I've gone over his head. Head office will deal with it. There's no point asking Blackie anyway, because Kevron doesn't sink shafts.'

More beard stroking. 'I've been meaning to ask you. Do you work for Blackie? What is your position here?'

'I work for Kevron's chairman, Kevin Marshall. My remit is to work out how the remains got there.'

'Surely that's now up to the police and the Procurator?'

'Mr Marshall wants his own person here. I was recommended to him.'

'He couldn't have chosen a more capable geologist.'

'Flattery, Cameron, will get you everywhere.'

'What was this place, do you know? What are all the concrete slabs and foundations?'

Thanks to my inspection of Kevron's documents I could answer his question confidently. I told him that one of the maps showed what looked like army buildings, with warehouses the size of small hangars. I had seen papers saying they were used for storage.

'Military,' I said. 'After that, the land and buildings were leased to private firms. Older plans show a big house nearby.'

The sound of an engine interrupted us. A digger appeared, carrying a pump slung under its bucket, its driver unsure where to go. Cameron waved to him and then sloshed off back to his team. I started to walk away. Then, remembering my need for somewhere to work, I followed him and asked him about the container promised by Blackie.

'No sign of it yet, Jessica. To be honest I haven't followed it up. I don't want to pester the man.'

I noticed Blackie, heading our way. 'Talk of the devil…'

Cameron glanced back across site and saw Blackie approaching. Then Cameron was gone again, back to his team. I felt sorry for them all. Working in such conditions was bad enough. Having no clear-cut aim was worse.

I waited until Blackie was close. 'Mr Blackie?' He wasn't coming to me, he was heading somewhere else. He stopped and stared. 'Professor Thomson is wondering when the container you promised him will arrive.'

'What's that to do with you?'

'He's very busy. I said I'd ask you.' A polite response. Not at all what I really wanted to say to him. He gestured upslope to the container row.

'He can't have any of those. They're all in use.'

'He said you promised to get another.'

He grunted. 'Go to the office. Speak to Margaret. Tell her to gee-up Harry.'

Then he was gone, taking long strides, leaning back in that way of his. Getting away from me, no doubt. A high pitched whine from the direction of the dig told me the pump was set up and working. A hose of pythonic proportions shot grey water well clear of the excavation, no doubt something else for Blackie to grumble about. From my limited experience of such things I reckoned it would take a few hours to pump out all the water. I guessed that even when that was done, digging and scraping in slimy mud would be impossible.

Later that day a flatbed lorry arrived on site carrying a large steel shipping container. At Blackie's suggestion I had passed on his message to his secretary. She'd listened to me, picked up her phone, then stared at me until I'd left her room.

I watched the lorry's progress as it lumbered across the site. It had its own crane, one of those angular, crab-claw things perched high behind its cab. When the driver decided he'd gone far enough he clambered out of his cab, climbed onto the roof of the container and attached chains from the crane arm to each corner of the container's roof. A tall man, he stood high up, pressing buttons on what looked to me like a large television remote. The crane jerked. The chains tightened.

The container, still with the man on its roof, rose slowly into the air. To steady himself he gripped one of the chains with his free hand, reminding me of a pirate in a ship's rigging – except that he wasn't in pirate gear. No pirate hat, no knee-length leather boots and no parrot. Despite that, he did look odd. Someone doing that kind of work would usually wear overalls of some kind. This man wore a collar and tie and a grey business suit.

Then, a shout from behind me, 'Where the hell do you think you're going to put that?'

Blackie had materialised as if from nowhere. The man on the container stared down at him but did nothing. Blackie shouted again. The man's stare became a glare. He topped the crane but the container kept moving, swinging around. All the time, the man glared down. I had the feeling that if he'd been on the ground he would have taken a swing at Blackie. Blackie moved closer.

'Where's Harry Sinclair? Where's your hard hat? Health and safety reg – '

'Who the fuck are you?'

Not a response Blackie expected. 'Blackie,' he called back. '*Mister* Blackie, site manager. Where is Harry?'

'If you don't want this here where the fuck *do* you want it?'

Blackie, dumbstruck, pointed towards the core shed. Then, 'Next to the other orange one, that's also one of Harry's.' Mumbling, he turned to me. 'If Harry had come himself instead of sending his pet ape he would know where it should go.' Said barely loud enough for me to hear. Definitely not loud enough to be heard by Harry's pet ape.

Half an hour later Cameron had a container. It had been positioned – after several tries – on the end of the row of others.

I spent time watching Cameron's team scraping mud. It was actually a bit less exciting than watching paint dry.

'Has anyone decided who will sink the shaft?' Cameron asked when he came to me. 'Do I have any say in it? I don't want it done by cowboys.'

'It's a skilled job. Six metres is not particularly deep. Though I suppose it doesn't matter how deep it is, the safety issues are the same.'

The beard nodded agreement. 'We are a good metre down in the clay already, Jessica. The shaft will only need to be five metres. I'm sure Kevron could excavate it if they wanted to. What they need is an experienced mining engineer to organise and manage it.'

'Plenty of those in Scotland fifty years ago.'

'Do I keep going, or do I stand down?'

'That's not up to me, you will have to call your own people. Best if you give them another hour or so because they might have heard from Kevron by then. Head office is trying to sort things out for us. Oh – and your container's arrived.'

'I saw. I even felt sorry for Mr Blackie, there was no need for that verbal abuse. Thing is, Jessica, I may have to store stuff in it after all. I wasn't expecting to be here for so long. Nor to be flooded out.'

Deciding to check out the new arrival, we plodded up from the dig to the row of containers. Cameron's had been over-painted in the same orange undercoat as the adjacent one, in paint not quite thick enough to obliterate its original paintwork. Cameron's container had no lettering; the adjacent one had words and numbers, stencilled in just-about-visible white paint, in Russian characters – the Cyrillic alphabet. There was no mistaking those backwards Rs and upside-down Ns.

Unlike the core shed, with its window and wooden door, Cameron's container had not been converted. It still had full-width, steel double doors at one end, locked by a hinged lever mechanism designed to be opened only by sumo wrestlers… and also, luckily, by a forensic geologist and forensic anthropologist using muscles they didn't even know they had. The doors groaned as we heaved them back.

I had expected an empty container. This one wasn't full, but it had remnants of occupation: trestle tables, several stacking chairs, and a metal waste bin still full of rubbish and tipped on its side. An old-style energy-saving bulb hung from the roof on the end of a short length of cable, which meant that some time in its life the container had been connected to electricity. It had, I guessed, been used as a contractor's mess room.

I knew as soon as I entered the thing that I wouldn't be using it. Even with the doors wide open it was dark inside. It also felt cold, even colder than outside. More importantly, my view of Cameron's excavation was blocked by the core shed. Though that wouldn't bother me unduly – because I could simply step outside periodically to check on progress – it may well trouble Curtis or Marshall. Even if Marshall never came to site, who knew what Blackie might tell him?

Cameron's voice echoed. 'Plenty of room in here for us all. Gloomy though. Are you sure you wouldn't be better off in that core shed?' When I didn't respond he made a point of looking at his watch. 'Jessica, it's my team's lunch break, I had better get back. Have you finished here? Do you want help to close the doors?'

I shook my head. I'd already worked out that the repeated application of a well-placed wellie boot would do the job admirably. He walked away and I stayed there to tidy the place. Even if didn't intend to use it, that didn't mean I should leave it untidy for Cameron. He was busy and I was not.

I lined up the table and chairs against the wall, righted the bin and refilled it with the used food wrappers strewn across the floor. Later I would find somewhere to empty it.

The container was indeed a gloomy place. Without light and heat it wasn't for me. I was the boss now. Thanks to Mr Marshall I could do whatever I wanted to do. The core shed had light and heat. I would use that instead.

Curtis turned up on site just as I was thinking about leaving. He said he had been close-by anyway. *In the vicinity*, he said. I wasn't sure I believed him. More likely he wanted to see progress – or the lack of it – for himself. No doubt he had been quizzed on events by his superintendent.

We walked together to the excavation. I found myself having to explain everything again to him from first principles – the way the drillers penetrate the clay, casing the ground with steel pipe as they go deeper. How they changed over from one type of rig to another when they reached bedrock. How the rotary drill recovered its core samples.

Even my students didn't need things explaining to them so many times. I knew that Curtis hadn't paid much attention to my earlier explanations because he wanted to believe the simpler one – that we would find what we were looking for in the clay.

'Seems you were right all along, Doctor.'

That was unexpected. It was the closest I'd get to an apology and I wanted to punch the air. I couldn't think of an appropriate response, so I attempted a change of subject.

'Do you have anything more on Morini?'

My question triggered one of his long silences. He was wearing shoes, not boots, and he took a dozen or so dainty, mud-avoiding steps before he responded.

'Nothing useful. We do know that the body was dumped there. We found tracks.'

'Through the undergrowth?'

'No, the same way we went in, around the edge of the field. If truth be known, we screwed up. We thought that by going around the field boundary we were keeping well clear of any route a vehicle might have taken. We even flagged it.'

'I remember.' My night-time walk through that mud, in darkness, was something I would never forget. 'Surely someone saw the tracks before they chose that route?'

'They weren't at all obvious. The ground had been firm and dry, there were no obvious tracks. We arrived there in a downpour. Next day, with the benefit of daylight, SOCO found tyre marks in a patch of soft ground.'

'Not made by the farmer?'

'The farmer uses either his tractor or his quad bike. These were different tyres, a different wheelbase. We believe that whoever dumped the body used a van. We are fairly sure Dr Morini was killed and dumped two or three days before the farmer found the body.'

Then silence again. To me, all that sounded fairly good stuff – especially if they ever found the van – and more work for me, possibly, comparing mud in tyre treads and under wheel arches with mud from the field. I didn't push it. What I really wanted to do was talk to him about the gold. But this wasn't the time or place.

'You said they need to sink a shaft here,' he said. 'Tell me about that.'

We had reached the edge of the dig. Most of the water had gone but a flawless, shiny veneer of soft grey mud remained. It looked treacherous, like wet concrete. I wouldn't be stepping down onto it and neither would Curtis, not in those shoes.

I explained to him that to have the best chance of recovering all the remains, a shaft would have to be four metres in diameter and five or six metres deep. His frown told me he didn't understand the four metres bit.

'I thought I explained all that?'

'Not to me you didn't.'

'The drill penetrated a skull. Let's assume the rest of the skeleton is there and it is lying flat and straight. Let's also assume that the victim is no more than six feet tall – that's one-point-eight metres – so to be sure, let's say two metres. We don't know which way the skeleton is lying, so we also have to assume it can be in any direction. Therefore, to be sure of recovering it all, we need a pit four metres across.'

'That seems excessive. Can't they go down a small shaft to the bones and then go sideways to recover the remainder?'

'I suppose that's possible. Cameron will prefer the big pit option. Going sideways risks damaging the bones. It's also dangerous. If the victim was killed by a collapse of rock then we don't want that to happen again.'

Another long pause.

'I've got a colleague looking into missing persons. I'm not holding out much hope because we are talking paper records, not computers. Until the mid-seventies this region was the Eastern Division of the Lothian and Peebles Constabulary. There were dozens of separate forces in Scotland at that time and all records will have been on paper. Bearing in mind that our victim might not have been a local resident, we're facing an almost impossible task.

'But most likely he was from around here.'

'Perhaps. Where's this professor, this Thomson? Where are they all, anyway?'

Unlike the pump, which was still doing its work, Cameron and his team had given up and gone home.

'Kevin Marshall says Kevron doesn't sink shafts,' I said. 'When they need to, they get subcontractors in. Cameron says he doesn't want that. He wants a choice. He doesn't want cowboys.'

'That won't be up to him.'

'Mr Marshall is going to ask around. He thinks all it needs is an experienced mining engineer to take charge. Not sure how Blackie will cope with that.'

'What about your father?'

It was my turn to stay quiet. My father had spent most of his life in mines of one sort or another. Though he was supposed to be retired he still did consulting work. Also, he had many mining contacts.

'I suppose I could ask him. He might know someone.'

'No, I was thinking of him doing it. Would he be interested? Is he still in Edinburgh?'

'He moved house. He no longer lives in The Grange. He has a small place in Peebles.'

'Considering what happened in his basement it doesn't surprise me that he moved house.'

Curtis came across my father some years ago. It was a bad time and I didn't want to talk about it. Thankfully Curtis stayed focussed.

'Is he qualified to do something like this?'

'Very well qualified. I'm not sure he would be interested though.'

'Is it worth asking him?'

'I can try. I'll let you know how he responds.'

16

As soon as Curtis left site I phoned my father. He had been in Perth for a meeting and was now driving home. Whenever he talked to me using his car's new hands-free phone it was like listening to a wartime bomber pilot.

'Hi Love, what can I do for you? Approaching the new bridge. Traffic's heavy.'

He was on the motorway, about to cross the Forth Estuary on the Queensferry Crossing. I didn't mention the shaft to him because it was the kind of thing best discussed face to face. Also, I wanted him to keep focussed on his driving. Our conversation was brief and to the point.

'Where are you going now, Dad? I'd like to talk.'

'Driving south. Heading home.'

'You don't need to shout, I can hear you clearly. I'm in East Lothian. Can we meet somewhere? I don't want to go to Peebles unless I have to, it's well out of my way and I'm fairly busy.'

'What, you mean now?'

'If you have time.'

'Bloody fool just cut me up… damn boy racers… what about?'

'I don't want to discuss it on the phone.'

'Police stuff?'

'Sort of.'

'ETA Peebles five-thirty.'

'ETA?'

'Estimated time of arrival. Surely you know that?'

I nodded to myself. Of course I knew that. I just wasn't expecting to hear it from him.

'No, not Peebles. Somewhere closer. I'm calling a taxi. I don't have a car.'

At the end of our chat I half expected him to say '*Roger, over and out…*' Mischievously, I was tempted to say it myself. I did not, because it would have probably led to a long explanation. We arranged to meet for coffee, in a café just off the Edinburgh bypass. He arrived there long before I did.

'So,' he asked. 'What's the problem?'

He was frowning. Lately, we had spoken a few times on the phone, though we hadn't met for a few months. Calling him, asking for an immediate meet, was not usual.

'No problem. Nothing serious. I mean it is serious, but it's work. It's not personal.'

It took me some time to explain my involvement with Kevron. I ran through everything I could think of, finishing with the need for a shaft. I found it easier talking to him than to Curtis because I didn't have to explain all the techie stuff. He sat listening, nodding occasionally. Only when I'd finished did he speak.

'I don't understand why Kevron can't do it themselves. Sounds to me like they just need to excavate a hole in the ground. More a pit than a shaft.'

'It's a health and safety thing. Kevin Marshall no longer has his own mining engineer and the forensic anthropologist – that's Cameron Thomson – doesn't want a third-party contractor involved. It's all very sensitive. They must not use an excavator. Cameron has to scrape the clay bit by bit.'

'What's the point of that? You said there is nothing in the clay.'

'What I say makes no difference. They have to go slow. It's how they do things.'

'And when they get to rock? You said rockhead is three metres down? That's ten feet.'

A bit of mansplaining from Dad. It is actually nine feet and ten inches.

'That's the time they will need someone with shaft-sinking experience,' I said. 'The rock is broken, we know that from the core. I'm betting the roof of whatever is down there has collapsed.'

'What are they thinking, a square-sided shaft or a circular one?'

I shrugged. 'I'm not sure they're thinking anything at the moment.'

'If the rock's as broken as you say it is then it will definitely need support. Circular steel shuttering may be easier than square. It depends what kind is available at short notice.'

'That's why we need you. Do you remember that detective, Curtis?'

'Detective Inspector Tom Curtis? How could I ever forget?'

'Now Detective Chief Inspector. He's my police contact.'

I explained the unofficial nature of it all, emphasising that I was working for Kevron. And, as far as I knew, he would be too.

'Sound interesting. Do you want a decision now?'

'It would certainly help. I need to bounce the idea off Kevin Marshall.'

'Does this Marshall know you are speaking to me?'

'Not yet. It was Curtis's idea. It might be too late anyway. Earlier, when I spoke to Kevin, he said he would sort it.'

My father nodded. 'I'm game. I have a couple of things on the go but they can wait.'

Kevin Marshall wasn't available when I phoned Kevron. He called me back later and I gave him my news, emphasising that it was a suggestion from DCI Curtis that I contact my father.

'You are too late, Doctor Spargo. I have made other arrangements.'

'Ah!'

'Luckily the arrangements are not yet finalised. I assume your father is qualified? Is he experienced in this kind of work?'

'Very qualified and very experienced.'

'Would you be happy to work with your father?'

'In practice he would be working for Cameron, not for me.'

'I'll be paying him, Doctor, so he will be working for me. Have you discussed this with your father? Does he know what is involved? Does he know we want an immediate start?'

'I've put him in the picture. I've made no promises, so if – '

'If he can start right now that's good with me. As I believe I told you, I would rather have my own engineer doing this than a subcontractor. What is your father's name?'

'John Spargo.'

'Ask him to email me his CV. Also copy it to James Blackie. While you are at it you might like to send me yours.'

After calling Curtis to say that all was well with my father and Kevron, I had a call from Andy Kuzuk.

'I asked around,' he said. 'About the gold. It is probably from Soviet military equipment, computers and radar electronics. The USSR had much old equipment, big electrical connectors and contacts. They used gold, so nothing corroded. Then it works okay when they press the nuclear button.'

Very funny. I wasn't at all happy. I distinctly recall telling him not to do this. 'Who did you ask, Andy?'

'Just a friend.'

'I hope you haven't dropped me in it. I can't afford stuff like this to get out.'

'I thought you trusted me.'

'Andy, I trusted you not to ask anyone.'

'I only asked if it is possible for me to buy old computers. My friend thinks I meant for me, to get gold to make jewellery. In modern equipment the connectors and terminals are microscopic, I told you that. Also, recovery of the gold is dangerous. Acid is used to – '

I interrupted him. 'Thank you, Andy. And of course I trust you.'

'You need to chill. When you last have a holiday?'

'That is not… how many computers would you need to – '

'– to get enough gold to fill a shotgun cartridge?'

'I wasn't actually going to ask you that. But yes.'

'We're not talking desktops and laptops, Jez. We are talking computers with tape drives and valves, big enough to fill a room.'

All very interesting. But why go to all the trouble of recovering gold only to throw it away – which was effectively what they had done by loading it into a shotgun cartridge. Silence now, from both of us. Then a suggestion from Andy.

'Hired killer, Jez?'

'I wondered about that. Are there really such people?'

'I am sure there are. But I think this is personal, so no hired killer. This man killed for satisfaction. He fired two barrels, yes?'

'I didn't ask.' I really didn't want to know.

More silence. Then, 'Jez, sorry, I have to go. I have an appointment with a client.'

I sat quietly at home, studying the documents from Kevron. The geological books and memoirs told me nothing I didn't know already. Most interesting were the maps I had spread out on my table. Some were original, others were copies. The oldest, a photographic enlargement of a hand-drawn map from the seventeen-hundreds, was rubber-stamped *The National Library of Scotland*.

Another map, an undated plan of the site stamped *War Office*, showed roughly the same area, with the boundary of what was now the Kevron site marked on it with a recently drawn solid black line. Inside this boundary a square grid of roads served long, rectangular buildings. At the far end of the site, just about as far from the site's entrance as possible, was the outline of another building. From its size and shape I assumed it had been a large house.

I nodded to myself. The large rectangles were the military warehouses, built on the concrete slabs that Kevron had been ripping up. The house – if it was a house – must have been demolished long ago. I had seen nothing like it on site.

I moved to an armchair and spread the maps on the floor. The oldest one, the photographic copy, looked remarkably uncluttered. The original had been drawn with a fine pen, with boundaries shown as dashed and dotted lines. Roads, probably little more than lanes at the time, meandered around woodland, itself represented by tiny, hand-sketched trees. Sitting dead-centre of this old map was an impressive house – a mansion, even – no doubt the one shown on the later, War Office map. A neat little pen sketch showed windows and chimneys. Even the wide steps to the front door were shown.

Next morning, standing side by side in the core shed with Cameron, I spread out both maps on the bench. I explained where they had come from and what I had found last night. He tapped a finger on each of the rectangles on the War Office map, as if counting them.

'These must be the concrete slabs Kevron are breaking up.'

I nodded. 'Old foundations. There were once warehouses on them. What do you make of this?' I placed a finger on each map, pointing out the now missing house. 'I've not seen anything like this on site.'

'Neat little pen drawing. I'd say this map was made for the owner of the house. He probably owned the whole estate.'

Together we looked out of the window, beyond Cameron's dig, towards woodland.

'If I've got it right,' I said, 'the house was near the boundary fence, this side of those trees. I'm wondering if Kevron demolished it. Perhaps you could ask Blackie.'

I said it tongue in cheek to see his reaction.

'Or you could, Jessica? Or we could ask that young engineer, Hamish. How old is the National Library map, do you know?'

'It's undated. Whoever arranged for the copy to be made by the library also made notes on a separate sheet in the Kevron collection. It is believed to be early- to mid-seventeen hundreds.'

'That old?' He traced a finger along a dark line that partly obscured the house. 'Shame about the creases.'

The original map had been folded and refolded many times. Photographic copying had picked out the folds as a grid of several widely-spaced dark lines. Cameron went for the light switch, switched on the fluorescents and returned to the old map. He moved a finger over it. 'Have you noticed this dot?'

'Looks like a speck of dirt on the original. Or ink, perhaps.'

'You think? Could it show the position of a well?'

'I doubt it. They show the house as a small sketch of a house,' I said. 'They show trees as sketches of small trees. Wouldn't they show a well as a small sketch of a well? You know what I mean, a circular wall with a winder thing on the top.'

'Some wells were simple, just a hole in the ground. You threw a bucket on a rope down a hole and hauled it back up.'

I rubbed the dot with a finger, to see if it came off. It didn't.

'I does look as if it could be close to the borehole. There's nothing shown near there on the War Office map, so if it was a well it must have been filled-in before that map was made. Did you come across anything in the floor of your dig? Anything that resembled a filled-in well?'

'Nothing. You saw it, Jessica. It was undisturbed clay.'

I stopped to think. If I'd had a beard I would probably have stroked it. 'I'm not sure anything we just said makes sense. When did they stop calling it *War Office*?'

'In the early nineteen-sixties. It changed to *Ministry of Defence*. Why?'

'Think about it. This place had military stores, so it was probably built in the nineteen-thirties or forties. If there is a well, and if it was filled in before this map was made, how can anyone have gone down it in the nineteen-seventies?'

'Good point Jessica, stupid of me. I still think we need to follow it up – no stone unturned, and all that. We know that there is some kind of underground opening. Somehow our victim got into it.'

'What are your plans?'

'Today? I don't have any. I told my team to stay away until someone sorts out what's to be done. Why do you ask?'

I suggested that as we had time on our hands we could search for signs of the old house. If we found it, then by taking a few measurements we should be able to see if the dot on the map was anywhere near the borehole.

'Can we do that though?' I asked. 'You know more about surveying than I do. Can we pace out distances?'

'We can do better than that. I have long measuring tapes.'

We talked as we walked to his van. I asked him why the drill recovered only the tooth and bone, given the young age of the remains.

'You mean why was no soft tissue recovered?'

'Soft tissue, yes.' That was exactly what I meant but hadn't wanted to say it. I had visions of Curtis, white-suited, bending over Morini. I think I must have shivered, because Cameron asked if I was all right.

'I'm fine. Just wondering if a body could decay that quickly.'

'In forty to fifty years? Down there? Most definitely. We have air and we have dampness, perfect conditions for decomposition. Also, didn't you say that when the drillers reached rock they started to lose the water they pumped down the hole? I've been meaning to ask you about that.'

'They lost their flushing water. It's pumped down the drill rods to lubricate the drill bit. It should bring the drill cutting back to surface, but according to their records that didn't happen, it all went into the ground. That indicates broken up rock and possibly a large opening of some kind.'

'That water will have washed a lot of the decomposed material away. What puzzles me is why the drill didn't penetrate both sides of the skull. Drilling into one side and out the other, I mean.'

'A cubic metre of this rock weighs around two and a half tons. Who knows what happens to a skull when it's crushed by a rock fall like that?'

Torn apart, probably. I didn't want to say it and didn't want to think about it. As I'd told Curtis. I'm a geologist. I don't do bodies.

17

I walked to the site office with Cameron. Blackie wasn't there, nor was his secretary. We spoke to Hamish Anderton, asking him if he knew where the old house had been. In the surveyor's room he thumbed through maps, finally producing the site's own copy of the War Office map.

Then Blackie was there, standing behind us. He elbowed Anderton aside.

'Can't you read? That sign on the front door not big enough for you? Or maybe you want it in Braille – *boots off at the door*, it says. That's what that bloody boot rack's for!'

I looked down at our mud-caked wellies. The site engineer wore trainers and Blackie was in long thick socks. I didn't respond. Cameron did, apologising for our oversight.

Blackie stared at me. 'What is all this? Not content with the core shed and Professor Thomson's container? You've decided to take over our offices?'

'There used to be an old house on your site. I want to know where it was. Your colleague was helping us.'

'Oh, was he now?' Then, to Hamish, 'I'll deal with this. Don't you have things to do?'

'The house, Mr Blackie,' I said. 'It is shown on old maps. We need to know where it was.'

'And why is that?' The engineer had gone. Blackie was now face to face with Cameron. 'Your brief is clear. Unless I'm mistaken, it is to recover the remains.' And then, turning to me, 'And yours is to report progress to Mr Marshall. Though why he needs you to do that when I'm running this site is quite beyond me.'

'My job is to also to help work out how the remains got there.'

He grunted. He hadn't mentioned dog bones again, so he must have been told the remains are human. If he had spoken to head office he would also know they were recent.

'Site's starting up again, anyway.'

'That can't be right. Mr Marshall didn't mention anything about you restarting work.'

'That's probably because it's none of your business.'

Squabbling wasn't going to help anyone. I could resolve this with a phone call to Curtis or Marshall.

'The old house, Mr Blackie,' I said again. 'We need to know where it was.'

He reached for the old map, swivelled it round and prodded it with a grubby finger.

'You can see for yourself where it was. That's it there.'

'Can it still be seen? The foundations, I mean.'

'One or two bits. Our site boundary is here,' he said, drawing an imaginary line across the map with his finger.

Blood and stones came to mind. He wasn't giving much away. 'Are you saying that the house is not in your land?'

'It's not part of the Kevron site, if that's what you mean. The military site was huge. We only have part of it. There used to be a fortified manor house just outside it, over our boundary fence. It burned down in the nineteen-fifties. The army had gone by then and the house was derelict. The fire left the place unsafe and it was demolished.'

'That's not in head office records.'

'Head office doesn't know everything.'

Cameron, silent until now, decided it was time to be Mr Nice Guy.

'Mr Blackie, there is a possibility that there was once a well on this site, perhaps associated with the house. There is also a possibility that the remains you found in the core box – '

'I didn't find any bloody remains!'

'Of course. There is a possibility that the remains are associated in some way with a well.'

'Associated? A well? What makes you think that?'

Cameron looked uneasy. He had started to blush. I decided it was time to step in.

'When I visited Mr Marshall he gave me a much older map than this. It shows the house, and possibly an old well. If we knew exactly where the old house was then we could work out how close this well is to Professor Thomson's excavations.'

Rare silence from Blackie. No doubt aware, for the first time, of my visit to head office. He strode to the doorway.

'Come!'

We were being commanded to follow him. He walked ahead of us, muttering what sounded to me like *bloody geologists... bloody professors.* Out in the small car park he stepped up on a pile of old sleepers and pointed across the site.

'See that wooden post with the floodlights on it? The one near the edge of the site?'

'You mean the one near your boundary fence?'

'Is there another one? If there is, then I can't see it.'

I held my tongue. In amongst his rudeness there could be something of use.

'I'm told that the building was somewhere near there,' he continued. 'Though I've not seen any foundations. Not that's it's of any interest to me, but there's a block of stone near the boundary fence, hidden by brambles. Whole site was overgrown when we arrived. We had to fell the trees. We burnt the lot.'

Cameron frowned. 'Burnt them? Perfectly good timber?'

I winced. Cameron, the man who didn't like conflict. I thought for a second or two that Blackie was going to ignore him. He didn't.

'I get shot of the media mob and along comes a bloody eco-warrior!'

Without another word he stepped down from the sleepers and set off for his office.

'Nice man,' Cameron said when he'd gone.

'Booby Prize for tact and diplomacy. Mr Curtis says he's an acquired taste.'

Instead of heading up the site towards the containers we cut straight across it towards the floodlight post. The walk wasn't easy. Smashed slabs of concrete lay at random angles, many pointing skywards as if hit by bombs. In the midst of this carnage sat a large rock crusher, now silent. From it, a conveyor belt led to the top of a large cone shaped pile of crushed concrete. Now I knew where Blackie got the chippings that paved the site's roads.

We reached the floodlight post. I stood there, looking around me. To one side of me, a long way off up a gentle slope, sat Cameron's gazebo. Behind it, just visible, were the tops of the containers and the core shed. Cameron stood next to me, looking back.

'Can Mr Blackie do what he said? Can he start work again?'

'I doubt it. Not without official permission.'

'Can you please find out if it is correct? I wouldn't like their work to interfere with the excavation.'

'I'll speak to Marshall. Curtis, too. If they stayed working in this part of the site, I don't suppose it would affect us.'

'Doesn't look good, does it?'

'What doesn't?'

He was talking about something else now. Either side of us a rusting, chain-link boundary fence disappeared into the distance. In front of us, beyond the floodlight post, dense woodland blocked our view. Whoever occupied this land before Kevron hadn't bothered to repair or replace the fence. There wasn't much point. The woodland beyond it looked impenetrable.

'That undergrowth. There isn't much chance of finding anything in there.'

'We don't have to go in there. Blackie said the block of stone is near the post, not in the trees.'

Cameron went one way and I went the other. To locate the position of that black dot – the possible well – accurately, we would need an array of measurements. At least one of them had to be from the house. I shouted to Cameron.

'No luck this way…'

He shouted back. 'Found it!'

We stood side by side, looking through tall weeds at a low stack of worn steps that led nowhere. The top step was capped by a huge stone slab.

'A mounting block,' he said. 'A *louping-on-stane*, used for getting on and off a horse. It must be a couple of hundred years old at least. There is one at Duddingston Church. There's a rare beauty at Aberlady.'

'More importantly right now, Cameron, where was this one? At the front door, back door or side door?'

'Right beside the front door, Jessica. There would be no point walking in the rain to a mounting block.'

Cameron walked to his van for a measuring tape. While he was away I called Kevin Marshall, whose mobile switched me through to his secretary. I left a message and then phoned Curtis.

'I've been meaning to talk to you,' he said. 'Kevron wants to start work again. Mr Marshall called me before he left for Sunningdale.'

'Sunningdale?'

'Playing golf with my Super. I thought you might know that before I did. Where are you now?'

'On site.'

'Is anything happening?'

'Nothing. And I've heard that too… about site work starting up, I mean. Blackie told me. The man is a pain in the arse. Sorry, that was unprofessional. I have just been with him. He is undoubtedly the most offensive man I have ever met.'

'I'm sorry I got you involved with this, Dr Spargo. I had no way of knowing how things would develop.'

'Don't beat yourself up about it. I'm being well-paid.'

'Is there any way the site can restart without affecting your work? Professor Thomson's work, I mean. I have cleared things with the Procurator's Office. Their only concern is that is reopening the site should not compromise the recovery work.'

'You've seen the size of the site. We are only in one small area. As long as we are left alone I can't see any reason why things can't carry on. I'm sure Cameron feels the same way.'

'Very well. Will you pass that on to Mr Blackie?'

'I would be happy to do that. I would be the bearer of good news for once and I'd like to see his face. But shouldn't it go through Kevin Marshall, not through me?'

'You may be right. I can call my Super and he'll pass on the message. Thank you, Jessica. I appreciate it.'

He hung up before I could respond. A *thank you* from Curtis? And he said Jessica, not Dr Spargo. He must have found his happy pills.

I spent the next hour with Cameron, measuring slabs and long distances. By late afternoon Cameron had fixed the position of the black dot to within one or two metres. We stood together in the core shed, looking at the map he had drawn. The dot was nowhere near the borehole. If it did show a well, then that well would have been right underneath one of the concrete slabs – so probably not a well, more likely a spec of dirt or ink on the original map. I didn't know whether to be disappointed or pleased.

For reasons I didn't understand, I felt tearful. Cameron noticed.

'You need to get home. Put your feet up. Switch on the TV. Open a bottle.'

I nodded. I liked those words.

18

I didn't open a bottle of anything that evening, nor did I put my feet up and watch television. Instead, I met Curtis in the coffee shop at Tollcross. Cameron had taken me to site that morning and was driving me home when Curtis phoned me. He wanted to *touch base with me*, he said, adding that he had things to say that he couldn't say on the phone.

Heavy traffic made me late. Curtis was in the coffee shop before me, slumped in an easy chair with a half-empty Americano on a low table in front of him. He had his briefcase open, the leather one with the brass clasp. I hoped he hadn't brought another vial for me. He didn't notice me until I settled into the chair opposite.

'Dr Spargo… you have bought yourself a drink.'

A self-evident truth from the DCI. I was tempted to compliment him on his powers of observation. He had probably intended to buy for me and I'd spoiled his plans.

'Mr Curtis…'

'Thank you for coming. How are things on site?'

'No change since we last spoke. Something of a wasted day.' He looked at me over his coffee cup, raising one eyebrow quizzically high. 'Kevron lent me a photographic copy of an old map. I've been looking at it with Cameron.'

'Do you mean a photocopy?'

'No, it must have been too large to photocopy. It's a full-size, glossy, black and white photo of the original. It came from the National Library's collection. We – that's me and Cameron – found a black dot on it that we thought might be a well. We thought it was close to the borehole but we were wrong on both counts. It's not a well. And it's nowhere near the dig.'

'Are you sure of that?'

'We took measurements. Even if the dot did mark a well, it is positioned under one of those concrete slabs. They were built in the nineteen-thirties or 'forties, so nobody could have descended it in the 'seventies.'

'Like you said to me, don't beat yourself up about it.'

I took a sip of coffee. 'I'm sure you didn't want meet me just to listen to my grumbles. Did you manage to get hold of your Superintendent? About the site starting up again?'

'I did. He has told Mr Marshall. Mr Blackie will know by now that he can continue work.'

'He's probably bulldozing everything in sight.'

Curtis sipped at his Americano. Once, twice, three times. It had gone cold. He must have been here for some time.

'Can I get you another of those?'

'No thanks. About those gold fragments…'

I sat up, attentive. A little man in my brain blew away cobwebs and I remembered how worried I'd been when Curtis said he wanted them back. I was about to admit that I had ground half of them away when he spoke again.

'Are you spending all your time on Kevron stuff?'

'About ten hours a day.' And the rest. 'Why?'

'I was wondering if you had any spare time. Now that you and Professor Thomson are awaiting decisions, I mean.'

'Spare time for what?'

'I have a young detective inspector, newly assigned to my team. He's a bright young man. He's been looking over the Morini paperwork. He is interested in those photos you took of the gold fragments.'

The temptation to respond '*but they didn't interest you?*' was strong. I let it pass. I had known Curtis long enough not to let his remarks upset me.

'The photographs are not as good as the real thing,' I said. A slip of the tongue. They no longer existed as loose grains and I hoped he wouldn't want to see them through the binocular microscope himself. 'I have done more work on the fragments,' I added, quickly. 'I have better photos. They show much more.'

I expected a rebuke for doing work without his permission. It didn't come.

'I know this is all unofficial, Doctor. I will get something to you in writing in a day or so.'

Yes, Mr Curtis. Preferably some form of contract. 'I'd appreciate that,' I said. 'My rates are still the same. Would you like your man to visit my lab? Does he know where it is? Don't send him to King's.'

I sat quietly, sipping my drink. Everything so far could have been done on the phone. I knew Curtis well, knew these silences. As expected, it wasn't long before he came out with something more.

'Dr Morini,' he said. 'What do you think? What have you learned from the gold?'

Another temptation fought. This time, the urge to shrug. I'm told not to do any work on the case and then, days later, I am asked what I have learned.

'Whoever told you that gold came from jewellery is wrong.'

I got full frontal raised eyebrows. 'Really? What makes you say that?'

'The work on the Morini job that I haven't been doing.'

'Yes, yes. Go on.'

'It is my belief, Detective Chief Inspector Curtis,' I said in my best lawyer-speak, 'that the fragments have been cropped from computer components.'

My attempt at humour met with silence. He sat quietly, nursing his cold coffee cup with both hands.

'Have you ever seen inside a computer?'

'Several,' I said. 'Years ago I helped my father build one.'

'Then you will know that the amount of precious metals they use in components is minimal. It amounts to no more than a microscopically thin coating on the circuit board.'

'They didn't fifty or sixty years ago.'

'Did we have computers then? I don't mean like that Bletchley Park thing from wartime with gears and valves. I mean real ones.'

'Universities had them. The military had them.'

'And you are suggesting they are still in use?'

'I am suggesting that they might now be available as scrap.'

I was being interrogated. Any second now he would find a bright light to shine in my face like they do in old black and white movies. I didn't want to let on that I had been discussing his case with Andy Kuzuk. I needed to steer the conversation.

'So,' I said. 'How is the investigation going?'

'DI Cavendish has taken over the day to day operations.'

'He's the one coming to see me?'

He nodded. 'As I said, bright lad.'

'Is he also taking over the Kevron stuff?'

'Unfortunately not.' He said it with feeling. 'I'll get him to call you. Brief him thoroughly, will you? He has been through the paperwork. I think you should get along.'

An ambiguity from Curtis. I wasn't sure if he meant this meeting was over, or that Cavendish and I should be friends. Both, perhaps. Because he clicked his briefcase shut and shoved his coffee cup away.

Detective Inspector Cavendish: Mid-thirties, taller than me and smarter than Curtis – more smartly dressed, I mean. He called me on my mobile shortly after Curtis left me and we arranged to meet at my lab. He arrived before me and was standing with his back pressed hard against the front door in an attempt to shelter from rain. For some reason I can't explain, I was not expecting a slim, fair-haired man.

'Tim Cavendish,' he said. 'Just in time for morning prayers.'

'It's an old church hall. Not an old church.'

I produced my dungeon door key and inserted it into the iron-clad keyhole. Iron levers clunked. Just in case Curtis had sent him to check that I wasn't working in a damp, rat-infested cellar, I showed my visitor round, first walking straight through the lab to the back room where I showed him my bandit-proof cabinet. He didn't comment. Back in the lab again he looked up at the high roof. I didn't have a ceiling, I had oak beams that came to a point, very high up.

'This place must cost you a fortune to heat.'

'If you mean it's too big for me, I agree. I'll know how much it costs to heat when I get my first electricity bill.'

I wanted to get down to business but I didn't mind the smalltalk. Curtis was never off-topic. Everything he said seemed relevant to his police work.

It wasn't long before I had Cavendish where I wanted him – sitting on a tall stool in front of my reflecting microscope while I explained how it worked and what it did. An hour later he was still sitting there, looking through the instrument at the resin block Andy had made for me, moving it millimetres at a time. I guessed from his questions that he was examining every single grain embedded in the resin. Craftily, I saw this as an opportunity.

'As I said earlier, these are the same grains you saw in the photos I sent to the DCI. I've set them in resin and polished them. To cut right into them and polish them meant that some of them have been ground away.'

'Impressive!'

He had definitely heard me. Whether or not he took on board that the grains were no longer in the same state they were when Curtis gave them to me, was doubtful. I felt better. And guilty. When I brought tea for him, and coffee for me, he seemed to relax. He swivelled on the stool and leant back against my workbench.

'I was told that these bits came from jewellery. Is that what you think, Doctor?'

'It's Jessica. Jez.'

Jez to my friends. I couldn't really call him a friend, not yet, though he did smile a lot. Not sure if smiling a lot was a good or bad thing for a policeman. I reserved judgement, too, on whether he was a bright lad or not.

'It doesn't look like it's from jewellery to me,' I said. 'What have you heard from Mr Curtis?'

'The general consensus is that it has been cropped from stolen bracelets and rings.'

'Now you have seen it, what do you think?'

'Hmmm, not sure. It isn't all gold, is it? There is some copper. That is puzzling. Why would a jeweller use that? Copper tarnishes. It goes green or blue.'

I was impressed. He had been referring to colour photos in an identification book that I use. Considering that the pale colours reflected by the metals were barely distinguishable from one another, he had done well.

Holding his mug of tea, he slipped down from the stool and wandered around.

'Old stuff,' he said, touching equipment. 'Is this a portable XRF analyser?'

I nodded. X-ray fluorescence. He had picked up my handheld spectrometer. The instrument is a point-and-click gun that identifies chemical elements. Twenty years old when I bought it, it had proved an invaluable tool on several of my jobs.

'Please don't drop that, it cost me as much as a small family car. Much of my kit is old, yes. The fact that it still works shows how well-made and reliable it is.'

He held the instrument like a pistol and pointed it at the floor.

'We had one of these at Uni,' he said. 'It didn't work. It needed a new battery.'

I didn't admit that mine also needed new batteries – expensive, rechargeable ones. Batteries I wasn't sure I could still buy and couldn't yet afford anyway.

It didn't surprise me that he'd been to university. It did surprise me that he knew what the instrument was.

'What did you study?'

'Chemistry.'

'Ah! And you became a copper.'

He smiled. 'Not right away. I did other jobs. If I'd stayed to do a doctorate I might have stayed with chemistry, then I'd be stuck in a lab with a few dozen others. Oh! No disrespect, Doctor,' he added, looking around. 'I don't mean you, and all this.'

'If I worked here every day I would go stir crazy. What about you? DCI Curtis says you have taken over the Morini case.'

'It should never have been his job. He only became involved because they were short staffed that night and someone called him out.' He was back on the stool, nursing the hot mug. Perhaps I should turn up the heating. 'I am told that you identified the body.'

'Morini, yes. At the scene. Not a pretty sight. Not something I thought I ever have to do as a geologist. Now it seems I have another one. Hopefully nowhere near as bad.'

'Another one? Ah, you mean Haddington Man? The DCI mentioned that. It sounds a weird one.'

'Weird is an understatement. Not a man, either.'

'A woman?'

'A lad, we think. A teen. We need to drop the Haddington Man thing, it's inappropriate.'

'I only know what's in the papers and on TV. Aren't you the one who said the bone wasn't a fossil?'

'I didn't realise I was a media celebrity.' I had been far too busy to bother with news. 'Was there mention of a tooth?'

'Not that I recall.'

I had the impression he was sounding me out, no doubt to decide whether or not he could trust me. I soon learned why.

'Not going well, mine,' he said, leaning back again. 'Morini, I mean. It's something of a poisoned chalice. No real progress. No suspects. No motive.'

'Has Mr Curtis stepped back from it completely?'

He shook his head. 'He's still the boss. It's my job, along with several other cases. Luckily I have my own DSs and DCs.'

Detective sergeants and constables. I knew the jargon, of course. Cavendish went quiet. I asked if he wanted more tea. He shook his head.

'I have read the DCI's notes. He says you work with Charles deWit. He told me he misidentified the victim as that man and you put him right.'

'Morini had an old university card of deWit's in his pocket. For some reason he was wearing deWit's jacket.'

He was nodding. 'But you know deWit? You do work with him?'

'I know him, I don't work with him. What has Mr Curtis told you about me? I used to lecture full time. A long time ago I set up a forensic geology course. Then I did this…' I gestured with an arm, waving at the room. 'I still run a forensic geology course for post-grads. It's part time.'

'And Charles deWit?'

'He used to be one of my students. Now he lectures.'

I did my best to remain professional, managing not to say what I really wanted to say – that I kept as far away from deWit as I possibly could.

'I understand that deWit and Morini live together?'

'No. They used to. *Live together* is probably an inappropriate expression.'

'Right. Yes. Can you tell me more about him?'

'Not much to tell.'

'I can't believe that. All those backstabbing academics? There has to be something to tell.'

I tensed. He was getting too pushy, too friendly. I had already intimated to Curtis that I had no time for deWit, that I couldn't stand the man. I daresay my comments were in Curtis's notes.

'Interesting that you want to know about deWit,' I said. 'Have you met him? Have you interviewed him?'

'The DCI did that.'

'So you already know how uncooperative the man is. And, presumably, how he dislikes the police. And how he dislikes me.'

'I would rather not comment on that.'

'So why this interest? I'm guessing he's a suspect. He has to be, doesn't he? He's the only one you've got.'

We talked some more, not about Morini but about everything and nothing. I had the impression that Cavendish welcomed the break from routine. I suggested we go somewhere for lunch but he declined.

'I have to get back. I've been here longer than I intended.'

I left the same time as he did. As I was locking up, his mobile got a signal for the first time in hours. It beeped half a dozen times, a string of missed calls and texts. I heard him cursing as he walked away.

19

I'd had a quiet couple of days. Nothing seemed to be happening. Then, unexpectedly, my father collected me from home and drove me to site. He had an appointment with Cameron Thomson, followed by a session with Blackie. He told me he had spoken with Blackie by phone.

'Helpful man. Sounded as if he knew what he was talking about.'

I grunted. 'Are you sure it was Blackie you spoke to?'

We parked at the site office and changed into boots, hi-vis jackets and hard hats. At the top of the gentle slope to the containers we found Cameron's van and then Cameron, alone in the core shed, its wall heater blasting warm air. Introductions over, we inspected the core. My father poked at it. Said very little.

Outside again we walked to the dig. The pump was doing its work, still thumping rhythmically, still belching water. We stood in a row, three wise monkeys that peered through the mesh of Blackie's temporary fence.

'So,' my father said. 'You want to sink a shaft around that borehole casing. Why does it have to be four metres across?'

That same question. 'The drill went through a piece of skull,' I said. Work it out, Dad.

'You assumed the remains are of someone six feet tall. You don't know in which direction they lie. You want to be sure of exposing the whole of the remains without excavating sideways.'

Ten out of ten for slick reasoning. Faculties still sharp in his seventies. Nice to know.

'But you now know that it's probably a teen. So not the height of a grown man? Can't you reduce the width of the excavation?'

'When did you last see a teenager? They might well have been five and a half feet tall when you were a boy, but not in the nineteen-seventies.'

'I don't suppose it makes much difference. Not when we get an excavator in.'

We both stared at him. Cameron looked horrified. '*Excavator?*' he said. 'Surely not!'

My father was adamant. 'You were doing an archaeological dig in the clay, looking for a shallow burial. Now you are not. What we need to do now is to get down to the rock as easily and as safely as possible.'

Cameron shook his head. 'It's all gone a bit pear-shaped. Frankly, I'm not sure why I'm here. I came because there was supposed to be a shallow burial.'

As far as I was concerned, things were far from pear-shaped. I'd had this negativity from Cameron before. When things were straightforward and clear, he was confident. I stepped closer to him and said, quietly,

'You are here because you are one of the best in the business, Cameron. You don't need me to tell you that.'

Without speaking, he went off towards his gazebo, plodding through mud. My father turned to me. 'What was all that about?'

'When things don't go as planned he needs his hand held.'

'Don't we all.'

'I was surprised he made professor. I have always thought of him in a strong supporting role. A number two. A second-lieutenant.'

My father admitted to me that he had already asked Blackie to arrange for an excavator to dig out the clay, right down to bedrock. No surprise, then, that the two of them got on so well.

The excavator arrived while the three of us were bagging up Cameron's gazebo, ready to carry it to his container. Again, the three of us stood in a row, this time gazing down towards the site office, watching the bright yellow machine trundle off the back of a low-loader and start its long run up the slope. Blackie was there, supervising. My father stood with us, his arms folded.

'Good man, Jim Blackie. Very efficient.'

Cameron said nothing. I bit my tongue. My father set off across the site, presumably to confer with, and probably praise, Blackie for his support and efficiency.

I muttered to Cameron, 'Perhaps it's just us?'

With help from Cameron's team we carried the bagged-up gazebo to his container. Eventually, when the dig was right down through clay and rock, we would probably need it again. Cameron was working in the gloom at the container's back end, rolling one of three gazebo bags with his foot. Something crunched, like treading on cornflakes. He stooped, picked up something and threw it across the container. Had the waste bin been empty, it would have fallen into it.

'Good shot,' I said. 'What was it?'

'A piece of old plastic.'

'I'll empty that. I know where there's a skip.'

I picked up the bin and took it outside. Some way off, set back from the row of containers, sat a yellow waste skip containing plastic bags, timber offcuts and general waste. As I upended the bin into it, what looked like more broken pieces of plastic clattered down through the rubbish. I managed to grab hold of two before they tumbled down further. I wasn't sure what they were so I put them into my pocket.

By the time I was back at the dig most of the fencing panels had been removed. I made my way over to Cameron, my father and Blackie.

'We thought we had lost you,' Cameron said. 'Where have you been?'

I ignored the question. I doubted very much whether Blackie thought he had lost me. If so, he probably wished I would stay lost. The three men had been pointing, no doubt agreeing, or maybe disagreeing, about what should be done next.

The digger driver clunked his machine right into the dig. It was a big beast with a big beast's teeth on a big beast's bucket. Slithering in mud, it manoeuvred towards the rusting steel casing, its caterpillar tracks churning, gouging the clay. Cameron stared. I felt sorry for him. This was not the way he did things.

By the end of the day the excavator had dug a huge conical hole in the clay. The area now covered by the pit seemed massive, three or four times bigger than Cameron's original dig. The sides were cone-shaped because according to my father that was the safest way to get down to depth without the sides falling in. With such low-angle sides, he said, support wasn't needed, not in the clay, only when they started to excavate down through the rock.

The casing remained in place. Though it was now three metres high, it hadn't fallen over. I knew from the driller's logs it had been socketed a short way into the bedrock.

I stayed there, staring at what now resembled a wide bomb crater with nice, neat sides. To finish it off the driver had changed the bucket for one without teeth, then moved his machine carefully all around the top edge of the cone, scraping the sides neatly. He did that all the way round.

"It's a work of art,' I said. 'An upside-down umbrella.'

My father muttered 'If you say so. And it's called a backhoe, not a digger.'

'*Digger* suits me. What happens now?'

'We'll call it a day. Tomorrow morning we start again.'

I admit I was miffed. It was a geology thing. The clay didn't particularly interest me. I wanted to see the rock, wanted to know what we had to go through to get to the remains. Seeing it in the core box wasn't the same as seeing it in place.

I nodded towards Edinburgh, to distant black clouds. 'Looks like rain,' I said. 'Shouldn't you put the pump down there?'

My father didn't agree. 'It won't rain. Mr Blackie says the forecast is good.'

Cameron drove off in his van. I walked to the site office with my father. When we reached the car park I remembered the pieces of plastic and took them out of my pocket. My father took one from me.

'I'm not sure what it is,' I said. 'Looks like plastic.'

'It's Bakelite,' he said, turning it over. 'Or some sort of early of resin. I haven't seen this stuff for years. Where did you get it?'

I passed him the other piece. Both were dark coloured, broken slices, each one no bigger than a playing card. He wiped both pieces on his sleeve. 'They are bits of old electronic circuit board. Corners broken from much larger boards.'

'Computer boards? Printed circuit boards?'

He shook his head. Until he wiped them clean the boards had been so dirty that I hadn't noticed the rows of tiny, regularly spaced holes, all clogged with dirt.

'Possibly from computers, but not *printed* circuits. Before printed circuits were invented they simply drilled small holes in boards like these. They fitted all the components to one side of the board, pushed connecting wires through the holes and soldered them together on the other side. These days they print the wiring directly onto the board.'

I knew about printed circuits. Instead of a tangle of wires linking components together, the whole electrical circuit is printed, neatly and in pure but microscopically thin gold, onto resin board.

My father handed the pieces back to me. 'Where did you get them?'

'Found them in a skip.'

'Best place for them. What were you doing in a skip?'

'I wasn't doing anything in a skip. Cameron has one of the shipping containers to store his stuff. I emptied a waste bin for him and these fell out.'

I didn't want to say more. I knew my father well enough to know it's unwise to feed him puzzles. Years ago he got himself embroiled in events that almost cost him his life. It's how we both met Curtis.

We stood at the back of my father's car, changing from boots to shoes.

'There's a waste bin over there, I'll take those bits for you.'

I had returned the fragments to my pocket. That was where they'd be staying.

'Dad, I've just remembered something I need to do in the core shed. Don't wait for me. I'll get a taxi home.'

I told him I had to go through the core logs again, a job that would take hours. I was hopping around, one shoe on and one boot off, trying to keep my sock out of the dirt. My attempt at distraction worked. He lost concentration, forgot about the circuit boards and hovered close by, unsure what to do.

'I don't like leaving you here. Are you sure you can get a taxi?'

'I'm a big girl. There's a taxi firm I use. She's reliable.'

Kitted up again I slung my day sack over my shoulder and set off for the skip. The core logs thing was a bluff, they no longer interested me. The bits of circuit board that had clattered down through the waste in the skip, did.

Luckily, the skip contained mostly dry waste. Gloves on, I reached in and pulled out everything I could reach. Then, using a plastic drum as a stepping stone, I clambered in, over the side.

Years ago I spent hours in a large industrial skip, hunting through a mix of food waste and paper for geological maps thrown out by mistake. Not by me, I hasten to add. Back then I had dressed in full kit – wellie boots, coveralls, rubber gloves, and hard hat to stop my head hitting the bin's roof. I also wore a face mask, that kept out the dirt but not the smell.

At least this waste was clean. I heaved things out over one end. When I was satisfied I had recovered all the pieces of board that had clattered down through the waste, I clambered out of the skip, my pockets bulging.

I was right about the rain. While in the skip I was aware of fading daylight, putting it down to the onset of evening rather than wall-to-wall cloud. The rain came like a rainforest cloudburst, a sudden, drenching waterfall dumped from on high. No wind, just water.

I ran, not to the core shed, because I knew it was locked. Cameron's container was not and I reached it, tugged at the handles, and swung open the doors.

Once inside I stood looking out, marvelling at how so much water can be held in the sky. To let in as much fading daylight as possible I pushed both doors wide and retreated to the dark end, to the gazebo bags, the tables and chairs and the waste bin I'd emptied. I sat on the edge of the table, deafened by rain that drummed on the roof.

Steel bars on the inside walls of the container reinforced its sides. They criss-crossed diagonally – top right to bottom left and top left to bottom right. Jammed behind one of these bars, down in a back corner, was what looked like a square of thin plywood.

I went to it. Tried to pull it out. It wasn't wood, it was another piece of circuit board, much larger than those I already had. Thin wires zigzagged over one side of it. Affixed to its other side, still jammed against the container wall, were a jumble of damaged electrical components, some as large as a matchbox. I had found a complete, unbroken circuit board.

I braved the rain. The piles of junk I'd left beside the waste skip provided me with a short length of steel reinforcing rod. Back in the container I used it as a lever to free the board. Inspecting my new treasure with the light on my smartphone, I saw that one corner was damaged, a sure sign that somebody else had also tried to unjam it.

As I'd told Curtis, I was familiar with personal computers. The size of a tea tray, this board bore little resemblance to anything I had seen in one of those. A black plastic connector, fixed along one of the board's edges, contained dozens of small gold plug-in terminals, each one shiny and untarnished. The board had been designed to be plugged into something much larger, perhaps a computer with many similar boards. My imagination, slightly out of control, pictured the huge computers in old spy movies, rows of flashing lights and whirring tape drives.

I had to find out where Blackie got his containers. If they came from Kevron, in Bristol, I'd be wasting my time. But that was unlikely. Why bring them so far when they are available to rent or buy almost everywhere?

The rain had eased. The taxi I phoned for was on its way, it was time to leave site. With the circuit board bits in my pocket and the whole board tucked under my arm, I set off for the site office at a steady trot, sticking to the site road, avoiding recently formed puddles and taking care not to trip. At such a late hour the site gates would be closed. I hoped the security man was full time, not one who turned up in a van every few hours.

I won't bore you with details of how I got home. How I got off the site is a different matter. The taxi lady took a good thirty minutes to arrive, which was just as well because it took me most of that time to convince site security that I wasn't an intruder. The man, in a small portable building near gates, said had no record of me being there and therefore couldn't tick me off as having left. His logic had a degree of validity. If the daybook didn't have me signed in, how could he possibly sign me out?

'*Doctor* Spargo,' I'd said to him, emphasising my title as if it were high rank.

That didn't help. Doctors, apparently, worked only in hospitals and surgeries, not on construction sites.

'I'm not that kind of doctor. I work here. I work for your boss.'

'Mr Blackie isn't here to prove that.'

'Not Blackie. Mr Marshall.'

'Never heard of him.'

'He owns Kevron. He owns Blackie. I guess he also owns you.'

And so it went on. I would probably still be there now had the taxi not pulled up to collect me.

Home again, I called Andy Kuzuk to thank him for the suggestions he'd made. I told him I had found a whole circuit board in a shipping container on a construction site. I mentioned that one of them had Russian markings, overpainted with orange paint.

I worked late into the night, checking and rechecking Kevron's maps and documents. I suspected it was pointless. Coming up with something new at this stage was unlikely. No amount of reading would help me now.

Research is nothing new to me, it is part of my life. Geological fieldwork depends on searching for clues and interpreting them, building a picture of what lies in the ground. Disappointingly, in the case of the Kevron site, that approach didn't seem to be working.

Cameron had pencilled-in the position of the borehole on my maps. Now, kneeling on my carpet under bright lights, I unrolled the National Library copy and stared disappointedly at the tiny black dot that had wasted so much of our time. For the first time I noticed that one of the creases in the original map, the one that passed right through the old house, also passed very close to the borehole.

I hadn't paid much attention to the map's creases. They hadn't troubled me because there weren't many features on the map anyway and the lines didn't seem to obscure much. Or I hadn't thought so until now. Seen under bright lights, the crease line I was looking at seemed to have a faint pattern, one that none of the other creases had.

Using my hand lens I detected a row of faint dots. They started at one edge of the map, ran a short way towards the borehole position and then vanished. Had I been looking at the original crease rather than the line it made on the photographic copy, I might have been able to smooth out the paper and reveal even more dots.

I was aware that I might well be doing that thing I warned my students not to do, *if something isn't there, then no amount of looking will find it*. But further along the line there *were* more dots. A row of five or six, each the size of a pin prick, ran from the back of the house and into same crease.

I now had two short rows of dots, one coming in from the edge of the map and another, a long way off, near the small sketch of the house. It didn't take much imagination to realise that they were probably two ends of the same dotted line, most of its length obscured by the crease line.

I didn't sleep well that night. I woke at five and lay on my back, dropping in and out of sleep, my mind flipping from maps to circuit boards and back again. Finally I got up and showered, dressed and returned to the map. The dots were definitely there. I had not dreamt them. Did they mark a footpath, long gone? If so, it once led from the house, up towards what was now Cameron's dig and the borehole, and then off site. Back then there would have been no boundary fence. Probably no overgrown woodland, either.

I breakfasted on toast and coffee. Then, at a more respectable hour, I called Cameron. Luckily for me he hadn't yet left home and he agreed to collect me and take me to site. He had done it before but it was a big ask. After leaving home near Glasgow he would join the motorway. An hour or so later, instead of heading further east on the Edinburgh bypass, he would join slow moving – often stationary – traffic and head into the city to collect me.

'I'm no historian, Cameron,' I said when we were well out of the city, 'but I do know that some big old houses down south had priest holes, used as hiding places for Catholic priests. Some even had escape tunnels. Did they have things like that up here?'

I had changed my mind about the dots marking a path from the house. We were, after all, searching for an underground void. What if the dots marked an escape tunnel, or a drain, or some kind of old water supply?

'I don't pretend to be an historian either, Jessica. I know that some Scottish castles have tunnels and I daresay others exist under fortified manor houses. Probably not for Catholic priests, more likely for Jacobite sympathisers. Is that what you are thinking? Would parish records help?'

I shrugged. 'For what purpose? At best you'll get names of previous owners, their births, marriages and deaths. Nothing about priest holes, tunnels and Jacobite sympathisers.'

Cameron muttered to himself as he signalled, changed gear and took an exit. 'You may well be right, Jessica. You may well be right.'

On site, the digger driver was using his bucket to bail water from Cameron's dig. During the night the wide, cone-shaped pit had filled to the brim and overflowed. What had been clear water now resembled *slip* – the clay mixture poured into moulds to make pottery. Unhappy about rivers of mud flowing across his site, Blackie had provided two impressively large dump trucks to carry the pit's liquid contents elsewhere.

The digger operations resembled a slow-motion dance. Its long arm swung out across the pit and then down, angling its bucket to scoop out the mud. Bucket loaded, it swung back through the air to dump wet clay into a waiting dump truck. Meanwhile, in the pit, more clay slipped from its sides, collapsing into the mud mix. It was going to be a long job.

'The clay is unstable,' Cameron said. 'It's a mess. All that water doesn't make any sense to me. If there is some kind of tunnel down there why doesn't the water drain away?'

'The clay is impervious,' I said as we left the dig and set off for the core shed. 'It seals the base of the pit. The water can't escape down the borehole because the casing is tight in the rock.'

We reached the core shed. I unrolled last night's map and showed Cameron what I had found. He could just make out the row of dots at the edge of the map, but not those near the house. Carelessly I had left my hand lens at home so he took off his glasses and used them to magnify the sheet. He shook his head.

'Sorry, Jessica, I can't see them. I'll take your word for it. Do you think the map is one of a series? The next map along might show where the dotted line goes.'

'I doubt it. It looks like a one-off to me, a map made for whoever owned the house and estate. I suppose we could check it out ourselves, it's not as if we are going to be doing much here.' I touched the map at the place the dots ran off it. 'We know the direction the dots are heading. Fancy a walk in the woods?'

'I don't want to spend the day walking in circles, Jessica. You are a geologist, you must know what it's like, trying to find your way when you can't see any landmarks.'

I rummaged in my bag and produced a compass, one I'd had since I first started geology. I held it in the air as if I'd done a magic trick.

'Shame I didn't bring my satnav.'

He stared at me. 'You have a satnav?'

'A hand-held one. A birthday present from a friend. Pocket size, like a phone. I didn't think to bring it with me. Didn't think I'd need it to find my way from the site office to the core shed.'

He took the compass from me, held it out and watched the red-tipped needle settle steadily on Magnetic North.

'So,' I said. 'Worth a try? The other day you did say we should leave no stone unturned.'

It was a long walk, in dense woodland that would have challenged a jungle explorer. There was no path, not even animal tracks. Machetes would have helped. To make things worse, my wellie boots had heavy steel toecaps and after a while, lifting my feet over fallen tree trunks and branches proved tiring. Cameron didn't have such problems. Before setting off he'd changed from shoes to the walking boots he kept in his van.

For the first part of the trip he stayed beside me, helping me in a gentlemanly way over obstructions, holding branches and brambles so they didn't whip back at me. All that soon changed. When he realised I was more than capable of negotiating such obstacles unaided, he commandeered my compass and left me behind.

I'd assumed, wrongly as it turned out, that eventually we would encounter the distant side of the old military site, perhaps come across high steel railings like those near Blackie's offices. Such a fence would inevitably stop progress. So far, there was no sign of it. Nor was there any sign of Cameron.

Our little adventure seemed pointless. I'd had enough and I wanted to go back. I guessed we had already walked – struggled, more like – more than a mile, with no guarantee that we were still walking the same line as the dots on the map. It wasn't as if we were in open fields, able to look back.

I called out. 'Cameron! Time to go back! We are wasting our time!'

Either he ignored me or he didn't hear me. I did cross my mind that if there was anything to find, he wanted to be the person to find it. A man-against-jungle thing. Delaying me further were small bits of woodland – twigs, I hoped, rather than creatures – that had found their way into my wellies. I stopped, leant against a tree, took each boot off in turn and emptied it out.

I tried to walk faster. Ten minutes later there was still no sign of Cameron, though I didn't need tracking skills to see where he'd been. Following a trail of broken branches and trampled brambles I eventually reached a clearing where animals, perhaps deer or badgers, had passed through. Like Cameron they had trampled the ground, breaking small branches, so many tracks I didn't know which way to go. Unsure what to do, I stopped and listened. All I could hear was the faint drone of far-off traffic. I called out again.

'Cameron! Where are you? I've lost you!'

I listened. Nothing at all now, not even distant traffic. A plane howled high overhead, making for the Firth of Forth and Edinburgh Airport.

'Cameron! This is crazy! We should go back!'

My imagination ran wild. Something had happened to him. Perhaps he had fallen. Perhaps, however unlikely, we were still on that dotted line and he had fallen down a shaft or a well.

Getting back to site, I thought as I shouted, wouldn't be a problem if I set off now. If I went much further then chances were that I would become confused by more branching-off animal tracks. If I got lost I might be there for hours. Even days.

Then I remembered my phone. Surprisingly it had a good signal. Having quick-dialled Cameron's number I soon had the phone to my ear. I let it ring several times before cancelling the call and trying again, this time realising that it would make more sense if I kept my phone away from my ear and listen for the ring of Cameron's phone instead. I did that thing birds do when disturbed, cocked my head one way and then the other, seeking faint sounds. I heard nothing.

People do stupid things. The stupid thing I did that day was to let Cameron get out of my sight. Another thing I did, a thing that took me some time to realise, was that I had used the quick-dial for Cameron's home number, not his mobile.

I tried again. This time things worked as planned. From far off came Cameron's tuneful ringtone. Expecting him to answer I put my phone to my ear but it went on ringing – an ordinary ring tone from mine and a distant jangling from his. It went to voicemail so I cancelled the call.

I shouted again. 'Cameron!'

Shouting was pointless. I had to go towards the source of the sound. I battled on, calling his phone frequently, heading as best as I could towards the source of the sound.

To one side of me the woodland looked brighter. More daylight meant that the bracken, knee-high before, had grown to waist-height. From the way it had been battered down I knew I was back on Cameron's trail. I guessed that he had armed himself with a big stick and then wielded it, cutlass-like. More Captain Blackbeard than eco-warrior.

I hadn't expected the ground to slope away from me. The giant stalks of bracken gave way to short, rabbit-cropped, slippery grass. The treads on my wellies failed to grip and with a yelp I fell backwards, my feet going from under me as I started a long slide towards the top edge of what I now realised was an overgrown quarry. A subconscious survival instinct kicked in, consisting largely of yelling and a flailing of arms.

The yelling didn't help but the arm-flailing did. One of my grasping hands caught a lifeline of brambles. Roots ripped from the ground. Thorns tore my skin as the tentacles ran through my fingers. Finally my nightmare slide came to a slow, painful stop and I lay on my back on the slope, too scared to move. My boots stuck out over the edge of what I guessed was a sheer quarry face, a vertical drop to whatever lay below.

Rather than put more weight on the brambles I dug my heel into the grass and pushed myself back. Still gripping the bramble stem lifeline and still on my back, I inched myself slowly up the slope, using my heels to dig footholds. At last I lay safely, breathing heavily and staring at clouds. Long skid marks in the grass, made by Cameron's boots, showed me he hadn't been so lucky.

I couldn't phone for help. My phone had gone. I had been holding it when I fell and it had followed Cameron, over the edge, down into the quarry.

There was no way I could go for help and leave Cameron. I had to find a way down to him.

20

From where I stood, safe now and well back from the edge of the quarry, I couldn't see down. Even if I could get closer to the edge, the vegetation that grew on the quarry floor was as dense as that in the woodland. I was level with the tops of self-seeded trees that grew up from the quarry floor.

Quarries come in all shapes and sizes. These days, some are the size of small towns. Back in the days when transporting heavy materials over bad roads was difficult, small local quarries provided stone to build farmhouses and farmworker's cottages. I couldn't help wondering if some of the stone from this quarry had been used to build that old house. If so, then this quarry could be three hundred years old. Such quarries can be found all over Scotland, disused for years and heavily overgrown, many backfilled with farm rubbish.

I knew from visiting similar places with my students that there would be an old entrance, somewhere low down, a track used to haul out the stone. No quarryman worth the name would dig a pit and then haul the cut rock up its steep sides if there was another way to get it out.

Walking around the top edge of the quarry proved impossible. I returned to the undergrowth and continued my battle with bracken. Finally, after negotiating my way down a wooded slope, I found myself standing in the quarry itself.

For a few minutes I forgot about Cameron. Long ago, when this quarry was abandoned, it would have been left as bare rock. Within a couple of years, moss – which does not need soil to grow and whose spores are carried by wind – began to coat the bare rock with a carpet of green. Seeds spread by birds and wind took root in the moss and the plants grew, died and rotted, building up a peaty mass that supported even more growth. Saplings sprouted into trees, whose leaves then fell, providing more nutrients. Strong tree roots penetrated cracks in the rock and helped release vital minerals. In short, nature took over.

Nature had certainly taken over here. I had entered an overgrown green jungle, an eerie and damp silent world with no bird song, no distant traffic sounds and no planes or trains. Damp leaves fluttered from trees, a gentle pit-pat as they touched the ground. Though I couldn't be sure, I thought I could also hear the sound of running water. The trickle of a distant stream, perhaps?

I made my way around trees and through greenery, calling out occasionally, heading towards where I hoped to find Cameron. Just as I began to think I was heading in the wrong direction, through the branches of trees I caught sight of the quarry's cliff-like sides and the place where I'd slipped – a vertical rock face, topped by the grassy slope I had slid down. I changed direction and battled ahead, no longer skirting obstructions but forcing myself through dense undergrowth.

I reached the cliff face. Years of erosion had left a bank of rubble at its foot, from which saplings sprouted and weeds grew. Most importantly of all, Cameron Thomson lay on it, face down and motionless.

'Cameron? *Cameron?*'

I reached him and shook him. Had his eyes been open, I would have despaired. My first aid knowledge is basic. I knew the ABC rule – *Airway, Breathing, Circulation.* Luckily the first two weren't a problem because I could hear him breathing, shallow and fast. Did the fact that he was breathing mean his heart was pumping? I wasn't sure so I checking his pulse, first on his wrist and then, because I felt nothing, by touching his neck.

A pulse, faint but present. Now, what else? *Circulation* – blood – thankfully there was no sign of that. Had he hit his head on one of the many rocks that studded the bank? I didn't know, nor did I know how to tell. He lay with his head steeply downslope, which did not look right. As I tried to swing him around into the recovery position I saw that one of his feet pointed backwards. Cameron had broken a leg.

Two hours later Cameron was safely in the ERI, the Edinburgh Royal Infirmary. I had used his phone to call an ambulance and also Kevron's site office. While I waited for help, Cameron returned to a groggy but painful consciousness. Lying motionless while waiting for rescue he had nursed the back of his head. He had, I discovered when I checked, a lump the size of a golf ball.

The most bizarre part of the rescue had been the sight of Blackie driving a bulldozer, entering the quarry on an old entrance track – the track I had assumed would be there but hadn't found. He was followed, not too closely, by a police 4x4, an ambulance and a paramedic on a motorcycle. After splinting Cameron they carrier him on a stretcher, down the track recently deforested by Blackie.

After the ambulance took Cameron the police gave me a lift back to site. I sat in Blackie's office while an officer made notes. I was concerned that she was taking her time, I didn't want to be around when Blackie returned. Also, I wanted to visit the ERI to check on Cameron, something I mentioned to her in the hope she'd hurry up.

Then I heard the distant clatter of bulldozer tracks, the sound I had been dreading. With Blackie at the controls, the yellow monster lumbered through the entrance gates, turned in front of the car park and disappeared up one of the site's roads. I had deliberately avoided him in the quarry, easily done because he'd remained with the dozer until the ambulance took Cameron away. After managing a multi-point turn that left even more trees crushed and broken, he had started his journey back to site at the pace of a snail. Later, we had overtaken him in the police 4x4. I hadn't waved.

'Now, Doctor Spargo,' the officer said, 'Let's go through this again.'

I sighed. The chances of me leaving site before Blackie came to the office were remote.

'Shall we move out of this room,' I said. 'The site manager won't like – '

Blackie burst in. Tugging off a pair of leather gloves finger by finger he strode across his office, took off his hard hat and threw it into a corner.

'Years since I've had the chance to drive one of those,' he said, addressing the officer after a quick glance at me. 'Bloody marvellous! You should try it. Did you see the size of those trees I brought down?'

'Sorry Mr Blackie,' I said, before he could start on me, 'We were following a line on an old map. We didn't know about the old quarry. Cameron went on ahead.'

Now, in his office, he stood looking down at me. I addressed both him and the policeman.

'I don't understand how you all found us,' I continued, as contritely as I could manage. 'Even I didn't know where we were.'

The police officer started to speak. Blackie interrupted.

'You said you were in an old quarry. Before Kevron tendered for this job I came here with Mr Marshall to reconnoitre the site and the land around it. Somehow we managed to do it without falling into any quarries.'

'Sorry,' I said again.

I caught the hint of a smile from the officer. Possibly from Blackie too. Though more likely an angry twitch.

'I see that Professor Thomson's van is here.'

Blackie said it to me, as if I was responsible for it. Ironically I was, because while awaiting rescue Cameron had insisted that I didn't come with him in the ambulance and that I should take care of his van instead.

'I'm taking it,' I said to Blackie. 'He asked me to.'

The way things were looking, Cameron wouldn't be driving for some time. The paramedic had suspected two distinct breaks, one in his ankle and another in his lower leg.

I signed my police statement with difficulty. I had damaged my hand. Thorns had torn the skin. For what seemed like hours I'd been clenching my fist to stop the bleeding. I hadn't bothered to mention it. Compared with Cameron's injuries it was nothing.

'Thank you, Mr Blackie, I said when the policeman had gone. 'Thanks for your help. For clearing the way.'

I had embarrassed him. For once he seemed lost for words.

'Your hand… what have you done to it?'

With difficulty I unclenched it and held it out. It was a mess of congealed blood. 'It's fine,' I said. 'I'll see to it when I get home.'

He left me there and returned minutes later with a first aid kit the size of a small suitcase that he set down on his desk. Opening it, he rummaged around. Got frustrated and upended the whole thing on his desk.

'One's bad enough, he said. 'But two of you? Site's been injury free since we started.'

'You don't have to report it. It wasn't on your site.'

He nodded. 'And I intend to keep it that way. If you are planning to repeat your daft bloody games, Doctor, make sure you do them off my site.'

I stood up to go. 'I told you, I'll sort it out at home.'

'Sit down, woman!'

21

Blackie's command surprised me so much that I obeyed without question. In ten painful minutes he cleaned my palm, painful for me because the antiseptic hurt like hell and painful for him because I must have jumped a hundred times while he worked away with tweezers, teasing out thorns.

I expected him to cover my hand with plasters. Instead he produced a bandage that he twisted over every time he wrapped it around my palm and wrist. I ended up with a pattern of chevrons that ran up the back of my hand and up my injured thumb. It was a work of art. My grandfather had done the same kind of bandaging on my knee when I was young and I remember how I was able to bend it afterwards. I was impressed back then. I was even more impressed now.

'First Aider,' he mumbled when I mentioned its neatness. 'Now, do you want me to call your father?'

'I'm not twelve years old, Mr Blackie. I'm probably older than you. Why would I need my father?'

He grinned. He actually grinned!

'Can you drive with your hand like that?'

'Just you watch me.'

'Because if not, you can leave the Prof's van here and I'll get your father to run you home. Where do you stay, Edinburgh?'

I nodded. 'But he doesn't. He's in Peebles. I can manage, Mr Blackie. Thank you for offering.'

'Good man, your father. Knows his stuff.'

I remember my father saying the same thing about him. I had stumbled upon some sort of engineer's mutual admiration society.

'So, what happens now?' Blackie asked. 'Now the Prof's indisposed?'

'It shouldn't make any difference. As he said to me, he was here to do a shallow dig and everything's changed now. Your digger... your backhoe... has dug down to bedrock. We still have to remove three metres of rock.' The embodiment of discretion, I did not mention dogs.

'That can't start until the shuttering arrives. Your father said we didn't need it through the clay and he was right. As you have seen, we have battered the clay right back to make a safe slope. Now we must support the rock as we go down through it.'

I nodded. I knew all that. 'He knows best.'

'Do you work with him often?'

'I don't.'

Not at all if I can help it. Not that my father was incompetent, far from it. He was an excellent engineer. His big problem is that he manages to get mixed up in things that don't concern him. Not that I would ever admit such a thing to Blackie.

'You told the police you were following a line on a map,' Blackie said. 'What was that about?'

Reluctantly I explained about the non-existent well, the crease on the map and the supposed dotted line whose general direction we had attempted to follow. I was impressed that he listened without asking questions. Later, as I drove away from site, I thought that perhaps he'd simply been bored.

On my way home I called in at the ERI. Cameron lay behind a drawn blue curtain, on a bed designed by a mechanical engineer – all levers and pistons and stuff. In his hospital gown he looked very sorry for himself. He nodded towards his leg.

'Do you mind keeping the van until I'm mended?' he asked. 'That's likely to be weeks rather than days, I'm thinking.'

'Won't your wife want it?'

'My partner. No, she's got her own car. She's on her way here now.'

I sat there, nodding. 'That's good. And good of you to lend me the van, I appreciate it. I'm sorry this happened. I shouldn't have pressured you into going.'

'You didn't pressure me. I'm a grown man, Jessica, I'm responsible for what I do. I should have been more careful.'

'It wasn't as if we found anything.'

'No.'

'We don't even know where we went. We were supposed to walk in a straight line.'

'That wasn't possible.'

'No.'

'Not sure what happened to your compass, Jessica.'

Forget it, I thought. Yes, it was a good compass, I'd had it for years. But I had Cameron's van for the indefinite future, which I though a fair swap. For the first time since I came into the cubicle he noticed my bandaged hand. He looked from it to my tousled hair.

'If you don't mind me saying, Jessica, you do look awful.'

'Oh? I didn't realise you were a graduate of the James Blackie School of Tact and Diplomacy. You don't look so good yourself. You could do with a haircut.'

He ran a hand through his hair. 'Chance would be a good thing. My barber is ten miles from my home.'

'Get one closer to home.'

'There aren't any.'

'I bet I could find one for you.'

This was becoming one of those hospital bedside conversations. I didn't want to leave. Nor did I want to stay.

'What have you done to your hand?'

'That place you slid over. I slipped too. I almost followed you down. I managed to grab hold of brambles.'

'Thank god you didn't slide over.'

'It might not have been that bad. I would have landed on you. You would have cushioned my fall.' He tried his best to laugh. 'Blackie knows where the quarry is,' I continued. 'That's why he was able to drive that dozer and clear the way.'

'Didn't know it was him driving it.'

'A man of many talents.' I held up my bandaged hand. 'He did this, too.'

The pointless chat continued until a nurse and hospital porter wheeled Cameron away. If his partner was coming, then me staying and waiting was just as pointless.

My mobile rang as I was driving home. As I prefer to stay law-abiding – and alive – I never answer my phone when driving. This time the caller was persistent, calling three times before I was halfway home. I pulled over and answered.

'Are you all right, Love?'

'I'm fine.'

'Are you sure? Jim called me.'

'Jim?'

'Jim… James… Mr Blackie. He said you injured your hand.'

'It's nothing. Did he mention what happened?'

'He said he had to pull out thorns.'

'No, I mean did he say what happened to Cameron? Professor Thomson? He's in the ERI.'

'Hang on, I'm in the car, I'm at crossroads.'

I could tell he was in his car from the way he was shouting. I waited while he negotiated his way through traffic or whatever it was he was doing.

'Cameron's got multiple leg breaks,' I said. 'Didn't Blackie tell you?'

'He only mentioned you. Oh – and he said he'd just had a call saying the shuttering is on its way. I'm to be there first thing tomorrow.'

'We were walking through a wood and Cameron fell into an old quarry.'

'What were you two doing in a wood?'

'We weren't doing anything in the wood. We were following what we thought was a line on an old map.'

'And was it?'

'Was it what?'

'The line on the map. Was it what you thought it was?'

Our conversation was getting complicated. I didn't like to think of him trying to work it all out while driving so I suggested we talk about it tomorrow.

'You will be on site too?'

'Like you, first thing. I've got transport now.'

'I missed that. Please repeat.'

'I said I've got transport.'

'Okay. Got you. On my way home now.'

'Okay, Dad. Over and Out.'

'What was that?'

'Nothing, Dad. I said nothing.'

My father wasn't my only caller. Tim Cavendish had left a message asking me to phone him. 'Quite urgent,' he'd said. I was tempted to wait until I got home, but that was at least fifteen minutes away. I called him. A mechanical voice said he wasn't available. I was about to drive off when he rang me back.

'Dr Spargo, yes, thanks for calling. Do you mind telling me where you are?'

'South Bridge. Near Blackwell's bookshop. I've just pulled in to take a call. Why do you want to know where I am?'

'Did my DCI phone you?'

'Not recently.'

'I'm not far from you. Would it be possible to meet?'

'What, now? Can you get to my place?'

'Your lab?'

'Either that or my home.' It was late afternoon and I didn't want to hang around on that side of the city. Another half hour and I'd be caught up in the usual peak time traffic chaos. 'My home,' I said, after a bit of quick thinking. Parking at my lab was even worse than parking at home.

Cavendish arrived before me. He had parked in front of my garage doors, his small unmarked car displaying POLICE on a sign in its windscreen. I nodded towards it.

'All right for some.'

'I don't use it that often. If I parked in some parts of the city I would get a brick through the windscreen.'

'Sorry I took so long. I couldn't find a parking space.'

He frowned. Looked at my garage doors. 'Can't you park in your garage?'

'It's full of unpacked boxes. Tell me why you wanted to meet.'

'If it's all right with you I would rather tell you inside.'

As I made coffee for me and tea for him I realised that my only callers since I moved to the mews were police officers. The rain-soaked policeman, then Curtis and now Cavendish. As he took a sip of tea he noticed my bandage and made me explain. I related to him, as simply as possible, my exploits in the woods and the quarry.

'Mr Curtis doesn't know about it yet,' I said. 'I'd rather you didn't tell him.'

He nodded. 'It's unlikely to interest him at present. He's tied up with a big case. It's sensitive.'

'Aren't they all. I'm used to keeping secrets, Tim. I've been in this business for years.' *Probably since you were in Primary 3*, I thought but did not say.

'Of course. It's just that the DCI hasn't told you about this yet.' Looking at me across the top of his cup he took another sip of tea. 'He seemed sensitive about me talking to you. He wouldn't say why.'

'He's feeling guilty. I've been doing bits and bobs for him and it's all unofficial.'

'If it helps, he did say that your lab's been approved. What about your time, do you charge for that? What about now?'

'I would if I could but I can't.'

'Not for this meeting?'

'Not for anything, Tim. It would help if you would chase that for me. I don't really want to trouble Mr Curtis.'

He nodded. 'Will do. In view of that I won't stay long.'

'Stay as long as you like. I'm used to twelve-hour days.' And the rest. 'So why are you here? Surely not to chat about contracts.'

'No, no. It's about Charles deWit.'

'Does Mr Curtis think deWit is connected? With Morini's murder, I mean.'

I had provided Cavendish with the real deal, a tray on which I'd arranged a teapot, real tea, a teacup and saucer and milk in a jug. I had a mug of coffee. I refused to be mother, so he had poured the tea himself. Now he was nursing the cup in both hands.

'I'm not sure I should be telling you this.'

Come on, Tim! I held my breath and waited. Had I upset someone? His superintendent, Ken Ripon, perhaps?

'There's been another.'

'Another?'

'Another shooting. Its Charles deWit. He's dead!'

22

I like to think nothing surprises me. That bit of news did. Cavendish watched for my reaction. Shock, definitely. Regret, too. Also relief… relief that Cavendish was not here about me.

'Was he found at the same place as Morini?'

Cavendish had taken a sip from his cup. He swallowed quickly, anxious to put me right.

'No, no, in his apartment. We are uncertain when it happened. It looks as if whoever did this finally got the right man.'

'You said he was shot. Did nobody hear it? He lives near King's Buildings, it's all residential. There must have been dozens of people around.'

'You would be surprised what people don't hear, or say they don't hear. What makes you think he lived there?'

'Doesn't he… didn't he? He did when he was a student.'

'That was where Mr Morini lived. Mr deWit lived in New Town.'

Old Edinburgh is split into two parts. High Street, and the rest of the Royal Mile between Holyrood House and Edinburgh Castle, is surrounded by ancient buildings, some of them five hundred years old. In the seventeen-hundreds a new town was built to the north, Georgian mansions, churches and banks for the gentry. And mews houses like mine for artisans, coachmen, and the middle-management of the day.

'It's Doctor deWit and Doctor Morini,' I said. 'Not mister.' Not that it mattered much now. Part of me wanted to quiz Cavendish about deWit's death. The other part really didn't want to know. 'Same as before? Gold fragments?'

'The DCI doesn't yet know.'

I winced. I had a flash of déjà vu, standing under floodlights at the edge of a field, looking down at deWit's jacket, worn by Morini, thinking the same thoughts I had now. Just because I didn't like deWit, didn't mean I wanted him dead.

It was after Morini's post mortem – his autopsy – that Curtis handed me that phial of gunge. I hoped it wouldn't happen again.

Cavendish put down his cup. 'I'm told you worked with him.'

'deWit? Yes. He was one of my students. Later he became a lecturer.'

'Can I ask when you last saw him?'

I told him the day, date and time. 'I lecture at King's. We met in the corridor.'

'What did you talk about?'

'Not much. He was offensive.' I almost said *offensive as always,* but under the circumstances it would have been insensitive and tactless. Ironically, just like deWit himself.

I told Cavendish that deWit had blocked my way and had warned me off.

'In respect of what?'

'Morini's death. His murder.'

I recounted the conversation to him, mentioning that deWit told me to keep my nose out of things that didn't concern me.

'You two really didn't get along, did you. What about his relationship with others? How was he with students and staff?'

'It's no secret that he wasn't liked. As far as I knew, not by anyone. I suppose Morini must have got along with him, seeing that they lodged together for a while. 'Why did you say what you said just now?'

'Which bit?'

'That whoever killed deWit finally had the right man?'

'Dr Morini was wearing Dr deWit's jacket when he was shot. You must know that, the DCI says he called you out. Whoever did it got the wrong man. They finally got the right one.'

I stayed quiet for some time, fiddling around. He'd put his empty cup down on the table and I moved it onto the tray. He tilted his head, quizzically.

'Is something puzzling you?'

'Yes it is. What if the murderer finally got *both* the right men?'

He frowned. 'Not sure what you mean.'

'Think about it.'

Leaving him to mull over my words I took my empty mug to the kitchen. 'Tell me, Tim,' I said when I returned, 'If you don't mind me asking, why are you really here?'

'I wanted to keep you in the loop. I'm actually on my way home. I have just worked twenty hours so the DCI sent me away. He is insisting that Dr deWit isn't my case but I don't agree. Both murders and the break-in to Dr deWit's apartment must be connected.'

'You mean they broke in and shot him?'

'No, no. I'm talking about last week. You don't know about that?'

'I don't.' Cavendish was under the misapprehension that Curtis actually told me stuff.

'Somebody damaged his apartment door. The DCI is furious that nobody made the connection.'

'*What connection, Tim?* Start at the beginning?'

'Dr deWit's apartment was broken into several days ago. The officer investigating it didn't realise deWit was a friend of Morini's.'

'You mean deWit didn't tell the officer that his friend had been murdered?'

'Apparently not.'

'That's bizarre! I can't see why Mr Curtis has his knickers in a twist. Unless deWit's name was circulated in relation to Morini's murder, the officer attending the break-in wouldn't link the two men. Was it the murderer who broke in, do you think? Was he expecting to find deWit at home and shoot him? What did he do when he didn't find him there, come back later and try again?'

Cavendish didn't comment. He stood up as if about to leave, but instead he tidied the tea things, returning his cup and the teapot to the tray. I realised he was about to take the tray to the kitchen so I took it from him, I didn't want him to go there because I had washed the fragments of circuit board and left them on the drainer to dry.

'None of this is general knowledge,' he said. 'The deWit shooting, I mean. I would appreciate you not telling the DCI that I have spoken to you about it.'

'I have no reason to tell anyone, Tim.'

He didn't leave. He sat down again and stared at the floor. I stayed quiet too, thinking things through. I had questions to ask. It wasn't often that I could share my thoughts with someone and I intended to make the most of it.

'The break-in at deWit's place…' I said. 'If my friend had been murdered I would have made sure the officer investigating the break-in knew all about it, especially if the murdered man had been wearing my jacket. Presumably deWit knew about that?'

'Knew about what?'

'That Morini had been wearing his jacket.'

Cavendish nodded. 'He did. It was one of the first questions the DCI asked when he interviewed him after Morini's murder. DeWit explained that last month Morini had visited his apartment and the weather turned cold.'

I nodded. 'I suppose that makes sense.' I sat quietly for a while. It *did* make sense, but something else Cavendish had said did not. 'I still don't understand why deWit didn't tell the officer about his link with Morini.'

'What if I told you that deWit didn't even report the break-in?'

'What do you mean?'

'What I said. DeWit didn't report the break-in to his apartment. The woman living in the adjacent apartment did that. She saw the damaged front door and called it in.'

'So there's a possibility that had she not called the police, deWit might not have reported it? Even though the perpetrator might have been Morini's killer? Why would that be?'

It was Cavendish's turn to sit quietly. I had merely pointed out something I thought fairly obvious. Perhaps it was not.

'Interesting point. I hadn't thought of that.'

'Fair enough. It's not your case.'

'It probably will be. As I said, when you next see the DCI, please don't mention any of this.'

'Learn to trust people, Tim.'

'What, in my job?'

After he left I made space for Cameron's van in my garage by moving boxes from there to my kitchen. I hoped that by seeing them every day I would have a real incentive to empty them.

Just before midnight I drove the van into my garage. Though I had checked sizes before embarking on the garage clear-out, I had to turn-in the van's side mirrors to make it fit in. Also, I couldn't open the van's side doors. To get in and out of it I had to clamber over Cameron's kit and use its back doors.

23

By coincidence I arrived at Kevron's site next day at exactly the same time as my father. I parked the van at the office beside his 4x4 and walked with him to the dig. Despite previous efforts, the dig had re-flooded. Not only had rainwater run in from around it, water had also leaked in from thin bands of sand in the clay. Those, I knew from experience, would probably keep on flowing.

The digger was there. The driver had fixed one end of a chain to its bucket and the other to the borehole casing. Blackie, in boots, hi-viz jacket and hard hat, stood with my father and others on the far side of the pit, shouting instructions. My father saw me and walked around the pit's edge to me.

'The casing has to come out,' he said. 'It's in the way. The excavator driver wants to get his bucket right down to bedrock to clean it off.'

I watched as the driver lifted the digger's arm. The chain tightened. The casing tilted precariously and then broke free from the ground. With an impressive sweep of its arm the digger swung the casing away from the sea of mud and lowered it carefully to the ground. A cheer went up from the watchers.

'Good man, that!' my father said. He set off around the dig again and joined up with Blackie. I stayed put, staring at the slurry of water and mud in the pit. Pumping it out hadn't worked. Bailing with the digger and carrying water away in dump trucks hadn't worked either.

To me, everything was a mess – the dig, the mud, and the foolishness that led to Cameron's accident. I felt tearful. I knew it was probably tiredness, I hadn't slept well for days. I hadn't eaten properly either. Too little food and too much coffee.

My father was calling to me. A cluster of faces, all topped by hard hats, had turned towards me. Arms waved and fingers pointed, some at the mud and others at the side of the pit. Unsure why they were calling and waving at me I panicked, paying attention to them and not to the pit. My father was running towards me again, shouting. As he neared me, I heard his words.

'Look at it! Look at the water, it's going! Look at the sides!'

I looked. I could see from the tide-marks around the pit's sloping sides that the water level was falling fast. Removing the casing was like pulling the plug from a huge bath. I watched, speechless. It wasn't long before a whirlpool established itself above the borehole, swirling and gurgling.

'Where's it all going, Love? If this was limestone you could easily lose thousands of gallons into caves. If it was chalk then it could go into wide fissures. But not here.'

Yes Dad. Tell me something I don't know…

'If you ask me,' he continued, 'there must be mineworkings down there to take all of that.'

'Not mineworkings, Dad. Not out here.'

It was time to tell him about the maps, the dotted line, the old mansion and the reason Cameron and I had walked to the quarry. Clearly, he was miffed that I hadn't told him about this before.

'I didn't want to sidetrack you. You have enough on your plate.'

He responded with a grunt. While others stayed to watch the vanishing mud, I took advantage of Blackie being out of his office by wandering in that general direction, back along the row of the containers and then down the site road. After dutifully removing my boots at the office entrance, I padded, in my socks, down the corridor to the engineers' room. I had hoped to find Hamish Anderton. He wasn't there.

'I'm looking for Hamish,' I said to Blackie's secretary. 'Is he around?'

'He's off site. Can I help you?'

'Possibly. I'm wondering where your shipping containers came from.'

'Why is that?'

'I just wondered. I've been thinking of hiring one. Perhaps buying one.' I knew from her frown that this wasn't going to be easy. I knew I should have waited for Hamish. 'Storage,' I said. 'I have a lot of equipment.'

'There are many places you can hire containers.'

'I'm sure there are. But those you have are perfect. The orange ones, I mean. I'm wondering if you have the name of your supplier?'

'I'm not sure I can give you that.'

'Because you cannot or because you won't?'

'Because our site records are confidential.'

'I thought I was working for Kevron, not the Security Service.'

For that verbal transgression I received a glare that would melt steel. I considered saying that I had a piece of paper from the top man saying that Kevron *would afford me every possible facility to aid me in the execution of my work*. It just wasn't worth the effort.

Outside, boots on again, I encountered Hamish, parking his car. Boots off again I accompanied him to the surveyors' room, where he logged on to his laptop.

'The quantity surveyor's records show that two of the shipping containers came from one of our previous sites,' he said, paging down a spreadsheet. 'Two others – the toilet and shower units – came from a supplier in Yorkshire. The core logger's cabin isn't ours, it belongs to the drilling company. That reminds me, I must put that one-off hire now the drilling is finished. Is that the one you are interested in?'

'No. What about the new one?'

'None are new.'

'I mean the latest one, the second of the two orange ones, the one that came for Cameron. The lorry it came on had no company name.'

'Ah… here… two containers, re-painted. Both from a supplier in West Lothian. Strange, though. I'm in the site's purchase ledger. There are no rental or purchase details for those two.'

'Should there be?'

'There should. There's a comment. It says *crushed*.'

'That's odd. It can't mean that the containers were crushed. They're undamaged.'

'I don't know what it means. I can ask Mt Blackie for you. He's out on site, trying to find out who's been emptying rubbish from one of the waste skips.'

I winced. 'No,' I said. 'Please don't do that.'

I thanked him, left the office and walked back to my father. There wasn't much to do on site so I decided to return to the quarry to look for my phone. I had been so concerned about Cameron that at the time of his accident I hadn't bothered to look for it. I was sure it would be damaged, if not from falling into the quarry, then from the overnight rain. Even if it didn't work, I needed to find it to have it repaired or replaced.

Like me, my father had time on his hands. When I told him I was off to the quarry to look for my phone he insisted on coming with me. I suppose it made sense. As he said, *two pairs of eyes, etcetera.*

No way would I being going through the woods with my father. I had already lost one person over the edge and I didn't intend losing another. Thankfully he had no intention of walking, and following my directions he drove me there in his 4x4. A hard-surfaced road gave way to a stony track and then to Blackie's environmental carnage. Tree trunks and branches, shoved aside by the dozer blade, still littered the approach to the quarry. Undaunted, my father battled on until finally, to my great relief, he admitted defeat. Years ago I had watched from far off as he drove a vehicle down what can only be described as a ravine. He'd as good as wrecked it. That one wasn't his. This one was.

We were walking now, making our way around crushed branches.

'You said Jim did this? What did he do, drive a herd of stampeding elephants through here?'

'Pretty much.'

I wondered who owned the land and what they would do when they saw the devastation visited upon it by our friendly neighbourhood site manager. Luckily, Blackie's transgressions were not my problem. I had enough on my plate already. Little did I know that by the end of the day I would have even more.

24

From somewhere in the beaten-down undergrowth came the sound of trickling water. I mentioned to my father, saying I'd heard it before.

'Quarrymen sometimes hit natural springs,' he said. 'The water has to flow somewhere. If there is no way out for it, the quarry fills up and becomes a lake.'

'I am a geologist, Dad. I do know that.'

I walked away, towards the source of the sounds. My father, glad for a break from the walk, stood with his hands on his hips. Finally, unable to hide his curiosity, he followed me.

'I can't hear any water. Are you sure it's not wind in the trees?'

'There isn't any wind.' I'd thought for years that he was going deaf. Now I was sure of it.

In a clearing I found a deep, overgrown drainage ditch. Extra daylight, plus running water, meant healthy, rampant undergrowth. So much undergrowth that although I could hear water, I couldn't see it. My father came up beside me.

'Sounds like a stream, Love...'

Shoving aside greenery, I stepped down. My boot touched running water. Thinking it wouldn't be deep I stepped right down, not onto gravel as I expected but into thick mud. I dipped my unbandaged hand down and scooped some up.

'It's grey!' I said, holding it out and up. 'Look at it!'

'Same as in the dig? Surely that's no surprise? It's glacial clay, the same as on site, it's going to be everywhere. And we've had a lot of rain lately, it's no surprise there's a lot of mud.'

'No, look at these weeds, their stems are grey from mud. A lot of mud has flowed through here. The ditch has been full of it.'

'Could it be from the pit? Could it have come through here?'

'It must be from there. You saw how quickly it drained away.'

I clambered out of the ditch and tried to follow the stream. It didn't go far before it vanished under boulders. My father had waited, watching me. I returned to him, more excited than I meant to be.

'There must have been a tunnel from here to the house. Could it have been a drain?'

'Who in their right mind would tunnel this far just to get rid of waste water? That doesn't make sense to me.'

'I talked it over with Cameron. We did wonder if the house had some sort of escape tunnel. We know the house was built in the seventeen-hundreds.'

He was shaking his head. 'Could be true if it was a castle, not a house.'

'Blackie… Jim… says it was a fortified manor house. What if the stone to build that house came from this quarry? What if the quarrymen also dug a tunnel for the house owner?'

My father was shaking his head. He sometimes had a *not invented here* way of dismissing other people's suggestions and I wondered if he was doing that now. I'd learned long ago how to deal with that attitude.

'Priest holes?' I asked. 'Escape tunnels for Catholic priests?'

I was using it as bait. I had been through all that with Cameron and I knew it was wrong.

'If the house was built in the seventeen-hundreds then it's much too late for all that. Also, you're thinking England, not Scotland. Escape tunnels up here would have been for Jacobite sympathisers. It would be interesting to know who built it, and if he was one of Bonnie Prince Charlie's men.'

I nodded furiously. 'Dad, yes, I hadn't thought of that. So you agree that there could be an escape tunnel?'

That, I told myself, was crudely unsubtle. I waited for a reply. He said nothing for a while and then glanced at me.

'If the mud in that ditch came from the dig,' he said, ignoring my question, 'there has to be an tunnel entrance in this quarry. Your victim must have got in from here.'

My victim. Yes, my secret thought for days, articulated now by my father. First a fossil, then a dead dog. Then ancient human remains that unexpectedly became recent. Much too recent.

Yes, Father, I suppose he is mine.

He suggested that we split up. I said I couldn't see the point. I reminded him that we were here to look for my phone and I knew roughly where it should be. My words were ignored. He was already walking away, avoiding the undergrowth, trying to skirt around the base of the quarry's cliffs. I was tempted to call out, to tell him not to walk too close to them in case loose rocks fell on him. I didn't. He had more experience of working with rock than I would ever have.

The quarry turned out to be much longer than it was wide. My father went off into the long bit, leaving me to search for the place where I'd found Cameron.

Blackie's bulldozing had changed things. My part of the quarry looked as if it had been hit by a tornado, everything looked so different. Rather than pay attention to where I was treading I gazed up ahead, seeking the quarry's top edge through the remaining trees.

It took me a good half-hour to find my phone. I had hoped that leaves or weeds might have broken its fall and sheltered it from the rain, but I had no such luck. Also, it looked as if it had hit every rock possible on its way down – its screen had cracked and turned misty-white on the inside. I wasn't daft enough to attempt to switch it on. If it was wet inside, that would kill it for ever.

I'd heard nothing from my father since he vanished through trees. I cupped my hands to my mouth. 'DAD! WHERE ARE YOU?'

I waited, listening attentively, hoping for some small sound.

'UP HERE!'

I jumped. And swore. 'What the hell?'

He was standing on a ledge, about as high up as the third floor of a building. He cupped his hands to his mouth and shouted.

'I thought I could get down this way. Seems I can't. I'm going back up.'

I stared up at him. I had already taken part in one rescue and had no wish to take part in another. Now wasn't the time to chastise him, that could wait until he got down. Small pieces of rock tumbled down as he started his climb back up.

'Are you sure you – '

I stopped mid-sentence. Distracting him wasn't wise. I imagined Cameron, his feet sliding on wet grass towards the top edge, unable to stop. I didn't know if my father was just lucky, or stupid, or what. When he called down that he was safely back on top, I directed him around the edge, the way I'd come after my own little clifftop adventure.

'If looks could kill,' he said when he finally reached me.

'Well! Of all the stupid – '

'I've found it.'

'Found what?'

'Your ditch. Your stream. I didn't fancy struggling through bushes so I climbed to the top and looked down. The quarry's much longer than I thought. It gets narrower towards the far end. That's the old part, I'm sure of it. It's a dump.'

A dump? The place wasn't pleasant, but it wasn't that bad.

'The far end,' he continued. 'It's been used as a dump, a rubbish tip, there's corrugated iron and rotten timber. Lorry loads of it, all tipped from the top edge. Many years ago by the look of it.'

Years ago was right. No lorries would have been able to get anywhere near the top edge for at least fifty years, not through that woodland.

'And the stream? You said you'd seen a stream.'

He waggled his hands in a *more or less* manner.

'So you didn't actually see one?'

'It's hidden under rocks, I'm sure of it. There is lush vegetation. It's starting to die off everywhere else but in places it's still very green. That's a sign of water. Beneath the surface, I mean.'

If you say so, Dad.

We set off, walking through the quarry. By *walking*, I mean bending back branches and balancing on boulders, frequently backtracking to find a less impossible route. My father stopped and held up a hand.

'Hear it? That's water, beneath us. If you listen you can just – '

'Quiet, Dad!'

He was right. I could hear it. A hollow, trickling sound some way below me.

'The quarry was once much deeper,' he said. 'Everything beneath us is waste rock, the stuff the quarrymen didn't want. They simply dumped it in a part of the quarry they no longer used.'

If he hadn't been with me I'm sure I would have worked that out for myself. I imagined stonemasons dressing the stone, chiselling it to size with hand tools and throwing aside their waste. Now, after a build-up of around two hundred years of rotting, fallen leaves, very little of that waste rock was visible. That didn't mean it wasn't there.

'So,' he continued. 'If they excavated a tunnel to that house, groundwater would seep into it, right?'

'Right.'

'And if the tunnel sloped towards this quarry, it would give the quarrymen a supply of fresh water, right?'

Yes, he was right. And that water would now be percolating through all that rubble beneath us. It keeps the vegetation watered, which is why it is so green, just as he had said. We walked on. Soon, rusty iron sheets replaced weeds. Long, rotting timbers replaced trees. My father had walked ahead of me and he stood waiting, high on a pile of rubble and old bricks. He called out.

'I'm betting these are the remains of old army huts, Nissen Huts. See how the iron sheets curve?'

'Yes, Dad. Shouldn't you be getting back to site? What if the shuttering has arrived? You don't want to upset your friend Jim. He's such a busy man.'

'He'll be fine. How long do you think this rubbish has been here?'

'I have no idea.'

He came down off the rubbish. I watched, hoping he wouldn't twist his ankle or do something worse.

'That way you came with Cameron,' he said. 'Over the top. I'm betting there was an army camp up there before those trees grew. After the war they dismantled it and shoved everything over the edge. Jim told me there were military buildings on his site. Those concrete slabs are the old foundations.'

'And later they became warehouses, yes. So why are we here? If the victim got into a tunnel then it's hardly likely to be behind all this junk, not if it was dumped here after the war. He wasn't even born then.'

'If he got into a tunnel here then obviously the entrance must have been accessible. 'Could it be in the rock face, behind that lot?'

134

I didn't comment. If it was, then it would have to stay hidden. There was no way were we going to drag away a hundred tons of old junk. We stood in silence, close to a high rock face – a vertical cliff – its lower half hidden now by a scree slope of rubbish.

'Quiet, isn't it?'

'Yes, Dad.'

He was right. No traffic noise. No birds. No planes overhead. Only that constant, barely perceptible trickling sound far beneath us. Just when I thought he might stand here for ever he sprang to life.

'Forgot to ask. Did you find your phone?'

'I did.'

'Is it okay?'

'It's trashed.'

'Ah, shame. Come on then, let's get back to site. As you said, the shuttering may have come. Don't want to upset Jim, do we?'

No, Dad. Been there, done that. Done that a lot, actually…

On our way back to site I used my father's phone to update Kevin Marshall. I also tried Curtis but couldn't get through. Back in the site office my father and I tackled Blackie. Tactfully, I left most of the talking to him. Blackie listened quietly.

'So, John,' Blackie said when my father had finished. 'Have I got this right? You heard running water. You think it comes from a tunnel you haven't yet found. If there is one, then it *may* once have led from the old house to the quarry.'

'The mud from the dig reached the quarry, Jim. There is grey mud in the ditch on the – '

'Could mud flow that fast, John?'

Listening to them was painful. I stood there, biting my tongue. Whatever scheme my father was planning needed full co-operation from Blackie and I wasn't going to jeopardise anything. Still talking, Blackie stood up from his desk, walked to the window, put his hands in his pockets and looked out.

'If there is a tunnel,' he said, 'Can we recover the remains that way? By going in from the quarry?'

My father and I looked at each other. I wasn't going to commit myself to any such thing.

'Yes, Jim. That might well be possible.'

'So you won't be needing a shaft? I can get on with the job I came here to do?'

'Not quite, Jim. Let's take this step by step. Demolition rubble has been tipped from the top of the quarry. My daughter here is sure that the tunnel entrance is hidden behind it. How else could the lad have got in there? We would like it moved. It's a big job.'

Thanks, Father. Not *Doctor Spargo*, but *my daughter*. A daughter who, by the sound of it, could guarantee that a tunnel entrance lay behind the rubbish. I shook my head. They took no notice.

Blackie's frown grew 'Can't do that. It's not on my site. Getting to the Prof was different, it was an emergency.'

'You did an excellent job with that bulldozer, Jim.'

The corner of Blackie's mouth turned up. It could almost pass as a smile.

'That was an emergency. No way will I be doing that again!'

'No?'

'It's not our dozer. We hire all our heavy plant. It comes with drivers.'

'A dozer wouldn't do it. It's mainly old timber and corrugated iron. Could we get that long arm excavator out to the quarry? The one that dug out the pit?'

I kept quiet. If he was wrong, he was the one who would have to face Blackie.

'I'll need to check this with the boss.'

'Mr Marshall? I thought you ran things here, Jim?'

Blackie scowled. 'I do.'

'I phoned Kevin Marshall on our way from the quarry,' I said. 'He says we have carte blanche to do everything we can to recover the remains.'

It was a mistake. I got the full-frontal scowl.

'Bloody geologists! If it wasn't for you people…'

I wasn't expecting that. Before I could think of a suitable response my father had placed his hand on Blackie's shoulder and guided him outside. I stayed in the office, cursing softly.

25

We were back in the quarry next morning in our hardhats and hi-viz jackets. Blackie had phoned my father to say his usual digger driver had reported sick.

'Jim says he's called in another driver,' my father said, as if I was actually interested. 'Young man. Very keen.'

We were accompanied in the quarry not by Blackie but by Hamish Anderton. Trundling behind his pick-up came one of the long-armed excavators from site. It clattered past us, its caterpillar tracks clambering over Blackie's crushed trees. My father, now up with the driver, hung on like a tank commander, no doubt in contravention of numerous Health and Safety regs. Waving his free arm he directed the driver through undergrowth to the far end of the quarry, stopping only when he reached the first rusty sheets of iron.

By the time we caught up with my father he was back on the ground, waving both arms and shouting instructions to the new driver – whose name, Hamish told me, is Macbeth.

Standing near the digger while it worked wasn't wise. Using the path I'd come down that first day my father and I, together with Hamish, climbed to the top of the quarry. From there we watched the digger rip a path through the rubble.

Hamish and the driver talked by radio. My father, ignoring such technology, attempted to direct the driver from on high, using some form of arm-waving semaphore.

'Good man, that!'

The digger driver handled the excavator sensitively, as if its bucket were an extension of his own hand and arm. Moving rubble aside with his bucket he clanked his way steadily through the waste. Chunks of brick wall, the bricks still cemented together, lay with slabs of concrete and rusted iron sheets. Rotting roof timbers, caked in green moss, stuck out from the rubbish like huge broken ribs. Hamish, who had watched silently while my father arm-waved to the driver, finally spoke.

'I've told the driver to stack the junk high. I don't want him picking up a bucket-load and tracking away with it, we'll be here for days.'

If I had expected anything from the day's work, I suppose it was that we would find a neat tunnel entrance, perhaps the height and width of a man. The hole we eventually found was nothing like that. After three more hours of watching the digger moving material, the three of us returned to the quarry floor in time to see its bucket drag back the final flat sheet of corrugated iron from the now cleared quarry face.

Macbeth saw the dark patch at the foot of cliff before we did. By the time we reached him he had climbed down from his cab and was peering down into a deep, dark, uncovered hole about twice the size of a street manhole. Though I couldn't see water I could hear it, a long way down, echoing as it fell. It wasn't just a trickle. More like a bath tap, full-on.

'Bloody big rabbits around here.'

A tongue in cheek comment from Macbeth as he walked away. In different circumstances I might have laughed. The man could not possibly have imagined what I was going through my mind – images of a teenage boy clambering down through boulders. A boy who would never again see daylight.

Macbeth returned to us carrying a torch. Steadying himself against the rock face he pointed its beam down.

'Grey water,' he said. 'Coming in from the quarry face like a waterfall, ten feet or so down. Looks like it drops down a few feet and then runs away through boulders.'

Handing his torch to my father, they swapped places. I stood beside him. I could see a small waterfall, shooting out from what looked like solid rock. It came, I realised, from beneath an overhang. If there was a tunnel down there then it had to be small.

'You know what I think?' my father said, peering down. 'The quarrymen used this as their fresh water supply.'

'Hardly fresh,' Macbeth said. 'Not if Mr Blackie's right about what's down there.'

All three of us stared at him. 'You've heard about that?'

'Oh aye. Word's got around. The body of a man. Did he go in through here? Is that what you're thinking?'

'It was fresh water once,' I said. 'The remains are quite recent, probably nineteen-seventies. And it isn't the body of a man, it's skeletal remains at most. Most likely a sixteen-year-old.'

Macbeth put his hand over his mouth. 'My god, really? James didn't tell me that.'

'It's not general knowledge, so keep it to yourself. Imagine the media circus if that got out.'

A reverential silence followed. Thoughts went through minds. There were no further comments until my father, as if for something to say, said I looked puzzled.

'Not really. I suppose I was expecting a tunnel entrance in the quarry side, not at the foot of a man-made shaft.'

That water issued constantly from such a long tunnel didn't surprise me. It lay well below the water table. Even before we messed around in the clay on site and caused a deluge of mud and water to flow through it, natural groundwater would have seeped into the tunnel and run into the quarry. It would have provided the quarrymen with a constant supply of water.

'When the quarrymen dumped their waste rock at this end of the quarry they didn't want to block off their water supply,' my father said. 'As the dumped rock got deeper they built it up like a wall, ending up with a manmade shaft. When they needed water they clambered down to get it.'

'I still don't see how the victim got here,' I said. 'How he got to this hole, through all that junk.'

Macbeth had the answer. He said that the last few timbers he shifted were propped against the side of the quarry, with corrugated iron sheets dumped on top of them. He asked us to follow him, walking away from us along the foot of the newly exposed quarry face.

'Look at the ground,' he said. 'Downtrodden. It's like a rabbit run. Someone made a passage under the junk.'

Nobody spoke. Fifty years ago a lad, probably following the sound of water like we had, discovered the old quarrymen's shaft and the tunnel. To get to it more easily – or perhaps to hide it from others – he made a covered access through the dumped rubbish.

I shook my head. 'But why?

'Why what?'

'Why go to all that trouble? Finding it and going into it is one thing. Bothering to make a permanent passage to it seems a bit fanciful.'

Macbeth again: 'It would have taken more than one person to move those timbers. I'm betting there were several of them. Here for a bit of adventure? A smoke? Who knows what they did down there.'

My father walked away from us. He still had Macbeth's torch and was heading back towards the hole.

'Dad! Don't even think about it!'

'What? I'm just going to look down it again.'

My pulse returned to normal. I moved to the hole with Hamish and we stood on its edge. I guessed he was there for the same reasons as me – either to stop my father falling down the hole or prevent him climbing down into it.

'I'm just going to sit here,' my father said, crouching down and then sitting, dangling his legs over the edge of the hole. 'The quarrymen couldn't have used it like a well because the water runs away. They must have clambered right down, carrying buckets.'

'What,' I said, 'every time they wanted a drink?'

'And every time they wanted water for their work. They were quarrymen. A shaft like this wasn't a problem. They could climb like monkeys.'

Macbeth came to our rescue by asking for his torch back, saying it belonged to his firm and should be kept in his cab. He winked at me as he took it. Unexpectedly, he sat down beside my father and then launched himself down the hole, clambering from boulder to boulder until he was level with the incoming water. His voice echoed back to us.

'It's a tight squeeze. Hole's just about big enough to climb into.'

Hamish and I chorused the same words. 'Don't go in there!'

'There's no way I'm doing that. Coming up. Take the torch.'

'So what now?' I asked Hamish, when Macbeth was safely back. 'You'll have to tell Blackie what we've found because he let us use the digger. I suppose I had better tell Mr Marshall, because if I don't, Blackie will.'

'I'm thinking he won't be telling Mr Marshall anything yet, seeing how he went off half-cock about the remains being those of a dog.' He smirked as he spoke. 'I'm thinking he will want to be more sure of things this time.'

The skies opened. Rain stopped play. After covering the hole with corrugated iron sheets, Macbeth and his digger trundled out of the quarry with the rest of us tramping behind it. No sooner had we reached my father's car than I had a call from Curtis. He sounded snappier than usual.

'I've been trying to call you for hours. Where are you?'

'Kevron site. With my father.'

I didn't mention the tunnel. My first duty was to Kevin Marshall and I didn't want him to hear about it from Curtis.

'We need your advice. I want you to look at something.'

I wondered who he meant by *we*. 'Is it more of that gunge?'

If he heard my question, he ignored it. 'Can you get into Edinburgh? Right now?'

'Tell me why. I'm due to have a meeting with Mr Blackie.'

'I can't say on the phone. I want you at an address in New Town. If you can't come now, when can you come?'

I checked the time. 'I can be there by three. Do I need to bring anything?'

I was thinking of kit. If he wanted me to bring stuff, I would have to go via the mews.

'Just bring yourself. I won't be there. If you are late or can't get there then call DI Cavendish.'

Back at site Blackie was waiting for us in the doorway to his office. 'Boots!' he snapped. 'I'd have thought you would have learned that by now.'

My father mumbled an apology. Balancing himself by pressing an elbow against the wall he tugged off one boot and then the other. I acted as nursemaid and carried his and mine to the boot park by the front door.

Hamish Anderton, Blackie and my father had moved to the surveyor's room where there was space for us all.

'Well?' Blackie asked after we explained what we'd found. 'What now? If you think any of my site staff are going down that hole then you can think again.'

His remarks were directed at me rather than my father. When I didn't respond he glanced at Hamish, then at my father and then back at me, plenty of time for me to compose an appropriately barbed response – though it was one I reluctantly decided to keep to myself. My father, standing incongruously in thick socks pulled up over his trouser legs as far as they would go, held up his hands defensively.

'Jim, Jim! You have enough on your plate, you have a site to run. Leave everything to us.'

'All very well for you, John. Thanks to you lot the clay dug from that pit is blocking one of my site roadways.'

'Can't you move it?'

'You lot had my bloody excavator!'

This was a pointless waste of time. I made a point of pulling back my sleeve and concentrating on my watch.

'Gentlemen, I have an appointment in Edinburgh with Police Scotland. Can we get on? Can we make some decisions?'

'We need cap lamps, Jim. Don't suppose you have anything like that on site?'

Blackie was shaking his head. So was I.

'Dad, you are not going down there. The last time you went underground you almost died.'

I'd said more than was prudent. Had I not said it he would soon be conspiring with others, making plans to go down that hole. Blackie was silent, no doubt wondering what I was referring to.

'That was different, Love. And who says I haven't been underground since then? Anyway, I wasn't thinking of going down there alone.'

I winced. Maybe if I stop calling him *Dad* in public he'll stop calling me *Love*.

'If the tunnel does lead to the house then we're talking about a mile-long crawl in water and mud. At least a mile.'

'I can do that.'

I changed to a whisper. 'No you can't. Not with your bad back.'

Rare silence from Blackie. Hamish, embarrassed, had moved away, pretending to look at pinned-up site plans that he must have inspected a hundred times before.

'Then who?' My father said, tilting his head quizzically, expecting an answer. 'Don't suggest the fire service or police because they won't do it, it's hardly an emergency.'

Hamish said, 'Surely the police will arrange to have it done if they suspect foul play?'

Blackie glared at him. Slamming his hand down on the table he turned to face me. 'Dr Spargo! As I understand things – though god knows how, because nobody tells me anything – you are employed by Kevron to keep Mr Marshall informed of progress, not to become involved in any kind of recovery work.' He turned to my father. 'John, you are retained by Mr

Marshall to advise on sinking a shaft to recover the victim's remains. You are not here to poke around offsite in old tunnels.'

That was us, told.

'But Jim – '

'John, thanks to you we now know how this person got underground. Let's stop pussyfooting around in that damn quarry and get on with the jobs we are paid to do. If that's not asking too much.'

So, my father found the quarry and the tunnel, apparently, not me and Cameron. I said nothing.

'Jim, Jim! We agreed that if we could get the remains out through the tunnel you could backfill the dig and reopen the site.'

'That was then. This is now. Most of my site is up and running again. The only bit that isn't is the bit you lot are messing around with.'

'Jim, I thought – '

'We keep digging. By the weekend we'll be down through the rock.' He looked at me. 'What happens then, now that your Prof friend's not here? Who is responsible for the removal of the remains?'

I didn't know the answer to that. I told him I'd speak to Curtis. In the silence that followed I had an idea… more like a flash of inspiration. I knew just who might be willing to explore that tunnel. Probably more than just willing. I would keep it to myself for now.

Blackie was fidgeting with the zip of his jacket. 'As you so rightly said, I have a site to run. Though you wouldn't think it,' he added as he moved to the doorway, 'not with half my equipment used off site. Who the hell pays for that, I want to know?'

Entering Edinburgh in Cameron's van, I crossed Holyrood Park in the mid-afternoon sunshine. I turned off at the Scottish Parliament, rattled along stone setts, and parked in the car park at Waverley Station. Though it would cost me dear – because I would not be charging it to Kevron – I had little choice. Parking spaces in this part of the city were even more rare than those nearer home.

Curtis had given me the address of a terraced Georgian town house in New Town, a ten-minute brisk walk from where I'd parked. When I say *terraced*, I mean terraced like in Georgian Bath, Brighton, or Regent Street, not terraced like in former mining towns. These New Town houses are stone built and three storeys high, their basements and attic rooms once occupied by a housekeeper, a cook, a housemaid and possibly a butler.

I was surprised to find that the front door to the house, at the top of a short flight of stone steps, had been propped open with an ancient iron weight. Even more surprising was that the door opened into a small foyer that itself had two front doors. Thought the house appeared on the outside to be one large dwelling it was actually two separate properties split down the middle. The arrangement should not have surprised me. My former house was a similar size... or it appeared to be. Mine, however, was split into apartments horizontally rather than vertically. One front door. One flight of stairs to the separate apartments.

The left-hand door opened. Either DI Cavendish was psychic, or he had been watching for me through one of the apartment's bay windows.

'Doctor Spargo, thank you for coming. And promptly, too.'

By coincidence it was exactly three o'clock. Unlike when we met at my lab, Cavendish now had a switched-on smile. *A happy to see you but this isn't a bundle of laughs* kind of smile.

'You look apprehensive, Doctor,' he said. 'There is no need to be.'

Apprehensive didn't begin to describe it. And queasy, too. Doing a strange grasping motion with one hand Cavendish beckoned me to follow him, into a carpeted hallway. A staircase, against the party wall and narrower than I would have expected in such a distinguished property, led up into darkness. The hallway continued past it, becoming a wide passage that led to closed doors. Cavendish opened the first of these and stood aside to let me to enter. I stood in the doorway, looking in.

'Lights?' I asked.

He clicked switches. Light from a simple chandelier, hanging from an ornate plaster moulding in the centre of the ceiling, flooded the room with brilliant white light.

'Didn't think to bring sunglasses, Tim.'

What should have been candle lamps had been replaced with tasteless daylight fluorescents that spoiled the effect. Surprising, I thought, because whoever this place belonged to had remarkably good taste. The room's furnishings suited the property so perfectly they might well have been made for it.

Stepping into the room, I wondered if the oak sideboard, the bookcase, and armchairs upholstered in red leather, were genuinely old or faithful reproductions. And the rugs, Afghan? Iranian? Turkish? Foreign, anyway, and wherever they came from they looked pricey. A wide-screen television, the room's only obvious concession to modernity, gazed out from one corner. Cavendish stood in the centre of the room, studying my face.

'Dr deWit had good taste, I'll give him that.'

'Charlie? Really? This is – was – his place?'

'You didn't know? The DCI didn't mention it when he phoned you?'

I shook my head. 'He didn't, he was secretive, couldn't say anything on the phone. You did tell me that deWit lived in New Town. I didn't imagine a place like this. Did he own it or rent it?'

'We don't yet know.'

Owned or rented it made little difference. Either way, you didn't get this on a lecturer's salary.

'I understand that his father had money,' I said. 'I also know that his father died last year. Perhaps deWit inherited enough to buy this place.'

I could speculate all I wanted to now, there was no danger of Charlie confronting me and accusing me of lies – and what I'd said about his father was what I truly understood, it had been common knowledge in the department. I had not been spreading rumours.

'Was he shot in here?'

'No, no. Not in here.'

'There's no police tape outside.'

'We don't want to advertise our presence. So far we have managed to keep it from the media. Scenes of Crime have done their stuff. We're as good as finished with the place.'

The room's bay window and its upholstered, fitted window seat, gave a view of the private park across the road, a park surrounded by iron railings, shared in fine weather by local residents, those with a key to a locked iron gate.

I looked up at the ceiling at the chandelier and the plaster cornice around the room, a tangle of leaf-and-berry clusters, the leaves picked out in gold leaf. Grapes and vines, probably.

What surprised me as much as the place itself was its tidiness. DeWit was a scruffy, untidy man. Years ago, when he shared my room at King's, he was the untidiest person I'd ever known. Did he have a cleaner, I wondered? Had his cleaner found him dead? That didn't bear thinking about.

'Why am I here, Tim?'

'Sorry, Doctor. That cabinet in the corner. The DCI wants you to look at those rocks.'

He nodded towards a tall, slender, polished oak showcase with a curved glass front and sides, doubtless made to display a Victorian household's best china and now holding an impressive collection of geological specimens. No surprise there, though. DeWit was a geologist.

Cavendish had abandoned me. Now over by the windows, he fingered a pile of neatly folded red velvet curtains piled on an armchair.

'Do you think he was going to replace these?'

Distracted, I walked to him. The curtains were new, still with their shop labels, and sitting on several large bags from the Princes Street department store, Jenners. Before SOCO came here they were probably in the bags.

'How much does a set of curtains like this cost?'

Cavendish again, assuming women know such things. 'For deWit's pay grade? A month's pay? Two month's pay?'

'We have accessed Dr deWit's bank account. I haven't yet seen it but we know he was spending money like it was going out of fashion. Earlier in the year he had his kitchen gutted and re-equipped. It would take me years to save up what that cost him.'

'Inherited money?'

Or maybe another source of income? I kept that to myself and returned to the cabinet.

'Can I touch this?'

'You can touch anything. Tell me what you think.'

I opened the cabinet door. It swung so smoothly and easily that I suspected that it was indeed a reproduction. I appreciate beauty as much as the next person, but the design of this thing was not my style, it would not look right in the Mews.

'Tell you what I think about what?'

'The rocks on the bottom shelf.'

My eyes hadn't got that far, they were still taking in the range and quality of deWit's small fossil collection on the middle and top shelves. All good stuff, all museum quality. Chances are he had bought them rather than collected them himself. I crouched down and examined the rocks. Doubtless they had been relegated to the bottom of the cabinet because of their dullness. And possibly their weight.

On the shelf sat five rock specimens, all unexciting shades of grey. They were arranged in a curve, a shoe-box size chunk at the rear and two fist-sized lumps on either side. I took out one of the smaller ones, stood up, and held it out to Cavendish.

'Coarse grained igneous,' I muttered. It was a geologist thing. Pretend you know what you are looking at right from the start.

'Oh? Volcanic, you mean?'

'Plutonic. Volcanic comes to the surface. It cools down quickly so there is no time to grow large crystals. Plutonic is deep down, it's a volcano's magma store. It cools and solidifies over millions of years so there is plenty of time for large crystals to grow.'

Then it came to me. DeWit was from South Africa. South Africa was the home of diamond-bearing rock. I didn't have my full kit with me but I did have my folding hand lens. Thinking of Blackie's comment that day, I did my Sherlock Holmes thing with it. Peered at it, pirate-like, with one eye closed.

'Kimberlite,' I said. 'Probably from a diamond pipe. That's the neck of an ancient volcano.'

'The host rock for diamonds?'

'You impress me.'

'Can you see any?'

'What, diamonds? Yes I can. Probably not what you would think of as diamonds and definitely not the Koh-I-Nor. Look at these. You don't need the lens. See those pinhead-size glassy bits? Not good enough for jewellery, but good for industrial use. Think diamond dust for abrasives, tips of drill bits and cutting tools. Is this what Mr Curtis wanted me for, to look at this?'

'No, no, he wanted you to look at the large piece at the back.'

I crouched down again and reached for it. It was long, heavy, and difficult to lift out. I could see already that it differed from the others. And not just because of its size and weight.

'Could diamonds be how Dr deWit made his money?'

I did an exaggerated headshake. 'From rock containing diamond dust? Only if he had a few thousand tons of it and the means to process it. As a source of industrial diamonds, that chunk is worth pennies. It's worth more as a geological specimen.'

I carried the rock to the window seat, sat down and placed it beside me. It didn't take me long to realise why Curtis wanted me here. This specimen differed from the others, and not just because of its size. On every side of it were short, hair-thin lines of gold. If I split the rock I would reveal a network of gold veins. Elsewhere in the rock were more flecks of gold, some the size of pin heads. Tim still hovered close.

'Gold,' I said. 'Definitely.'

'That's what we thought. We didn't want to influence you. So it is not iron pyrite, Fools' Gold? Are you sure of that?'

'Give me some credit. You are beginning to sound like your boss.'

'Sorry. I didn't mean to offend. Why would Dr deWit have gold?'

'Dr de… Charlie… was a geologist. He was South African. I suspect the whole collection is from there.'

'Could the gold in that cartridge have come from here? From rock like this, I mean.'

I couldn't help smiling. 'Perhaps originally. Are you thinking that he has more of this rock around? That someone has been picking out fragments of gold from it?'

'Is that possible?'

'Physically possible, if you have the patience of a saint and some very big hammers. To get gold out of rock like this you have to crush it almost to dust.'

'Are you saying the gold used to kill Dr Morini couldn't have come from here? From more of the same stuff, I mean.'

'You saw the fragments from the cartridge yourself. You saw copper and silver in with the gold, even lead and possibly platinum. You won't find a mix of metals like that occurring naturally in rock.'

'Yes of course. SOCO noticed the rocks here and told the DCI. He wanted you to check them out. Good thing he doesn't have to change his mind about the gold coming from jewellery.'

I could hardly believe my ears. 'The gold he gave me is NOT from jewellery, Detective Inspector! Surely Mr Curtis told you my take on all this?'

He frowned. Shook his head. 'Your take on it? No. What is *your take on it*?'

'I'm sure the gold comes from old computer parts. He really didn't tell you that?'

His expression changed from puzzled to totally blank. I wondered what was going on in his head, maybe a few theories shot to pieces. He moved from the cabinet and sat on the arm of a chair.

'The DCI has a lot on his mind.'

'Haven't we all.'

I hoped the amount Curtis had on his mind was the real reason he'd neglected to tell Cavendish about my thoughts – though it would probably have helped my case if I had got around to doing something about my fragments of circuit board. I might then have been able to prove where the gold came from.

'Talking of Morini,' I said, as if we actually had been, 'does the media know about his murder yet?'

Cavendish, no doubt glad I didn't labour my point about the gold, seemed to perk up.

'Doctor Spargo, where have you been? It was all over the press and TV!'

'I don't have time to watch much television.'

He smiled. Stood up as if to go. 'Well, Doctor, that's one thing out of the way. Only another thousand or so to deal with. It was good of you to come. Oh, the DCI asked me to tell you that the approval for your lab has been posted to you.'

I smiled back. I already knew about the approval, but it would be nice to have the paperwork.

'Tim… am I to assume that you have been assigned to this case? Morini and also deWit?'

'It was the obvious thing to do.'

'I just wanted to be sure. As it's now your case there is something I have to tell you. I was hoping to check it out myself but other things got in the way.'

He frowned. I had his full attention.

'Is it to do with this case?'

'It is very much to do with this case. You had better sit down.'

26

Cavendish did what he was told and sat on the arm of a chair. He listened attentively while I told him about the circuit boards. Then he asked if I still had them. I told him they were now in my lab.

'If you really think they are in some way connected with a crime then that is not where they should be.'

I knew that. I didn't need telling. 'They were in a waste basket that I tipped into a skip. At the time I didn't know what they were.'

'And you retrieved them. What about the big piece you mentioned? That whole board?'

'It's over one-foot square. I've sealed it in an evidence bag. Don't worry, I wore gloves when I retrieved it.' I didn't tell him they were work gloves from the core logger's cabin.

'I am surprised you haven't mentioned this before.'

'I didn't because I needed to be sure. I still don't know how relevant it is.' And anyway, it seems that it would have been pointless mentioning it to Curtis, seeing that he hadn't passed on my views about the source of the gold.

'Sure of what? Relevant to what?'

The frown intensified. The head-tilting questioning had gone, replaced by a full-frontal inquisition. I was seeing a different side of the man.

'The large board still has all of its components intact, relays and switches and sockets, still fixed to the board. I've been meaning to check to see if they contain gold contacts, perhaps even platinum ones.'

'Are you qualified to do that?'

'Pardon me? You mean to check for gold? Mr Curtis certainly thinks so. If he didn't then he wouldn't have given me that gunge sample to look at. He told me not to do any more work on it.'

'But you can now?'

'I guess that's up to him.'

'No, it is up to me and I would like you to proceed with it. Do you really have the time though, Doctor? I understand you are working full time for Kevron.'

'I'll make time.'

He nodded and smiled. A smile that, uncharacteristically, didn't quite reach his eyes. He went to the window seat, picked up the rock sample with both hands and replaced it in the cabinet.

'Where's the kitchen?' I asked. 'I could murder a glass of water.' Probably inappropriate terminology in the circumstances, but what the hell.

'Next door along.'

I didn't want water, I wanted to snoop. I left the room, stepped into the passage and walked to the next door. I turned the brass knob on the kitchen door, swung the door open and stepped into a darkened room that stank of strong bleach. Dull daylight leaked in around the edges of a closed window blind, giving enough light for me to see that the room was large, around the same size as the one I'd just left. As my eyes adapted to the gloom I made out a sink near the window, continuous fitted kitchen units around the walls, and a large central island with an additional sink.

I flicked switches. A battery of dazzling ceiling lights lit the white-painted room as if it were a film set.

I shrieked. 'Oh my god, Tim! You could have warned me!'

Cavendish came running. He took hold of my arm in a fatherly manner and attempted to guide me back out. I resisted. 'Sorry,' he said. 'I should have warned you.'

'A pump-action shotgun?'

'A twelve-gauge. Possibly pump action. Either that, or whoever did this could reload fast.'

The doors of a cabinet on the opposite wall were shattered, the cabinet's contents destroyed. A DVD player beneath the cabinet had been hit by stray pellets, several having passed right through a nearby television screen and also through a black plastic toolbox. A bare patch of kitchen wall had the appearance of an overused shooting range target, its modern plasterboard centre torn out to reveal the wall's original lath and plaster. Around the shredded edges of the central gash were holes pierced by scattered, wayward pellets.

'You told me that nobody heard it,' I said. 'Two shots? Really?'

'Whoever did this was standing in the doorway. Dr deWit didn't stand a chance. The first shot missed him, the second did not. And as I said, nobody heard it.'

'Or admits hearing it.'

'The woman in the adjacent property wears a hearing aid. The house on this other side,' he said, nodding towards the damaged wall, 'is now an office. We believe this happened in the evening, after staff had left.'

I took more steps into the room. Though deWit's body was no longer there it was obvious where it had lain. The firm called in for the clean-up had done a good job, but there was no way to hide what had happened. Only gutting and rebuilding the kitchen would do that.

I knew enough about guns to know that a normal, long barrel shotgun constrains the batch of pellets into a tight group. A sawn-off shotgun behaves more like a scattergun – think blunderbuss. This was a sawn-off, because from what I could see, half the shot from the last blast caught deWit and the other half tore off the corner of a polished stone worktop.

'This wasn't done with cartridges loaded with gold fragments.'

'That would have been a lot of gold, Doctor. As far as we know they used standard cartridges loaded with standard shot.'

'Have you got the used cartridge cases?'

'No such luck. Shall I get you that water?'

'Not thirsty. Changed my mind. I wouldn't mind seeing the rest of the house.'

'There is nothing to see. SOCO has been through the place. We have all Dr deWit's paperwork and we are going through that.'

My snooping was over. He was soon at the front door, holding it open for me. I thought he had finished with me, but he wanted to see the circuit boards, insisting we do it right away. I nodded my agreement. I was working for him now. Putting him off wasn't an option.

'My lab in thirty minutes?'

'Thirty minutes? That long?'

'My van's in Waverley car park. Ten minutes to walk there, ten to drive to my lab, and then ten – if I'm lucky – to find a place to park when I get there.'

'No, I'll take you to your lab. Afterwards I'll drive you to Waverley for your van.'

Reluctantly, because it meant doubling my car park charge, I agreed.

Using his POLICE sign – big blue letters on a piece of white card – he had parked around the corner, a fairly safe thing to do in this part of town. Then, driving as if he'd been taught by Curtis, he negotiated back streets at speed, as if he'd been born here. Police sign still in the windscreen, he pulled up on the double yellows outside my lab. I unlocked the dungeon door, placed my phone on the windowsill and took him to my storeroom. I no longer called it my office.

We stood under bright lights and inspected the large circuit board. If ever there was a piece of ex-military Russian hardware, this was it.

'Chunky,' I said. 'Isn't it?'

He was looking through the evidence bag at a code of small numbers and letters, painted in one corner of the board.

'As you said, Russian. What are you going to do with it?'

I couldn't help labouring the point about Curtis. 'I haven't decided yet. As I told you, Mr Curtis believes the gold came from jewellery. A circuit board found in a shipping container is unlikely to interest him.'

'But you think it should? Tell me why.'

'I thought I had done that. You came here, you saw those gold fragments. They did not come from jewellery.' I was tired of saying it.

'I'm hardly an expert, Doctor Spargo.'

'You don't have to be an expert.' I ran a finger down the electrical connectors at the edge of the board. 'These are gold contacts. If they are similar to those in the cartridge – think crop marks, size, kind of precious metals, etcetera – then there's your connection.'

'And if they are not?'

'Then obviously it's less likely. Though that doesn't mean the link isn't there. Those fragments probably came from many kinds of computer board. This is just one type.'

'Or many kinds of jewellery.'

He was annoying me. I thought I had him on my side over this.

'You sound like your boss.'

'That's because at some stage I'm going to have to convince him. Not just him, but perhaps a courtroom.'

'Where is he, anyway? I've been trying to call him.'

'What about?'

'The Kevron site.'

'Best not to phone him. He's at a funeral.'

'Will he be back today?'

'No. It's in Orkney.'

'Is there anyone else I can speak to? I promised to keep him informed.'

'Try me. I know a little about the case.'

'We have found a tunnel entrance in an old quarry. There's a good chance our victim entered that way.'

'Has anyone been into it?'

'Not yet. We only found it a few hours ago.'

'The remains have been there how long, fifty years?'

'Fifty at the most.'

'Did you secure the entrance to this tunnel?'

'We covered it with old iron sheets.'

'Then what's the hurry? The DCI should be back at the weekend, I suggest you speak to him then.'

He was right. The only person who wouldn't agree with him about there being no hurry, was Blackie.

Cavendish drove me towards Waverley. On the way we continued our discussion, coming to an agreement that I should check out the rest of the components on the board, on condition that I keep a record, including a photographic one, of everything I do. I do that anyway. I do not need to be told these things.

I needed a phone. At my request Cavendish dropped me in Princes Street. An hour-and-a-half later I walked from the phone shop with a new mobile containing my list of contacts and a string of texts and missed calls from Cameron. As I walked through the station concourse on my way to collect his van, I called him.

'Jessica, at last! I thought we had lost you!'

The very thought that had gone through my mind about him recently.

'Never mind me, Cameron. How are you? Are you recovering?'

'So-so. I'm bored. I'm reading War and Peace.'

'Good god! Really?'

'Really. I'm home and well looked after, all patched up. I never thanked you for taking care of me. How is my van by the way?'

'Your van is good. Do you want it back? And thanks for the thanks, but they're unnecessary, I'm glad I was there to help.'

'The van is safer with you for now. How is everything, are you down to bedrock? Have you found anything?'

'Not yet. They pulled the casing out and the water and mud in your dig drained away down the borehole.'

We chatted on. After what happened to him I felt bad about not admitting that we had found a tunnel and that I knew where all the mud from the dig had gone. It's not that I didn't trust him. The fewer people who knew about our finds, the better.

Back home I jammed the van in my garage and walked to my lab. On the way I called Kevron's head office to update Kevin Marshall. It was late and the office was closed. I tried his mobile, leaving a message that I had called to update him.

Working with pliers and sharp-pointed snips I spent the evening dismantling the circuit board, while making notes of what I was doing. And I did better than simply taking photographs. I videoed everything.

The board wasn't that complicated. It seemed to be some kind of switching system with mechanical relays, not unlike those in old telephone exchanges. As well as the connectors down one side, each relay had a bank of a dozen or so thin steel springs, all with gold electrical contacts. I cut all of these off, ending up with enough pinhead sized gold fragments to fill a teaspoon – a fraction of the amount I'd need if I was to fill a shotgun cartridge.

I had hit gold. Literally. The fragments looked remarkably like those Carrie and I recovered from Curtis's vial, except that these were all gold, there was no silver or platinum. I was about to inspect them with my binocular microscope when my phone beeped. I sprinted to the windowsill.

'Spargo…'

'Doctor, you left a message. I haven't heard from you lately. I understand that there are delays.'

'Mr Marshall… yes, Professor Thomson injured his leg.'

'So I hear. I also hear that you and your father found the entrance to a tunnel. Do you believe that this tunnel leads to our site? Do you think this is where the remains of this young boy lie?'

'The teenager. It is almost certainly the way he got underground.'

'Has anyone been in there yet?'

'Not yet.'

'Can I ask why not?'

'We found the entrance this morning. Mr Curtis is at a funeral up north and it has been suggested that we do nothing until he returns. With Professor Thomson indisposed we are not sure who else to ask to assist us. Mr Blackie says the quarry and tunnel isn't Kevron's responsibility.'

Dead silence. I knew I was making excuses. It was likely he had been discussing things with Blackie, so who knows what slants that man had put on our quarry exploits.

'Doctor, if part of the tunnel lies under our site then it is Kevron's responsibility.'

'Yes of course.' I didn't know what else to say. It was better not to comment. He was disagreeing with his own site manager.

'Do you know precisely where this tunnel goes? Can you plot it accurately on a map?'

'We're not that confident. At one end we have a borehole that we are sure goes into a collapsed void. At the other, a long way from it, we have a tunnel entrance.'

'Did you discover it, Doctor?'

'It was a joint effort. Me and Cameron – Professor Thomson – found a short, dotted line on one of those maps you sent to me. It appears to run from what was once an old house, an old mansion, close to your site. The dotted line runs off the edge of the map. We followed it. It's how we found the quarry.'

'So I hear. Yes, I know about the house. It was demolished in the nineteen-fifties.'

'We think the house may have been Jacobean. The tunnel might well have been an escape tunnel.'

'One my assistant engineers, Anderton, agrees with you. He says he was with you in the quarry.'

I nodded to myself. So perhaps he has been speaking only to Hamish, not to Blackie. That had to be a good thing.

'Doctor, if this tunnel runs beneath our site then we need to know exactly where it is. How do we do that? If I can possibly avoid doing so I would rather not pepper the site with more exploratory boreholes. Can we get someone into the tunnel? Should I be asking your father?'

Heaven forbid! 'No, please hold-fire on that. Can I get back to you?'

'Not this evening. It's late already and I'm at a dinner, I just stepped out to call you. If you feel confident about doing so then please make whatever arrangements you think fit and call me back no later than midday tomorrow. I do suggest that you talk to your father about this. Whatever you decide to do it must not compromise the recovery of the remains in any way, I do not want your Procurator Fiscal on my back. Nor do I want you or anyone else to take risks.'

'Should we be talking to the police about this? As I said, I haven't been able to speak to Mr Curtis.'

'Leave that with me. I will handle that side of things.'

When the call ended I locked up my lab and set off home. On the way there I called Carrie. Before I could explain why I was calling her she grunted into her phone.

'I'm hoping this is nothing to do with gold and glass vials, Girl!'

'It's nothing like that. You are a potholer… a caver.'

'You're not going to tell me you want to join me on a trip?'

'No I'm not. The last thing I want to do is to go underground. Listen please. I need some advice…'

27

Carrie rides a motorbike. I'm not sure if it is a Harley, a Honda or a Triumph, but it is big. I managed to persuade her to leave it at home the following morning so I could drive her to work. I wanted to talk to her during the journey.

It turned out that she had heard the media hype about Kevron, the site geologist and the so-called fossil bone. By the time I stopped the van at Bush she had also heard about James Blackie, Hamish Anderton, Cameron Thomson, Tom Curtis, Tim Cavendish, and my father.

'So you did find a tunnel?'

'Didn't I say?'

'You said that you thought there was one.'

'Sorry, yes. We found its entrance.'

'Are you sure this lad went in from the quarry end? Not from the old house?'

'The house isn't there, not even its foundations. We are thinking that if the tunnel led there it may have come out in old cellars, under the house.'

'Are you asking me if I am willing to go into the tunnel? What about the police, I'm sure they would be able to source someone.'

'I'm not asking you to do anything, Carrie. I just want to know the best way to find out exactly where the tunnel goes. The Kevron boss man has asked me how to do it, how to survey it. Recovery of the victim is another matter, that's not up to me. If we decide to get the victim's body out through the tunnel I guess that's a job for Mine Rescue.'

'I doubt they will do it, it's hardly an emergency. Now that there aren't any underground mines in Scotland they run training programmes in rescue techniques. And it's Mines Rescue. Plural.'

'Whatever. What about the cave rescue people, would they do it? Are they in Scotland?'

'The CRO? The Cave Rescue Organisation is based in Lancashire, that's two hundred miles away. I suppose the police could ask them. Best to ask your friend Curtis.'

'You once told me you were a member of the CRO thing.'

'That was years ago. Anyway, I thought we were talking about surveying the tunnel, not recovery.'

'Survey it, yes. I told Kevron that I'd find a way to do it, perhaps even organise it. I'm not sure how. I'm open to suggestions.'

We had reached Bush. I stopped in the road and waited with her. Rather stupidly I had spent most of the journey explaining about finding the tunnel rather than asking her who I could get to survey it. Instead of getting out of the van she turned to face me.

'Tell you what, Jez.'

'What?'

I frowned. She had a mischievous look that I hadn't seen since we were at school together.

'Tell you what,' she repeated. 'I'll do it.'

'Do it?'

'Survey it for you. But only if you help me.' With that, she slammed the van door and walked off.

The clock in Cameron's van said nine-fifteen. Three hours remained before I had to call Kevin Marshall. I wanted to call him before that. I didn't want to make it a last-minute thing.

Peebles is a half-hour's drive from the Dick Vet. After dropping Carrie, I phoned my father, said I was on my way to Peebles, and arranged to meet for coffee.

He was driving, he told me. 'In the car. Just left Tesco, now driving to Sainsbury. Traffic heavy. Turning into the car park. Spaces in the far lane… damn fool coming the wrong way! Hold on, Love!'

It wasn't long before we were sitting in his 4x4 in one of the town's car parks. We exchanged pleasantries. The weather had cheered up a bit, he said, but there could well be rain later. And there were more cars in the car park than usual at this time of day, etcetera.

'Just thought I'd bounce something off you,' I said, interrupting his pointless train of thought. 'I thought it easier to drive here than to phone. I was at Bush, so I was halfway here already.'

'Easter Bush? Why's that? Anything I should know about?'

'Carrie works there. I dropped her off at work.'

'Carrie? Is she that girl you were at school with?'

'One of them.'

'The one you brought home? The one who rode her motorbike across Bruntsfield Links? Didn't she get arrested?'

I marvelled at my father's memory. 'She didn't get arrested, she was cautioned. Anyway, that was years ago. We were at university then.'

'She didn't have a licence or insurance. She did wheelies on the golf links.'

I wasn't there for smalltalk. With difficulty I steered our conversation around to the tunnel, then to Carrie's frightening suggestion that I help her survey it.

'I can see why Mr Marshall wants it surveyed, but it would be better to do it later. Once we have recovered the remains we can explore the tunnel from either end.'

'He wants it done now. I'm guessing it might impact on whatever they are building.'

'I'm on site this afternoon, I'll bounce the idea off of Jim. He tells me the shuttering is in place and his crew has already excavated half a metre of fairly broken rock. He says it's getting difficult. He wants to use explosives but he can't get permission.'

'I should think not! He shouldn't do anything that could damage the remains.'

'I don't suppose blasting would damage them any more than they are already.'

'That's hardly the point.'

'Five metres across is a big excavation. Blasting would break up the rock and make it easier to excavate.'

'There is no point even talking about it if he can't get permission. It does sound to me as if you are all excavating more rock than you need to. The excavation need only have been four metres across, not five.'

'I told you already. Jim could only get the bigger size shuttering. He's now trying to source a long-arm excavator with a hydraulic pick that will reach down into the pit. Good man. Knows his stuff. Chipping away at the rock should do it. Hard going, though. Much quicker to blast.'

I shook my head. I'd been thinking about spending the rest of the day on site but had changed my mind. Watching my father and Blackie cosying up to each other didn't appeal to me at all.

'What did you want to talk to me about?'

Good point. I had almost forgotten why I was there. I had come to ask him about surveying tunnels. I didn't want to ask him outright in case he decided it was a job he should do himself.

'The tunnel…' I said. 'What would be the best way to survey it?'

'You don't need to survey it. Get a rock drill on site. I don't mean a coring rig, I mean a percussion drill, the kind quarrymen use for blast holes. Bang down a grid of holes over where you think the tunnel is. If the drill rods drop rapidly at around six metres down, that's where the tunnel is.'

I knew all that. I didn't need telling. 'Mr Marshall doesn't want a more boreholes.'

'Then what about a gravity survey? That should pick out any voids in the ground. You're the geologist. You must know plenty of geophysicists.'

'Geophysics might work, though probably not through three metres of dense clay.' He hadn't answered my question. 'You must have surveyed a lot of tunnels and mines. What's the simplest way?'

'Don't suggest using satnav underground, they need a line of sight to the satellites.'

I didn't bother to grace that with a reply. Satnavs need a line of sight to satellites. They don't work in road tunnels and they also screw up in narrow streets surrounded by high buildings. The last time I drove in Aberdeen a satnav tried to take me through a cinema.

'If he just wants to know where the tunnel runs, then a tape and a miner's dial would do it.'

Useful stuff at last!

'A miner's what, Dad?'

'Miner's dial. It's an accurate underground compass. Works well when there are no iron-rich minerals in the ground. It so happens that I have one, it's solid brass, a real museum piece. Cost me a fortune. Old but serviceable. Rather like your lab equipment.'

I ignored that. 'Does it work?'

'Of course it works. Though I've not used it for thirty years. Once we get down to the tunnel we can use it for the survey. I'll raise the matter with Jim. Are you heading to site now?'

'I need to phone Mr Marshall about the survey. I also have work to do in the lab, I've got the go ahead for a police job and I need to catch up.'

'You just don't want to encounter Jim. I don't know why you don't like him, he's a good man, he knows his stuff. He's off on holiday all next week. So is his secretary.'

'Oh? Both together?'

'Sometimes I wonder about you. Jim's off fishing, somewhere up north. Margaret stays in London with relatives. They take the same time off so he always has his secretary at work and not a hired-in temp. So what's the new police job? Anything I should know about?'

Over my dead body was probably not the most appropriate thought to have at this time. It came to me anyway.

'No Dad. All simple stuff.'

It was anything but simple. The Morini and deWit murders were about the most complicated jobs I had tackled. They were undoubtedly the weirdest, though I wasn't going to tell him that. I made my excuses and left. On my drive back to Edinburgh I stopped in a layby and called Marshall, explaining that I had put together an experienced team to plot the tunnel's position on one of his site maps. Lying had never been so easy. I mentioned my father's suggestion about surveying from the victim's end – but only because he might hear about it if my father mentioned it to Blackie.

'Oh? You just said you were ready to do it now.'

'It's my father's suggestion. I thought it right to bounce the idea off you.'

'No, Doctor Spargo, I want this information as soon as possible. Have you considered that there may well be a network of tunnels under my site?'

'I think that very unlikely.'

'But you do see my point?'

'I do.'

'Then go with your plan. Your father has other commitments. Let me know when this is to be done. I take it you will be one of the team? You are the geologist, I want you there when your team goes underground'

I winced. 'Yes Mr Marshall. I shall be one of the team.'

Can just two people be a team, I wondered?

'Do you feel happy about doing it, Doctor? You are aware of course that there is every likelihood that you will encounter the remains, are you prepared for that? I want your assurance that you will not do anything that jeopardises the recovery operations or the safety of yourself or those working with you.'

I considered every one of his words. No, Mr Marshall, I am not at all happy. And yes, I am aware of all of those things. Very aware.

'You have my assurance,' I said. 'I shall get back to you when I have firmed up on things.'

He hung up on me. I stared at my mobile as if it were to blame.

'Sunday?' Carrie asked me when I made my next call. 'Is Sunday good with you? I can't do a weekday, we've a big workload.'

'An elephant?'

'Be serious. Not that kind of big. There is a problem though, girl. I have two full sets of caving kit. I have a long tape. What I do not have is a compass.'

'Can't we buy one?'

'I'm not talking about a cheap plastic thing. I was hoping to get a friend of mine to come with us, he's got the right kind. Unfortunately he's in France right now.'

I didn't know what to say. Then I remembered my conversation with my father. 'Would a miner's dial do the job? Do you know anything about them?'

'A miner's dial? Have you been reading old surveying books? Fat chance of getting hold of one of those, they are as rare as hen's teeth. Finding a good compass isn't our only problem. If we can't get someone reliable to stay outside then we won't be going in. We need someone with a bit of sense who knows what they are doing, any suggestions? What about that young site engineer you told me about? Is he dishy?'

'Dishy? Hamish Anderton? You are old enough to be his mother.'

'So?'

'Not Hamish, Carrie. I don't want to ask anyone from site, there's a conflict of interest. The tunnel entrance is off site, so the site manager won't be happy about him doing it. Hamish is a good lad. I don't want to make trouble for him.'

For a minute or two our conversation dried. I sat there, watching the passing traffic.

'Carrie, my father has a miner's dial.'

'Does it work? Will he lend it to you?'

'Knowing him, it will work perfectly. Not sure I can get it though. He may want to be involved.'

'He was a mining engineer, wasn't he?'

'Still is. Still does consulting stuff.'

'Would he be happy being the third man?'

'Third Man?'

'Would he be happy to stay on the surface?'

'I doubt it. I don't particularly want to use him. He was there when we found the tunnel entrance, we all thought he was going to go in and I don't want that. He's retired, he's in his seventies.'

'Age shouldn't be a barrier. Not if he's fit enough.'

'He keeps telling me he's got a bad back. If he crawls into that tunnel we'll know all about it.'

'Didn't he discover a body in his basement a few years ago? I always meant to ask you about that.'

'Yes he did. And don't ask, I don't have a spare two hours to explain. I am really not happy about using him.'

'Up to you. He's got the miner's dial.'

We ended the call, having agreed that I would collect her from her home on Sunday. I then phoned my father and told him that Kevin Marshall wanted us to survey the tunnel as soon as possible.

'Me and Carrie,' I said. 'She was in cave rescue. She knows her stuff. She's got all the equipment.'

He wasn't impressed. 'A boiler suit, boots, a lamp and a hard hat are all you need.'

Arguing wasn't worth the effort. As far as I was concerned, Carrie was now the expert.

'Mr Marshall could have asked me to do it,' he added. 'I do have surveying qualifications.'

'He knows you are busy with the recovery operations. It's important you don't get side-tracked.'

'Is the site working this Sunday?'

'Not as far as I know. Why?'

'If you can spare the time you are welcome to join us in the quarry… with that miner's dial you told me about… I'd love to see how it works. Nine on Sunday, at the quarry? Is that too early?'

I waited. And waited. 'Six would be too early,' he said. 'Nine is fine.'

Still sitting in the van in the layby, I called Marshall again. He was in meetings so I left a message for him. Finally, back in my lab at last and determined to look at the gold I had cropped from those contacts, I settled down at my binocular microscope.

28

On Sunday I woke to thin drizzle. If it wasn't for an appointment I had in the quarry with Carrie, my father, and a tunnel that I really did not want to go into, I would probably have stayed in bed.

Though Carrie told me she could supply everything except a compass, I slung into Cameron's van a soft bag containing boots, gloves, a torch, and assorted bits and pieces including a waterproof camera – guaranteed waterproof to a depth of ten metres, a claim I was unlikely ever to challenge. I also put in a backpack containing my forensic field kit that I had exhumed from removal boxes deep in my garage. I hoped I wouldn't need it, but what the hell. Better safe than sorry.

At seven o'clock I collected Carrie from her home. Not just Carrie, but also her massive kitbag, the kind of bag macho young rugby players use to carry their kit. It took both of us to heave it into the back of the van.

'Got everything,' she said. 'I hope. Two complete sets of kit and some spares just in case.'

'Just in case of what?'

'Just in case the stuff I selected doesn't fit you.'

'I'm the same size as you.'

'You were the same size as me twenty years ago.'

'Are you saying I've put on weight?'

'I'm saying you look shorter.'

The roads were surprisingly clear and we arrived at the quarry earlier than I expected. I drove in and stopped in a safe spot. Carrie, out of the van and watching me park, stood with her hands on her hips, frowning as she looked all around her. Mist hung heavily in the trees, so thick it obscured the top edge of the quarry. The usual silence of the place was broken today by a pitter-patter of raindrops falling from leaves.

'Gloomy here this morning,' I said.

'It's certainly not a bundle of laughs. What the hell came through here, wild elephants?'

A madman on a bulldozer. No, that was unfair. 'The Kevron site manager cleared it,' I said. 'Blackie, the one I told you about. He made it a lot easier to reach Cameron Thomson.'

I stepped over crushed branches and opened the van's back door. 'Let's wait for my father. He can help us carry your bag.'

Carrie couldn't reply. She had taken a bite out of a bread roll and was attempting to recover shreds of lettuce and tomato that dangled from it. She shook her head. Chewed and swallowed.

'No, we'll kit-up here. Then we can leave what we don't need.'

We unzipped the bag and upended it. Orange helmets tumbled out, followed by cap lamps, batteries, heavy belts and three sets of tightly rolled orange suits made from some sort of rip-proof, waterproof fabric. Bulletproof too, for all I knew. I watched while she clipped a small camera to one of the helmets. I thought we were to survey a tunnel, not go white-water rafting.

At the sound of an engine we looked back through the quarry. My father's four by four trundled into view and came slowly towards us. He had his head out of the side window, looking out and down, as if bringing a ship alongside a dock.

'Early,' he said as a greeting. 'No traffic anywhere. Quite surprising.' He looked at me and then at Carrie. 'Caroline? Goodness me!'

I half expected a '*How you have grown!*' Thankfully it didn't come.

As we clambered into our orange suits he commented that when underground he just wore his old overalls – that he insisted in calling his blue boiler suit – and that he'd brought his own. Guilt hit me hard. He had been underground in mines, tunnels and caverns more times than Carrie had been in potholes and caves. I wasn't sure how to tell him that this time he was to stay on the surface and leave things to us.

We clambered into his cab and drove further into the quarry, over Blackie's crushed branches and the ground cleared by the digger. My father grunted approval.

'Did a good job, that Macbeth.'

Carrie mumbled, 'Bad luck to mention his name…'

'The Scottish Digger Driver,' I said.

Father shook his head. 'Stop it, you two... shall we stop here?'

We parked, stepped out, and walked to the quarry face. My father, in wellie boots and his blue overalls, tagged along behind.

Carrie whispered 'Does he think he's coming with us? What have you told him?'

I turned to him. 'Dad, we need you to stay outside. We need someone reliable there.'

'I know that. You didn't expect me to come in, surely? Not with my bad back.'

Relieved, I forced a smile. It was wrong of me to have left it so long without telling him, though I had the impression that he'd been teasing me. He'd had no intention of going underground.

'You brought a hard hat,' I said.

'I'll be standing under that rock face. Also, I brought this.' From his pocket he took a neat wooden box with its lid secured by two rubber bands. 'Miner's dial. Didn't forget.'

He pulled off the elastic bands and flipped up the box lid to expose a brass compass the size of a large pocket watch, nestling neatly in the bottom half of the box. I thanked him. He hadn't forgotten about it, but I had. He took it out, unfolded two short brass arms like rifle sights and sighted along them as if he were the captain of a sailing ship, taking bearings. Ten minutes later Carrie and I knew everything there was to know about miner's dials.

We moved the iron sheets away from the shaft. Carrie bent over the hole and looked down, her cap lamp lighting the gloom. Water from the tunnel fell a metre or so, like a miniature waterfall, before vanishing through gaps between shiny black boulders.

'Didn't expect a manhole. How deep is it?'

'About ten feet.'

'You didn't tell me there was water.'

'Forgot to mention it.'

'Did anyone go into the tunnel?'

'Macbeth went down and looked in. He said it's narrow.'

She was already lowering herself down the hole, straddling each side with her boots, stepping from foothold to foothold like a mountain goat.

'Dead things,' she said, looking down. 'Bones, down in the rocks. *Vulpes vulpes. Melles meles.*'

'Fox,' I said. 'You're a vet, so don't expect me to be impressed. What's *Melles?*'

'Badger. A few bones and the skull.'

'Nothing human?'

'Not expecting human, are you?'

No, Carrie, not yet, not out here. 'What does the tunnel look like? Can you see far in?'

She looked up at me, shielding her eyes. 'Don't point your cap lamp at me, it dazzles. The tunnel looks just like a tunnel. A tunnel in rock, dark and wet. Straight, as far as I can see. It looks as if the roof gets higher further in, so we won't have to crawl far.'

She stood to one side and guided me down. Our cap lamps, much brighter than I expected, dispelled the dark like small floodlights. Three sides of the shaft were built from waste rock, stacked by the quarrymen. The other side was the old quarry wall, a high rock face that disappeared up into the mist.

'Are you two all right down there?'

'Dad, we are fine.'

I stood uneasily beside Carrie, both of us squeezed into the shaft. We aimed our lamps into a tunnel little more than one metre high and half a metre wide, cut through solid rock. It reminded me of the entrance to the cupboard under the stairs in my last house.

'I never liked going into that, either.'

'What?'

'Nothing. Talking to myself.'

Then she was gone, stooping and walking fast, her boots splashing through running water. I followed her in, bent double and trying to keep up with her. Her voice boomed back to me as a loud, hollow echo. I had no idea what she said.

'Carrie, wait for me!'

She waited. I caught up. Turning to look at me, she laughed. I hadn't noticed that the tunnel roof was now higher, I no longer needed to stoop. I stood up straight. My caving helmet whacked against rock. She laughed again. I didn't think it was funny.

'Shouldn't we be surveying? Measuring angles and distances and things?'

'We'll do that on our way back. Let's see how far it goes first. There's a bend up ahead and if it's blocked beyond that, there's no point surveying anything.'

I couldn't see past her, couldn't see any bend. Our breaths and the warmth from our bodies had fogged the air. I worried that soon we wouldn't be able to see anything at all.

To me, the tunnel looked unsafe. Slabs of rock, some the size of manhole covers, littered the floor. In one place there was so much of it that it dammed the flow of water and we found ourselves wading through water knee-deep.

'Carrie, I can't see what I'm walking on. What if there's a hole? What if there's a shaft in the floor or something?'

'Then I'll fall into it before you do.'

'Not funny.'

'If I step into a shaft in the floor then I'll float.'

'That's not funny either.'

'Stop worrying.'

That was something I could not do. I wasn't happy that she seemed to plough on blindly. I knew that most naturally formed caves are stable, their roofs and walls are safe. Man-made holes can deteriorate with age and have to be properly maintained. How old was this place, two hundred years? Three hundred?

Now that the tunnel roof was higher, I managed to keep up with her. She stopped suddenly. With my head down, I bumped into her

'Another roof fall,' she said. 'Doesn't look bad. Keep close to me.'

Ahead of us, angular chunks of rock littered the ground. A slab of rock the size of my kitchen table had fallen from the roof and smashed to house-brick size chunks when it hit the ground. As if Carrie had suddenly realised she was not in a natural cave but something man-made, she walked more slowly, looking up, inspecting the roof. I knew from experience that if my father was with us he would be poking at the roof with a steel bar, testing for loose rock.

For the first time since I entered the tunnel I paid attention to the rock all around me. Despite the small collapse, the tunnel roof looked remarkably stable. Just because the people who made places like these didn't understand geology, didn't mean they weren't good at their job. Here, the miners or quarrymen had deliberately stayed beneath a strong, flat layer of rock.

Carrie stopped again. We had been walking for some time and had come to a bend. 'Three hundred and sixty-two short steps,' she mumbled. 'Let's record it. Where's that compass?'

She had changed her mind, saying that measuring on the way in and also on the way out would give a more accurate result. I took compass bearings of the tunnel, behind and ahead, while she made notes. Compass and notebook away again we splashed on, Carrie keeping the same steady pace, sometimes counting aloud.

At some stage, back on surface, she – or probably me – would plot angles and distances to scale and overlay them on a map. I thought about it as we walked. If we reached the big collapse then we would have two known positions – the borehole and the tunnel entrance. If we placed our tunnel plot onto these, then did a bit of adjusting, we would know the tunnel route. Not accurate if you are building a bridge. Accurate enough for Kevin Marshall.

'Carrie…'

'What? Wait a sec…'

She took out her notebook, moved it clear of drips from the roof and made more notes. Once, before the borehole was drilled, all the water that flowed through the tunnel would have come from the drips. Now that we were so far in, very little water flowed. To me, that meant we were not that far from the tunnel's far end.

'What?' she asked again.

'Your paces. How do we know they're accurate?'

'I try to keep them the same. I have a tape. On the way out we'll measure a short length of tunnel, I'll do my funny walk over that bit and we'll count the paces. Easy peasy and surprisingly accurate.'

'What if there are more bends?'

'I'm used to it. Not many straight bits in caves.'

'How do we know there's no gas?'

'In here? Shouldn't be any. You're the geologist, you should know that. There are no beds of coal or oil shale for miles. Anyway, I've got this.'

She tapped a black box clipped to one of her pockets. It was the size of a mobile phone and measured, she said, oxygen and three other gases. I gave an approving nod. As usual, she didn't see it. She was on her way again, walking fast.

Though she counted her paces I had no idea how far we had walked. Nor did I know the time, because my watch was sealed under the rubber cuff of the suit. I guessed we had been going for almost an hour, in conditions better than I could have hoped for.

She stopped suddenly. Head down, I walked into her again.

'Something up ahead…'

The fog had thinned. In the distance, picked out by our cap lamps, lay a mass of broken rock. The tunnel was much wider now, around two metres. It appeared to continue beyond the rock pile as a dark, square-cut void. I asked how far she thought we had come. She stayed quiet for a while as she worked things out in her head.

'We could be there, girl. We could be near your borehole.'

I felt sick. Every bit of me wanted her to leave me there and go ahead on her own. Then she was away again, counting. I kept close to her. Closer than before.

'Two tunnels,' she said as we approached the rock fall. 'This one goes on a short way and then stops, see its end? There's another tunnel coming in from the side. It looks as if the roof of that one has collapsed into this one.'

I could see that. The span of the roof at the junction was wide, too wide to be stable. Fallen rock almost filled the side tunnel, much of it shaly and loose like some of the rock in the core box. I shone my lamp at the tunnel wall. Though there was hardly any water flowing here, I could make out traces of grey mud, high up.

'Mud from the dig,' I said. 'We must be directly below it. A few thousand gallons of mud came through here when they pulled out the borehole casing.'

'What's casing?'

I explained, quickly and briefly. Then, 'Come on, Carrie, let's go! I don't like the look of that roof. We can't go any further anyway. And it's steaming up again.'

As if she hadn't heard me she started to clamber up the fallen rock. I stayed in the main tunnel, watching her clamber over the collapse.

'Don't, Carrie! Come back!'

She ignored me. I heard rock tumbling down the pile as she slid down its far side. Through the gap she had gone through I could see light from her cap lamp but I couldn't see her. I called out to her again. She didn't reply.

Then she shouted. 'Come here! Come and see this!'

Reluctantly I picked my way up the rock pile and eased my head and shoulders through the gap at the top. I didn't intend going further. At Carrie's feet a faded, black wellington boot protruded from beneath a slab of rock. She prodded it with her foot, then used her boot to shove away blocks of rock to expose a second wellington, this one embedded in a mix of gravel and slimy grey clay.

'Oh my god, Carrie!'

She continued to scrape away mud. I told her not to do it. Rock in the roof looked dangerously loose and I worried she'd disturb it. She stopped her prodding and scraping and turned round, pointing her cap lamp further along the tunnel.

'Can't see much. The tunnel bends. There's another collapse. Looks like the tunnel's completely blocked.'

'Carrie, never mind the tunnel. Let's get out!'

She returned to the boots. 'It's definitely your victim. The boots aren't empty.'

She bent down and moved rocks. I saw traces of what had once been blue denim jeans, tucked loosely into the degraded remains of one of the old wellies. I closed my eyes. I was in the wet field again with Curtis, averting my eyes from something I did not want to see.

'Carrie, we should leave. I have to tell Curtis what we've found.'

'If you can't stand the heat, Girl, then get out of the kitchen.'

However true that may have been, it was uncalled for. I was very happy in my own kitchen but I felt I had strayed into someone else's – and whoever owned it had turned up the burners too high for me. Crouching down, Carrie moved faded fabric aside between the finger and thumb of her gloved hand. 'Waxy,' she said. 'Some adipose tissue. Lower leg. Definitely the femur.'

'For Christ's sake, Carrie! Leave him! That's not your job!'

'We're all animals, girl. Just different kinds.'

29

I'd had enough. I slid back down the pile of fallen rock and set off alone. After walking a short distance I stopped and waited for Carrie. I couldn't leave her. I leant against the tunnel wall, imagining myself attempting to justify to my father why I'd come out alone. Carrie was stubborn. But I'd always known that. It wasn't long before I heard tumbling rock, the sound of her returning over the pile. Then her booming footsteps, walking fast.

'You're right. Mustn't keep your father waiting.'

I said nothing. At the final bend in the tunnel she stopped, took out a tape, measured out twenty metres and did her walk, along to a marker she'd placed and then back again, all the time making notes in her notebook. It was what we were there for, I told myself, to fix the position of the tunnel. For Marshall and Blackie and the whole damn lot of them.

As we neared the entrance the sound of falling water got louder, tumbling and splashing, echoing sounds that to me meant fresh air and freedom. Through those sounds I heard voices, strangely loud, one of them my father and others I didn't recognise. A powerful lamp shone in our direction. Someone – it turned out to be Curtis – had perched himself on a rung of a metal ladder that had been lowered into the shaft. Carrie, now in front, ordered him to stop dazzling her.

Six figures stood near the top of the shaft: my father, Curtis, Hamish Anderton, a motorcycle paramedic and a man and woman who turned out to be Scenes of Crime Officers. Curtis told me later that unbeknown to me or my father, Kevin Marshall had called Curtis's superintendent to arrange for a support team to be present at the quarry. The three of us had confused the arrangements by turning up an hour earlier than expected. We were already underground when they arrived.

Everyone gathered around Carrie as she streamed video from her helmet camera to her phone. I walked away, alone, not wanting to see what she had filmed. Someone else, a man I didn't immediately recognise, stood some way off watching events. As I got closer to him I recognised him as the first digger driver – not Macbeth but the man who went sick, the driver who handled his machine so sensitively when he dug out Cameron's pit. Wanting to be alone, I stopped well short of him and sat down on a long timber. I wasn't alone for long.

'Dr Spargo? Can I join you?'

I looked up. When I saw him in his digger he wore a hard hat and red overalls. Now he wore a grey suit, white shirt and a badly knotted blue tie. He held out a hand. I did the same. Introducing himself as Frank Sixsmith, he gave my hand a strangely personal squeeze.

'Do you mind if I sit down?'

I did mind. But I didn't have a choice, because he was already sitting beside me. Right now I really, really, did not want company.

'I'm sorry,' he said.

I frowned. Sorry for what, calling in sick? Sorry that Cameron had fallen into the quarry? He didn't elaborate and I didn't ask. I was not in the mood for more knowledge.

'You came out of the tunnel. You went underground with that other woman.'

Ten out of ten for observation. Hoping he would go away I didn't reply. Finally I nodded. 'Yes.'

'I'm sorry,' he said again.

So was I. Sorry for the lad whose remains I'd just seen. Sorry I ever got involved with this mess in the first place. Sorry I ever went into that bloody tunnel.

I turned and looked back towards the rock face, the shaft and the gaggle of figures clustered around Carrie – everyone except my father, who was heading towards me, perhaps to offer some words of comfort. I expected him to sit down beside me, the three wise monkeys. Except that he didn't, he stayed standing. Sixmith stood up and walked away.

'You okay, Love?'

'No. Have you seen it?'

'The video? The boots, you mean? Yes I have. Distressing. Proof that you were right about everything.'

That was no consolation. If he meant that I'd said the bone and tooth were not from a dog, that was just a simple observation. 'I'd rather I hadn't been right. I'd rather it was anything but another body.'

'Another?'

I realised I hadn't told him about Morini and deWit. 'Nothing,' I said. 'Mind's wandering. What's happening now?'

'Your friend Carrie is going back in. She says she needs your kit for the Scenes of Crime officer. I said I would get it from you.'

'What the hell does SOCO expect to find? Rotting wellie boots containing god-knows-what. The rest of the remains are under a ton of collapsed rock. You know that, you saw the video. You are the expert, Dad. You must have seen that there is no way the remains can be recovered from this end without causing another collapse, you will have to keep excavating Cameron's dig and do it that way. Can't he just be left where he is? Can't we just block-up the damn tunnel up and leave him in peace?'

'You know we can't do that.'

I stripped off my orange Telly-Tubby outfit and handed it, with my helmet and lamp, to my father who carried it all away. Feeling horribly cold and damp without the suit I sat down on the timber again. The digger driver,

Sixsmith, returned and sat beside me. Again, I willed him away. Again, it didn't work.

He spoke quietly. 'That old tunnel led all the way to a house. House wasn't there though. Just its foundations.'

I swivelled to face him. 'Sorry? You knew about the tunnel?'

'We all knew about it. All the lads.'

I wasn't sure what I was hearing. I frowned so intensely that I didn't have to ask him to explain.

'Back in the 'seventies we came here a lot. A load of us, all mates. Do you mind if I smoke?'

I shook my head. I did mind, but what the hell. Silently he made himself a rollup that he lit with a match. I watched as he inhaled long and deep.

'His name was Sandy Davison,' he said. 'The dead lad, I mean.'

I wondered, for a couple of seconds, if I had passed into an alternative universe. Or maybe I had fallen asleep and was dreaming. It has been known to happen.

I mumbled. 'Sandy Davison…'

'His name was Robby. We called him Sandy because of his hair.'

'Robert Davison?'

I had to choose my words carefully. If I started to question him he might clam up on me.

He nodded. Sucked on his cigarette.

'You called in sick,' I said. 'You didn't want to clear the rubbish here, did you?'

Another nod. 'Couldn't do it. Knew I was just delaying things. Knew that Jim would get someone else to do it for you. Knew you would find him eventually.'

My stomach churned. I might well be sitting next to a murderer. I glanced back at the still-clustered group. At least I wasn't alone.

'We came here every weekend on our bikes, usually three or four of us. In the school holidays we came most days. Kids explored places like this back then. No computers, no games and iPads and all that crap. Sandy heard running water and we moved tin sheets and all that wood. That shaft you went down was blocked by tree branches and we cleared it out. How did you find it?'

'Same as you. We heard water.'

'That woman you went in with. Is she police?'

'She's a friend.'

'How far did you get?'

This was bizarre. I wanted to hear what he was saying but it didn't seem right. He shouldn't be talking to me. 'You should be telling the police all this, not me.'

'I've spoken to him,' he said, turning and nodding towards the group. That one in the brown coat, the CID man.' Curtis noticed us looking at him. He ignored us and turned his attention back to the group, he didn't seem concerned I was talking to Sixsmith. 'He asked me to wait around. Not going anywhere though, am I? You know who I am, Hamish Anderton knows who I am. Good to get it off my chest after all this time. Lived with this hell for most of my life.'

I didn't know what to say. We sat side by side, alone with our thoughts. I wanted to know more and I had the impression it would come, I just had to be patient. He threw the damp stub of cigarette down and ground it under a shoe.

'We thought the tunnel would lead to the ruined house. We knew it had cellars because back then there were stone steps leading down from one of the rooms. I see they are gone now, like the rest of the house.'

'The tunnel? Tell me?'

'We explored it. It came to a dead end. Sandy wasn't disappointed like the rest of us. He worked out that a side tunnel, not the main tunnel, led to the remains of the old house. Blocked off, it was. Did you get that far in?'

'We did.'

'He was clever, Sandy was. He said whoever dug the tunnel wouldn't have been able to aim straight for the house.' He swivelled around and looked at me. Sadness had become enthusiasm. 'Think about it! If you were digging from here, how would you know the tunnel would end up at the house? How would you be sure your tunnel wouldn't go to one side of it?'

'I really do not know. A compass?' I wanted to know what had happened, not the mechanics of digging the tunnel.

'Sandy was bright, he knew about navigation. He said that even if the tunnel diggers had a compass, if you were one or two degrees out over that distance you would miss the house completely. He said the best way to be sure of tunnelling between here and the house would be to deliberately aim to one side of it. Then you start another tunnel from the house end, heading in the direction you know the other tunnel to be, until you meet up with it. *Dead reckoning,* he said it was.'

I suppose that made sense, if both tunnels were at the same level. 'So what happened? Did you explore the side tunnel? Did you find any cellars?'

'We didn't. Like I said, the side tunnel was blocked off.'

I frowned. I didn't understand. 'Do you mean that it had already collapsed?'

'No, it was blocked off by a wall of stacked-up stone – a stone wall, right up to the tunnel roof. We went back there every weekend, trying to dismantle it, stone by stone. Then it happened.'

He went quiet again, this time for so long that I wondered if there would be more. Self-consciously he used a finger to rub one eye and then the other.

'Tell me?'

'We cleared away enough of the wall for Sandy to climb through. He was like that. He had no fear.'

'And it collapsed on him?'

'Whole damn lot came down.'

'And you just left him there? You didn't think to get help?'

Bad question. He turned away from me. This time he used fists to rub his eyes.

'What good would that have done? We all knew he was dead. He was under a couple of ton of rock.'

'But his parents? Surely you…?'

'He lived with his nan.'

I was shaking my head. 'Surely you didn't just turn up at his grandmother's and say he'd disappeared? What about school, what did they say when he didn't turn up? What about the others, did they really not say anything? Never? Not in all these years?'

'It was summer. Sandy was months older than us and had left school for good. Police came round to us but we told the same story, that Sandy had talked about going to sea, that he'd been to Leith docks a lot. Ships still came there back then. Police put posters up in shops. I suppose they made other enquiries. They weren't going to find him, were they? They must have recorded him missing.'

'What about the others with you?'

'What about them?'

'Do you still see any of them?'

He gazed into the middle distance. 'Not around, not now. Callum might still be alive but he went off to Australia or New Zealand. Haven't seen any of the others. I was the only one that didn't move away when we left school. Can't blame them can you, not after what happened.'

'Didn't Sandy have any other relatives? Is his grandmother still alive?'

'None that we knew about. And his Nan would be well over one hundred now.'

'You could have saved us all a lot of trouble, Frank,' I said. 'You knew what we were digging for.'

'I didn't, not at first. I heard about the remains of a dead dog. It wasn't until I was asked to excavate the Prof's pit that I realised what you were all doing.'

I'd had enough. I left Sixsmith sitting on the timber and walked back to my father. I could hear Curtis down the shaft on the ladder, calling to someone in the tunnel. My father – thankfully still above ground – had promised to transport Carrie, who was not, back home with her equipment when all of this was over.

'Bad business,' I said to him. 'Sixsmith could have saved us a lot of trouble.'

'Sixsmith?'

'The other digger driver. The stuff he told Mr Curtis.'

He didn't react. I guessed Curtis had kept his new knowledge to himself. My father, preoccupied with whatever Curtis was doing down below, shouted down the hole. 'Is that SOCO coming up? Okay. Pass up their kit.'

I was being ignored. 'I'm off,' I mumbled. 'I have to call Kevin Marshall and update him.'

Brooding and moralising and avoiding Sixsmith, I walked back through the quarry and out to the van. I was at a loss to think of any laws Sixsmith and his friends had broken. Morally guilty of several things, yes. But nothing illegal.

I got a mobile signal, called Kevin Marshall and told him everything. I tried to stay calm and professional, saying that we had carried out the survey and by chance we had found the remains. Lastly I repeated to him Sixsmith's story, adding that Curtis was present in the quarry and that he and Sixsmith had spoken. I remembered to thank him for arranging support – support that Carrie said, as we'd clambered up that ladder with me, we hadn't asked for and didn't need.

'I wanted to ensure your safety,' Marshall said. 'I had a feeling you would attempt to do this on your own, on a shoestring.'

At any other time such a remark might have annoyed me. Shocked by what I had seen and what I had just heard from Sixsmith, there was no space in me for anger. Anyway, Marshall was right. He had me sussed.

Curtis called me that evening. I had just turned on the television and heated yet another a ready-meal, a habit I knew must stop. Without pulling punches he told me that Frank Sixsmith had driven into a tree on his way home from the quarry.

'Bad business. Ambulance crew said he wasn't wearing his seatbelt.'

'Oh my god! Do you think it was deliberate?'

'I really cannot say.'

He kept talking. I stopped listening. I'd heard *fatal injuries* and that did it for me. I hung up on him. I cried quite a lot that evening, tears for Sixsmith and Davison. Perhaps it was tiredness, perhaps it was something else. I tried to convince myself that nothing I had said to Sixsmith might have triggered him into taking his own life. I hadn't been particularly sympathetic. But surely, in the circumstances, that was understandable?

An hour or so after that first call Curtis phoned me again. Checking up on me, possibly. He sounded contrite.

'After I phoned you I remembered that I saw you speaking to Mr Sixsmith in the quarry. What did he tell you?'

'He said he had already spoken to you.'

'Yes, yes, we talked. He told me that a friend of his went missing back in the nineteen eighties. He wondered if the remains could possibly be him. I arranged to meet him tomorrow.'

I swallowed. My throat felt dry. 'He told me rather more than that,' I said. 'He was in that tunnel when the roof fell in. The dead boy is Robert Davison. They were exploring with friends. Sixsmith told me they left the boy there. He was obviously dead.'

Curtis went quiet for so long that I really did think we had been cut off. Stupidly I asked if he was still there.

'I'm still here, Doctor Spargo. Please go on.'

'There is nothing more. I assumed he had told you everything.'

I regretted my words. I had broken my first rule. *Assume nothing, Jessica Spargo. Nothing at all. Never. Not ever.*

'I'll need a statement from you, Doctor.'

'Now?'

'No, not now, it's almost midnight. Tomorrow morning, first thing. I'll be at St. Leonards.'

30

After speaking with Curtis last night I dumped my uneaten meal in the bin. I turned off the television, booted my laptop, and by two in the morning I had drafted a statement for Curtis, attempting a word-for-word recollection of Frank Sixsmith's story. I had to get it all down, not because I might forget details – I had a feeling that would never happen – but because Sixsmith was dead I was the only person, apart from those involved that day, who knew the truth about what had happened.

Perhaps, knowing what he was going to do on his way home, Sixsmith had unburdened himself to me rather than to Curtis. That fact, more than his words, distressed me unmercifully. I hoped that writing it all down was a way of passing it on. Perhaps. Perhaps not.

Curtis quizzed me next morning, sitting opposite me at a table in an interview room at the divisional headquarters at St Leonard's. Not only did he question me over my statement, he asked me what the hell I thought I'd been doing by entering the tunnel at all – though not in those exact words. In truth he asked me, very tactfully and no doubt bearing in mind that Kevin Marshall and his superintendent were involved, how a veterinary surgeon, a forensic geologist and her father had contrived to go underground to search for the victim themselves.

For once, I had all the answers. I told Curtis that from information I had provided to Kevin Marshall, he was concerned that a tunnel lay under his site.

'We were to do a survey. Mr Marshall asked me to investigate it and to map its position. My friend Carrie surveys caves.'

'She's a vet.'

'She is also a caver, a potholer. We had all the equipment, you saw that.'

Curtis is not easily impressed. He was certainly not impressed by what I was telling him. Resting both elbows on the table he cupped his face in both hands and sighed. I guessed it wasn't something he would do when interviewing real criminals.

'Late on Saturday Mr Marshall called my superintendent.'

'Had they been playing golf?'

'No, Doctor Spargo, they had not been playing golf.' Then, barely audibly, he mumbled 'But who knows.'

'I didn't expect to find the remains. I didn't think we'd get that far. I thought we'd find a collapse.'

'You did find a collapse. You did find the remains.'

'Another collapse, I mean. One nearer the entrance that would have prevented us going that far.'

'Did you know that your friend Carrie and Scenes of Crime returned with a wellington boot? And its contents?'

I frowned. Too much information. I didn't know about that and I wasn't sure I wanted to know. When I got home last night I had switched off my mobile and unplugged my house phone.

'If you had cleared everything with me beforehand,' Curtis continued, 'I could have arranged the SOCO team and the medic for you. Instead of that, my super had to hear it from Mr Marshall and I had to hear it from him.'

'I'm sorry. I was told you were away.' I didn't say that I knew he was at a funeral in Orkney or who had told me that. 'We weren't expecting to see you or the others when we emerged. Like I said, it was a surveying trip.'

He sat upright and fixed me with a *pull-the-other-one* stare. 'This,' he said, holding up a printed page, 'the statement you emailed. I've been through it. It tells me what Mr Sixsmith said to you. It doesn't tell me much about what you said to him.'

I got the Curtis frown. I looked down at the table top.

'Doctor Spargo?'

'Yes, sorry. I'm finding it hard. I was the last person Frank Sixsmith spoke to before he died.'

Curtis's frown deepened. 'Died? Really? The last I heard he was sitting up in bed in the ERI. Uniform has interviewed him. Concussion, broken wrist, broken nose and some serious facial bruising.'

Crossed wires, somehow? Had I dreamed it all? Were we talking about different people?

'Frank Sixsmith,' I said again. 'The digger driver, the man in the quarry.'

'Yes. What about him?'

'Last night you said fatal injuries.'

'Well, Doctor, you got that wrong. I said *facial injuries*, most likely incurred when his airbag inflated. Apparently he doesn't wear a seatbelt when he's in his excavator and often forgets to use one when he drives.'

I cried again, this time with relief – relief Frank Sixsmith wasn't dead, relief that the whole thing was over. Curtis was unsympathetic. Embarrassed, he left the room. He returned carrying what I hoped would be coffee but which turned out to be ultra-sweet tea.

'Can we get back to what you said to Mr Sixsmith, Doctor?'

'I said very little to him. As you have seen from my statement, he did most of the talking. He wanted to get it all off his chest.'

He dragged a hand through his hair. Then, self-consciously, attempted to smooth it flat again. 'So, Jessica. Where do we go from here?'

I smiled at his softened tone. *Jessica* sounded as if we might even be friends.

'We excavate,' I said. 'Continue with the site dig. There's no way we can recover the remains through that tunnel without endangering lives.'

'That's what I hoped you would say. Does your father agree?'

'I'm sure he does.' And when I switch my phone back on, Mr Curtis, that is what I shall tell him.

Curtis sat quietly, thinking hard, nodding slowly to himself as if agreeing with his own thoughts. Finally he shoved back his chair as if to stand up. Instead of doing that he stretched out his legs.

'About the other thing,' he said. 'Those two murders. I had hoped to have DI Cavendish in on this meeting but he has been called away. Do you have any more you can tell me about his case? I know you visited Dr deWit's apartment. Thank you for that.'

'Nothing since then. I did emphasise to him that the fragments came from computer contacts.'

'Contacts?'

'Contacts. Connectors. Relays. Things that switch things on and off or connect one bit of computer to another. They are made of metals that don't tarnish or melt.'

I couldn't believe I was saying this again. How many times had I told him?

'Yes, yes. You said all that before.'

'I had the impression from DI Cavendish that you still think the fragments came from jewellery.'

'I remain to be convinced either way.'

'DI Cavendish has seen the evidence. He visited my lab.'

Curtis nodded. That he was tired – exhausted, more like – was obvious. I was tempted to ask him when he last had a holiday. I didn't, in case he asked me the same question.

'Did DI Cavendish tell you that I found pieces of circuit board in a waste skip at the Kevron site? Also a large board?'

'A printed circuit board. Yes, I believe he did mention it.'

'No, not a printed circuit board, an old hand-wired board. They pre-date printed circuits. It's probably late 'sixties or early 'seventies. It still had its components.'

'Had?'

'I've dismantled it. DI Cavendish agreed that I should do it. I recovered a small quantity of gold contacts, similar to the fragments you gave me in that glass vial. I haven't had chance to tell him that yet.'

Suddenly I had his undivided attention. He pulled his chair back to the table and sat upright.

'Where exactly did you find these… bits? Kevron's site, you said?'

'Mr Blackie had a shipping container delivered for Professor Thomson to use as a store. The Prof said I could use it. It had a table and chairs in it, also a full waste bin that I emptied into one of the site's waste skips – '

'Yes, yes. Go on. That's when you found the bits?'

'They were in the bottom of the bin. They fell into the skip so I climbed in for them. I found the bigger board later, jammed behind a metal bar in the container.'

'Where did the container come from, do you know?'

'No, but Blackie does. I watched it arrive on site. It was placed next to similar one that has Russian markings. Both containers have been over-painted in the same colour orange.'

'Are there any markings on the container you found the board bits in?'

'Not on that container. Just on its twin.'

He pushed back his chair again. This time he did stand up, gathered up papers and files and walked to the door. He changing his mind, picked up the internal phone and tapped in numbers.

'So you're back,' he said into the phone. 'I've finished here, come on down.' Then to me, as he returned the handset, 'DI Cavendish wants a word with you. Make sure you tell him what you told me about the circuit boards. Not about the tunnel, that is not his concern.'

Cavendish looked as tired as Curtis. He arrived within seconds of the DCI leaving and sat in the same chair. We exchanged brief pleasantries and then, without giving him the opportunity to ask me why he wanted to see me, I launched into the things I'd told Curtis. The Russian markings on the other container was news to him.

'Russian? Really? Are you sure of that?'

He was beginning to sound like his boss. 'Yes, I am sure of that. We have two containers from the same supplier, one with partly painted-out Cyrillic lettering and the other containing pieces of circuit board. I have taken the big board apart and now have a small pile of gold electrical contacts, similar to those you saw at my lab. And I took photos. I also videoed what I did.'

He was nodding. 'You say the containers came from the same supplier. It sounds to me as if you have been making your own enquiries.'

'I saw it arrive. The lorry it came on had no company's name. Also, I checked with one of Kevron's engineers.'

'Are you saying the Russian markings were covered up deliberately?'

'No. I am not saying that.'

'Have you checked inside the other container, the one with the markings?'

'I didn't need to. Its doors are always open and pinned right back. It's empty.' He had been making brief notes on a pad and I waited while he circled something he'd written. 'The containers,' I said. 'There's a record of them on the site assets list but nothing to say where they came from.'

'Russia, you mean?'

'No, what I mean is that there is nothing to say who supplied them to Kevron. The same engineer looked it up for me, but the purchase ledger has no details, nothing about purchase or rental.'

'The name of this engineer?'

'Hamish Anderton. There's no point asking him where they came from, he told me all he knows.'

'Who will know more?'

'The site manager, James Blackie. And probably his secretary. There's no point trying to call them, they are both away this week. According to my father, Blackie switches off his mobile when he goes on leave.'

'Your father? What has your father to do with all of this?'

To give Cavendish the kind of frown I really wanted to give him would have needed big black bushy stick-on eyebrows. Imagining that I broke into a grin.

'Doesn't Mr Curtis tell you anything? My father is retained by Kevron to supervise excavation of the shaft we need to the recover the human remains. Surely you've heard that?'

If he hadn't, he didn't admit it. He thanked me for the information and said he would keep in touch.

Out in the street again I switched on my phone. Amongst numerous missed calls was one from Cameron.

'I hear you are almost down to the remains,' he said when I called him. 'We've been asked to attend. I can't be there, but Brenda can.'

'First things first, Cameron. How are you? How's the leg?'

'The ankle. It's not so bad. I am walking on it. I am using crutches.'

I pictured a pirate with a peg-leg, an eye patch, and a parrot on his shoulder. And no, I don't know why. Maybe it was simply Cameron's new beard, I just couldn't get used to it. I brought him up to date with site news and told him that his van and equipment were safe.

'You said Brenda, Cameron. Who is Brenda?'

'Brenda Douglas. You saw her on site that first day. She's one of my staff. She's young and competent. To be absolutely honest with you, Jessica, I'm surprised they still want us there.'

'Who asked for you, Mr Curtis?'

'The Procurator's Office.'

'What have you been told? You do know that we found the tunnel entrance and I went underground with a caver friend? Have you been told that we found the remains?'

'I've been told that SOCO recovered the remains of a human foot.'

As dispassionately as I could manage, I filled in the gaps. Cameron listened. When I had finished he came up with something I did not want to hear. He was now able to drive. He wanted his van back.

I was not prepared for the scene on site later that day. I managed to find a spot where I could stand safely and look down into the shaft. A small digger, lowered into the bottom of the shaft, scooped out broken rock with its bucket. In Blackie's absence my father appeared to have taken over, standing alone in the bottom of what had become a huge, circular excavation, its sides supported by curved steel plates bolted together.

Hamish Anderton came to me. 'It was your father's idea, putting that excavator down there.' Then a long pause and a change of subject. 'He says you were in the tunnel yesterday and that you found the remains.'

I nodded. 'The victim is under rock that fell from the roof. He's just inside the start of a side tunnel that heads for the foundations of the old house.' I hesitated. I didn't like what I was seeing. I pointed down. 'That digger should move away from that side, it's above the main tunnel. If the tunnel roof collapses it will fall through.'

He unclipped a radio from his belt. My father, radio to his ear, responded by waving the small excavator away from that side of the shaft as he talked. I heard his voice on Hamish's radio. He actually ended the call with *over and out*.

An hour or so later both tunnels were visible. I had visualised simply un-roofing them with the digger bucket, like taking off lids. That is not how it happened. The roof of the main tunnel, where the digger had been standing earlier, collapsed with a hollow roar as a jumble of flat slabs of rock crashed down into it.

Darkness fell and work stopped for the day. By then, the newly fallen rock had been lifted out to leave the original, collapsed rock, the fallen slabs that killed Sandy Davison. I stood with my father, looking down.

'You can see the borehole,' he said. 'See it? Right through that slab?'

Yes, Dad. I can see it. Didn't want to mention it, actually.

31

Curtis arrived on site 0mob-handed next morning. I recognised one of the SOCO officers from Sunday, also the pathologist who had stepped over Morini's body that night in the wet field. A team that included uniformed officers attempted, and failed, to erect screens in the clay around the top of the dig. Directed by my father they succeeded in erecting a gazebo-like structure in the base of the shaft. All accomplished, I'm glad to say, without anyone falling into either tunnel.

Brenda arrived. Recognising me, she came over. I briefed her on progress while we walked together to the car park to collect Cameron's van. With her sitting beside me I drove it as close as I dared to the excavations.

The media circus had begun. A camera drone, flying high, hovered above us. I was beginning to envy Blackie, wherever he was. The man was no fool. With all this going on there would be no real site work. What little there was could be handled by Hamish.

Two hours later the stab that had crushed Sandy Davison had been broken into manageable pieces by two overall-wearing policemen wielding sledgehammers. One broken chunk had a neatly bored hole in it, the width of my hand.

Rain stopped play, a cloudburst that sent all but those under the gazebo scurrying to Cameron's empty container or back to their vehicle cabs. Brenda suited-up and I sat with her in the van with rain beating on the roof. She turned to face me.

'Professor Thomson tells me that you are a forensic geologist. Do you work for Police Scotland?'

'I'm independent, they call me in sometimes.' It sounded as if I had other clients. Before the different Scottish police forces amalgamated, that was true. Now I had only one client. From a commercial viewpoint it was a vulnerable situation to be in.

'He says you used to lecture full time.'

'I did. I still do a bit of post-grad work.'

I was there to shelter from the rain, I was not expecting an inquisition. Though she was undoubtedly qualified to do what she was doing, she was young. And being young, however well-versed she was in theory, meant she was inexperienced.

'Have you done anything like this before?'

I asked the question as if I was the world's most experienced forensic expert, as if forensic geology meant a familiarity with dealing with human remains.

'I haven't. I've been on a lot of archaeological digs.'

'This isn't the same.'

She nodded her head constantly, like one of those nodding dogs once so common in the back windows of cars. Her apprehension was clear.

'I know that,' she said. 'Are you going to climb down there with me?'

'I'm not sure that's allowed. You, the pathologist, and maybe SOCO will be the only ones allowed under that gazebo. And him,' I added, nodding towards a police photographer who was attempting to shield his cameras from the rain.

The rain stopped. People moved. Rivulets ran across clay and made their way down the slopes of the pit. Spurting like gothic fountains they sprayed out over the edge of the shuttering and onto the roof of the gazebo. From there it sprayed again, down onto freshly dug rock. Absently and pointlessly I wondered how long it would take for all that water to reach the old quarry.

A man standing on the top edge of the dig raised both arms high above his head and waved in the direction of our van. So I could hear him I opened a side window.

'Doctor Douglas?'

'Looks like you're on, Brenda…'

She mumbled something I didn't quite catch, clicked the passenger door, slipped out of her seat, looked back at me but said nothing. Then she was gone.

With her gone I realised with some regret that my work here, my work for Kevron, was over. A few more hours and I would be phoning Kevin Marshal to tell him that the remains of Sandy Davison had been removed from his site. Soon I would submit my not insubstantial bill to him and the real world could start up again. Big deal.

The man who waved to Brenda was running towards me. I'd been fiddling with my phone, I hadn't been looking. He reached the van and opened the door.

'Doctor Spargo? The other one, Doctor Douglas. She says she wants you.'

The gazebo in the shaft had a roof but no sides. To reach it I descended a ladder fixed to the inside of the steel shuttering. Reaching the bottom, I picked my way over broken rock and stood beside Brenda. Another, shorter ladder, led down to the floor of the now unroofed, intersecting tunnels. They resembled sharp-sided trenches in rock, narrow but deep.

Bright lamps lit the scene, a brightness supplemented every so often by dazzling camera flashes. Down there, three white-overalled, masked white figures balanced uncertainly on blocks of rock.

Brenda's first words to me: 'You don't mind?'

She looked at me for a response and I shook my head. An ambiguous gesture. To her it meant no, I didn't mind. To me it meant no, I didn't want to be there.

'Blue jeans.'

'What?'

'Blue jeans.'

I take it that you want me here for a hand-holding exercise Brenda and I don't need a commentary, thanks all the same. And yes, I know they were once blue because I have seen them before. Close up. Just the bit that goes into the wellies…

There was more to come.

'Adipocere. Grave wax – that fatty tissue.'

Thank you, Brenda, for that unwelcome gratuitous information.

I nodded towards the activity. 'Shouldn't you be down there with them?'

It wasn't the response she expected. Or wanted, I guessed.

'I'm waiting for the photographer to come up. Shouldn't you be suited up, Jessica?'

'It's pointless. I'm not going down there.'

No way, Brenda. Definitely not my job. What I could see from where I stood looked bad enough. No point going closer.

'I'm not sure why they want you here, Brenda.'

'Professor Thomson says it's a belt and braces thing. We need to be sure it was an accidental death.'

I grunted. 'You mean in case that slab of rock fell on him deliberately? Sorry. Didn't mean that.' I wagged a hand. 'Move over. Camera man's coming up. Looks like it's your turn.'

The man came up and Brenda went down. That, I told myself, wasn't much hand-holding on my part, probably because I was as screwed-up as she was, avoiding looking down at what had once been a human being, now an almost unrecognisable waxy slab of crushed bone and rotted fabric. Much of what had once been flesh had been scoured away recently by drilling water and by the rush of grey water from Cameron's dig, down through the borehole and along the old tunnel, out to the quarry and into that ditch.

'Dad?'

I hadn't heard him come down the ladder. Now he stood behind me, under the gazebo, trying to see down.

'Not much of him left, is there?'

'Don't you start!'

Years ago he'd worked underground in Zambian copper mines. I'd heard his stories of how he helped recover bodies. I hoped he wouldn't repeat them now.

'He's no longer there, Love. It's just old bits.'

I nodded. I knew that. It didn't help.

'DI Curtis tells me that you found out who he was,' he said. 'He told me you spoke to the lad who was with him when the tunnel roof caved in.'

'He wasn't a lad. He wasn't much older than me.'

I stood quietly, looking down. Quietly, because all around me the tunnels, the shaft, and the site beyond, were appropriately silent and still. Even the pathologist and Brenda worked quietly and wordlessly, lifting remains bit by bit, inspecting them before placing them in containers. This was not just a case of removing a body. This was a slow and careful inspection.

Brenda, moving silently, turned and looked up. In each hand she held pieces of skull that she brought together – jigsaw puzzle pieces with a core-drill-size hole. I nodded. Turned to my father.

'I've had enough. I'm leaving.'

To my surprise he said nothing. He looked at me and nodded.

32

While driving on the Edinburgh bypass I missed three calls from Andy Kuzuk. At Straiton I came off on a slip road and called him. There were no niceties. His anxiety came through loud and clear.

'Jessica, are you okay?'

'Yes, Andy. Why?'

'You told me you found a computer board. Do you still have it?'

'I dismantled it. I managed to crop fragments of gold from the electrical contacts.'

'You have taken apart everything?'

'Yes. Why?'

A deep sigh. Then, 'A friend tells me that old military equipment from some countries can have explosive traps to destroy secret components.'

'Seriously?'

'Very seriously. But you are okay. If you have more parts then don't touch them.'

'I don't have any more.'

'Jessica, I think you do dangerous things.'

Just as well he didn't know about my trip underground with Carrie. As we ended the call I thought about what he said. It hadn't occurred to me that dismantling the board might have put me in danger. I had used a screwdriver to tear away a small metal box from the board, a box that contained – luckily for me – just a tight coil of wire. I shivered. I wondered, if what Andy said was right, what the likelihood was of encountering an explosive component in a shipping container holding thousands of boards.

I was about to pull away when Andy phoned me again.

'I forgot to say. I asked friends about orange shipping containers. I didn't say why, I just asked them to look for them.'

I had a strange feeling I was part of a dream. A bad one. Not just because of the conversation I was having with Andy, but the whole of the last few days.

'Andy, *you told your friends?* You have a spy network?'

He laughed. 'Not spies! I have Internet friends.'

According to Andy, orange containers had been seen in several places, including one in a field near the Queensferry Bridge, two on a construction site in East Lothian – no doubt the ones on the Kevron site – and several in a scrapyard well to the west of Edinburgh.

'The scrapyard west of Edinburgh. Did your friends say where it is?'

'Wait please.'

I waited. Andy gave a mumbled commentary while he booted his laptop and logged on to something or someone, somewhere. It was marginally more interesting than the usual *hold while we connect you*.

'This is what she writes. *Five containers, perhaps more. One is green, part orange. Look like paint job not finished.*'

'Where?'

'She says *No Man's Land*.'

'That's not particularly helpful.'

I'm fairly sure it was Ian Rankin who described vast tracts of former mining country west of Edinburgh as *No Man's Land*. It is a fitting description of some parts of West Lothian and Lanarkshire – mile upon mile of unattractive marsh and high moorland, prime sites for wind farms. Much of the region has a history of oil shale mining, the shale dug out like coal and the oil sweated out of it in massive retorts. The oil was shipped out to be used mainly as lamp oil – and later, as the only UK source of motor fuel. As with most mining land, once the mining ended there was no work. No reason for people to be there.

I thanked Andy, ended the call and pressed quick-dial for Curtis. Realising that I should probably be calling Cavendish, I cancelled the call. Cavendish had been more receptive than Curtis regarding containers and circuit boards.

I cancelled that call as well. I was shooting from the hip. Friends of a friend had seen orange containers, so what? How many orange containers were there in this part of Scotland, dozens? Hundreds? I placed my phone on the passenger seat and pulled out into traffic.

Home again, I called Kevin Marshall and updated him. With difficulty I described the remains found on site and how we had dealt with it. I said *we* when I meant *they*. In truth I'd played no part in the day's recovery work.

I corrected myself. 'The others, I mean. I didn't do much.'

'Don't belittle your contribution, Doctor. How long will it take you to get that tunnel map to me? Did you manage to obtain enough information to plot it?'

I made promises. Then, after contacting Carrie, I drove out to her place. Thanks to her cave surveying hobby she owned mapping software that, from our basic survey data, produced a printout that looked as if it had been drawn up by a team of surveyors. I offered to pay her and she laughed.

'Gaping Ghyll, remember? You promised!'

I swallowed. 'That I'd go down it? Not sure I did.'

'You owe me, Girl. So what now? You got plenty of work?'

I shook my head. 'Nothing really, not now Kevron's finished. There's the gold thing, but it's peanuts compared with what Kevron paid me.'

'The gold thing? You never explained what all that was about.'

By late evening Carrie knew about as much as I did about Charles deWit and Demitri Morini. Also about Tom Curtis, Tim Cavendish, Kevin Marshall,

James Blackie and Hamish Anderton. Unlike me, she won't drink when alone. Inevitably this means that when she has company she makes up for lost time. I left Cameron's van outside her house and took a taxi home

Next morning I woke late. For once it didn't matter. Carrie, inexplicably more clear-headed than me, had already emailed her tunnel map to me. Sipping coffee, I forwarded a copy of it to Kevin Marshall in Bristol and another to Hamish Anderson at the Kevron site.

Paging through unread emails I found one from Cameron. He said he had given up trying to phone me. I checked my mobile. It was in airplane mode. His email politely reminded me that he wanted his van back.

Driving to Glasgow today was not on the cards. It wasn't simply the drive that deterred me, it was the thought of sitting with Cameron at home or wherever, recounting everything that had happened since his rescue from the quarry. I had done all that, and more, last night with Carrie. I didn't want to do it again.

I typed a short reply: *Good to hear you are recovering. Brenda will have told you we have finished on site. Van much appreciated. Very busy at present. Okay if I bring it over at the weekend?*

Fortified by strong coffee I logged-on to news sites. Robert Davison and the tunnel were very much in evidence, most of it half-truths and guesswork. Thankfully, nobody had linked Robert's death with Frank Sixsmith. I watched a short video taken by the drone I'd seen. Though it had been hovering around for hours, it seemed to have recorded nothing of great interest.

I had intended to collect the van from Carrie's. Instead I spent the day in my lab, working on a small job I had from Police Scotland's Northern Division. I had difficulty concentrating. I couldn't get Morini and deWit's deaths off my mind. When I started in forensics I made myself checklists and flowsheets to use as memory-joggers. At the bottom of every sheet I printed WHAT HAVE I MISSED? Because there is always something. Nobody is perfect.

That evening I slumped in front of my TV. At ten I tumbled into bed and fell asleep almost immediately, only to wake again at two in the morning. The human mind is a strange thing. At night it rearranges itself, telling you nonsensical stories mixed from fiction and fact as it stores away memories. That's how I think of it anyway. Probably not a mechanism a neurologist would recognise. I swung out of bed, sat bolt upright and attempted to recall my dream. I had been flying high. Didn't know where or why. My lazy evening in front of the box had been spent watching comedy repeats, not skydiving or parachuting. Nor superheroes.

Then it came to me. The internet… the news… the aerial views of the Kevron site filmed from that drone. Wide awake now I booted my laptop and Googled *kevron recovery remains*. I then added *drone*. It took me seconds to find raw, unedited footage, a close-up of grass and a man with a joystick controller, caught peering up at the departing drone's camera. Then a dump truck, Kevron's site offices and Cameron's parked van. The drone then hovered high above Cameron's excavation, seen as a wide expanse of grey, with the shaft and shuttering.

The drone hovered high, giving a fifteen second view of the gazebo at the base of the shaft. Then something I hadn't seen on the edited footage, a uniformed police officer gesturing wildly at the drone, ordering it back the way it had come, mouthing what a polite person might lip-read as *puck off*.

As the drone backed away it passed high over the core shed and the row of containers. I watched the screen and then saw what had been puzzling me. The two shipping containers on the end of the row were not orange as I expected, they were green. Or rather their roofs were, because whoever repainted them orange hadn't bothered to repaint their tops. I banged off an email to Andy Kuzuk, saying I needed to know exactly where his friend saw that half-painted container.

My bedside clock showed five as I slipped out of bed for the second time that night. I wasn't expecting a message from Andy so soon, but his reply to mine was waiting for me.

Jez I ask Foxy. She say she drives in West Lothian, she get lost. She does not know where she saw container.

It wasn't the most helpful piece bit of information but it was better than nothing. I skipped breakfast and spent time on Google Earth, searching satellite imagery for scrapyards and storage yards in West Lothian and South Lanarkshire. I wasn't looking for green roofed orange containers because the satellite imagery was three years out of date and the street-view images even older. But I did find a number of scrap yards. At last I had somewhere to start.

I caught the bus to Carrie's house, unlocked Cameron's van and headed west out of Edinburgh. I had considered calling in to tell her I was taking it, deciding instead to phone her later. Carrie is not an early morning person. She would not thank me for waking her.

I stopped some distance along her road and stored several locations in the van's satnav. Driving again, I turned onto the motorway to join fast-travelling traffic. I came off on the same slip road as I had that night in the police car, this time more slowly and without blue lights and nee-naw horns.

I found the first location without difficulty – except that it had magically transformed itself and the surrounding countryside into a housing estate. The second place I visited turned out to be a building contractor's storage yard without a container in sight.

I pulled over for the umpteenth time and checked the satnav for the next location. Time passed, as did distance. So far I had driven thirty or so miles without seeing a single container, orange or otherwise. I was sure I was nowhere near the places Andy's friend Foxy had described.

No Man's Land was an apt description of the countryside I now drove through. I had seen very few other vehicles and only a scattering of houses. Apart from other drivers, I had seen very few human beings. I turned onto a dead straight road across boggy heath and put my foot down. Cameron's van responded admirably, purring along at around sixty.

Had the road been busy with traffic I would have missed the containers. A row of several sat behind a windbreak of tall firs, all painted in a washed-out shade of orange. Vertical stripes of colour had attracted my attention as I drove past, the orange painted steel alternating with the dark trunks of trees.

I didn't want to attract attention by stopping. A mile or so up the road I waited while a motorcycle passed me, then I turned the van around and drove back. This time, to get a better look, I slowed down, passing what appeared to be the yard's entrance – a wide track into the trees, newly spread with stone chippings. A short way in from the road the track turned sharply. If the entrance gates to the scrapyard were there, they couldn't be seen from the road.

Further along the road I pulled over. I managed to get the van up on the grass verge at a place I could look back at the scrapyard. It didn't need detective training to see that the containers arrived here coloured green and rust. Then, after receiving a thin coat of orange, they were sold on to companies like Kevron. Beyond the trees and containers were rusting shells of cars, piled five or six high, like high-rise buildings on a grid of streets. I could also make out what I suspected were once mine buildings, with blackened brick walls and asbestos sheet roofs. The place looked deserted. Perhaps a strange thing to say about a scrapyard, but it had seen better days.

I locked the van. A short struggle through tangled ferns brought me to the yard's boundary fence. What had once been strong, interlaced chain link, had unravelled like an old pullover, leaving gaps big enough to climb through.

I had rehearsed excuses in case I was caught. I would play the innocent. As I'd said to Blackie's secretary, I needed a container for storage… *and I just happened to be driving past and I saw you had containers and I'm wondering if they are for sale – I mean just one of them ha-ha I don't want all of them and can you possibly deliver because I can't collect something that size myself I only have a small van…*

I stood near the fence and reviewed my decisions. I wondered if I should call Curtis or Cavendish. Again, it would be premature. This was only one of the places Andy's friends had seen such containers. I would lose all credibility if the police came here mob-handed and found nothing.

So, what to do next? Walk back along the road to the entrance track and look for a site office? Stepping through a gap in the fence would be easier and quicker, and if I was caught then it wasn't as if I was a gang of kids hell-bent on trashing the place. Not that they would have to do much to succeed.

I negotiated an overgrown ditch and crossed into the yard. To my right, some way off, sat the row of orange containers, their back ends against the firs. Their doors, all closed, faced a lorry-width avenue, containers on one side of it and neatly-stacked cars on the other. The road surface I walked on had the same clean, fresh chippings I'd seen near the entrance track. I bent down and scooped up a handful. It wasn't crushed stone, it was crushed concrete.

And I knew just where it had come from.

To most people concrete is just concrete, a mix of cement, sand, and natural gravel or crushed stone. By spitting on the crushed fragments – an unattractive but useful geological habit – I enhanced their colours. This was crushed concrete made from rounded grey gravel and fragments of red rock, identical to the crushed concrete at the Kevron site. Whoever owned this yard had bought truckloads of the stuff and spread it on their dirt roads.

Things fell into place. Not bought, but swapped. Several truckloads of crushed concrete, traded by Blackie for two orange shipping containers. It explained the strange entry in Kevron's purchase ledger. No money changed hands. Blackie, and whoever owned this yard, did a deal. This of course did not mean that the yard's owner, or Blackie, knew anything about the circuit boards I'd found. Chances were that the scrap man simply bought containers, repainted them to cover the rust, and then sold them.

I hesitated. What if I was wrong? What if the containers arrived here full of boards? I walked on, less confidently. With every step my rehearsed reason for being in the yard seemed to get weaker and weaker. You don't buy containers by chance, you go on-line and compare sizes, prices, and delivery costs. You don't call at a deserted, isolated place like this on the off chance you'll get a good deal.

Opposite the orange containers, sandwiched between the stacks of scrap cars, sat another container, twice as long as the others and painted dark grey. A cable looped from it to tall pole after tall pole, revealing that this container had electricity and perhaps even a phone. It was a permanent fixture. A store or an office.

I stood and listened. The place seemed dead. If anyone was around then surely they'd have heard me or seen me by now. It wasn't as if I'd been tiptoeing through grass. Walking on the freshly laid roadway sounded like scrunching across a pebble beach.

One of the double doors of the grey container stood ajar. I called out, reasoning that by asking loudly if anyone was there I couldn't be accused of snooping. Crows in the firs croaked a response. I stepped closer to the container and tried again. Silence, this time. Even from the crows.

Since nearing the container I'd detected a chemical smell that I recognised. Years ago I had accompanied the police to a row of lock-up garages to take soil samples from tyres, and from under the wings of a van believed to have been involved in the theft of car batteries. The stolen batteries had been emptied of acid before being broken up to recover the lead they contained.

The ground around the garages had an acrid, chemical smell that caught in my throat.

The closer I came to the open container the stronger the smell became. And there was something else, a distinct smell of bleach. I grasped the edge of one of the twin doors with both hands, swung it back, took a deep breath and stepped inside.

Dismantling old cars for spares requires a well-equipped workshop. That's what I assumed this place was... or had been, until recently. Something had happened here. Something catastrophic.

33

The floor, the walls and the arrays of tools and equipment in the container had been hosed down recently, so recently that everything still glistened. I had thought – hoped – that the yard was abandoned, but clearly it was not. It was time to get out and call Curtis. The quicker I was back in the van, the safer I would feel.

I jumped and yelped. With a metallic clang the container door slammed shut behind me. Wishful thinking that a sudden gust of wind had blown it shut was dispelled immediately by the squeal of the door's twin locking handles being levered into place. Someone had shut me in.

Standing in darkness I beat on the door, shouting that I was inside, a wasted effort because whoever shut me in knew that already. Staying quiet, I listened for footsteps. Hearing none, I yelled again and again, beating and kicking the door like a child in a tantrum.

Unsurprisingly, panicking didn't help. Gradually my eyes adjusted to the dark, detecting dim light where the two doors joined, allaying my fears that these things might be airtight. Weak daylight also came past the blades of a fan, high up on one wall, so at least I'd have air, I'd be able to breathe. But it wasn't just the lack of air that worried me. Now that the doors were shut, the acidic fumes and reek of strong bleach caught in my throat.

My attempts to phone Curtis – or anyone – came to naught. I had no signal. My phone wasn't completely useless because I remembered it had a light. Using it, I found a grubby length of cord on a pull-switch and tugged it. A string of bulbs down one side of the steel roof lit up the place from end to end.

The length of the workshop surprised me. It was not one container, but two. The end of the one I was in had been cut off and joined to another, giving it the appearance of a well-lit pedestrian underpass. Workbenches and cupboards lined one wall. Floor-to-roof shelves lined the other, many of them stacked with strong boxes. Someone, or something, had ripped through the sides of several of the boxes and strewn small car parts across the floor.

Remembering the poles and wires I'd seen outside, I searched for a phone. What I found was a black phone without a dial, a museum piece, no doubt an extension to another, distant phone. I lifted the handset to my ear. As expected, it was dead.

Whatever happened here had not only damaged the boxes, it had scoured the container's steel floor so that some parts of it shone like a mirror. Other areas looked etched, as if attacked by strong acid. Tools lay scattered on the floor near one of the workbenches: pliers and snips, screwdrivers and spanners. Assorted bits and pieces seemed to have been thrown in the air and left where they landed.

Intent on making as much noise as possible I resumed my attack on the door, this time with a hammer. Every so often I stopped to listen. I heard big birds squawking, then a car on the road, travelling fast. Fifteen minutes later my head hurt from the banging, my arms ached from the effort, and my throat felt as if it had been sandpapered. I ended my hammering with a painful coughing fit brought on by the fumes.

Hammering was pointless and shouting made me hoarse. Whatever fumes I was breathing began to overpower me and to avoid inhaling them I pressed my face to the gap between the doors. Though I could breathe, I couldn't see out. I knew from Kevron's containers that these doors have an overlap, a steel flange-like thing to keep out the rain.

I tried to think rationally. I was trapped but I wasn't hurt. If the fumes were not poisonous then I could survive here without food or water for days. If the nights became cold that wouldn't be a problem – that's if the two convector heaters I found still worked. I walked over to one and switched it on. The warm air from it made the fumes worse.

I resumed my attack with the hammer. After two or three minutes of hard beating I stopped and listened. I'd heard an engine, not a car on the road but something much closer. Then, hearing crunching footsteps, I stayed still. Someone was coming. Someone was approaching the container.

The footsteps stopped. The door's locking levers lifted. I braced myself as the hinges on one of the doors groaned. Then I waited, terrified, hammer in hand.

I expected to see a human. What I got was top-to-toe shiny black leather, topped by a soot-black dome and smoked visor. A heavy, leather-strapped motorbike boot stepped up onto the container floor.

'What the devil are you doing in here?'

'Carrie?'

Definitely Carrie. Using both hands she lifted off her helmet and tucked it under her arm.

'The lock handles were down. You were locked in.'

'Tell me something I don't know. How did you…? What are you doing here?'

'Never mind that. Who did this, did you see?

I shook my head. 'The yard was deserted. Well, I thought it was.'

She looked past me, into the container.

'What is this place, a workshop?' Then, coughing, 'Good god, what's that smell?"

'Bleach, I think.'

'Bleach and strong acid. Nitric, by the smell of it. Why the hell does a scrapyard need nitric acid? God, my throat's already like the bottom of a hamster's cage.'

'The container door was open. Someone slammed it on me. I didn't see or hear anyone.'

'Seems like they saw you. Let me guess… you didn't notice the camera? On the telephone pole thingy?'

I shook my head. 'Didn't. Carrie… I don't understand why you are here.'

My mind was in turmoil. For a few seconds only I thought she might be the person who shut me in. For a few seconds only because, with a metallic groan and a thud, somebody outside swung the container door shut again.

I won't repeat what Carrie shouted. Taking the hammer from me she beat on the door. Frustrated with herself she flung the hammer down the length of the container and attacked the door again, this time with her fists. Been there, I thought. Done that. Doesn't work.

'There was nobody out there! I rode around the whole place!'

'Camera…?'

She grunted. 'Yes. Right. I should have stayed outside, shouldn't have come in here. Have you tried that phone?'

'Doesn't work. I tried my mobile but there's no signal. Do you have yours on you?'

'We're surrounded by steel. Waste of time even checking. You did physics at school. Faraday Cage, remember? Blocks all electromagnetic waves?'

Again, she took out her rage on the door, this time with a long spanner. I let her get on with it.

'I saw you take the van from outside my house,' she said when she'd calmed down. 'I wondered what you were doing so early in the morning, so I followed you. It was like following a wandering cow.'

'Not sure I like the comparison.'

'I caught up with you on the motorway. I'm surprised you didn't notice me following you.'

'I've been searching for orange containers. A friend gave me some locations. Two or three bikers did pass me. Was one of them you?' I nodded at the one-piece black leathers. 'Difficult to tell, Carrie.'

'The bikers were all me. The last time I passed you was outside here. I waited a few miles up the road and when you didn't appear I came back.'

She was pacing, right to the far end and back again.

'Stop doing that. You're making things worse.'

Glaring at me she stopped pacing. Instead she started to check shelves, opening boxes and looking inside them. It was something I hadn't bothered to do. All that had mattered to me was how long I could survive, locked in a container without food and water.

'Someone doesn't want you snooping here. Why's that, I wonder? Why did you come here, what did you expect to find? What's all this about containers, are you are going to explain?'

Carrie noticed the extractor fan, high above the workbench. She found the switch and set it to run fast. The air freshened. I told her everything, about the circuit boards, the cropped gold and the information provided by Andy. Also, Curtis's reluctance to believe that the gold fragments came from computer parts.

Carrie hadn't always been a good listener but today she stayed quiet while I told her my tale. When I finished she went to shelves at the far end of the container and returned with a box of computer parts.

'Wondered what these were for,' she said as she tugged-out boards. 'Plenty more boxes like this down there. What the hell happened in here?' She nodded to a workbench. 'Look how that wood is splintered. And those metal shelves, all twisted. Looks like something on the workbench blew up. Look at the floor, it's etched with acid. That glass container, the big one on the floor under the shelf, it's cracked, the acid's come from that. Looks to me as if someone's hosed the place down to clean away the acid. You'd probably be dead by now if they hadn't done that.'

I had been so concerned about getting out that I hadn't really bothered about the condition of the container or its contents. Nearer to the cracked glass container than her, I walked over to it and bent down. I was about to roll it out from under the shelves when she shouted.

'Don't! Don't touch it!'

I jumped up. She was beside me already, gripping my arm. 'That bleach smell isn't bleach, it's chlorine gas. You are right about the gold. Someone's been cropping it from components and dissolving it in aqua regia. It's a crude, low-tech way to recover it. It's also very risky.'

Aqua regia – a mix of nitric and hydrochloric acid that can be used to dissolve gold. I'd never had reason to use the stuff myself but I knew of the dangers.

'Can it be stored in glass?' I asked. 'Doesn't it dissolve glass containers?'

'That's not aqua regia. You're thinking of hydrofluoric acid.'

'What do they do with the acid afterwards? When no more gold can be dissolved in it, I mean.'

'Specialised firms buy it. A concentrate of gold dissolved in acid is more valuable than a mix of fragments still soldered to copper contacts.'

'What happened in here? Did the acid explode?'

She shook her head. 'If you mix the acids the wrong way – that's adding hydrochloric to nitric instead of the other way round – you get a reaction that can blow up in your face.' She looked around. 'Though that's not what happened here. Even a violent reaction wouldn't damage metal shelves and scatter things around like that. Something else happened.'

'You said the smell was chlorine. You get that same smell from bleach.'

She shook her head. 'Not a smell this strong. Aqua regia goes off, it decomposes into nitric oxide and chlorine gas. Remember your chemistry – chlorine – one of the gases used in World War One? That vent fan wouldn't have helped much. If someone had been dissolving gold in here they should have used a fume cupboard, protective clothing and full face masks. I don't see any equipment like that. It's a wonder anyone survived in here.'

'Perhaps they didn't. A friend told me that sensitive military components on circuit boards were sometimes linked to small explosive charges. If you try to remove them they destroy the component. I'm wondering if that happened here.'

Stroking her chin, Carrie nodded. 'If that's what happened here it did more than just destroy the component. It could account for the damage. Not sure about the acid though. That container was tipped up. It didn't break.'

'Perhaps someone fell against it.'

She shuddered. 'Doesn't bear thinking about. Blinded by an explosion and then stumbling back into one of the nastiest acids known to man.' She went quiet. 'Speculation isn't helping. If we don't get out of here soon, in a few weeks' time someone will be looking at our two bodies and asking the same questions.' She was looking up at the fan. 'If I can get my phone out past the fan blades…'

'There's no point. There won't be a signal. The place is surrounded by stacks of cars.'

'Worth trying? Unless you have other ideas?'

I shrugged. She switched off the fan, clambered up on the work bench and removed fan's mesh guard. Holding her phone, she manoeuvred it around the fan blades. Struggling and cursing, she pulled her arm back.

'Damn waste of time! Got it outside. Can't see if there's a signal or not. Can't get near it to speak. Can't even press the buttons.'

I waggled my fingers, beckoning for her phone. 'Text? Worth trying? Give it to me.'

'Not much point texting the emergency services.'

'Wasn't thinking of doing that.'

Taking phone numbers from my own mobile I keyed in a message to Curtis, copied it to Cavendish and my father and handed her phone back to her. She took it and reached outside with it again. The she squealed.

'I've dropped the bloody thing! *Dropped it!*' She pulled her hand back. 'Can't believe I just did that!'

Still cursing, she went to step down from the workbench. Something attracted her attention and she stayed up high, inspecting her hands and muttering to herself. 'Something up here…' Keeping one hand in the air as if holding it out to me, she jumped down. I expected her to hand me something but she walked to the nearest lamp bulb and held her hand up to it. Her hand was empty.

'Ugh! Dried blood! It's on fan's guard.'

I looked. The tips of her fingers were smudged brownish-red. 'Are you sure it's blood? Could it be rust?'

'Believe me, I know what dried blood looks like.'

'Is it human?'

'Is that a joke? I'm good at my job, but I'm not that good.'

She dug around in her pockets with her clean hand, tore open a sachet of antiseptic wipes and cleaned her fingers. Carrie, always prepared.

We had a go at the doors again, taking turns to beat them with the hammer. I went first, my arms soon tiring. Carrie took over, venting anger and frustration on the innocent steel plate. She paused for deep breaths.

'Didn't know you'd been a blacksmith in an earlier life, Carrie.'

She grunted but said nothing. Then, turning her head to one side, she seemed to be listening.

'What?'

'Footsteps.'

'I can't hear anything.'

Which did not surprise me. My head rang like big bells.

34

Carrie didn't do pleading. Convinced she'd heard someone outside she yelled abuse. Then, surprisingly, we heard thumps and groans, metal against metal as the locking handles released, this time on both doors as if the person doing it wasn't sure how to open them. Fingers came around the steel door edge. Carrie, spanner raised, stepped forwards.

'Don't, Carrie!'

The door swung back. Instead of the heavily-muscled scrap-man we expected, we faced a bespectacled youth no older than eighteen, his eyes fixed on Carrie's spanner.

'Did you lock us in, you little shit?'

I reached out and held her arm. The last thing I wanted right now was for the lad to take fright and slam the doors shut.

'I don't think it was him, Carrie.'

She waited for a response from the lad. He stood open mouthed, shaking his head, apparently as surprised as we were. My mouth, I realised, was wide open too, filling my lungs with fresh air. Aware of her threatening posture Carrie lowered the spanner.

'Well?' she said, taking a step forwards. 'Well? Who the hell are you?'

The lad took a step back. Nervously he raised a hand and wagged it at the container. 'What you doing in there, anyway?'

Still concerned he might slam the door shut I stepped outside, followed closely by Carrie. It was my turn to speak and I did so, calmly and quietly. Bad cop, good cop.

'Somebody shut us in there. Was it you?'

More headshaking. 'I heard the noise. I just come.'

'Do you work here?'

'Sometimes. Work for Harry. Weekends, mainly.'

'Who is Harry?'

'Old Man Sinclair.'

'Harry Sinclair?'

'Like what I said.'

'Is he here?'

Headshaking. 'Not seen him for days.'

Carrie made a point of examining her watch. 'Leave him. Let's get out of here.'

I ignored her and concentrated on the lad. 'But you still come here?'

'Owes me money, Harry does.'

'Harry owes you money.'

'What I said. Three weekends. Six day's money.'

Carrie hurled the spanner back into the container. The lad jumped.

'So, if Harry's not here and you didn't shut us in,' she said, 'who the hell did?'

The lad shrugged. I took out my mobile and started keying. 'I'll get the police. I'll tell them you shut us in.'

'Trespassing, youse were.'

'So you did shut us in!'

'Didnae do it. Wasnae me.'

'What's your name?'

'None of your fuckin' business.'

Sure I had no signal, I'd been tapping random numbers. I cancelled them and tapped in some more. 'Kidnapping's a serious matter.' I said, turning to Carrie. 'Shall I call DI Cavendish or DCI Curtis?'

'Just 999. Get a car here.'

Nervously the lad raised his hands to his ears and held them there. 'No… it's Den… Dennis. Den Stewart.'

'So, Den. Who shut us in?'

'Leave it. He's not worth the trouble. Just phone the police. He's not worth the bother.'

'Okay,' Dennis said. 'Must have been Murray. I came in on my bike as Murray drove out. Just now. In a van.'

Carrie again. 'Murray? Who is Murray?'

'Seen him before. Comes to see Harry sometimes.'

Blood from stone came to mind. 'So where is Harry now?'

I listened while he talked. Harry Sinclair, the yard's owner, hadn't been to the yard for two weeks.

'Not seen him since. He just vanished.'

'What do you know about this container? What's been going on here?'

He shrugged. 'Harry works in there. Does stuff with computers.'

'Circuit boards? Does he take them apart?'

'Never let me see. Said about acid and stuff. Wasn't safe, he said.'

Carrie nodded. 'Too damn right…'

'You said Harry hasn't been seen for two weeks.'

'I said I hadnae seen him. No' sure if others seen him.'

Smartass. Dennis wasn't as dumb as he liked to make out.

'Tell me what do you do here, Den.'

'Odds and sods. Work the crusher.'

Volunteered information at last. My threat to call the police had a positive effect on him. Time for us both to be good cops? I glanced at Carrie and raised my eyebrows. Detected a hint of agreement.

Dennis, apparently, was a dab hand at crushing cars. Harry, when not stripping computer boards, stripped down scrapped cars, removing any resalable parts and leaving the body shells for Dennis to flatten in the car crusher at weekends.

'Sounds like skilled stuff,' I said.

He stared at me. 'You takin' the piss? Presses buttons on the crane. Steers it around. Picks up cars. Drops them in the crusher. Presses buttons on the crusher. Lifts them out. Not fuckin' rocket science. All fucked up now though.'

'What, the crusher? You broke it?'

'Didnae say that. Came in and found it broke. Some bampot crushed a car with engine and wheels still on it. Crusher's for bodywork, no' for whole cars.'

Carrie had wandered off. She appeared to be attempting to squeeze herself between the outside wall of the container and a stack of old cars close beside it.

'No good,' she said, dusting herself down. 'Can't get down there.'

'She stuck her phone out through the vent fan,' I said to Dennis. 'Trying to get a signal. Dropped it along there somewhere.'

A couple of minutes later Dennis, small and agile, had squeezed himself between the container wall and the adjacent stack of flat cars. Halfway along he gave up and returned to us.

'Didnae get it. Got stuck, din' I? Jacket got caught on stuff.'

Dennis, now flavour of the month with Carrie for attempting to recover her phone, insisted on giving us a guided tour of several acres of scrapyard. After walking down alleys between stacks of scrap cars we ended up at the yard's office, at the top end of the lane we started from. During our tour Dennis let slip that one of the half-painted containers was still filled with old circuit boards. He was unable to open it, he said. All the site keys, normally kept in the office, had been stolen.

The weather had changed. We stood together in the office, out of the rain, looking out of its gridded windows, while Dennis lamented the death of his crusher. From where we stood we could see it. The size of a small bus, it sat near stacked cars, across from the office. The car it had failed to crush was still in it, jammed under the machine's huge top jaw. Instead of having been reduced to a flat block of steel scrap it looked three-quarters done, the crusher's powerful hydraulics unable to deal with the gearbox and engine.

'Hydraulics failed. Pump broke, I reckon.'

'Harry didn't have it fixed?'

'Harry don't know about it. Not been here since.'

'So who broke it,' I asked. 'Mr Murray?'

He shrugged. 'It's not *Mister Murray*. Murray's his first name. Couldn't have been him, could it? Never works here, does he? Just comes to visit Harry. Anyway, wouldn't have done it, not Murray. He and Harry are mates.'

'There are CCTV cameras. Didn't they record who did it? Do they work? Have you checked the tapes?'

'CCTV recorder didn't have tapes, had a hard drive. Keeps weeks of records then overwrites them. Couldn't check it, could I? Got nicked, didn't it?'

Of course it did. 'What's Murray's surname?'

The shrug again. 'Harry never said.'

'Is Murray young? Old?'

'You sounds like the polis.'

'I'm not the police. So? What about Murray?'

'Not young, is he? Forty, could be. Harry's older. Old man, he is.'

'So someone came into the yard, used the crane to lift the car into the crusher and then set it going. Sounds to me like they knew what they were doing.'

More shrugs. 'Could be. Not rocket science, told you that. Didn't know what they were doing or they wouldn't have put car in it with the engine and wheels.'

'Did the crane and crusher need keys to run them?'

He nodded. Pointed to a row of nails hammered into the wall. 'Kept all keys there. Place got trashed. Took the CCTV recorder from its box.' He went over to a steel cabinet and opened its door. 'Cut off the lock with an angle grinder, I reckon.'

Theatrically, I looked around me. The office didn't look trashed. 'Did you tidy the place?'

He shook his head. 'Trashed when I came here. Came back after a couple of days and it was tidy. Could have been Murray done that. Murray tidies Harry's stuff.'

The more I heard, the more puzzled I became. Unlike me, Carrie was losing interest. Bored, she stepped down into the yard and wandered off in the rain.

Harry Sinclair, despite his familiarity with computer boards, didn't use computers for work and kept everything in box files on shelves in the office. All, according to Dennis, were now missing.

'If it was a break-in then surely Harry reported it?'

'Wasn't a break-in. Door wasn't broke. Anyway, like I said, haven't seen Harry since before all that.'

'Murray, then. Did Murray report it?'

All I got was a shrug.

I stayed at the window, watching Carrie. Not exactly the most mechanically competent person I knew, she seemed to be taking a great interest in the crusher. I left her to it. More important things buzzed around in my head. I was willing to bet that whoever broke the car crusher knew their actions had been caught on CCTV. They came in here to get the tapes or to wipe the hard drive. It had no tape to take, so they took the whole thing.

'Because even if they wiped the drive, the video might still be recoverable.'

'What?'

'I'm talking to myself, Dennis. What puzzles me is that they didn't have to break in to the office to take the CCTV recorder, which means that either the office was open or they had a key. And why take Harry's files and papers? What incriminating information might they contain?'

Dennis, realising I was now asking myself questions, ignored me. He stood in the doorway, looking out.

'Woman's calling you.'

She was. Loudly too, yelling for me to come over. Dennis headed out across the yard with me at his heels.

'Smells,' Carrie said quietly when we reached her. 'Something's rotting in the crushed car…'

35

The five of us stood in the rain beside the crusher. Using the office phone, I'd left messages for Curtis and Cavendish and they had arrived in two cars. Calling 999 would have been pointless. There was no emergency. And the last thing I wanted to do was to have to explain the history of all this to uniformed strangers.

Whoever, or whatever, was rotting in the crusher had been there some time. Curtis sniffed around for a while, staying quiet while I briefed him about the orange containers and the grey workshop. I say *briefed*, but it was more him quizzing me on *why I'd come here in the first place, and what the hell did I think I was doing, poking around in a place like this?*

Carrie had been talking to Cavendish and she came to my rescue.

'Are you interested in what we're saying or not, Detective Inspector? There's something rotting in that crushed car. Something big.'

'Are you sure of – '

'Don't ask me how I know it. I just do.'

'It's Detective Chief Inspector,' I whispered to her.

'He's an inspector. He just happens to be a chief one.'

Cavendish stood stroking his chin. He pulled on latex gloves, stooped down beside the crusher, and poked around. He came back to us holding out his latex hand. Carrie reached out, held his wrist, and guided his hand to her nose. Sniffed twice. Sniffed again. Not for the first time in recent weeks I was glad I'd studied geology.

She nodded. 'The mud stinks. Blood in it, probably. Water pooled here some time ago. Either it rained hard or somebody hosed down the crusher.'

'When I got here there was water running out of the grey container,' I said. 'I'm sure it had just been hosed down.'

Carrie shook her head. 'Whoever hosed this thing down did it some time ago. The mud underneath it is thick, it's taken days to dry out. The rain we've had has softened it again.'

Curtis shook his head. 'Could it be a dead animal in the car? A dog? Fox? Badger?'

'You should get it sampled properly before more rain washes it away. If it's animal, okay. If it's human then you'll have to cut up the car.'

Curtis gave her a *tell me something I don't know* look. Without speaking he looked at Cavendish, who walked off, discarding his gloves and taking out his phone.

'If there's a body in there,' I said to Curtis, 'it could be the yard's owner.'

'What makes you say that?'

'We were let out of the container by a lad. Dennis something or other.'

'Stewart,' Carrie said.

'Dennis Stewart, yes. He works here weekends. He says the owner, Harry – '

Curtis frowned. 'Harry Sinclair?'

'You know him?'

'Sinclair is known to us. Where is this Dennis?' He swivelled on his heel, as if looking around for him.

'He cycled away when he knew we'd called you. He told us he hasn't seen Harry since before the office was broken into, a couple of weeks ago. Whoever did it took Harry's papers and files and also the CCTV box. He said Harry worked on old computer circuit boards in the container. Doctor Fitzpatrick and I are sure that Harry stripped precious metals from them. Also, there's been an explosion. A friend of mine says some old military components were fitted with anti-tamper devices, so perhaps that's what caused it. There's also damage to the floor. Carrie thinks aqua regia from a spilled pot flooded across it – that's an acid used to dissolve gold. As I told you, it looked as if the container had just been hosed down.'

By the look on Curtis's face, that was too much too soon. He seemed to be looking right through me.

'Show me?'

The three of us left the crusher and walked to the grey container. Cavendish, having finished whatever phone calls he'd been making, came trotting down the yard to us. Curtis, handkerchief to his nose, told us all to wait outside. Carrie mumbled, just loud enough for him to hear, 'You think the smell's bad? You should have been locked in the bloody thing!'

'This Murray,' Curtis called to us, his voice muffled. 'How do you know about him?' He came back to us, dabbing watering eyes with his handkerchief.

'Dennis told us. He said Murray was here today, driving out of the yard just as he cycled in.'

'So it could have been Murray hosing down this container?'

'I think so. I'm not saying he also hosed down the crusher.'

'Yes, yes, I understand that. Then he shut you both in?'

'Only me. He shut Carrie in later.'

His puzzled look told me he didn't understand. I didn't elaborate and he didn't ask me to. He opened his mouth once or twice as if to speak but changed his mind.

Then, after a long pause, he said 'Harry Sinclair is elderly. He is Murray's father. Murray spells his name St.Clair, that's Saint Clair. The man has history, he has previous, he's served time. He was born up here but he now lives in Chiswick. That's west London.'

'I do know where Chiswick is.'

'Murray St.Clair is a clever piece of work, clever enough to have been involved in some complex scams. Nothing violent as far as we know. He's been inside down south for the last few years and was paroled a few weeks ago. Are you sure it was him who shut you in?'

'Of course we're not!' Carrie now, impatient. 'We didn't see him. And we wouldn't know who the hell he was if we had.'

I was sure I'd heard the name Harry Sinclair before, but I wasn't sure when and where. My thoughts were far from clear. My head was aching. From the fumes, I guessed.

'There are traces of blood around the fan,' Carrie said. 'It's not been hosed down. Perhaps whoever did it kept the water away from the electrics. Must have been a big bang and some serious injuries.'

Curtis said, 'To Harry Sinclair?'

She gave a shrug. 'If it wasn't him, I can't think who else it could have been.'

I faced her, then turned to Curtis. 'Could it have been Morini?' I asked. 'You said he wasn't shot in that field, that his body was dumped there.'

While he mulled over what I'd suggested, I gazed up at the CCTV camera, high on its wooden post. I hadn't been seen on CCTV after all, not if the video recorder was stolen two weeks ago. Murray St.Clair must have simply been watching me as I came into the yard, there were so many places he could have hidden. Later, he heard Carrie's bike and he watched her too. Dennis came to let us out simply because he heard our noise. Not that any of it really mattered now.

I stood quietly, alone with my thoughts.

Carrie came to me. 'Penny for them?'

How appropriate, Carrie. The penny had indeed dropped. I turned my attention to Curtis.

'Tell me, Detective Chief Inspector,' I said quietly. 'Why would Charlie deWit have a video player in his kitchen? I can understand someone having a television there. But a video player?'

He didn't respond. Carrie, bored again, said she had work to do and excused herself from the scrapyard. Ignoring Curtis telling her she couldn't leave, she strode towards her bike, still in black leather, now with her full-face helmet tucked under her arm. Cavendish couldn't take his eyes off her.

'I saw an old black and white movie once with a headless horseman in it,' he said. 'Carried his head under his arm, just like that.'

'Stop looking. She must be at least twenty years older than you.'

'So?'

Cavendish, human after all.

Curtis had left us and was waving his arms, attempting to direct the movements of a convoy of police vehicles that had turned into the yard. He called out.

'Tim, go and sort out that lot. Keep them away from the office, the crusher, and the grey container. Get someone to tape it all up.'

I hadn't spoken to my father for days. He called me that evening, saying he'd had an impressively large payment transferred from Kevron's bank account to his own.

'I was in Edinburgh around lunchtime,' he said. 'I came to your place but you weren't there. Your new lab, I mean.'

'You should have phoned me first. I've been in a scrapyard in West Lothian. Don't ask!'

'Have you finished with Kevron?'

I nodded at the phone. 'I have. I'm still working for Mr Curtis. Though that's almost done, too.'

'Why have you been to a scrapyard? Are you looking for a new car?'

Very funny, Father. 'Looking for the scrapyard owner. A man named Harry Sinclair.'

He was quiet for some time. 'Harry Sinclair? The scrap man? I went to school with him.'

My father never ceases to amaze me. He was brought up in Kilcreg, a coastal village in the north of Scotland. His father – my grandfather – had managed Kilcreg's long-dead metal mine.

'You went to school with him? Really? Do you mean at Kilcreg?'

'Yes, Kilcreg. His father looked after the mine's plant yard.'

I knew about the plant yard. These days there was nothing there but overgrown green fields. Years ago it was where the mine once stored its contractors' plant – things like compressors and diggers, ventilation fans and electric motors. My father took me there once or twice when I was young to visit his mother. I was there again, years ago, when he got himself mixed up with the wrong crowd.

'Like father like son, then.'

'What do you mean?'

'You once told me that the mine's plant yard was rather like a scrapyard.'

'I did? Yes, I suppose it was.'

'Then it's no surprise that Harry's son should end up doing that kind of thing.'

'I suppose not. No surprise that he came south, either. When the oil shale mines closed down there would have been scrap – '

'Dad, listen to me! Harry has disappeared.'

'Disappeared? Harry?'

Caution kicked in. Part of me wanted to tell him everything and part of me didn't. The latter part won. 'Probably nothing,' I said.

Nothing I was prepared to tell him, anyway.

'I haven't seen Harry for over twenty years,' he said. 'I'm not sure I would recognise him now.'

I shivered. No, Dad. You probably would not.

36

Two days later I found myself in a claustrophobic, sparsely furnished room at St. Leonards. Curtis had called me there, having refused to give me a reason. I sat at a table between Curtis and Cavendish, looking like one of three wise monkeys. A DVD player and an impressively large computer monitor had been placed on the table in front of us. Cavendish spoke first. Curtis seemed preoccupied with files and papers.

'We have you to thank for this, Doctor,' Cavendish said. 'The device you saw in Dr deWit's kitchen was not a DVD player, it was the CCTV recorder from Harry Sinclair's office. The front was so badly damaged by shotgun pellets that we, like you, didn't realise what it was.'

Curtis started to talk over him. 'Luckily for us its hard drive was intact. We were able to have it installed in an identical recorder. We have made copies of the footage. DI Cavendish here considers it necessary to allow you to see the recordings.'

I guessed, from the way Curtis said that, he wasn't in favour of me seeing it.

Cavendish again. 'Recording was triggered by movement, so we have edited-out recordings of birds, rabbits and the occasional fox. The scrapyard has four video cameras. We have compiled recordings of interest onto one video. Are you happy with that?'

I nodded. Presumably they had done that for some future court case. It would save time looking through hours, perhaps days, of recording.

'Do you mind if we record your words?'

'Not at all.'

Cavendish tapped at a keyboard, one-handed. He told me to *remain aware* of the date and time on the digital clock in the corner of the screen. I resolved to remain aware.

The video started with a full colour view of the office taken several days before Curtis sent that car for me. One of the scrapyard's large double gates, just visible in the corner of the screen, opened slowly, shoved wide by an elderly, stooping man. He walked out of view, returning as the driver of a small car that came slowly into the yard.

'Office door's locked,' Cavendish said.

'Let her see for herself!'

'Old Man Sinclair?' I asked. 'Harry Sinclair, I mean. It was Dennis who called him *old man Sinclair*.'

Curtis nodded. 'Sinclair, yes. Have you seen him before?'

'Never. I told you. Dennis said – '

'Please keep watching.'

I watched. Sinclair, out of the car now, walked unsteadily to the office door, produced keys and went in. The recording went blank and then restarted.

Curtis commented, 'An hour later.'

I knew that. Dutifully I'd checked the screen's clock. Sinclair walked from the office and out of range of one camera. He reappeared near the grey container, picked up by the camera I'd seen high on that pole. Holding keys, he removed a padlock from one of the container's doors, heaved the door back, went inside and pulled the door closed. The video clock jumped forward an hour or so.

'Not exactly a hive of industry, is it?'

They ignored me. 'This bit,' Curtis said. 'Watch it. Watch the top of the container.'

I watched. Nothing happened.

'Stay watching. The system records thirty seconds before it detects movement.'

'Sorry? How can it possibly do that?'

Curtis started to speak but Cavendish talked over him. 'The cameras work constantly. Their footage goes to the recorder's memory, not to its hard drive. Whenever the software detects movement, the previous three minutes already on memory is dumped to disk.'

'Got it!' I lied.

'Watch it, Doctor. This bit!'

Curtis again. Whatever I was supposed to watch, I had missed. His interruption hadn't helped. Cavendish rewound for me. 'One-eighth speed,' he said. 'Easier to see.'

Jerky video showed what appeared to be a flash of light from the thin gaps around the double doors. Then smoke, a sudden gust of it, blasting out from the far side of the container.

'That's an explosion! That's smoke, sucked out by the vent fan.'

I studied the screen while Cavendish tapped keys. The container doors remained closed. The video ran for another minute or two but recorded nothing new.

'There's nothing more until later,' Cavendish said. 'Harry doesn't come out. Watch this next bit.'

The digital clock said five. A Renault came into the yard through the open gates.

'Green car,' I said, pointlessly. Seconds later the images changed from colour to black and white.

'Camera's changed to infra-red night vision. It's dusk.'

Mansplaining from Cavendish. I knew all that. I also knew the man who stepped out of the driving seat of the car, the man I now watched walking to the office door, trying it, opening it, looking inside and then returned to the car.

'That's Demitri Morini!'

Curtis spoke. 'Are you sure of that?'

'Absolutely. Don't you recognise him?'

'I have never seen him alive and walking, Doctor. Please keep watching.'

Curtis saying *keep watching* was probably the daftest thing I'd ever heard him say. I sat there, perched on the edge of my chair, unable to keep my eyes off the screen. Also, I couldn't help commenting on what I was seeing. Partly for my own benefit and partly for Curtis's audio recorder.

'Only four or five seconds in the office,' I said. 'So it wasn't him who trashed the office and took the video recorder.'

'That comes later. Watch, please.'

Morini, in the car again, drove out of view of one camera. Another, the one on the pole near the grey container, caught him as he pulled up and parked.

'Do you know of any reason why Dr Morini should be at the yard?'

'No. Why should I?'

'University business, possibly?'

'No, Mr Curtis. We don't do degrees in scrapyard management.'

Ask a stupid question, get a stupid answer. Morini, out of the car again, sniffed the air. Clearly puzzled, he stared at the container doors. Using both hands he tugged back one of them, recoiled involuntarily, lost his footing and fell backwards, striking his head on the wing of his car. On his feet again and with a hand over his mouth, he stepped back to the container. He peered in, turned back to face the car and vomited violently.

Curtis commented. 'Not a pretty sight in there.'

'That spilled container would have held around twenty litres of acid,' I said. 'It went everywhere. If Sinclair fell back on it, he didn't stand a chance.'

The image of Sinclair falling into the acid had troubled me for some time. I secretly hoped the explosion killed him before he fell.

'What's Morini doing now, is he locking up?'

'Watch, please…'

My attention was back on the screen. Morini, standing outside, had closed the container door and seemed to be messing with the padlock. Though the screen image was good, it wasn't clear enough to show detail. I shook my head.

'He can't be locking the doors. We know that Sinclair has the keys with him. Morini didn't go right in so he couldn't have got them.'

'No, Doctor. He is locking it. He didn't need keys because it's a Yale-type padlock. Also, you will see later that there is more than one set of keys.'

Morini didn't stay long. Soon the car was gone.

Cavendish, unusually, was fast-forwarding. 'Foxes,' he said. 'And two badgers. They triggered the recording. I missed that bit when I edited. Check the time and date, it's nine-thirty next morning. A delivery van drives into the yard and a package is left in the open office. We have checked it out, it's nothing suspicious. I shall fast forward through that too.'

'It's not exactly the world's busiest scrapyard.'

Curtis again: 'Watch, please, Doctor!'

He should hold up those words on a card, like at live broadcasts. *Clap now…*

Morini was back in the yard. His car, green again in daylight, turned in from the road and drove slowly past the office as if to ensure it was empty. Then, surprisingly, it drove on, out of view of the office camera. It reappeared unexpectedly – for me, anyway – on other cameras, deep inside the yard.

'Checking the yard?' I asked. 'Making sure nobody's around?'

Curtis and Cavendish said nothing. The car emerged at the far end of the lane, near the fence I'd sneaked through that day. It stopped some distance from the grey container.

'Two men,' I said. 'Morini driving.' The car doors opened. 'Oh! That's Charles deWit!'

'Are you are sure of that?'

'I'd recognise that swaggering walk anywhere.'

Morini was the first to reach the container doors. With a key from his pocket he unlocked the padlock, leaving it hanging on the door's locking bars. He then stood well back.

'I see what you mean about more keys. And he doesn't want to go in, does he? Are they arguing?'

'Please keep watching.'

DeWit, not Morini this time, tugged open both doors and stepped inside. He stayed inside for a minute or two before returning to the car. I stared at the screen.

'They've come prepared. Disposable coveralls, boots and full face masks. Acid resistant gloves. Jeez!'

'You can see the men more clearly now,' Curtis said. 'Is it definitely Dr deWit and Dr Morini?'

'Definitely.'

Harry Sinclair looked very dead. Thankfully I couldn't see the gruesome details. Like rubber-masked aliens in a sci-fi movie, deWit or Morini – this time I wasn't sure which – emerged from the container, walking backwards with his gloves under Sinclair's arms, dragging the limp body head first over the container's step.

'Harry Sinclair's wearing wellie boots and blue overalls.' Like my father's old boiler suit, I thought but didn't say. 'He wasn't wearing those when he went in, he must have changed into them in the container.' All said for the benefit of Curtis's audio tape. 'It looks as if he's wearing rubber gloves and a white paper dust mask… or the remains of one. Fat lot of use that would have been.'

Curtis again. 'Can you see any injuries?'

'Poor man looks like a life-size rag doll. Looks like his hair's burnt off.'

Masks still on, the two men dragged the unfortunate Sinclair out of view of the camera, picked up again by one pointed at the office. Part of the crusher, and Denis's small crane, could also be seen on the screen.

'What are they doing now?'

'Watch, please.'

For the next thirty minutes of video I watched in silence as the two men, having closed and padlocked the main gates to the scrapyard, took keys from the office and inspected the crane and the crusher. Occasionally Cavendish fast-forwarded the action. At other times he slowed it down to make the replay seem like an old silent movie – deWit in the cab of the crane, moving it backwards and forwards as he learned the controls. The crane rolled out of sight of the camera and returned dragging a car. Curtis asked me if I recognised the car.

'No. Should I?'

'Just wondered. Did Dennis Stuart make any mention of the car in the crusher?'

Make any mention of it… I loved that police-speak.

'Surely you've asked him?'

'According to him he was never there. He is not a very helpful young man,'

'He told me there was a car in the crusher that still had its engine and wheels. He said that's what broke the crusher.'

I watched the screen as the two men threaded a single heavy chain through the car's open side windows, in through one and out through the other. DeWit, back on the crane, lifted the car, carried it towards the crusher and dropped it beside Sinclair's body. Still protectively kitted up, both men dragged Sinclair into the back seat of the car.

Soon it was all over. DeWit, at the controls of the crane, dropped the car clumsily between the jaws of the crusher. Morini, holding a remote attached to the end of a thick black cable, eventually found the right buttons to lower the crusher's huge top jaw slowly down onto the car. The car started to flatten. Tyres burst. With the car more than half-half crushed, the steel jaw stopped dead. DeWit snatched the controller from Morini and thumbed buttons. Then another argument, deWit waving his arms. Without sound it all looked unreal.

'Why?' Curtis asked. 'Why Dr deWit and Dr Morini? Why Harry Sinclair?'

'Surely you don't expect me to answer that?'

'I'm hoping you can throw some light on this whole sorry business. What is the connection between the murdered men and Harry Sinclair?'

'What, apart from the obvious? That Sinclair cropped gold from circuit boards and some of those cropped fragments were loaded into the shotgun cartridge used to kill Morini?'

'No, Doctor Spargo. Not that. I accept that.'

And about bloody time, if you don't mind me saying, Mr Curtis. Had my future work for Police Scotland not depended on keeping him sweet I might have voiced those thoughts.

Cavendish had paused the video. I asked if there was more. If there was, then a mug of coffee, even police coffee, would be in order.

After comfort breaks, screen watching resumed. With coffee.

'What are they doing now? What are they looking at?'

'Keep watching. They're looking back at the container. They've seen the camera on that post. Now they are looking up at this one.'

If there was ever any doubt that the figures in the yard were deWit and Morini, these full-face views dispelled it. Masks off and car crushing apparently forgotten, both men entered the office. Curtis wagged a finger at the screen.

'Skip the next bit,' he said to Cavendish. Then to me, 'They are in there for fourteen minutes, we are sure they are attempting to retrieve the video recorder. For a while it goes dead. We believe they are trying to open the cabinet, perhaps even move it and take it away. Harry Sinclair was no fool, Doctor. He had the CCTV unit sealed in a fireproof cabinet that was bolted to the floor. It has a combination lock. The power supply and the cables from the cameras are inaccessible, under the floor.'

I kept watching. Clearly, whatever the men had been doing had not been a success because the video was still recording, Morini left the office and brought his car close to the door. Together they carried out box files and papers and threw them into the car boot, together with their gloves, boots, masks and disposable suits.

'Taking away evidence?' I asked for the benefit of the audio.

'But evidence of what, Doctor?'

I shrugged. I had no more idea than they had.

'There's nothing more of them for now,' Curtis said. 'They open the gates and drive out, closing them behind them. Skip to the white van, Tim.'

A rare lapse of protocol from Curtis. *Tim*, rather than *Detective Inspector.*

'It's two hours later,' Curtis said. 'Other vehicles have arrived at the yard but they've stopped at the gates and driven off. There is nothing suspicious. Then there's this. Have you seen this van before, Doctor?'

A white transit-type van with a hire firm's name on the doors had stopped at the gates. The driver removed the gate's padlock, pushed both gates open and entered the yard, stopping where Morini had stopped hours earlier.

'I've not seen the van before but I know the driver. I've seen him before, I mean. He came to the Kevron site, he was the lorry driver who delivered one of the containers, one of the orange ones. He made a right pig's ear of unloading it.'

'Are you sure it's the same man?'

'Ninety-percent sure. Who is he, one of Harry Sinclair's employees?'

'Not an employee. That is Murray St.Clair, Harry Sinclair's son.'

37

I studied the video. St.Clair stayed in the cab of the van. I guessed, but didn't say, that he was staring at the office door, left open by deWit and Morini. As if unsure whether or not to step down from the cab he peered down the lanes between stacks of scrap vehicles.

'What's he doing? Why doesn't he get out?'

'Keep watching…'

St.Clair concentrated his gaze on something distant. Though the screen didn't show it, I knew he was looking towards the grey container.

'Looking for his father, perhaps?'

'Why do you say that?'

'Because Harry Sinclair hadn't been around for some time. I'm guessing St.Clair is also wondering where he is.'

'How do you know he hadn't been around?'

'Dennis said. I told you that. Also, Cameron Thomson had been promised a container for site storage. It was supposed come from a man called Harry but it hadn't arrived. Someone, I can't recall if it was Hamish Anderton or Blackie, said they hadn't heard from this man Harry for some time. When the container finally came it was brought by him.' I pointed at the screen. He and Blackie had words.'

'Had words?'

'The container came to site on a flatbed lorry driven by St.Clair. He had trouble unloading it. Blackie tried ordering him around but came off worse.'

'Physical, you mean?'

'It probably would have been had St.Clair not been high in the air at the time, up on the container he was unloading.'

'Strange,' Curtis said. 'That doesn't sound like St.Clair. He might be a bad apple but he's not known to be aggressive.'

'Am Dram?' Cavendish said, turning to face Curtis. 'You saw the Parole Board's report.'

'Remind me.'

'Amateur Dramatics. He was a leading light in the prison's theatrical company.'

'You're kidding me!'

Curtis and Cavendish had an advantage, they had already seen the video. For me, key questions remained unanswered. Rather than ask them and receive another *Watch please, Doctor…* from Curtis, I studied the screen again, this time seeing St.Clair step down from the van. When he delivered the container to Kevron he'd worn a suit. This time he wore grubby blue overalls that looked far too small for him. I watched as he walked from the van to the office, all the time looking around him.

'Cautious,' I said. 'Why?'

'Men like St.Clair don't take chances.'

'It's more than that,' I said. 'He knows something is wrong. His father wasn't a young man. I'm betting they were in regular contact, then unexpectedly his father goes off the radar. Maybe Dennis contacted him to say Harry had disappeared.'

It was speculation. Curtis glanced at me and gave me the raised eyebrow. 'As I said, we've spoken to Dennis. He was no help. He admitted that he works there weekends. He doesn't know anything about what goes on there.'

The screen flickered. 'Check the new time,' Cavendish said. 'St.Clair stayed in the office for twenty-five minutes.'

'Understood. What's he doing now, is he leaving the yard?'

They ignored me. St.Clair, back at the van, opened the drivers' door but didn't get in. When he again faced the camera he was wearing a baggy jacket and carrying something, keeping it half-hidden under his arm.

'What's he got?'

'A shotgun. A sawn-off.'

'Jeez! I thought you said he wasn't violent.'

'Maybe he's fooled us. There are things about him we don't know.'

Still perched on the edge of the chair I watched St.Clair stride towards the grey container.

'Looking for his father?'

'No, Doctor, he's not. He knows exactly what happened to his father. We are sure that he spent time in the office watching the video. Look at him, look how he's staring at the crusher. When I saw this bit of the recording I actually felt sorry for him.'

'What do you mean, seen the video? He can't have done. Just now we saw deWit and Morini take everything.'

Cavendish came to my rescue. 'No, Doctor, they didn't take the recorder. If they did, how could we be watching St.Clair on the following day? We told you they couldn't get at it. Later you'll see that they return with an angle grinder to cut open the cabinet.'

'Don't tell her what happens. Let her see for herself.'

'Okay,' I said. 'Silly of me. But if they knew they were being recorded, why didn't they just cut the video cables? The ones on the poles. The ones to the cameras, I mean.'

'What would be the point of that? Their actions were already recorded. They knew they had to destroy the video recorder.'

'They could have set fire to the office.'

'The fireproof cabinet, Doctor? Even without that, a fire wouldn't necessarily have destroyed the hard drive. Keep watching, please.'

St.Clair walked from the crusher to the grey container. Like Morini, he opened one of the doors and recoiled from the fumes.

Time passed. The video flickered. St.Clair stepped out.

Cavendish spoke. 'He was in there almost forty minutes.'

'He had to be loading gold fragments into that shotgun cartridge,' I said. 'Wouldn't he need some kind of reloading tool for that?'

'It's possible to prise open the crimped plastic case and replace the standard shot with gold. Not that we know that is what he was doing that in there.'

'You said he was in there for forty minutes. Can you think of anything else he'd be doing all that time? If that is what he was doing, then he knew what his father did in there. He knew where the gold was hidden.'

'What makes you think it was hidden?'

'If it wasn't hidden, then surely Morini and deWit would have already taken it?'

Curtis was nodding, stroking his chin. 'That is a very good point. We now know that Morini was shot with two cartridges, both of them filled with gold.'

'One for Morini and one for deWit?'

'I suppose that's what he may have been thinking at the time. Possibly he expected to find them together. Watch please, Doctor…'

Still holding the shotgun, Murray St.Clair, sped-up like an actor in a silent movie, headed for his van. He stopped on the way to stare again at the crusher and its flattened car. Then he was gone, into his van and away. The screen changed to black and white. 'Just gone nine,' Cavendish said. 'Evening, same day.'

I sat through the arrival of deWit and Morini. Thanks to Cavendish's explanation earlier I knew they had returned to the scrapyard to remove the video recorder. Though the night video wasn't that clear, I saw DeWit, angle grinder in hand, enter the office. That, of course, was the end of the video.

'Clears up so many things, doesn't it?' I said. 'One thing still puzzles me though.'

'Only one thing?'

'At the start of all this you were sure the killer mistook Morini for deWit. The jacket and Uni card?'

Cavendish glanced at Curtis as if for permission to speak. 'As you saw, we got it wrong. St.Clair was after them both. We are sure now that Dr Morini returned to the container for some reason and St.Clair shot him there. He transported the body to that field, hopefully in that hired van.'

'Hopefully?'

'Hopefully because we've got it. He returned it to the hire company some time ago. With luck we'll find traces of Morini's blood in it.'

'Any luck so far with the swabs you took from the fan grill?'

'Early days, Doctor. These things take time. If it is Morini's blood then that will clinch it. He was killed there.'

'What about St.Clair?'

'You mean his whereabouts?'

'Where he might be now, yes.'

'Nothing yet. We'll get him. We will or the Met will. He really is a strange piece of work. A bit of a Jekyll and Hyde by all accounts.'

'Got in with the wrong crowd?'

Curtis answered me. 'No, not at all. From what I've heard he was bad inside.'

'Meaning?'

'His deviousness came naturally. He learned it all himself. The first time he was arrested he denied all knowledge of his crime. Even when they'd got him bang to rights.'

'That's an expression I've not heard for years.'

'When he was a lad he had a racket up here selling stolen motorcycles. We got him for that and he spent time in Polmont. Later he moved to London. The Met tell us that since then they've picked him up and charged him with several jobs. He always manages to find friends to say he was elsewhere at the time.'

'But they got him for something eventually. You said he was inside until recently.'

'Even the best of them make mistakes. Murray St.Clair, a right piece of work and no mistake. Though I'm told he's changed a lot.'

'In what way?'

'The last two jobs they got him for he admitted everything. Admitted it to them, that is, not to the court. When it comes to court he pleads not guilty. He's boastful. He's become a showman. I'm told he brags about his crimes. The police are sure they have him and then in court his brief lodges the defence of alibi.'

'But surely the Met records his confessions?'

'Last job they got him for he told the court that everything he told the police was a fiction. *I told them what they wanted to hear*, he said. Met says it's because he wants his time in court, he pleads not guilty so he can have an audience. Wasn't so clever that last time though.'

I frowned. 'I'm still not with you. You said audience?'

'A captive audience. Court, jury, media. His cleverness and deviousness, all on show, everything the police, SOCO, forensics and witnesses have had to go through in their attempts to secure a conviction is paraded in court. He needs the publicity.'

'Needs a psychiatrist, more like. I'm wondering if he didn't approve of what his father was doing. What if Harry Sinclair was talked into it by deWit and Morini without being made aware of the risks? Harry would have welcomed the extra cash. The scrapyard is run down, it's obvious it wasn't making money.'

Curtis shook his head. 'So what else is obvious to you, Doctor?'

Ouch! An unusually dismissive tone from Curtis that I put down to tiredness. Perhaps, if he'd had an open mind about the source of the gold fragments right from the start, he would have had more time to think things through properly. I glanced at Cavendish and detected a faint, embarrassed smile.

'If you and Doctor Fitzpatrick are right about what Harry Sinclair was doing,' Curtis continued, 'then an explosion and acid killed him, not Dr Morini and Dr deWit.'

'And your point is?'

'It was an unfortunate accident.'

'An accident that should never have happened,' I said. 'An accident that was the direct result of two educated professionals taking advantage of a less knowledgeable, elderly man. In Murray St.Clair's eyes they were responsible for his death. They as good as killed him.'

38

So that was it. My contract with Kevron had ended, as had my work on Curtis's gold. Kevin Marshall – or his treasurer, or accounts department, or whoever dealt with the financial aspects of construction – had transferred an unexpectedly generous sum to my business account. Similarly, smaller amounts had trickled in from Police Scotland, all of them gratefully received.

As I drove Cameron's van home from St. Leonards I wondered what I should do with my life now. Back to lecturing, possibly? I didn't want to do that, but my department head at King's had asked me to call in to see her. I'd had a hint from Uni friends that two lecturers had recently left, one retired and the other to a lectureship in London. A departmental staff shortage, then.

A break was called for. Taking Cameron's van back to him would mean a day trip to Glasgow, not a journey I wanted to do. At least I felt that I could now spend time with Cameron, thank him for use of his van and fill him in on all the news. And there was Carrie to thank. I owed her. Perhaps a girls' night out was due.

Carrie had, I remembered as I drove into the Mews, sacrificed her phone on my behalf. From what I knew of Carrie, her phone would not have been cheap, it would have been the latest all singing, all dancing, phone costing a couple of hundred at least. Daydreaming on my way home I had worked out how to recover it. Like Dennis, I could squeeze myself to within a couple of metres of where it lay. Then, by using a long piece of wood or metal – easily found in a scrapyard – I would be able to drag it towards me.

I knew from Cavendish that police work at the yard was over. With Harry Sinclair dead, Murray St.Clair in London, and Dennis Stewart unlikely to return to a scrapyard recently swarming with *the polis*, I felt the time was right to revisit the place.

I did wonder if I should clear things with Cavendish before I returned to the yard, but there wasn't much point. The police had finished there. The owner was dead. Who could possibly object to my presence?

I knew I might be wasting my time. Even if my phone recovery job was a success, it had rained since Carrie dropped it. Phones, like mine and Cameron's, and like most other electronic gadgetry, cannot tolerate moisture, let alone the night-time downpours we'd had recently.

It was raining now, a fine drizzle with a dazzlingly low sun shining through it. Strange weather. A strange day. A day that was to become even stranger.

I parked Cameron's van on the grass verge opposite the yard, close to where I'd parked that first day. Though Cavendish said they had finished with the place, blue and white tape still adorned the main gates, its loose ends flapping like streamers. I entered the yard through the gap in the fence, the same way as before. No tape there.

Police tape, I'd realised years ago, deters only the law-abiding. Strips of white polythene with blue stripes and words stops nothing. It did not stop me walking through the scrapyard. It did not stop me ducking under even more of it when I reached the grey container.

From where I stood I could see the office and the crusher. The office door was closed and the crusher jaws were open. Cavendish had already told me that the half-crushed car had gone, lifted out and taken away. That part of the yard no longer interested me. I turned my attention to the container.

Dennis, struggling between the scrap cars and the container in his attempt to recover Carrie's phone, had become trapped by his loose clothing. His jacket had allowed him slide in easily one way and then acted like the barb on a fish hook when he tried to pull back. That would not happen to me for the simple reason that I'd slipped into one of my disposable, one-piece white suits. Close-fitting and sleek, it wouldn't get snagged.

Armed with a long light pole I found nearby – the kind that supports TV aerials on house roofs – I lay down in damp dirt and slithered snakelike into the narrow gap. Though I couldn't see Carrie's phone, laws of gravity dictated that it would be directly beneath the container's fan. Things like phones simply fell vertically. They didn't bound around at random, like feathers.

A few uncomfortable minutes later I reached the phone and managed, with the help of the pole, to drag it towards me. Struggling and sweating in the suit I reached for it, grasped it, and attempted to put it in my pocket. Like Curtis in the field that night I remembered that these oversuits do not have pockets. Abandoning the metal pole and still clutching the phone, I reverse-thrusted my body. Going in, I had propelled myself forwards using my elbows and toes – my toes in my boots, of course. Reversing this action wasn't easy. The human body, it seems, was not designed to lie face down and go backwards.

'Do you mind telling me what you are doing here?'

I froze. Whoever had just crawled into the space behind me and grasped my ankles was now hauling me back, attempting to drag me out from between the container wall and some unfriendly, angular metal parts of scrap cars. I would like to say that once I was out I twisted around, got to my feet, and then ran like hell. I did not. Running away was not on the cards. Instead I simply sat up and stayed there. Hoping, I suppose, to talk my way out of things.

Looking down at me was the man I'd seen high on that orange container, the man in the video footage. That it was Murray St.Clair was obvious, but not from the sound of his voice. Shouting down at Blackie that day he had sounded rough and gruff, a tough guy with an East End of London accent seldom heard this far north. This version of St.Clair was inexplicably well-spoken and I wondered, for a minute or two, if Murray St.Clair had a twin.

'Well? Are you going to tell me?'

He stood, hands on hips, in the same well-fitting suit he'd worn that day at the Kevron site. There was no sign of the accent he'd used to curse Blackie, nor of the thug-like behaviour. Nor, I was relieved to see, was there any sign of his sawn-off.

Apart from having been dragged backwards by strong hands, St.Clair was politeness personified. Murderers, it seemed, weren't all thugs.

'So? What are you doing here?'

I stayed sitting, gazing up at him. Last time I saw him he was even higher, rotating slowly, pressing buttons on a remote in an attempt to guide an orange container into place while verbally abusing James Blackie. I held up Carrie's phone.

'Recovering this. I dropped it.'

He shook his head. 'Dropped it from where?'

'The ventilator fan. After you shut me in there.'

I expected a denial. Instead, I got a nod. 'You and that biker, yes. Who is he?'

So, not an identical twin. Maybe a doppelganger, or a Jekyll and Hyde. 'He's a she,' I said. 'A friend. She has nothing to do with all this.'

He stared down at me. 'What do you mean, *all this*? I caught you prying. Why were you both here?'

I hesitated, unsure what to say. Perhaps, if I played dumb, he would simply let me leave. 'I came here to look for a container, something like those orange ones. I need one for storage.'

'And your friend? Did she need one too?'

The sarcasm wasn't lost on me. 'Of course not. She agreed to come with me.' I tried hard not to sound nervous. My story sounded pathetic.

'Tell me why you called the police.'

That floored me. If he knew that, it meant he had been talking to Dennis.

'We were suspicious. The lad who let us out said his boss had disappeared.'

Had I said too much? It was impossible to know.

'You mean Dennis.'

'Dennis, yes. He tried to retrieve the lost phone for us. Well, as you can see, I've found it. I'd better get going before the rain gets worse.'

'The rain won't get worse. It's stopped.'

'Ah… so it has.'

'Dennis said he told you about the crusher.'

'He said someone broke it. My friend thought that was suspicious. Well, more than suspicious. She thought the owner of this place might be in there. That's why we called the police.'

'*The owner of this place…* Yes, my father. But you will know that by now, Doctor Spargo. You will also know that I shot the bastards responsible.'

My sharp intake of breath was audible. After an admission like that, what did he have planned for me? Then I remembered what Curtis and Cavendish had told me, that St.Clair admitted everything and later denied it. He held out a hand, offering to help me up. I took it.

'We know about the acid,' I said. 'We know how your father died.'

'Who's *we*?'

'Everyone. The police. We know what your father was doing in there. We know there was an explosion. The police have the CCTV recorder. They have seen everything.'

'That explosion was caused by your friend deWit. You worked with him.'

'He was no friend of mine.' I was once told it was wrong to speak ill of the dead. To me, that made no sense. DeWit being dead didn't change my opinion of him. 'What makes you think deWit caused the explosion?'

'Did you know Demitri Morini?'

'I knew of him. I can't say I knew him.'

'He was a chemist. The explosion was caused by something he and deWit did. It killed my father.'

I found myself nodding. Trying to humour him, perhaps. 'The explosion might not have been their fault,' I said. 'We know your father was stripping gold contacts from old circuit boards. Some board components used by the military have a small explosive charge, intended to destroy the component if tampered with.' Thanks to Andy I sounded quite knowledgeable. 'The police think that's what happened. Your father then fell into the acid he was using to dissolve the gold. You know the rest. You also saw the video.'

He stayed quiet for a while. I guessed he was considering what I'd said about the explosive. He wouldn't have known that.

'If one of those boards blew up then they as good as killed him. Until they came along he had a nice little sideline, stripping gold contacts from those boards. He sold the contacts to a precious metals refiner.'

'If he was doing all this before he met deWit and Morini, how can you blame them for his death?'

'My father kept it simple. Before you lot came along he didn't use acid. He didn't process container-loads of boards. Those two bastards suggested he'd make more money if he dissolved the contacts in acid and sold the gold concentrate, rather than simply selling the cropped contacts.'

'You said *your lot*. Just because I happened to know deWit didn't mean I liked him. And I certainly didn't know what he was doing.'

'I realise that, Doctor.'

For a murderer he seemed so friendly, scarily so. I wanted to say that if his father was stripping contacts long before he met deWit and Morini, there was a fair chance he'd have blown himself up anyway. I thought it prudent to keep such thoughts to myself.

'How did Harry meet deWit and Morini?' I asked. 'Do you know?'

'I don't. Two years ago he told me he was collaborating with two academics who could increase his profits. They wanted their cut, of course. I tried to talk him out of it.'

'Not exactly illegal though.'

'Not illegal? You saw that video, you saw what they did to him. Was he even dead? They killed him, Doctor Spargo. They put him pressure on him to increase output. They even got extra workers to help him, workers that turned out to be illegals. Last year the police got him for that. He was given six months inside.'

I didn't argue. If Curtis ever learned that I'd talked these things through with St.Clair, he would ensure that I never worked for the police again – that's if I survived this encounter. I didn't doubt that I was fighting for my life here. St.Clair had murdered two men. Adding a forensic geologist to his list of victims would make little or no difference to his sentence.

'What am I going to do with you, Doctor?'

So much for my belief that I was building some kind of rapport with him. I cursed myself for getting into such a vulnerable position, miles from anywhere in what was now an abandoned scrapyard, a place where my body might never be found. Soon, Cameron's van would be stripped of its engine and wheels, crushed flat, then stacked with hundreds of others.

'I'm no threat to you, Murray,' I said. 'The police know everything that I know.'

'Don't call me Murray. You don't know me. You are no friend of mine. You and your biker friend are a pair of interfering bitches.'

His Jekyll and Hyde change of attitude frightened me. 'My friend has nothing to do with this. And I *do* know you. I know about your father. I even know about your grandfather. '

'Don't bullshit me!'

'It's not bullshit. Your father and my father went to the same school. According to my father, they were good friends.'

'Don't lie to me!'

'Back in the nineteen-forties your grandfather worked at the Kilcreg mine, managing the yard where they kept all the scrapped equipment. My grandfather was also at the mine. He was the mine manager.'

A plane droned overhead, one of the few remaining propeller driven, island-hopping aircraft inbound to Edinburgh. St.Clair turned away from me, took a few steps and stood motionless, gazing at the sky, watching the plane until the sound faded away. He stayed quiet for what seemed an age.

'I know about that place,' he said quietly, turning back to me. 'Harry told me about it when I was young.'

He came back to me, grabbed my wrist and guided me back towards the crusher. As we walked past it my heartbeat returned to near-normal. Then he turned down one of the lanes between stacked cars. Still gripping my wrist, he hauled me into the body of an old rusting bus.

The shotgun, hidden in the rotting fabric of a bus seat, could hold only two cartridges. Was the first shot for me and the second for him?

'Come, Doctor. Let's get this over with…'

39

We walked out of the scrapyard gates and down the road to Cameron's van. Because I had entered the yard at its far end, the van was a good five minutes' walk away. For much of the time St.Clair paid more attention to his mobile phone than he did to me and I desperately hoped that a vehicle – a car or van or bus or anything at all – would come along the road so I could flag it down. Though what were the chances of a passing driver stopping for a mad lady, standing in the road waving her arms? Being followed by a man with a sawn-off shotgun tucked under his arm probably wouldn't help.

The opportunity didn't arise. Because the scrapyard really was in the ass end of the world, nothing came.

I walked faster than St.Clair, managing to increase the distance between us. I could hear him making short phone calls, cursing quietly when he couldn't get through. I had a horrible feeling he was making goodbye calls to his mates.

I had the van keys in my hand. Did I really have time to make a run for it, time to click the remote, open the driver's door, get in and start the engine? It might work. Even if he shot at me through the van's back windows it was unlikely the pellets would reach me, not with Cameron's equipment piled up in the back.

Common sense kicked in. I reasoned that if St.Clair intended to murder me then he would have done it in the scrapyard. I would like to say that my logical reasoning was what prevented me from running. It wasn't. My somewhat iffy escape plan was foiled at inception by St.Clair pocketing his phone and then trotting along the roadside to catch up with me.

We sat side by side, St.Clair in the passenger seat and me at the wheel. Disturbingly, he sat with the shotgun between his legs, the wooden butt on the floor and the barrel resting on the front of the seat, aimed up at his face. That the gun wasn't broken disturbed me even more. If you don't know what I mean by *broken*, I mean the barrel unhinged from the wooden stock to expose both cartridge chambers, the way gamekeepers and killers of game birds carry guns safely.

'Where are we going?'

'Just drive. Keep off the motorway. Take the next right turn. When we reach Edinburgh, head for Fettes.'

'The school?'

'Just do it, Doctor.'

I did what I was told. As instructed, I took backstreets. Not far from Fettes I passed the end of my mews. St.Clair waved an arm at the windscreen.

'Turn here. Then turn again at Waitrose.'

As I turned into Fettes Avenue, St.Clair leaned forwards, peering out. He shook his head. Kept shaking it as I drove up the road.

'Where are they all? The bastards!'

'What?'

'Police headquarters? Where is it?'

So that was where were heading. 'Moved years ago,' I said. 'After they all became Police Scotland. It's no longer Edinburgh and Borders, it's now Edinburgh Division. Their main office is now at St.Leonards.'

'Where the fuck's that?'

I swallowed. Mr Hyde again. Or was it Dr Jekyll? No, right first time – Hyde was the bad guy. What was St.Clair planning to do, go in there armed with the gun? And then what?

He looked at his watch. 'How long?'

'To drive to St.Leonards? Ten minutes. Maybe fifteen.'

'Fuck fuck fuck!'

Fifteen minutes later I turned into The Pleasance, the hill that leads up to St.Leonards. Surprisingly the road was gridlocked with vehicles. Was it road works? An accident up ahead? One of Edinburgh's protest marches? I managed to drive as far as a short row of shops before St.Clair seemed to lose it.

'Stop! No, not here! Closer, opposite the shops. Tidy yourself up. Get out of those coveralls. When we get out you will stay close to me. Don't do anything stupid!'

Not prepared to argue with a man with a shotgun I pulled onto the double yellows. I switched on the van's hazard lights, struggled out of the coveralls, and joined St.Clair at the roadside. Somehow he managed to conceal the shotgun, tucking it from armpit to wrist like he'd done in the video. I had no way of knowing if any of the drivers in the queue of cars noticed it. Not sure what they would have done if they had.

My mind spun with thoughts. That he was heading for St.Leonards headquarters was clear to me. Why he was going there was not clear at all. Was it some kind of vendetta? If so, then against who? Curtis, perhaps? Or Cavendish?

I could make a run for it, out into the road and around gridlocked cars. By doing that I would be safe. Alternatively, by staying with him, perhaps I'd get the opportunity to warn others.

Traffic started to move again, creeping cautiously forwards. Way up ahead, two large vans manoeuvred in the road and again blocked the traffic. Near the entrance of St.Leonards headquarters a small crowd had gathered, marshalled by police in yellow jackets. St.Clair stopped for a few seconds, turned to me and passed me the shotgun. I shook my head.

'No! That's crazy! I don't want it!'

'Take it. It's not loaded. Break it… no, not like that. Here, I'll do it…'

Holding the barrel, he pressed a lever. The gun unhinged.

'Carry it under your arm. Like a gamekeeper.'

I obeyed. Sinclair, I told myself, had completely lost it. This had to be some kind of breakdown. For the first time in hours I relaxed. I had the gun, I wasn't in danger. It wasn't even loaded.

'Hold my wrist, Doctor.'

'What?'

'Walk beside me. Grab my wrist. No, not with that hand, for god's sake! With your free hand. That's it. Now walk. Shove your way through the crowd.'

I didn't have to shove. The crowd, now blocking the pavement and half the road, stepped aside to let us through. No doubt it was the shotgun – or maybe the fact that I appeared to be dragging St.Clair, a man bigger than me, behind me. I still haven't worked out how he made it look like that.

A forest of arms raised mobile phones high. Cameras flashed. Some – those held by press men – flashed blindingly. By now, satellite dishes had been raised on the roofs of the vans and at least one TV camera, high on a cherry-picker, swivelled towards us.

'Amateur dramatics,' I mumbled. 'Those phone calls. To journalists? Why, Murray?'

'Smile for the cameras, Doctor. You've brought me in. Hold up my gun.'

'I've no wish to play your games.'

'Too late for that.'

I ignored him. No way was I going to be photographed looking like a trophy hunter. They all knew who he was, of course. Even I had seen some of the media coverage, the '*wanted in connection with...*' and the '*do not approach this man…*' stuff. And here I was, holding the idiot's wrist, having in some mysterious way managed to disarmed him and deliver him to police HQ.

Two of the uniformed officers controlling the crowd stopped and stared. It didn't surprise me that for a good few seconds they did nothing. Then one of them sprang, leopard-like, grabbing both me and the gun. St.Clair yelled at him.

'Leave her, you numptie! It's me you want!'

Carrie phoned me that evening. She had seen the news, watched me carrying a shotgun while apparently dragging St.Clair along the pavement. I put her right about a few things.

'Carrie, I thought he was going to kill me! He must have decided that enough was enough. He was going to hand himself in.'

'But why you?'

'I know it sounds weird, but I told him my father and his father knew each other.'

'That story worked?'

'It's true, Carrie. They really did know each other. It seemed to change things. The showman took over. He saw the opportunity to make a big scene.'

'As you say, weird.'

'Inside St.Leonards they split us up. I haven't seen him since, so I don't know what he said to them. I demanded to see Curtis but I got Cavendish instead and I told him everything. He couldn't keep a straight face.'

I talked with Carrie for a good half-hour. I explained that St.Clair had been involved in amateur dramatics.

'And real dramatics,' she said. 'Like murder. Don't lose sight of that. I hope this isn't Stockholm Syndrome.'

'Are you suggesting I'm sympathising with him? There's no chance of that. Oh… did I tell you he made me leave Cameron's van on double yellows?'

'No, you didn't tell me that.'

'It got clamped.'

I had been expected a call from my father. I later found out he was in Chile, on a consulting contract for a mining company. Some people get all the luck. Even at his age.

Like Carrie, I had watched the TV news. Scottish television had the best shots – or as far as I was concerned, the worst. If their cameras had caught St.Clair handing the shotgun to me and then making me grasp his wrist, they had edited it out. Viewers get what viewers want – sensation.

It seemed that everyone had watched the news that night. Everyone, apparently, except one of the geology professors at King's.

'You have of course heard about Charlie deWit?'

'Yes,' I said. 'Bad business.'

'As you say, a bad business. He will be sadly missed.'

He paused after each statement as if expecting me to respond. I didn't.

'He will be missed,' he said again. 'Which is why I am phoning you, Jessica. I am aware that you are no longer a full-time member of staff. I do know that you have other commitments.'

He waited again. I stayed quiet, wondering what was coming.

'With the loss of your good self and now Charlie, we are now several staff members short. I have been wondering if you, well… how is business going, do you have plenty of work? Would you consider coming back to us?'

AUTHOR'S NOTE

Many years ago I was a caver, a potholer. That developed into a love of geology, I wanted to understand how and why caves formed. At the time there was no way my school grades would get me into university to study my favourite subject so I became a police cadet and then a policeman (you have just read Ground Rules, so I'm sure you are seeing connections here, understanding how the story took shape).

Later I was fortunate enough to study for a degree. I graduated as a geologist, becoming not a forensic geologist like Jez, but an engineering geologist. At first, that involved spending many months describing rock cores. I do hope my descriptions of doing that didn't bore you. It was an essential part of the story (and you did continue reading!).

My work took me into mines and tunnels worldwide. It also took me to the most frightening job I ever did – called in to help recover bodies from a collapsed tunnel. Unlike in Ground Rules we didn't succeed, it became too dangerous to continue. Perhaps, in my mind, Jez helping to recover Sandy Davison's remains is some kind of compensation for that failure.

Jessica Spargo appeared in The Man Who Played Trains as the daughter of John Spargo, the novel's main protagonist. Reviewers of that book so liked feisty Jez – their description – that I wrote Ground Rules just for her. And for me. And for you, of course.

Kevron Construction also appeared in my first novel, Playpits Park.

I write because I love writing. If you enjoyed Ground Rules, please write a review of the book on Amazon or Goodreads, it is easy, just a one-liner will do. Most authors make very little from royalties and depend on reviews for sales. Only a handful of writers make real money from their books.

Thank you for reading Ground Rules
Richard

Printed in Great Britain
by Amazon